SALOMÉ

SALOMÉ

LONDON TO CAIRO TRILOGY:
BOOK I

ALEX DAVID

First paperback edition 2019

Cover by Alex David
Set in Baskerville Old Face 11.5 pt

ISBN: 978-1-69230-952-7

Author's Note:

Imprint: Independently published

Prologue

LEANING on the desk, I let my father's note absorb the sweat of my palm. Tapping my finger, I stared out the window, desolate. What did my father expect me to do with this bit of useless rubbish? How is this note going to help me find the girl?

...William, here are my notes on the subject dated 09 December 1941:

...News of the Japanese attack on American Hawaii reaches Cairo and the implications of such an attack are not lost on me. An English diplomat, I get the latest news.

Crossing the thoroughfare in a hurry, the cacophony of Egyptian streets agitates my nerves. The fetid air of Cairo nauseates me and when I pause, I hear footsteps.

A girl in a muslin veil comes to a halt. Her skinny arm shoots out, thrusting a letter.

"For me?" I recognize the hectic scrawl and ask sharply, "Where is your employer?"

The girl is silent.

Unaware that Señor Marcelo is in Cairo, I lean close, "Señor Marcelo?"

The girl responds with a hesitant nod.

"Do you speak?"

She quickly averts her eyes, staring at the ground.

"I see. Well, come along!"

She fidgets.

"You have nothing to fear. Follow me." Uneasily, I wonder how my wife, Lady Westbrook, will accept the arrangement. I can sense that there will be complications. Besides, my political position and my involvement in such a clandestine rescue organization clash. What will happen if this is discovered? What will happen politically if my activities are known? I walk a little faster, hoping that somehow my burden will lift, or the girl disappear...

William, I end this account with a reminder that you search for the girl with utmost care.
Niles Westbrook
...Cairo, 1943

Chapter 1: Homecoming

MY pulse raced as I crossed the gangplank, rushing to the taxi stand.

The Port of Alexandria roared with noisy activity in that December of 1941. A torrent of boots pounded on creaking pallets. Vendors, laborers, and officers bustled about, shouting.

Glancing at my wristwatch, already sticky with perspiration, I realized just how late I was, when a high-pitched whistle ripped the air.

Bedecked with the Eighth Army insignia of an officer, a man in khaki blew his whistle then bellowed orders in English at his confused, swarthy crew.

"Arabic," I shouted. "Speak Arabic. And blowing your whistle in their ears is only liable to make your men deaf."

"Who the devil do you think you are?" Between the officer's starched collar and heavy jaw, a vein throbbed. "Better yet, why aren't you in uniform? You're an Englishman. Won't you fight for your King? Afraid?"

"Are you calling me a coward?"

"Yes, I am," he shot back, pugnaciously.

Then a deep voice boomed, "William!" My father's head, bald under a bowler hat, rose above a group of hairy hawkers. Standing by a taxi, he was already surrounded by a crowd, his well-tailored suit clashing with the pajama-like dirty robes of the bootblacks.

The officer slewed his head back. "You're with him?"

"What's it to you?"

"I'd met him. He's Lampson's man...Sir Niles. GHQ Cairo."

"I doubt that you'd met him at General Headquarters."

"But you must be William Westbrook...the youngest son who volunteered in London and is joining GHQ...William Westbrook...with the London rescue units," he stammered. "It's all over GHQ Cairo. Look here, I must apologize."

"William!"

"Here."

Just then, his crewmen dropped a crate. The wooden frame broke and cans of bully beef rolled out.

"Pick it up, then," the officer ordered, casting a fulminating glare at the sun-scorched cans full of processed corned beef, the staple of the British army.

Repeating his command in Arabic, I jumped off the elevated platform. "Father, over here."

My father plowed through the swarm of flies and peddlers. "Making a martyr of yourself already?"

"Not exactly."

"We are at war, William." My father wanted to say more but held back, clasping my hand instead. "Welcome back."

In the interior of the taxi, I croaked, "Father, things have changed since I left Egypt."

"I suppose so. London too must be a completely different place than the city I'd last seen."

"It is."

"Is our townhouse still in being?"

"In being, yes. I stopped in before I left."

"And?"

"Well, the War Office has filled it with some odd military types. Who are those creatures?"

"The creatures, as you call them, are an old brigadier and his entourage."

"Well, I wish that they would clear out. They've turned the place into a gambling hell!"

"It's part of the war effort," Father said, sotto voce, gazing out the window as the taxi hurried to Alexandria's Sidi Gaber rail station. "We'll take the next train to Cairo. It's difficult to be away from home. Especially now."

"I'm here, Father. I am home."

He held my gaze and for a brief moment his pensive cobalt eyes lit up and his dimples appeared. "Home is still England. My eccentric father's Egyptian estate could never be home."

"Didn't August of '36 change your sentiment?"

"My appointment with Sir Miles?" He shook his head. "No. Recollect, William, that we relocated to Egypt when Sir Miles Lampson became the first British ambassador to Egypt since 1882."

"True enough."

"And for the time being, I am his advisor. But this will change soon enough."

"Alexandria's different."

My father issued a low rumble. "On the surface, Egypt serves England."

Staring out the window, I saw what my father had meant.

Petrol, ammunition, and rations weighed down porters. Lorries and machine-guns came off Royal vessels. And men in uniform popped in and out of buildings.

A shred of my childhood memories of Alexandria was still about. The stagnant water in the streets still hosted swarms of bluebottles and the rubbish blowing in the warm breeze continued on, dusty and directionless. Buzzing and ceaseless, the flies and dust reassured me that indeed this was Egypt.

'War has followed me to Egypt,' flashed across my mind.

But war did not follow me.

Early in December 1941, Japan attacked the United States of America and overran its neighboring Asian countries; Europe was crumbling under air raids; Africa was getting dismantled. As wild dogs fight over meat, the great nations were tearing at the world. And regardless of my position, a large chunk of the world was in the midst of a ruthless, widespread mêlée.

"Any news?" I asked.

"We have not heard from James yet." Concern for his oldest son etched every word. "As a field surgeon with the Eighth Army he should have had leave by now."

"Or paper, pencil, and postage. But maybe that's rationed."

I won a faint grin from my father. "James has never been one to write. William?"

"Sir?"

"Officially, you are no longer protected from conscription as a student. Will you join us at General Headquarters? Elliot did, you know."

"Elliot? Really?"

"Are you surprised?"

"Why, yes, I suppose I am rather. You know what Elliot's like."

"Don't I just!"

"Well, I can't see him working at GHQ, that's all. And neither do I see myself at GHQ."

"No?"

"I am twenty now. I'll have to look into my options. Will you help me?"

His head moved with approbation, but, forever the cautious diplomat, he added, "I will help as long as your choices do not upset your mother. She worries, you know."

"Is Mother all right?"

"She never shows it if she is not. You know how it is with her. But she worries."

"It's James, isn't it?"

"It always is."

Despite the breeze, the heat inside the taxi was unbearable, and I was relieved when we reached the train station.

"Where's Elliot now? GHQ?"

"GHQ? No. Your brother comes and goes as he pleases."

"But..."

"We planned to travel to Alexandria together. Elliot, however, left several days ago and has not returned."

"Elliot wanders, and often in secret."

"He hasn't been writing you?"

"No."

"So, you are unaware that your brother has offered for Elizabeth Baker?"

"Elliot and Ms. Baker? Elizabeth Baker? That boring, tedious, self-absorbed ninny of the very rich Mr. Baker?"

"Apt."

"Is it some kind of a joke?"

"No."

"A dare?"

Exhaling, my father only grumbled, "It's a suitable match."

"How so?"

"I haven't figured it out yet," my father choked, an undignified snort escaping him.

"It has to be some sort of a dare. I don't see how it's possible. Elliot's wealthy. He's good-looking. He can have the pick of them all. In fact,

I'm pretty sure that he has! Why Elizabeth Baker then? And why are you, Father, finding it amusing?"

"Don't you?"

"No. It's farcical."

"I wouldn't worry too much about it. I'm certain that Elliot will soon shake her off, like he did with all the others."

Chapter 2: Salomé

DUMBSTRUCK in Elliot's bedroom, I surveyed the welter of shirts and jackets, and the empty bottles and odd containers that littered the floor. Elliot's own private bird's-nest!

"Doesn't anyone tidy this mess up? And where are you now?"

But Elliot's cluttered room looked back at me with cheeky insolence, whispering, "Not here."

When a heavy thump shook the wall, I ran out to the hall only to tangle up with Ali Jamal's feet.

Sprawled on his buttocks, the boy stared up at me.

"Ali! Here, take my hand."

A short, hairy boy of thirteen, Ali was our gardener and stableboy. A year earlier, his father had passed away and Ali took over his father's duties at the estate.

"Effendi, you are back. Good."

"Good to see you Ali, but what was all that noise?"

"Oh, Cook, you know."

"The Horrible Cook? Still?"

Ali twisted to look back down the hall.

"Cook's after you? And you're making off like a lost mongrel, are you? Well, I don't blame you."

"No Effendi, the maids told me that I would find you here." Ali used a mixture of Arabic and English when he spoke, resorting to using the title Effendi when addressing me.

"You've grown since I last saw you."

"Of course, Effendi. You have changed too. You are much taller and more...white."

"Pale. You mean pale."

Ali nodded, his dark brown orbs resting on my crystal pale blue ones for an instant then, rather clumsily, he continued, "I last saw you before the war... Were you really in London when bombs fell from the sky?"

"That's right."

"Sir Niles explained that you worked with ambulances. We feared that..."

"Well, I'm back. Alive and well."

"Thank Allah." Ali, his palms pressed together, raised his eyes heavenward.

"We best step outside. You could send your prayers out there without worrying about Cook catching you."

Ali cast anxious glances about. "He's like a terrier when he hunts me down."

"But you came to see me, Ali."

"And so I did, but Cook, you know, he's always after...somebody."

Outside in the courtyard, I offered Ali a Woodbine.

"English cigarettes," Ali purred. "Oh, yes, please. The fig tree here shades this bench." Ali swept sand off the bench, raising his eyes as I pulled the last cigarette from its packet. "Effendi, cigarettes are hard to come by now. If this is the last Woodbine, then all that is left for me to enjoy is camel dung."

I choked.

"Effendi," swelling his chest and always at the ready to recite the chronicles of the kitchen, Ali howled, "Effendi, Cook must be mad."

"Of course he is."

"He shouts and yells and says such horrible things. We hoped that since parties are rare at the estate, the war you know, the Devil would calm. No, he is not calm! He is worse! He is always out of humor."

"No parties? Of any kind?"

Ali shook his head.

"What a relief!"

"But Effendi, only days ago, Fatima broke the tea service. Fatima saw an afreet in the kitchen. So, Cook sent her home, without notice, or approval of Lady Westbrook or Mrs. Judd!"

"Ali, Cook has always been disagreeable, the maids regularly see ghosts, and our timid housekeeper, poor Mrs. Judd, finds it difficult to control the staff. She is on her own. Our butler, followed by your father..."

"God rest their souls," Ali bleated.

"Well, they passed away and Mrs. Judd alone remains to supervise."

"Supervise?"

"Manage the maids."

"Manage the hellcats! That's what Elliot Effendi calls the maids."

"Yes. Even Joseph's gone now."

"Not gone! Joseph's retired," Ali interjected, pronouncing 'retired' with great difficulty and yet relishing the complexity of the word on his tongue.

"Dear old Joseph. He was good with the horses."

"He is good with horses and anything else that walks and breathes, Effendi."

I shot Ali a rueful grin. "You have the right of it. I keep referring to old Joseph in past tense yet he lives. He no longer works here and no longer tends to our horses, but he lives. Where precisely?"

"Back in his own village. Not far."

"So, Ali, what news have you?"

Ali waggled his finger. "Ah, Effendi, I do have news. Weeks ago, Sir Niles brought a girl. He said that we needed another maid. But Lady Westbrook announced that there was little for her to do, Effendi. And the girl is thin and lazy. Besides, she does not speak."

"Does she utter any sound?"

"Utter? She shakes her head when I talk to her." His voice had an unsteady pitch. "Effendi, she hangs out in the stables. It is not fitting."

"Ali?" A sense of foreboding gripped me.

"And she brushes the horses."

"Ali?"

"She chips clay..." then realizing his solecism, Ali fell silent.

"Not Marlena, Ali, surely you yourself take care of my Marlena. I trained you, and you gave me your word. You gave me your word, Ali, just before I left to England, that you, and no one else, will care for my Marlena when Joseph retired!"

Ali had the decency to blush.

"How could you?"

With an oriental shrug, Ali explained, "Marlena is in good hands."

"Thin, lazy hands."

"Yes, but she carries water buckets to wash even the donkey."

"Nick Bottom?"

"Yes. He's alive and full of energy," Ali remarked, almost complaining as he made a frenzied hand gesture, indicating the beast's vivacity.

"Well, that's odd. Do you remember how we found the ugly brute tangled up in barbed wire in a gully?"

"It was sick."

10

"He wasn't sick. His legs were bruised and scratched. His cuts were infected, that's all. And you, Ali, you were first to flatly refuse to shoot him when Elliot suggested it."

"You did not want to shoot him."

"True. It was rather a relief when we realized that none of us had a gun."

Under the guidance of our old groom, Joseph, I had dressed the donkey's infected legs. "Ali, you used to wash Nick Bottom yourself."

"The donkey was sick." The boy picked his teeth, then added, "The girl brushes it now. She walks it too."

"You're certainly well informed of the girl's routine."

Ali simply looked away and kept quiet.

#

Thin shafts of cool light dappled the stables. A girl stood in a recess on an upturned tub, brushing the donkey named Nick Bottom, her back to the door.

According to Ali, the new girl had not spoken a word to any of the staff. I wondered whether she was mute and whether she could hear.

"Top of the morning," I hailed.

Her footing shaky, the girl turned to glance at me, then stared at the ecstatic flies all about the swishing donkey's tail.

"Well, Nick Bottom. How do you do?" Bowing low, I accidentally brushed my hair against the muddy floor. "Damn! My hair!"

Eyes bright, the girl handed me her wet brush, the same brush she used on the old donkey.

"You won't dare!" My eyes narrowed.

Her wide, hazel eyes on level with mine regarded me as she wiped dry her free hand. Then, she ran her fingers through my hair, picking out bits of mud and straw.

"I'm William, William Westbrook."

The girl paused.

"And you, who are you?"

She remained silent.

I essayed Arabic, English, and even some French but my attempts were met with steady silence.

The girl's fingers were thin and so were her wrists. Her oversized robes hung loosely over her shoulders. And her eyes scrutinized me from an aperture in a conservative veil.

11

"Good day, then," I turned to leave, a bit thrown by her silence and the intensity of her stare.

The girl dismounted the tin tub. But it was a clumsy move. The hem of her robes caught in her heels, and she tumbled, flailing her arms and smacking the donkey's rear.

Her fall set events into motion like collapsing dominoes.

Insulted, the donkey kicked back then bolted outside, braying a litany of complaints, leaving the girl sprawled on the floor, splattered with mud.

"Are you all right?" I asked, giving her a hand.

Her eyes met mine with silence.

"Here, sit down. I better get to that beast before he disappears."

Indeed, outside, Bottom already headed to the river.

"Hold it!"

A sassy flick of the tail illuminated Nick Bottom's intentions.

"Bottom!"

But Bottom took off, fast.

I was hot on his trail.

Then, mercurially, Bottom turned, heading back.

I kept running after the beast, calling for Bottom to halt.

And so Bottom lured me into a second round of chase, only this time in a tighter circle.

Still running round and round, I caught sight of the girl, gentle shivers rustling her robes. Then came two claps and Nick Bottom's capers ended.

Grabbing the rope tied round Bottom's old neck, I whispered, "You're a snake in the grass."

Bottom replied with a twitch in his ears, a swarm of insects lifting off.

"Well, here's Bottom, hold his rope."

But the girl only scratched behind Bottom's ear then led my donkey along a path in the sand, her hand resting on his back.

"Use the rope."

Bottom and the girl ambled up a hillock, as the fields and the web of irrigation canals stretched below, soft green against stark brown desert, with shimmering pyramids far beyond.

An average of one centimeter of rain a year fell on Cairo. Agriculture was only possible along land close to the Nile. Man-made canals and nitrates made the soil fertile enough to produce maize, cotton, tobacco, and wheat.

"Workers are in the fields today. The fellahin. Winnowing grain!" Their motions seemed indistinguishable from those in antiquity and their voices carried to the dunes beyond the echoes of their ancestors. "Amazing, is it not? Rural Egypt continues to labor with the technology of the pharaohs. Crude wooden plows still in use on the fields. And fellahin still reap with the sickle and water their masters' fields with the *shadoof*, it's that bucket that you see on a weighted pole."

The girl did not respond. Caked with mud, the girl's robes whipped about while her eyes fixed on the green fields.

"A peaceful aspect. From afar," I added darkly but almost choked with surprise when I turned to the girl.

In the steady breeze, her veil had come undone, and she clutched it in one hand while the other stayed on the donkey. Her hair, cropped and brown, much like the style soldiers sported, stuck up. She had high cheekbones and her lips were full. Her nose, small and well-shaped, was freckled.

"Who are you?" I asked brusquely.

Her head swiveled.

"Who are you?"

She veiled herself but without the deftness of practice one might expect.

"Do you speak?"

Silence.

"Do you understand me?"

Her head moved but only slightly.

"Who cut your hair so short?"

Her gaze fell then lifted back to me.

"Do you have a name?"

She held my gaze, then returned her eyes once again to the Arab peasants in the fields.

There was so much melancholy in her motion that the impulse overcame me at once. "You cannot be a nameless stranger, a shadow."

The girl faced me once more. Her veil hiding much of her face.

"When I see you, what should I call you? How will I get your attention? Oi, you there, mind the hoof! That won't do. You'll need

13

some sort of a name. What if I were to give you a name? At least, for a little while."

The girl's hazel eyes rested on me.

"Look, you must have a name. My Great Aunt Clara used to name all her lady's maids Betty. But you don't look like a Betty and neither are you a lady's maid and I'm not as batty as that."

Silence.

"Salammeh?" I faltered. "No, no, you are more like a Salomé..."

The girl kept her silence.

"Salomé...Would you like it? It means peace and besides, it has a pleasant ring to it. Peace. Not the raging madness that's our world."

The wind picked up once more and whipped the veil about so that I saw her smile.

"Salomé, then?"

She nodded.

Chapter 3: Aziza the Beast

"WAR or not, it won't do, you know."

Father turned a blank expression at my stack of papers.

"We cannot let it all go to ruin."

"William?"

"Our gardens and orchards must thrive again, Father."

"William, the entire estate is in shocking disrepair."

"It is."

"But I have little interest in the estate just now. I'm at HQ at all hours."

"Can't we hire help?"

"Ever since Muhammad Jamal died and now with the war going on little has been done to maintain the grounds, especially the irrigation network to the orchards." My father shifted closer to the French windows. "What do you have in mind?" He asked then bent to examine my rough sketch.

"Revive what is still alive and replace whatever trees died."

"Not a bad start. But I must maintain what staff we have. I cannot have seven maids, with seven mops, and let them work for six months here!"

I laughed. "The Walrus and the Carpenter? Really, Father."

"I cannot hire new help."

"None at all?"

"Militant groups target diplomats in Cairo. Employ Ali in your project. The boy has been neglected, I should say. His minimal duties leave him free to loll in cafes, associating with nationalists."

"Nationalists?" I scoffed. "More like impetuous student mobs..."

"Not all are students, William. Some nationalists are former militia."

I stared.

"I don't want Ali to get hurt. Ali's just a boy."

"That's not what Ali believes! To his way of thinking, he's a man."

"Yes, he does think it, doesn't he? However, he works for me. My political and social standing endangers him. The boy must stay out of coffee shops."

"I'll have quite a lot of work for him. But as for keeping him out of the coffee shops, I can only try."

"Well...William, you had something else to discuss with me?"

"I hear that local hospitals are undermanned."

"But another general hospital was added near Ma'adi."

"Makeshift huts with corrugated metal roofs house the wounded, yes. But skilled help is hard to come by. I have experience; it would be foolhardy not to help."

"You won't join the journalists or clerks at General Headquarters?"

"Father, I'd like to help but not at HQ."

My father regarded me with mild surprise. "You worked with the rescue units in London during the Blitz. But I was certain that once back in Cairo you would join us at GHQ. It'll be a good opportunity to use your other talents. You have extensive knowledge of the country, its language and its people, and you write well."

"I went through emergency rescue training in London. It would be a pity to waste all that effort. You need not doubt my sang-froid, Father."

"No, there's no question about your composure and dedication. We can arrange that you join a medical unit here, in Cairo. But we will have none of that nonsense of roaming the deserts or joining a military campaign far away like your brother James. You will apply your recently acquired medical skills at a hospital nearby."

And just like that, and under the aegis of Sir Niles, I plunged into the horror of work at a military hospital during a world war.

#

Sauntering into the sitting room a day before Christmas Eve, Elliot startled my parents. Their expressions of surprise soon changed to disgust as the miasma of squalor gripped the room.

"Elliot!" Mother squawked, backing away. "Pooh! What did you roll in?"

"Mother..." he drawled. A seraphic smile lighting up his features. He was dressed in authentic fellahin panoply of barbaric beard and almost indecently dirty and torn Arab robes. He was remarkably convincing. And his dusky curls, pasted to his tanned forehead with sweat, hid his English identity.

"You've had your fun at our expense, Elliot. Now change for dinner," Sir Niles directed the smelly fellah who bowed in unexpected obedience.

16

"Fun? He smells like a sewage rat!" I grumbled.

Elliot's head swiveled. "William! I didn't see you hiding in the chair in the corner. Are you in disgrace? What have you done? Joined up with James?"

"No. But I'll join you as long as you postpone any display of welcome."

"Follow me then."

Elliot ordered a bath to be drawn and thrusted his smelly robes at a reluctant maid.

"Burn it, Effendi?" she suggested.

"Give it to the poor, Rahma!" When the brief staring match ended, Elliot called for his shaving implements while the maid looked dubiously at the robes, clucking and shaking her head. "And that's enough cheek!"

"What beggar would want your robes?" I asked after Rahma left us alone in Elliot's room and Elliot had settled comfortably into a warm soapy bath.

"You'd be surprised. But here William I have not greeted you properly!"

After Elliot's proper welcome, I retreated to my own room to change into dry clothes, spitting and hissing oaths under my breath.

Later at dinner, Elliot, groomed and cheerful, regaled us with amusing anecdotes about society people milling about at Cairo Central Station. Then, his smile frozen in place, he asked, "Any word from James, our heroic Eighth Army field surgeon?"

"None."

Here it seemed that Father needed to have his say. "Elliot, your antics are charming. And mischief has always been your raison d'être. But have the decency to tell your mother not where you are going, but when you intend to return. I shudder to think that Cook has to be told of an extra plate for our holiday dinner. Where will he find yet another athletic piece of leathery old camel to carve at table?"

Shaking his head, Elliot cast a reproachful look at her and complained, "Mother, when are you going to get rid of that old horror?"

The worried look her eyes had held while Elliot asked about James snapped into haughty petulance. "I like Cook and that's that."

#

"It's not too late for a walk, is it, William?"

"Elliot!" I stood up, tossing aside the Penguin paperback I had been reading in the study. "No, of course not! But rain's coming."

"Then put your jacket on."

Outside, wavering lights faded as gusts of wind rattled a flagpole, and treetops swayed against a dark sky. A dilapidated taxi careened round the corner, its engine rebelling with an eldritch screech.

"Nice of you to return in time for Christmas."

"I'm surprised that you keep track of holidays, William." Elliot yawned. "Rather rude of me to push off like this as soon as you arrive. Don't you agree? But it was necessary."

"I doubt that. Elliot, you disappear for days on some Paphian debauch, no doubt, and mask it with cloak-and-dagger tales that can never be supported nor believed by anyone."

"Did you miss me?"

"Don't be silly!"

"But you have been poking round my room in my absence, William. What were you looking for? Not a shirt, we're not of a size. A hint where to find me?"

"Funny thing that you should ask. Why the secrecy? Why not leave a note?"

My brother chuckled. "Would you've gone in pursuit of me?" His arm settled round my neck.

"Maybe. No...certainly not. You stank something dreadful tonight. Where were you? Gamboling in the underworld?"

"Do you remember Aziza the Beast?"

"I know of Aziza the Beast. A formidable female thug of the previous decade."

"Well, do you know of Aziza's granddaughter?"

"A rare Coptic beauty she is! And you two had recently met at the suk. A charming love story. But you've already spun that particular yarn, Elliot, so do try to come up with some new material."

"New material indeed," Elliot scoffed.

A rebel and a racketeer, Aziza the Beast was romanticized in the Cairene suks. And she, as well as her beautiful granddaughter, had become our idée fixe.

Like my brother, I was in awe of Aziza the Beast. And I was thirsty to hear more, true or false, about her elusive granddaughter but I certainly was not going to give Elliot the satisfaction.

18

"William, I've been trying to locate the girl."

"The girl?"

"The granddaughter. Last I heard, she was in Luxor. So, I went there."

"To Luxor? How?" I was still under his tight hold and so Elliot gave me a squeeze.

"Never-mind the details. My story begins in Luxor. I planned to join Father, to meet up with you in Alexandria. But I was detained. I was in jail."

"Oh, come off it, Elliot!"

With one arm still wrapped round me, he withdrew a cigarette and jammed it between his lips. "Jail." He paused to light his cigarette. "Well, my hotel turned out to be a suspected hideout of an Arab nationalist leader. The police rounded up the guests. And will you believe me when I tell you that they called your brother forward and took him as the guest of honor?"

"Impossible."

He stopped to remove his jacket and, under the street lamp, he bared his back.

Anger welled up. "Elliot! What's this?" I spluttered questions that piled up, disorganized and confused. "Who did this? How is it possible? Why were you beaten?"

Elliot fixed his shirt.

"How could anyone mistake you for a nationalist? You are the son of Sir Niles, Cairo's most prominent political advisor!" A touch of pain or panic crept to my voice. I was unsettled because our nationality and rank had always protected us before.

"You are mistaking Luxor for a modern city. Local law enforcement is merely a charade."

"But your height, your blue eyes! Your facial features! Could they not see that you are not an Egyptian? Could you have not convinced them at least of your innocence if not your nationality?"

"But what a bore would that be! Besides, I could have been a German spy."

"Elliot! Be serious!"

"Cairo is crawling with spies. Luxor, too. You begged me to tell you what happened. Are you still interested in my story?"

"Well?"

"Be silent then."

I looked away.

"The prisoners had been planning to break out with outside help. But they were clueless, like the authorities, and they too mistook me for one of their leaders. Then, it came." Elliot rubbed his hands together, delighted. "The chance of a lifetime. Would you believe it, I was put in charge of their explosives. Explosives! All those weeks spent in the school laboratory finally paid off. You, of course, remember the chemical experiment to which I am referring?"

"We set our dormitory ablaze, Elliot, how could I forget?"

"We were just experimenting!"

"And yet we were sent down."

Elliot was proud of his 'chemical experiment.' I, on the other hand, tried to bottle up that particularly nasty memory and the shame of being ejected out of a prestigious school.

"William? Are you listening? Do you remember that we used ten times the necessary mass?"

"How can I forget? There was too much of the explosive powder mixture in the milk churn. But, no matter! Go on..."

"You can't still be angry?"

"We could have killed somebody."

"There were no injuries."

"A lucky break."

Elliot could only recognize the farcical aspect of the explosion. "Never mind all that! William, my escape from prison was brilliant. The dazzling coruscation of the explosives! Unholy noise! Policemen everywhere! Large pieces of stone flying up in the air, and prisoners running in a stampede through the dust. Then I made for the Nile. I ripped off my clothes, jumped in, and swam, hoping beyond hope that I don't fall prey to the crocodiles lurking in the reeds. But there were enough of us swimming and the deafening cacophony must have been a great deterrent for the crocodiles and the police. The bastards are probably still looking for their Big Catch." Elliot's eyes shone until suddenly his shoulders slumped and he croaked, defeated and tired, "But I never saw her, William."

"Aziza's granddaughter?"

"I never found her."

"Well, no wonder! How could you find a mere woman through your cloud of dust, smoke, and coruscation?!" I rejoined. "What did you expect? And in the ensuing cacophony, she probably wouldn't be able to hear you calling."

#

Next day, stepping outside, I saw Salomé in the courtyard. Her straw broom scratched the sand off of the footpaths, casting shadows before her slender body.

Popping out of nowhere, Ali, without words or tact, snatched the broom from Salomé, and began sweeping. His dark features, distorted in the irresolute light, turned him into a jinn, deftly maneuvering the handle of the broom.

Salomé, her back straight and her head held high, waited. When Ali next paused, she hurried to him and tapped on his shoulder, gesturing for the broom.

"Go to the kitchen."

But Salomé stood in his way.

Ali grunted.

Now Salomé pulled on the broomstick handle, her stare steadfast. "Ali!"

Since neither saw me approach, both Ali and Salomé turned, surprised.

"Cook will fly into a rage if we don't buy his spices today. It's Christmas Eve, you know, and we've been putting off shopping long enough. Come along."

His face in shadow, Ali thrusted the broom at Salomé and followed me into the car.

"Does he want cardamom?"

"Ali?"

"Cook, the devil take him. Do you have his list, Effendi? It's never just one thing, it's always a list, a long list, for Cook!"

"A list?"

"Is it really only spices? It's usually not. Caraway seed? Wine, maybe? He has lists, and they never remain unchanged and, in the end, it is I who gets a pot or a plate to the head and nothing to eat or drink."

"Honestly, Ali, I haven't a clue. I assumed that you had it sorted out."

21

"No, Effendi. Cook did not write anything down for me, and I cannot remember what he murmured between his fits of shouting. Perhaps, we should go back."

"Absolutely not."

"Why can't Cook go to the suk himself?"

"Haven't you picked up on the nature of Cook? Sending you on an errand gives him an excuse to bully because you're bound to fail."

"Effendi! You volunteered to help me when you stepped in last night."

"Certainly. The maniac would have killed you, hammering his pot into your head like that!"

"So why do you say that I will fail."

"You will. I will. What do we know of the ways of spices and cookery? Pot sizing? Goat meat or goat milk? Oils and wines, and such odd things? Our old butler is dead or things would be different. And we don't even have a housekeeper with strong enough a personality to keep the old horror in check."

"And Sir Niles allowed Joseph to retire. Our dear old groom went back to his village."

"Joseph would have been able to treat your wounds at least."

"What wounds?"

"The wounds Cook will surely inflict on you."

"Effendi!" Ali squawked. "Can't we call Joseph back?"

"Dear Joseph is so very old. Ali, you cannot grudge him some years of peace and quiet in his sleepy little village."

"Joseph set my leg when I broke it while you were away, Effendi. But I doubt even he would have been able to stand up to Cook. Not when Cook is in a rage."

"Cook's a cockroach."

"He is a bad man."

"Ali, leave off Cook. Who cares about the maniac? Have you ever heard of Aziza the Beast?"

Ali crinkled his nose. "Another monster? I don't like your fairytales."

"No, no, not a monster," I hurried to put him at ease and stretched the truth. "A lady."

The motorcar groaned as I made a sharp turn.

"A lady. And a legend in Cairene history! Elliot revers her."

"James Effendi?"

"James? Well, James is more careful."

Ali murmured a quick prayer, then asked, "What about the spices?"

"Later."

Except for a sigh, Ali made no further objections.

#

Staring at the Bentley wide eyed, the Jewish businessman slowly vacated his wide bench. His white linen robes danced across his massive body as he rose. And his lips parted into a smile, his hands extended out.

"Faraj!"

"Welcome back!" Faraj boomed. His arms moved in fluid motions, welcoming. "William Westbrook! My dear boy! Come here! How are you? It is good to see you. In good health? Happy? How is James? Tell me, is Elliot all right?"

"James and Elliot are well enough," I managed as my mouth pressed against his shoulder in the embrace.

"Well enough?" Suspicion and concern crept into his voice as Faraj held me at arm's length now. "William, is something wrong?" Worry spread across Faraj's face and his deep brown eyes narrowed.

"Not at all."

"Where is your brother?"

"Elliot? Recovering from his carousing, I suppose."

"Well, that's good. James?"

"No word from James yet."

"I see," the big man looked away, unfocused eyes following Ali. Then, recollecting himself, Faraj exclaimed, "Ali! The young boy is a man now!" And as he pulled Ali into an embrace, he offered coffee, Turkish delight, and a water pipe.

"Faraj, young Ali has never heard of Aziza the Beast."

Rather of a nostalgic nature, the businessman was often keen on telling a story in mixed Arabic and French, seesaw like, and interlarding his long strenuous descriptions with some posh English aphorisms. So, after settling his bulk on a cushioned bench in his shop and seeing to our comforts, Faraj cleared his throat.

"Well, it was a long time ago," he began, then turned to Ali, "So, don't look for this woman. She's gone." His eyes snapped at me, too. "Aziza the Beast. She was a marvel from an age when women played a larger role in Cairo." Faraj scratched his silvery stubble and sighed to

23

prolong the suspense. "Well, life was hard then. Englishmen were moving in and there was chaos. And as more newcomers swarmed Cairo, prostitution, crime, disease, and poverty prospered. Shop owners were terrified. So, Aziza, the head of a certain gang, offered landlords and shop keepers protection from, eh, criminals...for a fee. They called her 'Aziza the Beast.' She had pale skin and beautiful almond-shaped eyes, the color of amber. Long eyelashes. Red lips. Masses of long black hair. She was grand. And there were none of those veils covering her beauty, thank heavens." Faraj's resonant voice rose and fell in his oriental fashion. "Few were the shop keepers unfamiliar with her skills. She had her good looks, true, but Aziza was famous because she dished out knockout blows to the head. Confused, Ali?"

"No, Faraj Effendi." But Ali's deep blush gave the lie to his words so Faraj elaborated.

"A shop keeper fancied a woman called Sayyida. One day, while making sheep-eyes at Sayyida in his shop, Aziza blew in. He tried to impress Sayyida. He refused to pay Aziza's protection fees and waved Aziza away. Well, there was nothing to it. Aziza brushed her hair back with a flick of her wrist, took a step forward, and dished out one of her knockout head butts. In an instant, our fellow fell unconscious to the ground. When he came back to his senses, he was tied to a chair in the kitchen of a restaurant with a pot of fava beans boiling and bubbling inches away from him. Hot, very hot! Then he saw her: Sayyida! *Très jolie*! Sayyida was beautiful, and he adored her. So absorbed was the young man, he never heard Aziza's footsteps. And when Aziza laid a hand on his shoulder, the man started. Aziza was willing to wed him to her lieutenant, Sayyida the Vein." Faraj chuckled. "Do you know why she was called that?"

Ali shook his head.

"Sayyida brought men to their knees by pressing this vein, right here," he pointed to his robust neck, somewhere under the folds of skin. "Well, our fellow was dangled above the steaming pot just so he would clearly understand Aziza's proposition. Fear. And when he married Sayyida, the cost of protection doubled. He paid the family rate. He also had to sign a will, leaving everything to his relict."

"What's that?" Ali asked.

"Should the fellow die, all his property and wealth go to his surviving wife, Sayyida."

24

"Oh!"

"Shop owners welcomed Aziza, showering her with gifts of patchouli, bread, sweetmeats, gold bracelets, silk scarves, ivory statuettes...Anything Aziza desired."

"But why?"

"My dear boy, protection was important. Under Aziza's protection, the suk was orderly."

Open mouthed and wide eyed, Ali listened to Faraj. He had never heard a story told with such delivery.

"Aziza," Ali uttered minutes later, adopting Faraj's French accented Arabic.

Faraj slapped Ali's back and blessed him.

#

Swinging open the heavy iron gate, Ali's gaze fixed, unseeing.

I drove past but when I switched the engine off and joined him, I asked, "Ali, do you fancy her?"

"Who? Aziza?"

"Aziza was a thug. And she's dead now. I'm talking about our new maid." I nodded at Salomé's retreating form. Then, crooning an oriental love song, I teased the boy.

"She is too thin. She will bring bad luck."

I paused long enough to say, "Ali, you watch her often,"

"May Allah protect you, Effendi," Ali spoke uneasily. "Allah Karim," he patted my back, reminding me that his Allah was a generous deity.

"Have you no poetry in your heart?"

"What about Cook and his spices, Effendi?"

"You know, Ali, we never got to the spice shop."

"We never got to the suk beyond Faraj's coffee shop! I won't eat tonight," he bleated.

"A trifling matter now that you know of Aziza the Beast."

"I know of a dead thug. Now I am hungry." And muttering a prayer, a plea for protection against kitchen utensils hitting his head, Ali left me to face Cook.

A lamentable tyrant of his pots and our maids, Cook terrorized us, excepting Mother. According to James, Mother had hired Cook against the joint protest of our, now deceased, butler, and Mrs. Judd, the housekeeper. And alone Mother championed Cook. He had little culinary talent, and he was frightfully ugly. His bulging eyes were insect-like and had a sickeningly penetrating power that matched his bad temper.

In the kitchen, ready for anything, I said bracingly, "I'll get it later, or, perhaps, tomorrow. Send a proper list with Ali and I'll see what I can do."

"Later? Tomorrow? A proper list? No problem." Cook radiated an oily smile. His yellow teeth were wide and square.

A wave of revulsion gripped me.

The old horror took a step forward, advancing like a mantis, pinchers extending out to grab hold. Clicking.

"Excellent. Tomorrow then. I must be off," I babbled, backing out.

"William!" Elliot's robust shout reverberated in my ear as my brother and I collided at the kitchen door.

My legs itched to run.

"William, here you are. Elizabeth dines with us tonight. Did you know?" Grimacing at Cook, he propelled me down the long gallery.

"No, I didn't know. And her stern father?"

"He declined the invitation."

"Oh, that's odd." But I was somehow relieved.

With a whisper that sounded more like a plea, Elliot invited me to the sitting room.

I agreed.

It could not be so bad to spend time with Elizabeth Baker. After all, my brother had proposed to her and she accepted. But I was wrong about that.

Tapping her expensive high heel pumps on our Persian rug in the sitting room, Elizabeth chattered about her Boxing Day plans, parties, and newcomers to Cairo. She prattled on endlessly in her modern metallic voice, smiling, yet describing with veiled malice shortcomings of people she would normally introduce as her 'dear friends' or assigning most unfitting nicknames to her 'dear friends' and all along she played with Elliot's brown locks, her fingers working their way round his wavy curls. Digits restless as her large breasts over her solid mid-section were never far from Elliot's head and never still. Yet, despite fingers and breasts thrust at him, my brother's expression remained bovine-like and his hair settled into a bleak mess while his cigarette hung in his mouth, smoldering. When it scorched his lips, Elliot jumped, surprised. And that was as lively as he got.

26

"Elliot, where is Mother?" I finally managed to interject.

"She'd telephoned to say that she'll be here shortly."

"That's surprising."

"Why? She's rarely on time."

"Mother dislikes the telephone. Haven't you noticed?"

"No."

"Where's Father?"

"With a guest. He too will join us shortly."

"Who is your Father's unusual guest?" Elizabeth asked, her restless expression suddenly sharpened with keen interest.

"Unusual? Florid and fat, more like."

Elizabeth bridled her expression and smiled at Elliot, appreciating his joke. "Beast, you tease me. But who is he?"

"Some old school chum of Father's, that's all," Elliot supplied.

"Elizabeth," I began but could not go on as Elizabeth took possession of my hand and entertained me with her favorite anecdote: Elliot's rescuing her from a group of natives that accosted her after a dinner party and their consequent romance.

Driving me to distraction, Elizabeth tittered on as her sharp voice and empty nonsensical words reverberated in my head. She fired the word beast or beastly often, and utilized darling almost as a weapon. I could scarcely imagine how Elliot tolerated such company and then to my relief dinner was announced.

Father walked into the dining hall and introduced his guest.

When Señor Marcelo approached me, he asked, "The youngest?"

"William, my youngest son."

Señor Marcelo spoke with a faint Spanish lilt, "Are you the towheaded boy I've heard so much about? Working at general hospital, are you?"

"I am."

He must have been to a military hospital because I detected some awe, some pride in his tone. "William, I salute you. But you do look quite young."

"Looks can be deceiving," Elliot mumbled at my side and at the same moment Mother sailed into the room, silk scarves aflutter and an assumed air of carelessness that belied her exhaustion. She had been playing tennis and spearheading charity committees, she explained, excusing her delay. Then she bestowed a frosty smile on the company.

"So, you have been absent all day?" Elliot asked her but did not wait for her answer before launching lugubriously into a complaint. "I hope Cook behaves himself. You know, Mother, he dislikes it when you're gone. And I certainly would hate to have our guests plagued with the shits!"

"Elliot!"

"Beast!"

"He jests, of course. Well, shall we?" Father escorted his companion to the table, shooting warning glances at Elliot, a pathetic figure as Elizabeth clutched rather tightly to his arm.

I followed, observing Señor Marcelo's short and fleshy form. His white hair was slicked back with aromatic pomade and his attire and manner were formal, matching Mother's cold stiffness.

#

"Elizabeth has left? Good. And your mother? Where is your mother?" Father asked.

Elliot drew on his cigarette and affected a surprised look. "Improvising on the piano. Can hear it a mile away."

"I'm only grateful that it's not a harp. Can you imagine a harp, twanging away at an evening?" I commented, well aware of Father's growing consternation.

"You have a point there, William. Cards?"

"All right."

Father halted, surveying Elliot as if trying to foresee what would happen next. "Señor Marcelo and I will retire to the study."

"We won't disturb you. Marcello's all yours." Elliot growled like a naughty child. "Now keep it a fair game, William!"

Later, when Señor Marcelo and Father emerged, Elliot shot up, gushing breathlessly, "I am pleased to have met you."

Señor Marcelo shook my brother's hand. "By the way, I haven't heard what it is that you're up to these days. What of war effort?"

A surreptitious smile altered Elliot's face. Then, my brother stepped close to Señor Marcelo to divulge his secret. "I'm an FF."

"An FF?" the old man tilted his head.

"Freelance Fighter."

I grinned. "What is it that you fight, the carousing crowds at the races? Or is it the overcrowded clubs that you subdue with your barrage?"

28

Señor Marcelo's melodic laugh dispersed my father's tension. Nevertheless, Father's pride made him add, "Elliot had joined the staff at GHQ."

I shook the guest's hand next and offered to show him round the hospital.

Señor Marcelo indicated that it would be unkind to his health and then followed Father outside.

Sotto voce, Elliot prophesied, "He'll rush to your hospital when he gets diarrhea from Cook's delicacies."

"Elliot, must you?"

"Well, what's he talking of 'unkindness to his health' for? This Spaniard appears to be in fine fettle. Why is he afraid of hospitals?"

"Military hospital, Elliot! He doesn't want to go into a military hospital," I snapped.

"Steady on! Why don't you go get some fresh air? No, you needn't worry, your precious cards are safe with me."

But as I stepped outside, still hidden from view because of the overgrown wisteria, I heard them talk.

"Where is the girl, Niles?"

"Would you like to see her?"

"I would."

"Wait here a moment."

Minutes later, Father returned, Salomé in tow, skipping to match his long stride.

"Let's see you child." Señor Marcelo tucked his cigarette between his lips and took Salomé by the hand, gently pulling her close. "Has she spoken yet?" he asked.

"I'm afraid not."

"No wonder! Have you read the latest reports, Niles? Nazis are now marching people off to camps throughout German-conquered territories. Horrific reports of cruelty and, worse, genocide. Machine-like. Calculated. Whoever can't work or serve the Nazis in some way, in any possible way, is eliminated. Inconceivable," he added and gave Salomé a kiss on her head. "Well, you are looking better now." Señor Marcelo's tones reached my ears. He was holding Salomé's chin in his palm. "Stay with Sir Niles, my little child...Just a while longer." He was talking softly, but something in his gestures made me believe that Señor

Marcelo was comforting himself as well as Salomé. "I am trying to find them." He glanced at my father.

Salomé, in response, embraced Señor Marcelo again.

What was going on?

"I'll see you again soon. Here, this is for you." He pulled out a thin package from his coat pocket and handed it to the girl.

Salomé accepted the golden parcel and turned to the servants' quarters.

"What was in the package, Albert?"

"Chocolate. Bonbons," replied Señor Marcelo. He dropped his cigarette in a temper then exited. He did not bother to bid farewell to my father, and when he made to open the heavy iron gate, he did so with his walking stick.

Leaning against the wall in a listless squat, I dropped my head in my hands. Who was Señor Marcelo? Father had never bothered to mention him before. What was Señor Marcelo's relationship to Salomé? What reports was he reading? Who was he searching for? And why did he give Salomé bonbons?

Exhausted, my thoughts drifted from Señor Marcelo and his business with my father to Salomé.

Salomé.

No one ever mentioned her real name, her identity. Even Salomé refused to acknowledge it.

Chapter 4: Truths Unveiled

"WHERE'S James?"

Elliot returned a look of utter bewilderment.

"Why have we not heard from him?"

"Ah, yes, William, you do keep on asking about our James," Elliot replied slowly.

"And you seem rather unaccountably nonchalant about our brother."

"James is an army surgeon. He can take care of himself. It's his patients you should worry about. Poor old chaps."

"Tobruk is under siege, and yet the garden parties continue." I gestured toward the lavishly decorated Shepheard's hotel.

"Such is life." Elliot nodded toward the hotel's exclusive bar. "Will you join me at the Long Bar?"

"And the press supports this jovial mood with reports of conquests in North Africa. Elliot, you know that these reports are wholly inaccurate!"

"The jolly celebrations uphold positive morale," Elliot drawled.

"How is it that you're rarely among the jolly crowd then?"

Elliot kept a stony expression.

"I am not opposed to socializing..."

"A recluse, William, that's what you are."

"Certainly not. But you agree, Elliot, do you not, that now, parties are inappropriate?"

My brother and I were at the historic and surprisingly still popular Shepheard's hotel. Outside the hotel, the streets bustled with the New Year's Eve festivities despite England's staggering losses in Europe over the Yule Season of 1941-1942.

Elliot stared morosely at his hands.

"Europe's in shambles! And in the Pacific, Japan is bashing into Australia and American Hawaii. And why's Japan an ally to Germany and Italy? Don't they know better?"

"Apparently not."

"And we're not doing too well in North Africa. In the Mediterranean Sea, British troops are under constant attack. Malta's still under siege.

Fascist Italy invaded Greece and the Greeks are now calling on England's promise for help. Russia, too, is struggling to repel Nazis."

"It is harder for you, William," Elliot finally offered in measured tones. "You working in hospital, I mean. It's difficult to think of anything else. I nearly fainted when I walked in on you holding down that fellow's feet while the surgeon sawed one off. And the smell! Good God. So, why, yes, to you, William, there is a deeper meaning to the clinical word 'casualties.' You see such gargoyles, their injuries and pain every day of the week. Most people experience this war through rationing or through the wireless. Most of them probably read the daily newspaper and can only relate to the fighting through news reports or letters from loved ones. And then, they get busy knitting, or joining some charitable committee. That's not the same as being in hospital and picking up the pieces so to speak. It's not the same at all." Then he snapped, "And just why the devil I can't shake off that dreadful rhyme of Humpty Dumpty out of my head now?"

"You work at GHQ. How is it easier for you?"

"It's not easier. I just get a different perspective. It's probably worse for me because I know when you will be receiving a shipment."

We fell silent.

Then, Mother and Father flashed across the dance floor before us.

"Father's colleagues are in attendance and keeping up appearances means so much to him. Look, will you oblige and stand in for me for the next dance with Mother?" Elliot asked. "All this noise. I'd like to step outside, only I promised her, you know."

"Go on, be off with you then."

Dazzling jewelry adorned her neck and wrists as I led my mother to the dance floor. Her golden hair was arranged to perfection, displaying a blue ribbon of pure silk, threaded, serpentine-like, into clusters of diamonds. She carried herself beautifully, arrogant and content. She was carefree and, for a moment, some of her insouciance pulled me in. The desire to forget the war and enjoy my privileged position was alluring. And it would be easy to become oblivious to a world war in Cairo.

The enchantment, however, was short lived.

"Are the rumors true, William?"

"Rumors, Mother?"

"William, the latest *on-dit* has you in company with a nurse from hospital. Are you involved with Miss Wright?"

Confused, I asked, "Do you mean Mrs. Wright? Do you know her?"

"Normally the matron allows only sisters to work for her but Miss Wright is an exception, isn't she? She is a certified nurse," Mother replied. "Now, William, dear, you have not answered my question. Are you and Miss Wright an item?"

"My affairs are no one else's concern."

"You are my son, William, so it is my concern."

"She's married. Did you know?"

"No."

"She is also a vicar's daughter. She helps the poor and frequently volunteers at local hospitals. She is a talented nurse, and I respect her. Mother, Mrs. Wright and I work together. There is nothing romantic between us. She is devoted to her husband and her work. And I do not feature much in her life, except as a lowly medic who removes putrid dressings or pungent bedpans now and then, I assure you. Would you be able to kiss someone over a pot of shit, Mother? Oh, I am sorry."

My mother raised her eyebrows. "I simply meant to say that Miss...eh, Mrs. Wright is...Not at all suitable."

"And I dislike gossip, particularly when there is not a shred of truth to the rumors. And why is it Mrs. Wright? She is about ten years my senior and not precisely a looker! Honestly, I'm a little hurt!"

"Oh, William, don't be so unkind. She can't help her age nor her looks," my mother leapt to defend the very person she had just condemned as unsuitable.

"I am young and unmarried and Father is a leading figure here in Cairo. You, Mother, are also popular and your charitable work is commendable and so your sons make a wonderful target for such whispered rumors at the club. Brace yourself for a season of spicy *on-dits* that have absolutely no ground, at least, whatever you will be hearing about me. I am too busy."

She smiled, relieved.

Feeling impish, I whispered, "Besides, it's Madame Sukey you should concern yourself with. She came into our hospital yesterday and caressed my cheek at tea time."

"William! Not that old Levantine dragon!"

"She is rather mature, true. But she is a wealthy widow who wants to help our cause. And she is generous, Mother."

"With her favors!"

"If you define favors as supplying patients with necessities and other odds and ends, or some fine wine and sweets and cards."

"I don't mind the necessities she provides, it's the odds and ends that I object to. Like her relationship with some of the patients and even that doctor!"

An unmanly giggle escaped my lips. "The information that reaches your ears is remarkable, Mother! And rather sordid."

Quite proud, she cast a roguish, challenging look at me and admitted, "Wonderful is it not?"

"I've always admired your humor." I bent to kiss her cheek, my thin, pale face against her delicate, rosy features, my lank, pale-straw hair against her golden pomaded coiffure.

Making our way back to our table, I inquired, "Will you be all right here? By yourself?"

Scanning the crowd, she answered, "Of course."

"I'll be on the terrace, keeping watch over Elliot. He's outside."

"Very well, dear, just don't go roaming. Cairo is such a wicked city."

"No more than London."

"William?"

I took her hand in mine and smiled into her eyes and promised to behave myself.

On Shepheard's terrace, Elizabeth and her friends, a gaggle of posturing debutantes, fluttered round Elliot. Mr. Baker, Elizabeth's father, hovered at a nearby table, talking to his business partners, while darting anxious glances at his daughter and making his distrust of Elliot quite clear.

Alone on the top step of the terrace, I stared at the shut shop windows across the street. The dull signs of Sinclair's Pharmacy and the Anglo-American Bookstore crouched before me as I escaped the noisy hotel.

"Effendi!" a boy popped out of the shadows of an alley lined with booths and handed me a leaflet. Catchy slogans urged Muslims to rise and defend the Honor of *Misr*, regain the Lost Honor of Egypt, defy British overlords and reinstate the Muslim caliphate. Hitler and the Mufti of Jerusalem busily concocted the scheme of championing Muslim rule over the Middle East to fuel dissent internally, necessitating diversion of British forces to deal with civil unrest, and thus weakening another front.

34

"Here, boy, take this rubbish back." But when I noticed a pile of pornographic cards, I summoned him. Dropping into the boy's brown hand the packet of naughty cards, I promised, "You'll get more baksheesh for this!"

The pamphlet brought Ali to mind. Ali, an orphan, joining the ranks of 'Young Egypt' seemed impossible. Nevertheless, my father expressed concern for Ali. And then I realized, suddenly and forcibly, the centrality of my father's role in our family. Father was aware enough of Elliot's character to comment however obliquely on a poor match in Elizabeth; he acknowledged Mother's meddlesome habits and James' unaccounted reluctance to write home; and he was informed that Ali had joined a radical group. What did he know about me? But what was there to know about me? I shivered and walked on into the teeming city.

#

"Ali! Wake up! I'm taking Marlena! Has she been exercised properly?"

Ali had been sleeping on bales of hay in the stables and was not amused to see me ready to go riding as he lazily stretched his limbs.

"Saddle her up."

It was the first day of 1942.

"Get to it, Ali."

In the far end, a shadow moved.

"The girl's here?"

"Every morning, Effendi," grumbled Ali, then turned to his duties, yawning and scratching every inch of his body.

Edging away from the boy and his fleas, I drew nearer to Salomé.

The girl moved across the variegated floor quickly and silently, but not quite gracefully. Her cotton robe got in her way.

"Salomé!"

She turned and raised her hand, returning my greetings.

"Effendi?" Ali's voice reached the far end of the stables.

"I'll see you when I return," I indicated to the girl.

She stood between the shadows. Alone.

I wanted to make her smile. But the damp earth smell smothered my senses and I could think of nothing amusing. At last, I saluted Salomé. I meant my salute in jest.

My fingers touched my forehead punctiliously, then I dropped my arm at my side with exaggerated mockery and force.

35

Salomé turned rigid; her stare blank, lifeless. Then, a tremble seized her, and she collapsed on the muddy floor.

Leaning close, I pulled her veil off to ease her breathing then continued to pat her thin cheeks, whispering her name, rubbing her face, her arms and noticing her rigid back.

"Ali? Ali!"

Silence.

I shouted, "Ali!"

The boy sidled up. "Effendi?"

"Bring water. Hurry."

Salomé's breathing was shallow and her pulse faint.

"Ali! Water!" My hands busily rubbing her temples, the nape of her neck, and her arms, I called her name all the while.

Then, after some time, like an orangutan in a circus, Ali showed up with a tiny glass of water in his hand. The boy stood by my side.

"You must be joking! Where the devil have you been all this time, Ali?"

He blinked, long hairy arms still clutching the glass of water.

I took my handkerchief, dipped it in the water and patted Salomé's face and lips, calling her name, urging her to wake up.

There was no response.

I was not sure when he left, but suddenly Ali stood by my side again, thrusting a bucket full of water upward.

"Ali, hold it!"

I was too late.

Water rushed down then splashed up as Ali soaked Salomé.

Dripping wet, I stood up relieved that the girl opened her eyes. But as soon as she noticed Ali, Salomé covered her face with her thin fingers.

Ali spat, clicked his tongue, and left.

When I crouched to check her pulse, the girl inched away. "Are you all right?"

Her only response was a slight nod.

"What happened?" Standing up now, wet and embarrassed, I felt utterly inadequate.

Salomé looked away as she got up slowly. A gentle stretch of her lips was her only display of gratitude.

"You better get another one, a dry one," I pointed at her veil and walked out.

Riding was no longer on my mind, but when I approached him, Ali grunted, "Effendi, Marlena is ready."

"You can be an efficient chap when it suits you."

Proceeding to pick his teeth, Ali managed, "You are the doctor, Effendi."

Surveying the ruins of my riding boots, I let out an oath.

#

On a cold February evening, a little over a month after Salomé's collapse in the stables, I returned home from hospital, dirty and exhausted.

A shrill voice recounted a day's events at the suk.

Curious, I bounded up two steps at a time.

Mother and Father glared at each other on the veranda.

"A mob surrounded us," Mother complained.

"Were you out today?" I asked.

"William, you're back," my father tried to smile but the result was a grimace.

"But really, Sir Niles, we couldn't get away. No, we could not–not until he took her."

"Her? Who?" I asked.

"William, there were riots in the suk today."

"I know. You wouldn't believe the damage a brick does to a man's exposed head! Especially when it's hurled from above. But, wait a bit, what happened? Was Mother out today? Mother, where you out today?"

"There were riots throughout Cairo," my father explained. "Your mother was indeed shopping. Ali and the girl accompanied her."

"Salomé?"

My mother's blue eyes snapped and she took a step forward. Her stance reminded me of Cook. "I always knew how it will be! Only I expected it to be Elliot, not you, William. You have always been such a good boy. But this is beyond..."

"Really!" Father interposed. "Let's be sensible. William, Salomé is gone."

The floor fell from underneath my feet.

"Ali explained it all," Mother interjected.

"Precisely what did Ali say?" Father asked.

"Ali handed her over to him."

"Handed the girl over? Who took her? Where? Is she still there, in the suk?"

Ignoring my questions, Mother continued, "She is William's lover, Sir Niles!"

"Lover?"

"Oh, for God's sake!"

"Lover!"

"Salomé's a child! Really, Mother, I cannot keep up. Is it some dalliance with a married nurse or sex with a little servant girl, a child at that? And where do you get these ideas?"

My father covered his eyes with his palm, and croaked again, "Lover?"

"Look here, Niles, I've often wondered why you employed her. She has been such a useless girl..."

I took off, running down the stairs.

"William! You need to hear your mother out." Father stood at the top of the steps.

Looking up at him, I shook my head. "I must go."

"William, it's not yet safe!" His calls echoed behind me as I sprang to the stables.

"Ali! I can smell your cigarettes. I know that you're here."

"I am here." Ali, smoking, slowly uncurled himself from the shadows.

I seized him by the shoulders, shaking him.

Ali's cigarette dropped out of his mouth. "Effendi!"

"Where did you leave her? Where is Salomé?"

Silent, Ali eyed his cigarette, smoldering on the damp earthen floor.

"Where is she?"

Another shake and I got Ali's attention. His face hardened. His body stiffened. "She...she was taken."

"Taken, Ali? Who took her and where? Answer me! Where is she?"

"A man took her. He ran into a crowd of people."

"There must be more to it than what you're telling me. Where is the girl? Was Salomé forcibly taken away without anyone noticing?"

"It's true, Effendi."

If Ali were telling the truth, then I underestimated the size of the insurrection. "Why did you not stop the man or follow him?"

"Her Ladyship was in greater danger, Effendi."

"Come, hurry." Unsatisfied with his answer, I propelled Ali out.

"Effendi, where are we going?"

"To the suk. But which one? Where'd you go?"

"I can drive you to the Khan el-Khalili, Effendi."

"I'll drive. And, I'll also wring your neck if we don't find her."

Ali called on his god for help.

"And leave off your Allah. I don't care about deities right now. Get in the car."

"I can drive."

"No, no. You sit here. Tell me, Ali, where did you last see her? Where did you leave the poor child?"

"Allah..."

"Answer me."

I feared for Salomé. And with a strong urge to kick every camel that blocked my path, I pushed hard on the brakes then the accelerator, swerving and slewing round Cairo's busy narrow roads.

Taking a deep breath, I tried, "Ali, she's but a mere child. A little girl. And she's all alone. Can you help? Can you recall where you last saw her? Ali, there's no telling what could happen to a girl in the hands of a mob, a rioting mob. But, how is it that you ended up in the suk with Lady Westbrook and Salomé? What were you doing there? What was my mother doing there?"

"Cook, Effendi, the horrible cook."

"Of course. It always is Cook."

Ali groaned and continued in rapid Arabic. "He had more requests and he threatened to leave, to quit. Her Ladyship, Effendi, heard the cockroach shout that he quits if no one attended to his needs. So, Her Ladyship offered to get new pots, and who knows what else. The girl joined us. I drove them to the suk. It's not such a bad place, Effendi, the Khan el-Khalili."

"No, you're right. It's the one marketplace most favored by foreigners. And on any other day, this suk is just a jolly walk. There's the pushy vendors and booming music to contend with of course but no one gets hurt. But you weren't to know, Ali, that today of all days the Khan ... the Khan el-Khalili would not be such a good idea."

Outside the windscreen of my motorcar, a veil of dust smothered the suk. The outline of the shops faded into a faint brown layer, still and mute.

"Ali, I'm stopping here. I can't possibly go on driving into this mess. Streets are narrow and I can't see a yard ahead of me. Park the motorcar someplace safe. Though, I can't see how it matters. There's nobody about."

"Yes, Effendi."

Pulverized dung, vegetable matter, and rubbish flew up in small puffs under my feet. And again, I was struck by the silence.

Some horrible stink hung over the stalls and the narrow, meandering paths were desolate.

The riot had progressed to another part of town.

The linen boutique where Ali maintained he had last seen Salomé was deserted. The scraps of wood and the layer of sawdust in front of the adjacent carpenter shop indicated a hasty retreat. At the onset of trouble, the merchants pulled down their rolling metal shutters and disappeared inside, afraid of the rioters and afraid of the aftermath.

"Open up!" I banged my fists against the shutters. "Open up! Salomé, are you in there?"

But my calls were futile. Even if Salomé were there, she would not respond. She had yet to make a sound.

Would I ever find Salomé in such a maze, such a labyrinth of narrow, dirty alleys? Was someone harming her?

My throat constricted with dryness. My hands were shaky. And still I called for her, sprinting, darting across tricky bends of a byzantine path.

I needed to find Salomé. Beyond the simple, humane urge to help a person in need, there was that inexplicable emotional bond to the girl that drove my search, and my fear.

Pausing to look into a shop, I heard footsteps behind me.

"Effendi?"

"Ali? Is that you?"

"Yes, Effendi."

"Here, Ali. I'm here, at the copper-ware stall."

Doors ajar, cluttered wares covered every surface without the ubiquitous hustler shouting and bargaining.

A mangy cur slunk away with half eaten flatbread between its jaws when I stuck my head in and shouted, "Salomé!"

Ali banged his forehead with a thud on one of the dangling pots.

"Mind the pot, Ali."

"It's hanging low."

"Come, let's go inside."

"Inside, Effendi, is very dark." Then Ali, his dark lashes flapping against his swarthy cheek, tugged at my jacket with hesitation.

"You can touch the jacket, Ali. My uniform is stained with blood and other fluids. But it's dry now."

"Blood? Oh!"

"It's all right I tell you. But what is it?"

"Effendi, your Salomé is far from here by now," he rasped.

"What do you mean?"

Ali's head turned away.

"Where is the child?"

"Do not worry. We will find her. Effendi, it is not a nice place of Cairo where we go but follow me."

Recognizing the futility of my search in the deserted suk, yet hesitating to trust Ali, I sighed in resignation.

"Lead on then," I prodded the boy into a run, back to the car.

Clutching at his chest, Ali rushed to the driver seat.

"Steady on, Ali. What are you doing?"

"Driving."

"Should you drive? Can you? I'd meant to ask you about driving my mother to the suk earlier. And parking the car..."

"Elliot Effendi taught me."

"Are you certain?"

In a remarkably good imitation of Elliot's British drawl, Ali replied, "Cairo is lawless enough. And this way, Cook will never again plague me with his outrageous demands." And with that, Ali slid inside, hairy arms stretched forward to switch the engine on.

As we flew out of the suk, I asked, "Where're we going?"

"Al-Khalifa," Ali announced and swerved round an equipment carrier that was stopped in the middle of the street.

"Al-Khalifa?"

"The man who took her...I recognized him. I know where he lives. We will go there and get her."

"In Al-Khalifa?"

Ali looked ahead.

41

"Al-Khalifa, Ali? Why go there? So what if you recognized the assailant?"

Ali darted a hurried glance.

"Why are you so confident that he took the girl to such a district? We are driving away from Salomé." Why did I trust Ali? Had he not just misled me to the suk?

"I recognized the man."

"Let's go back!" I wanted to grab the wheel from him and turn the machine around, back to the Khan el-Khalili. "I can't stand this. We're going the wrong way and into such a crowded, filthy part of Cairo!"

"No good going to the suk, Effendi. Better go and look for the man who took your girl."

I lit a cigarette.

"We will find her, Effendi," Ali promised, deftly avoiding collision with a watermelon cart. "Do not worry, we will find her."

"You should hope so."

"I hope so," he announced then cast a longing glance at my cigarette.

#

The Al-Khalifa district bordered with the mighty desert cliff, the Muqattam. Infamous for its dilapidated huts and graveyards crowding the foothills, the district was also one of the dirtiest in the area.

Ali sped up.

But what was the rush? And what horror was awaiting us in Al-Khalifa? Would I ever see Salomé again?

When Ali finally parked the car, slowly squashing melon rinds and some indistinguishable rubbish under the wheels, daylight was rapidly retreating and the temperature dropped.

In front of a group of derelict bungalows crouching under crumbling tenements, dogs lolled on the earthen walkway. Every so often, the mongrels mustered enough energy to scratch and lick their infected flea-bites, letting out low, tired growls.

Instantly, as we marched into one of the huts, the unmistakable miasma of human waste assailed us. Then, a buzzing noise broke through the heavy silence as, sensing a disturbance, bluebottles scattered to perch on every surface.

Ali hurried from one room to the next, glancing at the inhabitants but saying not a word.

"Ali?"

But he hushed me.

There were naked toddlers packed into a small common room. Their dark eyes followed us, in silence. A pile of rags served as a coveted bed upon which three older children crowded.

In the pit of my stomach, a hole formed, and it was growing larger. Would I find the girl here, in this squalor, miles away from the suk?

"Ali, where the hell are we?"

He proceeded bullheadedly into a courtyard, pausing only to claim, "Salomé will be here!"

"But where is everybody? Don't these children have any parents?"

"They ran away. They know something bad has happened, and they are afraid of the police. And the police will come. Police always come!"

So that at least explained the stillness of the children. The adults had fled, leaving their young behind.

Outside in the courtyard, Ali and I were alone.

"There's nothing here, Ali. We best head back to the suk."

Squinting, Ali's gaze swiveled about. Then he walked to a stack of deadwood by the communal cooking oven that still gave faint light from the fire within. Not far from Ali's feet, on the hardened earth, was a heap of rags.

"Salomé!" Ali declared. He looked like a stooge in a conjuring act that had gone terribly wrong.

Was that jumble of dirty rags really Salomé? Was she alive?

In just a few quick steps, I was staring down at the girl. "Wait by the door."

"Effendi, I..."

"Wait there and hold the door open."

I knelt down. Slowly, gently, I untangled the mess of torn fabric, sticky with blood, bluebottles ecstatically bussing about.

"Effendi, *yallah*! Hurry."

"Salomé?" Leaning over the girl's face, I placed my ear to her mouth, then to her heart.

Alive. She was alive.

Her hazel eyes flew open, watchful, but when she heard Ali's calls, Salomé quickly shut her eyes again.

Salomé's robe was ripped and she had no undergarments. Open gashes on her ear and upper brow were covered in dirt and flies. A trail

blood ran down her temple and cheek, and scratches
her face.

ie fragments of fabric covering the girl, I bit my lip in anger.
rd to the raised welts on her shoulders and abdomen, her
s. A wide bruise was taking shape under the left side of her
blood and caked dirt stained her inner thighs.
this to you?"

Ali whimpered.

ran quickly yet gently over the girl. "You have no broken
n going to pick you up and carry you to the car..." But
l explain that I was taking her home, a new horror leapt
es.

ieart was beating faster and my mouth drier yet.

ng and bruises disfigured Salomé's face and body. The
w extremely dirty and attracting innumerable flies, needed
ention. But it was the tattered yellow star that fell out of the
ier robe that made me choke with fear.

smothered the unlit courtyard, and there was the possibility
trator was nearby. Wiping sweat off his forehead, Ali
ndi. *Yallah! Yallah!*"

Salomé in the shreds of her robe, I took her in my arms.
r."

you going to do with her, Effendi?"
i."

i, we trampled through the dreadful house. Beads of sweat
my back and forehead, some falling on Salomé.

she done to deserve this?

l stirred in my arms during our ride back. And when Ali
igine off at the estate, the girl made sounds.

was under the impression that she could not speak, or
l at all, I brought Salomé's face close, and listened.

by my side. He offered his help while murmuring some
all the while.

are we?" I remarked acidly.

his palms and looked heavenward. "Lady Westbrook,
great danger."

y her into the stables then," I snapped, disappointed,
ther the girl's murmurs.

"But she's not a horse!"

"Do it, Ali! It's the closest place to the car. Do you want to run into Cook, or my parents just now? This girl needs privacy. A sojourn from the inquisitive maids and the sharp tongue of Cook could only help."

The boy reached over and, with unexpected tenderness, carried Salomé into the stables. He laid her on top of some bales of hay.

"We must bathe her. We must clean her wounds. These cuts will go septic otherwise."

"I will bring water, Effendi."

"Boiling water! Bring hot water, Ali," I shouted, but Ali was already gone.

Moonlight poured softly into the stables as I bent low to look at the girl.

Salomé's eyes locked with mine.

"It's all right. You're home."

She stirred.

"Be still, you're badly hurt."

She raised her hand and reached for my arm; her thin fingers wrapped round my wrist.

"What is it?"

She squeezed my wrist.

"You must be in terrible pain. But it's going to be all right."

She was nervous, perhaps scared. Talking to her would ease both our minds. "It's going to be all right, you know. You have no broken bones, no bullet wounds, no stab wounds, well, maybe a small one, or maybe it's something else, I need better light. Be glad for that. I'll clean out the cuts. I need to stitch the gash over your eyebrow. We'll have to stay here in the stables tonight. In fact, I much rather that you remain here for some time...until you're better. It's likely that you'll contract fever."

Her eyes still on me, her hold on my arm loosened.

"Nobody will bother you here. You needn't worry. I'll let my parents know that you are back." I talked to her to keep her mind off of her pain, and to keep my mind off of that bit of yellow cloth shaped like a six-point star and bearing the word 'Jude.'

I reached into my pocket and pushed the star-shaped bit of fabric further inside.

When Ali returned, bath sheets and bed linen tucked under his arm, candles and matches threatening to slip from his grasp, he hurried to the back of the stables, to a vacant stall. He flicked his torch on, then fashioned a bed from small squares of straw-bales. He hung up a sheet at the entrance, a privacy curtain, and got out again. He must have gone to the kitchen on his first excursion, because he quickly returned carrying a steaming pot of water. Carefully, he hobbled back into Salomé's new quarters.

I dragged a trough into the girl's room, my muscles straining against the weight of the old, wooden container.

"Here, you can use this, Effendi," he handed me a wet rag. "But I keep the troughs clean." He filled the trough with water, mumbling incoherently. When finished, the boy looked up. "Good?"

I dipped my fingertips into the tub. "Now soap."

Ali looked down and shuffled his feet.

"What is it? What's the matter, Ali?"

"Effendi," he whispered. "Do you not think we ought to have a woman take care of her? This is not a man's..."

"We'll manage. I don't have time to call on anyone. And I don't wish to disturb my parents...my mother, especially."

"You will not be calling for a doctor? You...you will do it all by yourself, Effendi?"

"Get soap and don't worry. And, Ali, get vinegar, all that you can find in the kitchen."

"Vinegar? All the vinegar? From the kitchen?"

"Go already and fear not. Cook's asleep."

"Are you sure?"

"Cook must be asleep. I don't hear him shouting, do you? Devil take the man."

#

The arid night air was cold.

After bathing the girl, I got Salomé into her makeshift bed and covered her with several sheets.

Her face was contorted with pain.

"You're brave."

She shut her eyes.

"I'll get iodine and dressings from my room. I have some ether, too. It's late, so my parents are already asleep. In fact, it's only you and I who are still awake. I'll be back shortly."

46

A jackal raised its voice and dispersed the stillness. The wind picked up, blowing about ferociously.

Crossing the courtyard, the crisp air lashed across my back. I wondered what my brothers would have done. James, the oldest, was in the army, but no doubt he would have marched straight into our house with Salomé in his arms, demanding our entire staff to be at his service. Elliot was misbehaving in town, but, had he been there tonight, he would have vomited at the sight. Elliot never could tolerate the sight and smell of blood. So, I was alone. At least I was spared having to explain what had happened and what I was going to do.

Had Salomé been violated? It certainly appeared so. What had happened? And what to do with a girl who was carrying a Nazi mandated yellow star? Who was she? How did she come by the star? Had she been in a ghetto? Or worse yet, was she in one of those horrific Nazi concentration or death camps?

I recalled an article I had heard my brothers discuss eight years earlier. I was only twelve and they excluded me from their discussion. They called Dachau a Hitlerite concentration camp in southern Germany and talked of forced labor and torture and of maltreatment and death.

Since 1939, since war broke out, bits of news had escaped Nazi occupied Europe and the information leaking out was shocking, almost inconceivable. Could humanity sink so low? But now, after handling the girl's yellow star, the war presented an uglier side yet.

The yellow star ended in my pocket. But what would become of Salomé?

Chapter 5: A Dark Hour

UP until the attack on her at the suk, I had had little to do with Salomé. I was either working in hospital or in the gardens. And when I had time to spare, I accompanied Elliot on his scandalous outings. Consequently, I found Salomé's eating habits, domestic responsibilities, and living arrangements rather mysterious. Where did she sleep? And where were her clothes, those shapeless, dark robes she wrapped round herself to resemble a Muslim woman? Clearly, Salomé was not an Egyptian. And, now, I suspected that she was not Muslim either. The robes and the veil were a masquerade. But who orchestrated the pretense? And why? Why go through all the trouble of impersonating an Egyptian maid on an English estate in Cairo?

Outside the stables, Ali was washing Salomé's robe in a tub by moonlight. The soapsuds shone, giving an illusion of purity.

"Still here, Ali?"

He stood up. "Effendi, I went to get her box from her balcony."

"Her what?"

"Her box, Effendi. She lives on the maids' balcony. They told her to sleep there. The Hellcats, eh, do not like her because she does not speak and because she has large eyes that watch them." Ali indicated with fingers stretched wide apart the gesture the maids used to describe Salomé's eyes. It was crude and cruel. Ali went on categorizing Salomé's possessions. "She has a box and had two robes and a veil. Ah...I asked the maids. That's what they told me," he explained, embarrassed. "And I told them that she moved to the stables where she can watch over the donkey."

"All right, Ali. Where are her box and robes?"

"Her box is in there," Ali replied, pointing to the stables.

"Good."

"Effendi, she wore two robes today to the suk. It was a cool day today. There is only one here, and it is torn." He fished out the wet fragments.

"She's going to be in bed for a while. You can buy robes for her later."

"Effendi? I? Buy women's clothes?"

"You'll figure something out."

"But, Effendi..." the boy bleated.

Stepping back inside the stables, I paused. What had happened in the suk? What was Ali's role in all this and why was he suddenly so determined to help?

The main door behind me blew open, letting a cold gust of wind into the sturdy structure. Marlena made an odd sound, echoed only by Bottom. I walked over to the mare and calmed her. When I went to shut the door, I noticed that the stars dimmed. Clouds took over the heavens and fearful noises filled the stables as the squall outside hurtled twigs against the old, thick walls.

Pushing aside the curtain at the entrance to the back room, I walked into the now torch-lit space.

Salomé raised her head from between the sheets then brought it back down.

"The bath was a trial. I'm sorry about that. But I had to bathe you. You can call it debridement. And, I'm afraid that you'll have to be strong a bit longer," I whispered as I dabbed cotton wool in iodine. "This is going to be a little..."

Her body shuddered when I applied the soaked cotton wool. With my palm on her forehead, I tried to get her to relax. The shiver that ran through her body subsided. Again, I tried the antiseptic. Again, Salomé shook with pain.

I had morphine. One Syrette worth.

I looked at the frail little girl lying on the straw-bales. She was morbidly thin. Deep cuts and bruises covered her face and body. And she was certainly dehydrated. Will I find a vein easily enough?

"Will you look there?" I pointed to the window opening. "Look away. Look over there." Again, I pointed at the window. I wanted to keep her from watching the Syrette, its long needle that was going into her skin at a low angle, at my thumb and forefinger squeezing the tube.

#

Macabre routine in bombed out London or in hospital could not prepare me for the sight that met my eyes on the following day. Squinting into the light slicing through the aperture, I saw Salomé still asleep. Her bed sheet tumbled to the ground, exposing a grisly map of cuts and bruises. I picked up the coarse white sheet and shook it, ready

49

to replace it on the girl. Her eyes flew open and I leaned close, whispering her name.

Her lips remained pressed as pain held them shut.

My pulse quickened. I had my duties to attend to in hospital. I had to leave. But could I leave her here in the stables? Could I trust Ali? What was his role in her abduction? And why was he helpful now? Could it be remorse?

"Stay in bed and sleep. I'll be back this evening. Wait for me, Salomé."

She closed her eyes.

In the evening, when I returned from hospital, Ali struck out to meet me at the gate.

"Effendi?"

"Ali."

"She slept through the day."

"I don't wonder at that."

"I looked in. I even got clean robes for her. And veils."

"That's good."

"Effendi, she never cries!"

Recalling the noisy wailing and public weeping at Cairene funerals, I did not wonder at Ali's bewilderment. "Salty tears probably sting her open cuts, Ali! She was brutally beaten, you know. And worse." I leveled a darkling stare at the boy.

"Effendi? Are you going in now? She is asleep."

"I'll wake her then."

Salomé's bruises were tender. Her bruising was a result of heavy impact. Her legs were atrocious. Because her body was recovering from internal shock, the discoloring and the accompanying pain were going to linger.

I looked for signs of infection. Dreading that the gashes and raised weals would go septic, complicating treatment, I applied antiseptic again and stepped outside.

"Still here, Ali?"

"Yes, Effendi."

"Fever often results from wounds like that due to infection."

"Effendi?"

"Call me as soon as you notice anything different about her."

"Different?"

"Anything that's different like smell, look, sweat, discoloration, anything unusual at all."

Fever did grip Salomé, sending her into unconscious, unpleasant sleep for three days. Then, the sweats and chills appeared as the fever broke.

At the end of the week, my father checked in on the girl in the stables.

"Father!" I stood up, rather surprised but mostly pleased that he came.

Salomé opened her eyes.

"William, you're here. What's this smell?" Father twitched his nose at the unlikely mixture of herbs, disinfectant, and horse.

"Ali's been boiling thyme and sage in here. I suppose that's what you're smelling, aside from horse or vinegar or..."

"Thyme? And sage?"

"A rather mild form of antiseptic. We dip the bath towels in it and soak up the sweat. Keeps her more comfortable as the fever breaks."

Father stepped close to the girl and reached for her hand; cobalt blue locked with hazel.

Then Salomé, who had given up trying to smile while her bruises were healing, blinked.

"How is she?"

"The fever's breaking."

"Good."

"Father, let us speak outside."

He bent close to Salomé. "You're in good hands, child." Then he walked out to the dark courtyard, hands thrust lazily into his pockets, slouching elegantly.

"The child is markedly thin. Father, I am quite concerned that her body would fail to heal."

"She is thin."

"She's malnourished. So much so that I was actually surprised to see the fever begin to break. I did not expect her to...recover. Her injuries, her weak state, her body, and the trauma all made me rather expect the worse."

"That bad?"

"That bad."

"Well, I'll have a few words with Cook. As much as I dislike it, I see that I must take it up with him." He gave a slight shudder. "The child must recover and thrive while under my care. What else does she need?"

"Food and water in small portions but frequently throughout the day and fresh, clean linen." I looked into his eyes and commented, "I doubt that this event is going to help her recover from her conversion hysteria."

"Conversion hysteria?"

"Did you ever wonder why she does not speak?"

Father simply stared.

"Shell shock."

"William?" He slid his hands deeper into his trouser pockets and tilted his head.

"In certain cases, mental distress is converted into a physical disorder."

"William, speak plainly!"

"Her body, her nervous system, is reacting to something that she experienced or saw. I suspect that that is the reason she is mute."

"I see." Then he changed his tone and remarked flippantly, "Well, let us hope that Cook and Ali will be able to turn that round!"

"Is it wise? Do you trust Ali?"

"He took you to her abductor, did he not?"

"Well, yes."

"And has he not been helpful to you? You mentioned it yourself. He does go in and out of the stables at rather frequent intervals like a Jack-in-the-box, if I can believe your mother's observations."

Sounding petulant, I conceded, "I suppose so."

"Then it's all settled. I'll have Cook employ Ali for any extra tasks. That should keep Ali close to home and under supervision, and the girl will get her much needed nourishment and rest. You must admit, the wretch in the kitchen has his uses! I doubt anyone could keep a lad in check better than Cook."

#

Perhaps it was her strong constitution or her desire to live that brought on Salomé's recovery, yet, over time, as days turned into weeks, I watched Ali's methods of care giving. And I suspected that Ali's rich Egyptian cuisine did wonders for the girl.

52

Father's instructions to Cook were interpreted liberally but generously. Ali brought what the rest of the servants would consider an indulgence, lamb and lentil stew, to Salomé daily. This hearty dish was religiously accompanied with sweet mint tea, datecakes, and, of course, Turkish delight.

But there were other offerings.

I was passing through the kitchen when I saw him.

"Ali? What's this?"

"For the girl," Ali explained while furtively scooping bits of *konafa* dessert onto a plate. "Look, Effendi. It's cooked in butter and stuffed with nuts. Delicious," he warbled.

But Ali was hurried, terrified of Cook's return. He was fishing bits of *konafa* out of a heavily greased pan, dripping oil and syrup onto the floor, tracing an elaborate, serpentine pattern on the tiles. While a bit of batter dangled precariously between his fingers, he raised his hand. "It is my favorite. It is very good, Effendi. Try some," he purred.

"I'll take your word for it." I backed away, eyeing the treacle and grease with the direst foreboding. "But Ali I must remind you that while I'm in hospital you must bring Salomé boiled water to drink. Boiled, Ali."

"Boiled water, yes."

The sound of clogs clopping along the hall reached our ears and Ali oiled out of the kitchen, holding the sticky plate close to his chest.

I quickly followed suit.

And there was also the occasion when I walked into the stables unnoticed by Salomé and Ali.

The boy was demonstrating how to eat Om Ali, rich, warm bread pudding drenched in milk, coconut, raisins, and nuts. He dipped his fingers into the pudding and, tilting his head heavenward and opening his mouth wide, posted the dripping goo.

"Why not use proper utensils?"

Their heads slewed.

"Well, don't look so scared. What's in the bowl, Ali?" Next to a glass of mint tea and Om Ali was a bowl full of thick, brown broth.

"She won't eat it."

"Well, what is it?"

"Cook, that devil, refused to make stew, so I cooked stew myself." Ali stiffened.

"Have you ever cooked anything in your life?" I leaned over the murky broth. "Do you know your way around the kitchen?"

"Well, a little."

"What is this? *Fuul?* Fava beans?"

"Not exactly."

"What the devil are you feeding this girl?"

"Eh...boiled fava beans, onions, and lamb. Boiled, Effendi, boiled, just as you always tell me."

Salomé eyed us warily from under her iodine-stained sheet.

"All right, Ali. You made your point." I took the dish. "Let's have a taste of your hellbroth." A hateful smell wafted, and my eyes opened wide. "Damn! What's in it?"

A bit of blubber floated to the surface and then rolled over again. The fat was tainted with the same brownish hue that characterized the dish and I half expected to stare down at the eye of a newt!

"Are you sure that it's lamb?"

"It is boiled," Ali, with deprecatory gestures, sang the stew's praise.

"Yes, and so was the fillet of the fenny snake."

"Effendi?"

"Shakespeare. Well, let's have it."

"Are you going to eat it, Effendi?"

"I am going to taste it." I placed the edge of the bowl against my lips and closed my eyes, then sipped. "Merciful heavens!"

"Effendi?"

"Did you boil a cat?" I snapped. "Take it away and dump it."

The thin sheet flung off of Salomé, and the girl got up like a shot. She grabbed my jacket and held tight to the bowl.

"What, you're going to drink this?"

She nodded.

"You see? It is good. I tell you, Effendi. Lamb not cat! Not hellbroth!"

There was nothing left for me to do but watch.

Salomé gulped the broth, the entire bowl, standing up. She grimaced, and then slowly creaked to her straw bed. Her stiff motions revealing what her abrupt reaction cost her, the pain that still kept its grip on her body.

A ruffled hen, Ali rushed to Salomé's side. He bustled about, nudging me out of his way.

Then Salomé ate Om Ali and drank her mint tea, purportedly to aid digestion.

"She'll be glad for anything that aids digestions after all that!" I growled.

Ali lifted his head, rather aggrieved.

"Well, I see how it is. I'm off." Marching out, I murmured in Arabic, "May Allah be kind and merciful, Ali."

"He is, Effendi. He is!" Ali's religious fervor chased me out of the stables.

And so I learned that I should not intervene with Ali's choice of menu for Salomé. For him, it was a matter of duty. For Salomé, well, she probably did not want to let food go to waste. And, although bruised and in pain, she looked well rested and was putting on much needed weight.

#

Even at work, though attending to patients, filling out paperwork, and addressing letters to parents conveying condolences, I found myself thinking of Salomé. Who was she? Was she safe in the stables? And was she safe at the mercy of a boy who had already allowed her to fall into the hands of a vicious man?

Ali. He had little interest in the girl until after we brought her back from Al-Khalifa. Now, Ali furnished Salomé's room with bales of hay and knickknacks he had rescued from the *zablaneem*, the handlers of Cairo's refuse. He fashioned a bedside compartment in which was hidden Salomé's mystery box. He even managed to purchase robes and veils for the girl. And while Salomé remained bedridden, he delivered food and drink. Ali also arranged her medicines like a parade ground. He refilled the supplies of iodine and dressings. But, of course, Ali would never apply the antiseptic or dress Salomé's cuts. He left such tasks to me.

Yet although I was glad for his assistance, the greater the physical distance Ali kept from Salomé, the better. At times when I returned home from hospital, and upon glimpsing Ali near the stables, a rush of anger or mistrust hit me. I mistrusted the boy because although I called him a boy, he was rapidly losing any signs of boyhood and was now a muscular, hairy young man. And he was so very near Salomé.

55

Why was Ali so attentive? Was it due to a guilty conscience? Should I find out more about his relationship with the man who attacked Salomé?

I had to be patient and wait for the right moment to make my inquiries. I could not demand answers because I wanted the truth.

Mid-February of 1942 brought cold nights to Cairo and on one such cold night, Ali sidled up to me and reported that the maids were getting curious and suspicious of Ali's, and my, motives for keeping the girl in the stables.

"Guarding the donkey was a poor excuse, Effendi. So, I told *Rahma* and Fatima that Salomé had fallen ill. Effendi, we must bring the maids here to see her."

"Nonsense, Ali. Don't be so gullible. The women are trying to feed their insatiable curiosity. I'll take care of this."

"You will?" he doubted.

"Of course. What have those gossip fiends to say?"

Ali recounted some of the gossip.

Face reddening, I relented, "I suppose I should've expected that keeping a girl hidden for so long might incite suspicions of the worst kind. Contagious diseases or pregnancy? Damn, if this bit of gossip reaches my mother, I would never hear the end of it! I'll take care of it tonight, Ali." I pulled cigarettes out of my pocket.

"Thank you, Effendi."

Then, offhandedly, I commented, "It was good that you knew where to find Salomé."

"Oh. It was a lucky guess."

Lucky guess, my foot! "A guess?"

"Effendi, I recognized the man who took Salomé."

"And who was he?"

Ali lit his cigarette. "Mahmud."

"A friend of yours?"

"He grabbed Lady Westbrook," Ali continued, ignoring my question. He blew white smoke through his nostrils. "Effendi, do not be angry with me."

"No?"

"I let Mahmud take her," he blurted, his eyes staring at the ground.

I kept silent.

56

"I told him that she wore gold jewelry. And I promised that you will pay to get her back. I told Mahmud that she was yours. You see, Mahmud loves money more than politics. Then police closed in on the suk, and he got scared and even crazier, so he grabbed the girl. Effendi, it was the only way to get Her Ladyship out of the Khan el-Khalili alive."

His rapid-fire words left me speechless. So, my mother's account was not entirely inaccurate. "You?"

"I did not have a choice, Effendi."

"But Ali, who is this Mahmud?" I asked slowly, afraid to say too much, afraid to reveal my outrage.

"A thief."

"Thieves steal money and gold, not little girls."

"Thieves are thieves, Effendi," he opined, sagaciously. "Mahmud joined the nationalists. And now he steals English people. I do not know how he recognized Her Ladyship. But he made to take her away."

"Lady Westbrook looks foreign enough. Not too many natives have fair hair, fair skin, and clear blue eyes. And few people wear such clothes as my mother does." My tone was laced with contempt. "Ali, can you tell me the whole story, not just snippets?"

Salomé stirred in her bed.

Ali made to go into the stables but I held him back. "I'll go."

Sitting on the edge of her straw-bales, Salomé smiled. Her thin legs, discolored by bruises, dried blood, and iodine, dangled from beneath the sheets.

Looking at her unveiled face, I wondered what did Ali know about Salomé's identity.

Because of her thinness, she looked like a little girl. But her increasing height, and other features I had noticed only recently, suggested that she was not a child. Perhaps she was fifteen, perhaps older. I also appreciated the value of her muslin veil. Her light complexion, her delicate features, and her short but soft coppery-brown hair cast doubts on her assumed 'Egyptian' identity. Now, iodine and bruises masked her fair visage.

"How are you? Are you feeling any better?"

She extended her arm.

"What is it? Ali's outside."

My eyes raked the girl. Where did Ali get the preposterous idea that Salomé was 'mine'? Thin, child-like Salomé as my lover? Or perhaps he

57

had meant my father's? Ali's words were vague as they were a blend of Arabic and English. The implausible idea was nevertheless acceptable because, in the Arab world, boys were considered mature in their teens. A twenty-year-old man would have an established family of wives and children. And girls were married off as quickly as a match could be arranged, if they were lucky. Many little girls ended up in brothels.

"Salomé, what do you remember of the events at the suk and Al-Khalifa?"

Silently, she pulled the sheets to her body.

"Do you trust Ali?" I whispered.

Silence. Either she did not understand or would not answer.

Could it be that Salomé knew nothing of the boy's role in her nightmarish assault?

Salomé patted the bales with her hand, disturbing the small box resting beside her.

"Would you like me to sit by your side?"

She nodded.

"I'll be back in a moment."

I wanted to finish my conversation with Ali.

Outside, Ali sat cross-legged under a lone, gangly fig tree. A shriveled-up fruit hung over his head resembling a thought that could not quite materialize. He leaned against the thin, twisted trunk and chewed on a reed.

Looking at the boy, I found that my temper was rising.

How much truth was in Ali's story? Was my mother at any risk? Was there legitimacy to Ali's motives? And why was it necessary to substitute Salomé for my mother?

Purchasing patience from recollecting his youthful innocence and the absence of parental guidance, I commented, "Rather brave of you, Ali. Saving Lady Westbrook."

Ali nodded.

"Lucky, really, that you know Mahmud so well."

"He is no friend of mine, Effendi." Ali placed his hand on his chest.

"But you knew where to find him."

"He used to be ...ah...well, he was known as a thief, maybe a murderer. He is a criminal. But he's also connected with political groups. They like him. He is not afraid of anyone, and he knows how to use a gun."

Would a fourteen-year-old boy like Ali associate with nationalists and criminals?

"Ali, where did you hear all that?"

"Hear?"

"It's café gossip, no doubt. Who told you of Mahmud? Do you really know the man?"

"Gossip? I don't gossip. I help the party. Mahmud was at a meeting. And I carried weapons to hide in his house."

"You cannot be serious. You're only a boy..."

"A boy?" Ali got up.

My father had the measure of the situation. Ali was a member of a nationalist gang. And I had erred in calling Ali a boy. I insulted him.

"Ali, before you go, there's something else."

"Of course, Effendi," he replied, his voice restrained and his eyes averted.

"Do you remember the gardens your father was so very proud of?"

Turning to me, his lips parted in surprise.

"It was art, really."

"Yes, Effendi."

"Well, I am going to bring it all back. The gardens, the orchards! But I need help to get the irrigation channels cleared up. Do you remember your father's methods?"

Again, Ali nodded, still unsettled.

"Cigarette?"

His gaze wandered for a moment, but then returned. "I can help," he said and accepted the cigarette.

"Good, because I'm tired of having to carry water buckets. The saplings I bought are already dead. Help me up, will you?"

Clasping my hand, Ali pulled me up, then looked to the gardens. "We need to start soon, Effendi."

"Yes, before spring, before the rain and winds begin."

"Will you have the water running in the ditches again, Effendi?"

"Absolutely. Ali, you will clear out the main ditch."

"And what about the diversion?"

"I've already added brush and more supports to the diversion your father constructed. It's working again. You can go see for yourself."

"Yes, Effendi, thank you. I will take care of the delivery channels. Only, Effendi, please let Cook know."

59

A soft shuffling noise came from the stables.

"Salomé's calling." I brushed the dusty grit off and walked to her room.

Supine on her bed, the girl was covered in white sheets soiled with purple, brown, and blue stains from her various ointments or tinctures.

"Let's check your pulse." But when I placed her arm back under the covers, I murmured, "You're healthy enough."

She looked round.

"Are you looking for Ali?"

She nodded, pointed to her wooden box, then turned her gaze to the exit.

I stepped out. "Ali, come inside."

"Inside?"

"Salomé called for you."

"Effendi?"

"It's something to do with her box."

Salomé was now seated on her bed, the box on her lap. Her face shone with the Vaseline ointment that I had applied to soften the healing scar tissue.

"What's this?"

As I took the box from the girl, I noticed that the wood was thin, warped, and weathered. "It's nailed shut. What should I do with it?"

She wanted it opened.

Ali peered at the box.

"It's nailed shut," I repeated.

"I know. I put the nails in." Ali stepped out to another stall.

"Where're you going?"

"Effendi, I'll get the tool." Ali returned and handed me a rusty pry bar.

Dreading what's inside, I forced the lid off then handed the box back to the girl.

Ali and I took a step forward as Salomé pulled out a satchel wrapped in golden tissue. She placed the attractive bundle on her bed and unwrapped it.

Breathing with a sigh of relief, I recognized the packaging. It was Señor Marcelo's gift for Salomé.

Gingerly, Salomé extracted a narrow carton.

"Chocolate bonbons?"

60

Her head bobbed. With her tongue slightly sticking out, she offered the open carton.

Ali plunged his brown fingers and grabbed a bonbon. He eyed and sniffed the chocolate. He then placed the entire ball in his mouth. Sucking and chewing, Ali's eyes seemed to pop out, surprised at the flavor yet going about it with obvious delight. Ali sucked the bonbon ardently until it melted.

Salomé and I, mesmerized by Ali's noisy approach to chocolate, stared.

With an effort, I wrenched my attention back to Salomé as she pushed the bonbons toward me, silky, bittersweet chocolate bonbons.

"Thank you. It's the kind I remember from pre-war days in England." I omitted the last bit of my thoughts, that it was a European import.

Salomé's legs and body gave a short dance-like wave. This was her way of thanking us.

Recognizing the meaning of her gesture, Ali nodded. Then, crooning a love song, he sauntered outside.

Salomé turned to me and I could not help but smile. But as Ali's voice faded, I wondered again whether the girl understood Ali's part in her misfortune. Perhaps Salomé had little understanding of Arabic. Or maybe she had no memory of Ali's role in her attack. And perhaps she was well aware of all that came to pass but she was choosing to forgive the boy.

"Salomé, there's been something I have been rather reluctant to do. I don't want to cause you pain or bring back bad memories but I must return this to you. It might have some special meaning," I spoke as fast as I could then thrusted the yellow bit of worn fabric, her yellow star, at Salomé.

She paled and her legs which, up until I pulled the star out of my pocket, were moving rhythmically, were now still. She stared, clutching that yellow fabric.

I had not the courage to remain. Calling over my shoulder, "I'll stop by later," I left, feeling gauche and unsettled.

Penitent, I headed to the kitchen.

Leaning on his workbench, Cook slurped arak and leered at a pretty maid.

In the tense silence, the servant dried a bowl with shaky hands.

Failing to attract their attention or to recall the maid's name, I cleared my throat. The servant let out a cry and nearly dropped the crockery. Cook, curse the man, ignored me.

"Look here!"

Cook swung round.

"The thin servant, the one Ali calls Salomé, needs rest. She's unwell."

Cook turned back round then asked slowly, his eyes once again fixed on the young woman and her chest, "Unwell?"

"Unwell, yes. Salomé was injured at the riots in the suk. She suffers terribly. See to it that she is undisturbed. Ali took over her responsibilities. I am sure that Sir Niles had already mentioned that to you."

"I wondered why Ali has been robbing my kitchen, sneaking off with delicacies I cook for the staff."

"You sent Salomé to the suk, did you not?"

"Lady Westbrook took her along."

"But why have Lady Westbrook go to a common suk? Why do you not venture out yourself? Afraid?"

Cook swiveled his protruding eyes in my direction.

My legs felt a bit unsteady. I had never spoken so to Cook. And why not? What control had he over me? Emboldened by my words and by necessity, I added, "Let Ali provide nourishing meals for the child. She does not require of you anything else. And certainly not your malicious gossip. She is injured. She suffers. You must open the kitchen to Ali while he assists me in taking care of her. And guard your tongue. She is but a child."

"Same age as Ali, and he's no child." Cook's words sounded dirty and crude.

"She is an innocent child."

Cook returned his protruding eyes to feast on the pretty servant, hungrily watching her neck.

"So, no more nasty tittle-tattle," I insisted.

Cook gave a slight nod.

Cook would not go back on his word, or rather his nod. I was sure of that. And I hoped that the servant would regale the rest of our staff with a colorful account of my conversation with the horrid man, and thereby explain Salomé's absence from their quarters. But as I walked out of the kitchen, I felt rather guilty because I abandoned the pretty servant in Cook's lair.

#

In early February of 1942, the same period as the attack on Salomé, Nazi and Fascist armies threatened Egypt and the Middle East.

Cairo plunged into a whirl of political disquiet. Now more than ever, Egyptian loyalty was of paramount importance to the Allies. But would the Egyptian King Faruq uphold Britain's interests in the Suez Canal?

In a daring move, British Ambassador, Sir Miles Lampson, left off acting as a diplomat as delineated in the Anglo-Egyptian Treaty of 1936-37. Sir Miles, and, according to the Egyptian press, British and Australian tanks, persuaded King Faruq to put into effect a pro-Allies government.

"Sir Miles has to secure Egypt as a loyal host to British military bases," Father defended the position of the British government. "Drink your whiskey, Elliot."

Elliot tossed it off neat. "The *wafd* is a bourgeois party. Would the *wafd* support England?"

"That's what Sir Miles believes."

"But do you? Sir Miles acted irrationally," Elliot opined. "Forcing the king like that brought national humiliation to the Egyptians."

"Perhaps you have the right of it. But we must maintain military presence in Egypt if we are to secure North Africa and the Middle East. If we lose our hold of Egypt, the Canal, or Palestine, we've lost quite a bit. Our safe flying zones from India to Europe, for example, would be undermined. And the Canal is a major artery to the Royal Navy. And what of Malta?"

"Not to mention the rich crops we get from the region," Elliot averred.

"And petrol supplies. But could Sir Miles have secured a pro-British Egyptian parliament less forcibly?" I asked.

"That's what he should've done," Elliot sighed. "Now, protests pop up everywhere. Cairo University students think that the Ambassador's actions proved that Egypt's merely a puppet at the hands of the British Empire."

"Sir Miles had to act swiftly. The streets of Cairo would be ablaze regardless."

My fists clenched, recalling how one such riot had left Salomé with lasting scars. "And maybe the riots on the streets will go on regardless, but does this mean a parting of the ways between Ali and our family? He's joined one of the nationalist gangs, you know."

"He did," Elliot grumbled. "But, for now, Ali's still undecided. The boy's torn between old loyalties and the sweeping wave of nationalism."

"I wonder, what side would he choose when the time comes?"

Elliot was in the right. Ali was an orphan, working and living on a British estate. He was an easy target for nationalists, or even for people with less admirable causes.

"Our estate has been his home all his life. Surely, he is grateful for having a home. He must be sensible of his good fortune," I postulated.

"William, you underestimate the appeal of the nationalists. Ali is young, naive. He's strong. And he's yearning to belong to a group, to have a purpose in his life. And you underestimate the power of persuasion."

My father smiled at Elliot's poetic statement. "I'd hoped, William, that your garden project would ease Ali's restlessness."

"I could find him a wife," Elliot suggested. "There's nothing like a wife to keep you distracted."

My father gazed fixedly at Elliot. "Cairo today, Ali will need a harem."

#

My visits to the girl in the stables continued. Often, I spoke of the patients in hospital. It was a dismal topic, but it was on my mind.

Leaning her lightweight head against my shoulder, her warm body pressed against mine, Salomé listened.

Did she understand me? I doubted that but she appeared to care to hear me speak. And I kept talking, finding solace in letting the words out, words that contained monstrous memories, tainted with pain, unbearable smells and the night terrors and cries of pain.

Somehow, I drew strength in Salomé's company and returned to the operating room, to the overcrowded wards that should have been better equipped. I returned to the soldiers who trusted me, to the fast pace of care giving and to the slow pace of recovery. I returned to the daily battle against pain and death and emotional misery and took heart in the courage and resoluteness of the patients and especially admired the sitting-up cases who kept up a running fire of wit and hilarity. And I

64

slogged through the mire of paperwork and petty complaints that often plague such institutions.

While with Salomé, I tried to make her talk. But despite the illustrations that I showed her and my slow pronunciation of words, she remained silent. Her understanding of my monologues improved, and she learned to recognize and understand more words in English. But she never spoke.

Her silence kept my curiosity piqued. What had happened to the girl in the suk? How did she end up in Al-Khalifa?

Salomé would only shake her head and lower her eyes when I questioned her.

At the end of February, returning home from hospital on a cool evening, I ran into Ali in the courtyard.

"Any news of Mahmud?"

"Mahmud has disappeared, Effendi."

A breeze blew about my tousled hair.

"He's been gone since the riots." Ali watched my hair, avoiding my eyes. "I tried to ask what happened, but I did not get far, Effendi. You understand me."

"Yes. I mean, no. Who were you questioning? When?"

"I talked to people in our party. No one knew much."

"I see."

But I did not! Was the boy loyal to us? And how creditable were his bits of news?

Chapter 6: Desert Wars

BENGHAZI fell to the enemy in late January 1942.

The winter campaign in the Western Desert that, at first, pushed and shoved the enemy out of western Cyrenaica and reached as far west as Benghazi, fizzled out. Deep into February and March, the Allies retreated halfway back across Cyrenaica, to the Gazala line, closer to Egypt, losing vital port towns on the Mediterranean Sea.

It was a staggering loss.

"Within two weeks of this campaign, the Allies lost 1,400 men, 40 tanks, and 40 field guns," I explained to Salomé one evening as we brushed the horses and the donkey. "And this was the winter campaign that was to have bullheaded the Allies to Tripoli, the principal Italian port in Libya, a port with facilities to match that of Alexandria's. Without Tripoli, German and Italian troops would have quickly run out of supplies in the Western Desert. And perhaps Malta would have been liberated."

Salomé paused and edged closer. She rested her cheek against my shoulder as her hand stole into mine.

Standing next to the great mare, my Marlena, brush in hand, I pressed on, my words marching in orderly progression out of my mouth. "Malta, by the way, is an important island in the Mediterranean Sea. Our Prime Minister calls it an unsinkable aircraft carrier. But the Italians and now the Germans as well have been bombing and strafing Malta since June of 1940. Allied soldiers and the people of Malta are starved and isolated. And it now appears that Malta will remain under siege for a while longer. So, do you see now why this winter campaign was so very important? Now, our people in the desert are caged along the Gazala line. Waiting."

Just like you, Salomé, I reflected.

War raged on but Cairene indifference dominated. A stalemate followed the winter campaign in the Western Desert in the spring of 1942. Now desert correspondence amounted to nothing more than non-committal news wired to Cairo sporadically and mercurially, never revealing the extent of the butchery.

But all nonchalance ended on 06 April.

Axis bombers attacked the port of Alexandria. A wave of anxiety coursed through the streets of Cairo.

Well, not exactly.

At Geziera Sporting Club, Elliot and I overheard a discussion of Axis movement.

"The Africa Korps will be here shortly," a towheaded officer commented, British nonchalance etched into his serene features.

His audience, all officers, huddled close, raising and lowering glasses of wine and bottles of beer, calling for service, then snorting with laughter.

"But not to worry, if all else failed, I mean, in the unlikely event of a Nazi invasion of Cairo, Shepheard's dilatory service would defeat the Germans."

"To Shepheard's torpor!"

An old man in a pale suit, who also overheard the crass remarks, approached the towheaded officer. Flicking his wrist, he splashed whiskey in the officer's face.

"An admirable gesture," Elliot commented. "But useless. They're tight."

As soon as the old man creaked away, the officer made a funny face and his comrades brayed with drunken laughter.

"Come."

"Where?" I asked.

"To hospital. Morale is high when I show up," Elliot boasted.

"True."

#

There was no escaping war talk.

"Yes, but we've Tobruk!" Elliot howled.

Elliot and an Australian patient argued strategy while playing darts on the second-floor ward.

"So you've met my friend, Mr. Tom Sullivan," I startled both men. "Elliot enjoys lecturing, Sullivan. Playing darts is pretense."

"Excellent!" Sullivan's smile made his slanted blue eyes and thin lips disappear. It lit up his narrow, boyish face. His short, sun-bleached sandy hair stood up, bringing his freckled nose and cheeks into focus.

Injured behind enemy lines during a sabotage mission to an Axis airfield stationed in the wasteland between Gazala and Benghazi,

Sullivan was finally mobile. He was one of few, selected fighters who penetrated the desert on such secret raids. Entering the Nazi airfield in pairs, he and his comrades attached Lewis bombs on aircrafts, machines and supplies by moonlight. And just when the camp was thrown into disarray, the commanding officer drew off his men. In pairs, they crept back to their jeeps. Sullivan's comrade however stepped on a mine. The comrade was killed. Sullivan made it to Cairo.

On his arrival, Sullivan's sunny disposition won me over and now I was happy to find Elliot in the company of such a remarkable man.

"Why is capturing and holding onto Tobruk so encouraging?"

Elliot looked at me through his lowered lashes. "William, you mean to ask, why is it vital to hold onto Tobruk?"

Limping to the board, Sullivan slowly extracted the darts as his desert sores on his hands were still raw. "Westbrook?" he handed me the darts.

"Don't! Oh!" Elliot growled.

A loud thud followed and then, "Oy!" Sullivan cried out as the dart left my fingers to connect with the center of the target.

"Archery lessons. I never play darts with my brother!"

"Westbrook!"

"I should've warned you."

"Yes, but you're forgiven Westbrook."

"So, what about Tobruk?" I asked, trying to deflect attention.

"Tobruk is a coastal port town in Cyrenaica. It's a key point."

"By key point Sullivan means that strong garrisons of more than one division each are centered at Tobruk and other similar towns," Elliot interjected.

"Right. Men, supplies, and even...hospitals," Sullivan added, his nose crinkling, sending his freckles into oblivion.

"Did William tell you that our brother, James, James Westbrook, is a field surgeon with the Eighth?"

Sullivan looked rather uncomfortable.

Warming up to his grievance, Elliot elaborated, "And that's why I understand your grimace at the mention of hospitals. Lean-tos in the middle of the desert are not hospitals. They are staffed with two doctors at best, and with minimal supplies, minimal disinfecting or sterilization."

"Often true," Sullivan offered.

"So, what about Tobruk?" I asked before Elliot could launch into a tirade about conditions in the field which had become Elliot's favorite complaint.

"The Eighth was supposed to get to Tripoli. Tripoli is now the chief supply port for the Germans and Italians. We get Tripoli, we get Africa. We can even relieve the siege on Malta. And we squash the Italian efforts to expand fascism and parallel forces with the Nazis."

While the two were talking, the ceiling fan circled flies round and round, over rows of bunks. Other patients began to throw in their comments and I wondered whether I sounded just like them when talking to Salomé. A little excited, a little anxious. Where was Salomé now and what was she doing?

Elliot chimed in, "That's what Mussolini's after besides the rich resources of Africa."

"Oil, they all want oil!"

"That too but there's more. Mussolini wants to prove Hitler that his brand of fascism is as strong as Nazism," Elliot insisted.

"But Hitler doesn't trust Mussolini and 'Italian-made' men or tanks."

"He sent General Rommel and his Afrika Korps to the desert."

"He reckons Italians lack discipline," one of the lying down cases piped up.

"You cannot have discipline when you have dysentery!"

"Elliot!"

"Well, really, William, how can you take aim when you have the shits?"

"We all have the shits, mate." Sullivan extracted a pencil and tore the paper wrapped round a fancy jam jar.

"That's a nice jam jar," Elliot observed.

Cat calls, "Jam for Sullivan...Madame's jam..." rang about and Sullivan's face darkened. Even his ears turned red.

Ignoring the jeers and bawdy remarks about Madame Sukey, a generous benefactor but also a lascivious widow, Sullivan talked on, explaining troop movement techniques. Using faint chicken scratches and a series of arrows and marker points, he summarized desert offensives. "We advance from one key point to the next in a pivoting fashion, never fanning out too far from the focal point." Australian accent blazed on as Sullivan continued, "Supplies, like petrol, water, food, and ammunition, are essential to the success of a desert offensive.

Yes, we have airplanes and, yes, the Royal Navy is backing us up, but land convoys could never traverse too long a distance in desert topography without supply trains to support them."

"But the Italians and Germans are using similar tactics. So, who will have the upper hand?"

"We have Sullivan, so we'll have the upper hand," interposed Elliot.

"What do you mean?"

"William, your Sullivan blows enemy aircrafts up before they can scramble and take flight, before they send our men to smithereens."

"Well, there's no need to wait for Germans or Italians to finish us off, mate. We have fleas, lice, mice, what else have we?"

"Rats. Don't forget the 'abominable' rats," a deep voice thundered.

"Actually, bedbugs, fleas and mice made me join the Desert Long Range Group."

"The what?" a patient asked.

"Reconnaissance units."

Elliot growled, "Reconnaissance my ...!"

"Well, we do occasionally sabotage supply and communication lines."

"Fuel dumps, storage stores, aircrafts," Elliot listed, sotto voce.

"You see, following our evacuation from Crete..."

Another roll of grumbles shakes up the ward as Crete is another sore topic.

"We regrouped in *Ma'adi*. I was billeted just outside *Ma'adi*," Sullivan lowered his voice. "And, by God, my armpits burned with flea-bites. I couldn't get any sleep. The mice danced on me, tails and whiskers whipping my face from the time I crawled into bed until I tossed the sheets off me in the morning."

An appreciative rumble echoed Sullivan's remarks.

"So, I used benzene."

"Oh, dear God!"

Another Australian patient, a giant of a man made of bulging muscles over large bones, croaked, "He soaked the furnishing in benzene."

"I did." Sullivan shot a rueful smile at his oversized mate, Bill Tate.

Tate ran his palms through his crop of dark brown hair, his generous lips stretching into a shy crooked grin.

"I wanted to exterminate the vermin."

"But I lit the cigarette that did it. I could smell the smell but I was dead tired and didn't put the two together: Smell of benzene and a lit match." Tate brought his palms together and closed his eyes, his open, guileless face a mirror of regret. "I flicked the burning match. Everything went up in a whoosh of flames. And we were both brought before our commanding officer."

"And, actually, this is how I joined the LRDG. We monitor the desert road."

"Both of us, Sullivan and I, together."

As Sullivan and Tate told their story, their young enthusiastic faces lit up.

I guessed that despite the hardship and pain, both were bound to each other. Brothers in arms now took on a new meaning.

Elliot and I sought their friendship too. I enjoyed their company and easy going back and forth banter. But for Elliot it was different. He finally found two men who inspired him, and won his admiration. Elliot, too, recognized the special bond between Tate and Sullivan, commenting once, "War rips us apart yet brings us closer together. But, William, I don't buy their story of igniting their camp. Such commando units are usually comprised of officers, or of some such military paragons, often attracting young aristocrats too who volunteer their services to the unit. Besides, few make it through their rigorous training."

"So, they're being modest. Why?"

"Not sure. Maybe they want to keep the unit's activities hushed up for security reasons. Cairo is crawling with enemy agents, spies, and busybodies. Besides, if their activities and talents, if their worth, were to be known, then the enemy would expect such attacks, defend the airfields and communication lines, and go as far as look for the men of the LRDG, and other such commando units like David Stirling's Special Air Services, and exterminate them."

#

Winter yielded to spring as February and March of 1942 brought rainstorms. Although brief in duration, the storms nearly wiped out our web of ditches. The torrents of rain resulted in rapid overland flow that choked the earthen canals with silt and debris.

Losing his patience, Ali battled desert flash-floods. By mid-March, thoroughly woebegone and frustrated, Ali wailed, "I thought that I dug

71

the channels deep enough. Effendi, I have never seen rain like this before in Cairo."

"Neither have I."

"What now?"

"Get the sand and debris back out of the channels. We have no other choice. It's in the nature of flash-floods to be destructive."

"Effendi, I will dig deeper."

"You know, we could shore up the slopes. Shoring means more work. But we'll armor the sides of the channels. Like so." I gestured with my hands to indicate the angle. "Elliot might agree to help you. He loves the exercise, as he calls it."

"Will he?" Ali's tone was dubious.

"Why not?"

"Ah, Effendi, Salomé wanted to work today."

"I was afraid of that. But ditch work is difficult, and I don't want her to reopen those cuts on her arms and legs. Besides, that fever nearly did her in. I told her to rest indoors."

"Effendi, she does not stay inside. Today, she took my shovel when I was not looking."

"The devil she did."

"She digs slow."

"Why did you not keep her indoors?"

"But, Effendi, you are the doctor."

"Not exactly." I grinned recalling how Salomé and I had argued. I ended up covered in straw.

With March of 1942 over, I could scarcely claim that the girl needed rest. And, at her request, I let Salomé pick up a shovel.

Together now, Ali and Salomé worked in the gardens and orchards. They removed debris and burned deadwood. They dug sediment out of the mother ditch and its tributaries with an energy that spoke well of their enthusiasm if not their prowess.

By mid-April, Elliot joined Ali and Salomé in their ditch warfare. He took up a shovel and introduced music to their work. And as the wireless spurted out itchy jazz, my brother worked with unparalleled zeal, sunshine bathing his shirtless back. Ali and Salomé barely kept up, and had I been there, I would've found it difficult, too.

The Battle of Gazala ripped the silence of the desert on 26 May 1942.

72

Carnage ensued.

Ambulances plunged out of shell dust and jostled for position on the track eastward, delivering the injured soldiers from the desert in unsightly cavalcades, their cargo piled up, heap-like, one on top of the other, and underneath the men, at the bottom, was the equipment, collecting dust and drips of blood and other body fluids.

Volunteers, nurses, and doctors carried the wounded inside the various military hospitals. The collaborations became known as 'Stretcher Parties.'

May 1942 shifted into June 1942. The desert war raged on.

Merciless sun, dry winds, and cold nights inflicted hell on the soldiers. And with rising temperatures, the flies increased in numbers.

"The same flies that settled on their bottoms while communing with nature, were the same flies that would later flutter over the soldiers' lips the next time they ate their biscuits and jam," I had explained to Salomé and several days later I shuddered at the memory of that conversation. Staring at a lump of jam on a biscuit at the cafeteria, I growled with anger. How could I have relieved the tedium of her evenings with such horrid tales?

"Anything the matter?" Elliot, sitting across from me asked.

"No, I just remembered something that I had said to Salomé."

"Salomé? What do you say to her?"

"Oh, not much. There's a book of medicine that I..."

Shaking his head and banging on the rickety table Elliot roared, "You cannot be serious!"

"Keep your voice down."

"What on earth does she want with a medical text book?"

I better not tell my brother about last night's monologue on rodents. True, rodents and insects were effective agents at spreading disease and discomfort. But did I really have to explain the details of it all? Did I have to list dysentery, malaria, typhus, infective hepatitis, tuberculosis, and diphtheria as diseases that incapacitate or even kill our soldiers? Was it wise to describe the symptoms and manifestation of each malady?

"Elliot, what does Father and his cronies at GHQ think of the retreat? How will the Eighth push back the Afrika Korps?"

"Well, the rout from Mersa Matruh was particularly hard on us. On the Eighth, I mean. Morale's low, very low."

73

"I know. It's been doing terrible things to the powers of recuperation. And it's not just low morale, Elliot. I'm beginning to doubt the efficacy of hospitals stationed hundreds of miles away from the front. Possibly, the wounded were already too far gone. But for some, the jostling ride across the rough terrain is just a little too much."

Elliot stared into his cup of tea.

"It pushes them over the edge."

"What pushes them over the edge?" he asked.

"Fatigue. Stress. Motion. Of course, now field surgeons developed creative methods to transport the injured. They insist, whenever possible, on letting the patients rest a few days before they travel by ambulance to Cairo or to Alexandria."

"But William, isn't there a good number of Mobile Dressing Stations close to the front?"

"It's a fluid battle that shifts rather unexpectedly. You know that as well as I. Besides, the men can't stay there above an hour or so. Then they get transferred to Casualty Clearing Station. But quiet rest and clean conditions, without the shelling and the flies, could make a big difference."

"Where do they go from the Casualty Clearing Station? Hospital?"

"No. Ambulance Station, then hospital train, and if they make it through, they arrive here or at the other hospitals in Cairo or Alexandria."

Elliot made a harsh sound then thrusted before me a packet he had stashed in his jacket. "Here, Mother insisted that I give you this."

"What is it?"

"Your razor and clean clothes. Oh, don't fly into a rage. I told her you need whiskey not your razor, but she would send razor and clothes and told me to remind you to present a calm and dignified appearance."

"Oh, Elliot. What would she say if she saw me now?"

"That's why I did not let her come along. But I grabbed some good brandy! What else do you need?"

Feeling a little churlish, I replied, "Morphia tablets, pentothal, ether..."

"Why?"

"Why?" I did not expect Elliot to take so much interest. "We use pentothal and ether as anesthetics. Morphia tablets are available sometimes but often not enough."

74

"I better have a word with your quartermaster."

"Oh, no, Elliot. You cannot mean to go about disguised as that monocled, old Frenchman. What name did you use? Guillaume? Dr. Leclerc?"

Elliot paused and stared into space.

"No. I won't be able to stand it again, Elliot. It was bad enough when you were ogling Madame Sukey earlier this month."

"Ogling?"

"Madame Sukey is a generous lady."

"A bit too mature for you, don't you think?"

"Elliot, we've been through this already, have we not? I like Madame. She is charitable, a generous benefactor. But, no, I am not one of her courtiers!"

"So why don't you want me talking to your quartermaster?"

"Because I'm familiar with your methods. To get what you want, you go about it in the most flamboyant way possible, and I can't let you go round calling out the quartermaster. I can see it all now: You brandishing a sword, yellowing lace handkerchief aflutter! Or worse, you might wave at him forged signed orders. Probably signed by no less a personage than Churchill himself! Besides, what's the use. Elliot, it's not just us who have insufficient supplies. Field surgeons I spoke to say that eight tablets of morphia, or two grains, in each emergency kit is not nearly enough in case of an injury! But there's general reluctance to provide tablets lest the common soldier misuse them."

Should I tell him that, for field surgeons, supplies like dressings were scarce too? And that it was an uphill battle against infections? It seemed that the only thing they had quite a lot of were flies, fleas, mice, and bombs. American soldiers often shared their rations of sulfa, the American military anti-bacterial agent. Just a sprinkling of sulfa on an open wound could prevent infection. But instead, I smile at Elliot. "Look, I must be off."

"I'll stop by again as soon as I can, William. And cheer up."

Elliot left me with my two packets. The brandy I passed round the sitting up cases, and the razor and clean clothes I stuffed into my cubby.

#

Pother and mayhem erupted at the British Embassy in Cairo. My father and his colleagues wanted to boost public morale so the Ambassador initiated a remodeling project at his estate. A crew painting

75

the estate by the Nile launched the charade flawlessly with the cheeky message that the English were here to stay.

Nevertheless, Cairo tumbled into chaos.

In June 1942, the Eighth Army retreated further back to el Alamein, a natural line along the Egyptian border, about 60 miles from Alexandria, protected by the Mediterranean Sea to the north and the Qattara Depression, a salt pan over which armor cannot ride, to the south.

This time, however, bureaucrats dreaded the worse.

At British General Headquarters in Garden City, officials gathered crucial documents and burnt paperwork of Empire archives.

"Up Rommel! On you go, Rommel," Egyptian nationalists cheered for Germany, reaching for the ashes carried in the wind from GHQ.

And sweaty hordes trying to escape Egypt crowded the Cairo Central Station, seeking travel visas to Palestine and elsewhere.

#

"Insufferable noise," Elliot grumbled and slumped into the divan.

"But you're fond of pianos."

"Not this one." My brother leaned forward and spewed out black, wrathful imprecations.

I handed him a drink. "Ignore the piano. You'll do yourself mischief and your rough language is not ingratiating yourself with me."

"It's a raging inferno outside."

"Will Father arrive shortly? Is he still at HQ? He's been there for days now."

"How would you know, William? I haven't seen you for days! Where were you? Hospital? By the way, where do you sleep when you stay away, at Mrs. Wright's?"

"I've a cot."

"A peculiar time for khamsin to blow into town. Hot and dry. But sand storms are in the springtime, not now in the summer months."

"Khamsin and Nazis."

"What's worse? Infinitesimal bits of sand hurtled at your face, your car, your house? Suffocating dust that smothers you in your sleep? Or the Nazis?"

"There's no comparison between the two, but if you must, then it's the Nazis. The khamsin is just a passing sandstorm. If the Nazis get

76

here, we would have a hard time driving them out. They're after the Suez Canal, the oil fields, and the crops."

"Among other things." Sweat ran along Elliot's temples and down his cheeks. His shirt, like mine, clung to his shoulders and back, wet with perspiration. He forced a smile as he got up. "Come, let us begin taping the windows. Who would you have assist us? Ali?"

I paused.

"Maybe that lovely creature, the girl, could lend a hand."

"There's black fabric to tack over the window frames. We must not let any light out during an air raid. Blackout confuses enemy pilots. They cannot target populated areas of a city."

"All right, but the staff need not know this great bit of detail. It's more likely that a sandstorm would hit us. An air raid is an unfamiliar evil, whereas khamsin is feared throughout Egypt. Besides, we should also get some soap for everyone."

"Soap?"

"It's difficult to wash sand out of one's arse without it."

"Elliot, don't be so crass!"

"Don't be so patronizing! I know damned well what's a blackout!" Then, with a hint of humor, Elliot said, "Well, William, I am ready when you are."

"I'll call Salomé."

"Oh, good. I prefer her over Ali. Now that he has grown up, he struts his machismo, day and night!"

I paused by the door and asked, "Should we wait for Father to return from Headquarters?"

"What for?"

"Maybe he'll have news of enemy advance. Perhaps all this preparation is in vain."

"No, if it's not Nazi bombers then it's the sandstorms! We need to get this business done and over with, and, besides, there's no telling when Father will return. He's been gone for days now."

"What's he doing at HQ?"

"Celebrating Guy Fawkes' Day."

"What?"

"Burning papers. Come William, there's not a moment to lose. And we cannot expect the piano to shut up, damn the thing. The world is at war, and Mother plays her piano, or tennis, or goes to the opera. Call on

77

that lovely girl for help. I won't be a finely outlined target for Nazi bombers."

"What shocking sights! The retreating bits of the Eighth Army return to Alexandria and Cairo." Elliot was somber. He had glimpsed the ambulatory cavalcades coming into Cairo from Alexandria. "I had to get to Alexandria yesterday, and all along the road between Cairo and Alexandria soldiers were piled up on top of each other with exhaustion and they cannot help but feel defeated. Many were badly wounded but they did not look like they cared very much. They were so hot, so exhausted that pain and bleeding probably played such a small role in their long list of discomforts!"

"Long list of discomforts? Elliot, that's an understatement!"

"Well? What of it? It's all the same."

"But why are the Egyptians pro-Nazi?"

"Can't blame the natives for wanting the foreigners out of their country."

"Egypt's long history is strewn with foreign rulers. So why curse the English but cheer the Germans?"

"Cunning Nazi propaganda. It's been infiltrating the region for years now." Elliot's voice drifted and his gaze fell on the girl, unfocused.

Salomé watched us stretch the tape across a window, then she touched my shoulder.

"They reckon the enemy is within a two-day drive from Alexandria," Elliot continued as I handed Salomé a roll of tape.

I took Salomé's arm. "Get on my shoulders. You can tackle the upper set of windows."

Salomé looked as I gestured my request. With dawning comprehension, she nodded.

Pointing at the topmost set of windows in the dining hall, Elliot exclaimed, "They're over eleven feet high! And there's an awful lot of these window panes. She'll have to stand up. Can she do it?"

"Let's hope so."

Holding the tape between her teeth, Salomé wrapped the cloth round her neck. She stepped onto my thigh, her arms on my shoulders and her face inches from mine, sun reflecting gold in her hazel eyes. Slowly, she climbed up on my shoulders.

Elliot watched.

78

Straightening up, Salomé tried to stand, balancing herself, when she suddenly tipped forward, nearly falling out the window.

"Hold her, William!" Elliot pounced and balanced Salomé in time. He shot me a glance, biting his lip as he kept his hands on Salomé's thighs.

Echoes of piano music and shouts from the kitchen filled the void of conversation while Salomé was taping X's on the windows.

"William!" The bellow came as a surprise. "Haven't we a ladder? What on earth is this? Put her down. Can't Ali do this job?" Sir Niles demanded.

Startled, Elliot looked at me then at Father and tightened his grip on the girl.

Noticing Elliot for the first time, Father called in agitation, "Elliot? I expect you to behave sensibly, and here I am walking into a street circus. A fine circus this is, a troupe of tumblers. And under my own roof!"

I could not turn and unbalance Salomé, and at the same time, I did not want to upset Father. A glance at Elliot confirmed that he too was at a loss.

With piano and Cook as background noises, my father breathed, "buffoonery," as Salomé kept uncoiling, stretching, and ripping the tape.

When Salomé tapped the window to indicate that she was finished, Elliot moved closer. The girl dismounted with a hop into Elliot's arms.

"Light as a feather!" Elliot smiled in surprise when she was in his arms.

"Well, you could hardly wonder at that! Cook barely feeds us!" my father complained. "I cannot imagine what our staff gets. Is dinner ready yet? What is that old horror up to now? Damn the fellow, I can hear him shouting again." He turned and marched to the noisy kitchen.

"Never saw him in such a temper. Have you?"

"Must be the strain of the army's retreat," I whispered. "Is he really going into the kitchen?"

Salomé pointed to the cloth, still draped over her shoulders.

"Oh, right, time for the dark fabric. Mother will not like it at all. It's hideous. Here girl, get on my shoulders." Elliot knelt by Salomé. "I am stronger."

"But smelly...ah, ouch!"

79

Elliot jabbed my arm and tripped me. He was about to straddle me when Salomé flung the black fabric over his head and wrapped her arms round his shoulders.

"Get off me."

"William, I can't breathe!"

"Get off."

"I'm off," he shouted.

In a flash, Salomé let go just as Elliot picked her up in his arms and bolted outside.

Salomé's eyes shut.

Would Elliot's trick startle the girl? Would she faint again?

"Elliot?"

Already outside, Elliot ran for the irrigation canals.

"Elliot, stop!"

And he did. He put Salomé back down and smiled as he gently fixed her veil. "Did you say something?"

Salomé's gaze locked with Elliot's cobalt stare.

"She does not speak, Elliot." My voice startled them. "If Father spoke to Cook, dinner will be served soon. We'd better go."

As Salomé turned to the kitchen for her dinner, Elliot rasped, "William, I could be wrong, but she said something."

"You sure about that? You'd made such noise, and I called you."

"Not sure, no. But..." Then, Elliot fell silent and uncommunicative.

#

Throughout the summer, one by one, British destroyers pulled out of the port of Alexandria.

Conversations grew desultory.

"No one will enter Cairo while the British defend it."

"Mother, at the moment, it's the Ninth Australian Division that is holding the Line," Elliot commented.

"Some British, New Zealanders, South Africans, Indians and a few others are in the mêlée, too," I was obliged to add.

"What Line, dear?"

"If Mother stays, I have to stay here in Cairo. And I'll help William when the convoys arrive from the desert. I can carry the men in, on stretchers."

"We could use a tall man like you. The ambulances arrive with wounded piled high."

80

"Nonsense! Elliot, you turn giddy at the sight of blood! No, no, you and your mother are taking the next train to Palestine. All the necessary arrangements have been made."

"But Father!"

"I have no intention of leaving," my mother objected. "The Ambassador is throwing a party at the Mohamed Ali Club."

Chapter 7: Demons in the Desert

MID July of 1942 violently shifted to late July. Rommel and his German Afrika Korps lunged at the Eighth Army. But Sir Claude Auchinleck commanded the Eighth to hold the Line along the Egyptian border between el Alamein and the Qattara Depression. And the indomitable Eighth pugnaciously held the Line.

When August fumed in, at that time of summer when the sun scorched the desert, GHQ in Cairo determined that Egypt was safe.

It was a somber victory or rather a costly stalemate.

"Ten thousand casualties in the month of July, and Egypt's safe!" a surgeon in my ward spat, wiping his forehead with his bloodstained sleeve. "The Canal is 'safe.' Ten thousand boys - dead! And every hospital in and around Cairo is overflowing! They're sending them to convalesce in Palestine."

Still, when the Prime Minister came to Egypt, he demanded a victory in the desert and a purge in upper military ranks, two fingers raised in a V sign.

Elliot's interests changed too. Whatever work Elliot had at GHQ, it did not ground him. Mischief moved to the forefront of Elliot's affairs almost as a defiant act against his work at GHQ or perhaps against his betrothal.

Elliot marked the housemaids. And he had good reason to do so. He took umbrage at the insolent remarks they made when he worked with Ali and Salomé.

"William, they stare."

"But aren't you pleased and flattered?"

"Well, at first, it was all right."

"Yes, I can see you flexing your muscles and winking."

"I did no such thing and if you're going to be odious about it you can bugger off."

"All right, Elliot, so the housemaids stare and titter and crowd close to you. What's so terrible about that?"

"They cannot take such liberties with me. It offends!"

"You've bronzed, Elliot. You tantalize them."

"Shut up."

"Temper."

"And I cannot tolerate the maids' ill treatment of Salomé. They can gawk at my bare torso. Fine. But to follow me from behind windows is the outside of enough!"

"What ill treatment of Salomé?"

"Hanging the washing, they ogle me. Lecherous beasts!"

"What about the girl?"

"They jeer at Salomé. Damn them."

"So, what have you in mind?"

"I'll contrive...And I'll use their own senseless superstition. What's more, William, we'll manipulate servant gossip!"

"What? We?"

Smiling seraphically, Elliot said, "William, we will stage a conversation within earshot of the housemaids."

"A conversation? Elliot, you cannot be serious."

"The Hellcats will believe it because they are superstitious and they will repeat it because they gossip."

"A conversation isn't exactly going to stop the maids from mistreating the girl. Call me when you have a better plan," I scoffed.

A day later, Elliot stormed into my room.

"William?"

"What is it?"

"Do you remember our plan?" Elliot stood in a cloud of dust that hovered over his dirty trousers and shirt. He was sweaty and muddy.

"Your plan to converse?"

"Well, it's time. When the maids clean my room, enter and demand that I stop digging. Warn me not to dig because of something dangerous! And make sure that you speak Arabic."

"Wouldn't they be suspicious if I spoke Arabic? With you?"

"No, no, they are far too stupid. And they'll be too scared."

As I followed Elliot outside, I noticed movement in his bedroom window. "She's there now."

"Who?"

"The ugly one. Fatima. Didn't you say that she was the ring leader?"

"Well, well, well." Elliot sprang back inside, with me following close behind.

There were two maids in Elliot's room.

"Fatima and Rahma. Cleaning my room again?"

"Effendi!"

"Elliot," I put my hand on his shoulder. "You cannot go on digging!"

The maids pricked their ears. And I hoped that they would not wonder why I used Arabic.

"A tall tale," Elliot dismissed my warnings as he marched to the sink to splash water on his face.

"It has been awakened. How else would you justify what happened to you?"

"Think nothing of it! A simple accident!"

"You nearly died!" I howled, relishing the impact that my Arabic guttural staccato had on the eavesdroppers.

"I merely slipped."

"The jinn," I insisted. "The jinn nearly devoured you. You heard its calls, its shrieks as you dug deeper. Sir Niles said that this estate was built on a sacred burial ground of royal pet monkeys."

For a moment, Elliot stared, disappointed. "Pet monkeys?"

"Royal pet monkeys."

Then he snorted and threw, "Nonsense!" over his shoulder, and shot out of the room, coughing and choking, with tears of mirth in his eyes.

The maids stood dumbfounded, clutching now mangled bedlinen between them.

"A jinn attacked my brother because he opened up burial grounds," I told them, nodding slowly, clicking my tongue, delivering my *coup de grâce*. "I told him not to dig into the sand."

From then on, the help spotted afreet. "The jinn," became a common whisper.

"It glowed in the dark."

"It looked like a monkey."

"A giant of a monkey. And it howled."

I congratulated Elliot on his clever use of sheets and torchlight. "But who howled?"

"Ali, who else?"

"All it now requires is a thistle-eating ass and some nonsensical beings that frighten people out of their wits!"

"For a charm of powerful trouble, let it brew and bubble?" Elliot burst into laughter then asked in faltering tones, "But why is it that you and Father always thrust Shakespeare at me? And always either Puck or

Macbeth's three witches, those Weird Sisters! Can't you find better quotes?"

"No, not I. You know that I read little and the quotes originated with Father. I am just reiterating."

#

Outside, on the following afternoon, as Fatima regaled her companions with her latest demonic encounter, Elliot picked up on their agitation. He made loud grunting noises then howled.

Frightened, the maids jumped and clucked. Then, after a brief silent pause, their frenetic exclamations filled the air.

"It is He."

"The jinn sounds like that."

"Jinn!"

Caterwauling behind bushes, Elliot stripped naked and dipped himself in the murky water flowing in the ditch. He rolled in mud and sand, then returned to the bushes to lie in wait.

The maids, their nerves worked up to a pulp, saw what they had been led to believe.

A demon erupted from the earth. Nude and gritty, he pantomimed a dance, haka-like, and his stretched mouth spattered curses in antique languages. Then he sprung toward the cultivated land.

Terrified of the apparition, the maids dropped the washing and, screaming, they stumbled to the kitchen to consort with Cook.

Later, across a beautifully arranged dinner table, but with a peculiar menu of Cook's ill-humor, my father cleared his throat, and quoted,

"Are not you he

"That frights the maidens of the villagery;

"Skim milk, and sometimes labor in the quern

"And bootless make the breathless housewife churn;

"And sometimes make the drink to bear no barm

"Mislead night wanderers, laughing at their harm?

"Those that Hobgoblin call you and sweet Puck,

"You do their work, and they shall have good luck:

"Are not you he?"

When Father recited the final "Are not you he?" his gaze fell on Elliot. It was a penetrating stare, one that sent chills down my spine.

How had Father learned about the sand demon prank? It was harmless. Nevertheless, he was aware, and in this subtle approach asked

85

Elliot to cease the mischief before his staff abandoned his 'haunted' estate.

A wide grin brightening his features, Elliot turned to me, "Shakespeare. Puck. Again!"

"Well?"

There was nothing for it. Elliot simply had to continue the verse from Midsummer Night's Dream. "Thou speakest aright; I am that merry wanderer of the night. But I can't quite recall the next line. Can you, Father?"

"Make sure that Elizabeth does not catch wind of your merry wandering in the night, then. I had the devil of a time calming our staff. Your fiancée might find it difficult to cope."

#

Squinting in the mid-August sunset, I spotted Elliot thrusting the shovel in and pulling out a mound of sand and roots. His white vest was soiled, its sleeves rolled up to let the muscles work freely. Elliot's cigarette hung loosely from his lips and sweat dampened his dusky hair. His motions matched the bizarre sound coming from the house, an upbeat rhythm of piano clanking against heavy drumming, and a loud trumpet that competed for attention, competed to be heard over the drums, piano, and American soloist.

Not far from Elliot was his swarthy apostle. Ali, equally inspired, launched his shovel with his simian arms. Removing the silt blocking the narrowest ditch, the boy cast questioning glances at Elliot, seeking his approbation.

With folded arms, Salomé stood nearby, watching.

"What's happened?"

Elliot paused then examined his fingernails.

"Salomé's upset. Why?"

"How can you tell she's upset?"

"Folded arms."

"Oh."

"Well?"

"She's taking a break," Elliot replied.

Ali spat.

"Why?"

"She fainted a little while ago."

"Did she have enough to drink?"

86

"Probably not." Elliot tossed his cigarette butt and ground it.

Salomé shifted her weight, arms still folded across her chest.

"She fell, you see, right over there. I had some refreshments for her..."

"What kind?"

"Beer. But we couldn't see her. Ali found her sprawled on the sand. I checked her pulse...you know, touched her wrist, while Ali brought a bucket of water..."

"Water again?" I snapped, turning to Ali. "One of these days it's not going to work. Then what would you do?"

"Leave it, William. She's fine now. I'm keeping her shovel away because she wanted to keep on working. She's a headstrong child!"

Ali opened his mouth when a quick look at Salomé brought out a squawk instead.

"Damn the child. She's digging and pulling roots out with her bare hands. I told her to rest. Can't she follow orders?"

I ran to Salomé. "Stop."

The girl's hands sank deep in the sand. She dug and tugged, but the root did not budge.

Emulating her behavior, I wrapped my arms under Salomé's chest and pulled.

But she squirmed and turned round to face me, trying to get away.

I held her close. "It's too hot now. It's warm, and it's dangerous to work outside. You can do this later."

She relaxed and I immediately let go of her because the pressure of her body against mine electrified me. She was not a girl child. Her firm breasts had pressed against my chest. Her wriggling body sent her scent up while her thighs pressed against my legs, making my senses reel.

I was out of breath. "Elliot, let's check the channels," I gasped.

"We'll meet you on the other side. Get over to the mother ditch, the biggest one over there. It's looking good, William. The ditches are clear of debris and sediment. The slopes are at a good angle."

"The sluices?"

"All operable, and the diversion's in good order." Grinning, Elliot marked the elevation drop. "All right, then, William. You can open up the gates."

When I screwed open the gate, murky water gushed into the intricate web of ditches that irrigated the palm and fig trees, the abandoned citrus grove and the skeletal grape vines. Even the last surviving members of the hibiscus and rose bushes took a long, thirsty gulp.

#

August of 1942 blistered with infantry engagements along the el Alamein Line barely sixty miles west of Alexandria. The Axis and the Allies snarled at each other in a series of 'offensive defense.' Both sides were cramped between the Mediterranean Sea and the Qattara Depression, a teardrop shaped region of the Western Desert boasting impassable salt pans, salt marshes, and salt dunes. And both sides tried to push on.

"Mother, the desert war now sounds like Hit and Run."

Strolling through the courtyard with Mother, I talked of some of the information I had gleaned from patients and doctors in hospital that week.

"And by no means is it over. They call the fighting desert campaign but from what I've seen it's more like desert carnage."

"William, don't."

"Don't?"

"Don't be so coarse."

"Coarse? Mother, if only you saw the bits we get! Piles and piles of remnants of human bodies! And somehow, we have to patch them back together again, Humpty Dumpty like. And it's a good thing that plastic surgery has come a long way since the last war or we would have another generation of gargoyles."

"Several ladies of my acquaintance have joined the war effort. And Lady Lampson helps the Red Cross, as do I, but William, the evening is fine, let us talk of something else."

Walking in silence, listening to the remote sounds of Cairo, reminded my mother of a rumor she'd picked up. "William, dear, you'll have to give up your guesthouse."

"My schedule is so erratic. That's why you suggested I move into the guesthouse. Not that I mind where I sleep. But, why the sudden change?"

"No, not immediately. Only once Elliot is wed. Your brother and Elizabeth would surely stay with us after their wedding, and they would want privacy."

"Yes, of course."

"It does not mean that I approve of you hanging about the stables day and night."

"No, Mother, I'm much too busy now. I rarely ride Marlena. I can only hope that Ali takes care to exercise and groom her properly."

"I'm not talking of horses, William. I have been hearing rumors. Rumors about escapades in the stables and stained sheets needing washing. The rumors concern young Ali, too. You frequent the stables with the thin one. Ali must see to his duties. You must see to your duties."

"Mother, I'm at hospital every day and, often, overnight."

"But you have your duty to your family, to our name, to your reputation."

Silence.

"William, I made no mention of it when you rescued the girl and brought her back. No one deserves to be thus beaten, and you are to be applauded for your actions, for rescuing her, and for bringing her back, going as far as nursing her to health, too. I am proud of you, William. But the girl is well enough now. So, send Ali into the stables if you must ride. And do keep out. Servants will gossip, you know."

"When I do find time to ride, I'll certainly do so."

"Oh, don't be cross, William. It's good advice. Gossip is odious. And one must avoid giving rise to unsavory speculations."

"Mother, I had barely seen Salomé over the last month."

A dull ache clutched me. I craved Salomé's company. No longer a nameless waif, she stirred my interest, yes, but it was more than that. Her touch, her scent even, roused my senses. Routine dictated otherwise. Throughout the day and many nights, I was in hospital. Salomé, already recovered, worked in the gardens. I doubted that I would be an invited guest at Salomé's makeshift room when I did manage to return home late in the evening or rather early in the morning.

"William, is something the matter?"

"Just tired, that's all."

She patted my hand again and led me back into the house. And as our housekeeper, Mrs. Judd, ushered my mother in, I turned to cast a longing look in the direction of the stables.

Chapter 8: Monnayeur's

WHINING, stinging mosquitoes swarmed the tawny reeds, their monotonous drone clashing with the gurgling whisper of the Nile. Little eddies along the banks bubbled and ebbed while crustaceans bore into the sand. There was deliberate frivolity in the late afternoon of a sweltering day in late August. An insect flirted with air bubbles, and when a bubble popped, the insect dove, head first, into a hole in the sand, kicking up mounds of earth with its needle-thin hind legs.

With sudden squelchy sounds and shifting reeds Elliot burst into my secluded retreat. "Watching the fellahin again?"

Looking up, a ray of sun hit my eyes and so my lip pulled away from my teeth.

"No need to snarl."

"Leave me."

Elliot stood still.

"I'd like to be away from noise, Elliot, away from blood and pain, smelly bedpans, and limb stumps, desert sores, dysentery, and those filthy dressings!"

"I am none of those things!"

"No, but you are noisy."

"William, brooding here isn't the answer. The fellahin are not a sight to behold. They're morbidly unhealthy."

"True."

"As you're well aware, infant mortality's high. A mature fellah rarely sees more than thirty years. Leave all this. William, come to Monnayeur's tonight." Elliot dropped heavily on the crushed reeds by my side.

"You'll ruin your suit, you know."

"I don't mind. Not-a-bit." He pulled a stem and chewed it. "Will you come tonight? Will you help?"

"Do you need my help?"

"It's been a busy week."

"And Elizabeth?"

"I need to work, and my work is at Monnayeur's."

"Work? Monnayeur's is your club."

"What am I to do, William? I must supervise my club. Who would run the place?"

"You cannot call it work, Elliot, when you go there dressed in the latest fashion."

"Well, I cannot go there looking a fright. I'd scare the customers."

"And you strut about the place surrounded with beauties, scantily dressed beauties."

"A chap needs his ornaments."

"Elliot, you watch dancing women and play cards all night then drive home for breakfast!"

"Am I not entitled to some food? What do you expect, William, that I work all night and skip a fine English breakfast?"

"You know what I mean!"

Lips now stretched in a wolfish grin, he rose, humming a seductive version of Lilly Marlene. His body moved in deliberate, sensual motions. "We will create...a world for two...I will wait for you..." He gyrated his hips disrespectfully. "The whole night through..."

"Where'd you learn to dance like that? It's shocking! You'd do better joining your dancers on stage."

"It's you, Lilly M-a-r-l-e-n-e..."

"Sod off!"

"Temper, temper. William," he leaned close, his eyes locking with mine. "You are my alibi." His hair fell on his sweaty forehead and curled. He was irresistible. "Dance?"

"Why not?" I reached for his outstretched hand. But instead of dancing, I left a wet mud ball in his palm and sprang off.

#

Monnayeur's was Elliot's nightclub. In a surprisingly short time, the club blossomed under Elliot's management since my brother's purchase of the venue in June of 1942 from Madame Sukey, a charitable Levantine widow.

Literally, *Monnayeur* referred to one who coined money. The cheeky name suited the establishment.

Valiant as ever, Elliot had combed the streets of Clot Bey, a district that for many years had been trying to get European attention other than that of laymen, prostitutes, and drug addicts. Elliot discovered the structure, and immediately saw its potential. He purchased the building

91

and constructed a magnificent venue, dubbed it Monnayeur's and turned it into a thriving cabaret and a secret gambling hole almost overnight. The disguise was the classy crooners and beautiful belly dancers who behaved themselves on stage and controlled the dance so that the performance was only suggestive rather than raunchy.

But behind the stage, and well-hidden, was entertainment known only to a select set of wealthy gamblers. Plagued with ennui and bored with the racecourse, they sought refuge at Elliot's secret gambling hall.

At each table, a corpulent woman reigned over the cards. The portly dealers had a disgusting aura of fleshiness. Dark lip-color, a lush shade of red, and a bold line of kohl traced round their watery, brown eyes left no room to doubt their carnivorous motives. The weighty golden earrings dangled low. The hoops rubbed against the women's thick necks and united with the heavy links of the necklaces to resemble shackles on beasts of burden, noisy and threatening.

Elliot reveled in it all: The reputation, the smoke, the cards, the money, and the entertainment. Monnayeur's was Elliot's playground and kingdom.

#

Remarkably at ease, leaning against the bar and a stunningly beautiful woman by his side, Elliot beckoned to me.

"What took you so long?"

"Car problems."

Elliot tapped his foot and traced his jacket buttons. His tracing motions, like his foot tapping, were erratic.

"Aren't you going to introduce me?"

"Right you are. And when the artificial niceties are exchanged, my dear little brother will show you round, Lady Jane. William, Lady Jane wishes to perform here so you two can talk about schedule."

It was only after Elliot had flashed me a smile and walked out that I realized that I landed in a sticky mess.

How was I supposed to show Elliot's beautiful singer round and talk schedule when the club was busy and noisy and I had little notion of club management much less schedules! Besides, ladies do not sing at Cairene clubs, or any club! Ladies are supposed to host tea parties for charitable foundations. Why did my brother call her Lady Jane?

"Let's sit down."

Elliot had said, "You're my alibi." Did he really need me to cover his absence? But how and for how long? And why? He must think that we look enough alike to fool someone, but whom? Was he in trouble, perhaps with a loan shark?

Elliot and I certainly had similar features. We were almost of the same height but I was thinner and less built and my hair was certainly fair, not as dark a brown as Elliot's and of course our eyes had different shades of blue. But in the dim light of the club, engulfed in lacing cigar smoke, the differences were negligible.

"Are you new in town?"

Lady Jane inclined her head.

Excellent, as a newcomer she'd have few acquaintances. And true enough, we were left to ourselves.

Now seated at Elliot's grand table by the open window, I fixed my gaze on the stage, scarcely looking at the beautiful woman.

The stage represented a Grecian courtyard. The band played energetically as the belly dancer heaved her bosom in steady, cat-like rhythm. Her abdomen undulated salaciously just below her bulging breasts. Slowly her brown stomach rose and dropped, matching in tempo with the brassy music, which dramatically sped up, and with it picking up the recurrence of the convulsive waves of feminine curves. Ample breasts rose and fell within the glittery bra, sweat and oil reflecting a shiny sheen in the light. Harsh, loud tones urged on the dancer's thrusts, pushing, pulling as the coins on the belt and skirt cascaded over her thighs.

The atmosphere at Monnayeur's became still. Men brought their lukewarm beer to their lips, but they never sipped lest they miss a second of this exhibition of feminine tortuous dancing that had them entranced.

Legs spread apart and body pushing and pulling, her lascivious gyrations reached a peak.

Wiping their perspiring faces, the spectators looked on, their eyes fixed on the serpentine slinking of the dancer's torso.

Alas, the dancer began her deflective string of turns in wide circles, attempting to blur the suggestiveness of her performance. Scarves and shawls fluttered, letting the dangling golden coins and bells chink, so as to confuse.

And as the dancer danced away, the drumming picked up. Violinists appeared on stage and a singer popped up.

"The dancer must need a respite."

"A respite?"

"To catch her breath after all...that..." I added a wave of my hand toward the stage. "Of course, this entire district needs a respite. Did Elliot tell you? Decades ago, Australian soldiers rioted here, in Clot Bey, throwing furnishings from balconies of..."

"Sounds like the high tales you get decades after a war has ended." Then Lady Jane smiled, put her hand on my arm, leaned close, and thanked me. She was remarkably beautiful in a classical sense. Her caramel hair was artistically pulled back in a chignon complementing her shapely nose and pretty eyes set in a perfectly oval face. "It was good of you to be my escort for this evening. I wanted to attend this particular performance only Mr. Westbrook could not escort me tonight."

"What of schedule and showing you round?"

She cast me a conspiratorial look. "No need. Just stay by my side and say not a word of my confession to Elliot."

"Well, this is all very odd and unexpected!"

And excepting another quick flash of a dazzling smile, I got little conversation from Lady Jane as she turned her attention to the performance on stage.

The crooner ululated her final note and the belly dancer returned, oiled up and ready, and suddenly I heard, "Soad is the best in Cairo." Elliot's voice was confidential and proud. "She is the real thing, not like a painted Hollywood girl just shaking a leg and bending over. Soad's the best belly dancer in Cairo!"

Where had Elliot been all this time? And how did he get to stand next to me so inconspicuously?

"She just danced with a sword balanced on her breasts. She has to be the best. And what with all that mythological set up you have on stage, I half expected a cobra to pop out of that basket over there or a white tiger to leap over her head," I commented, as if Elliot had been there all along.

Lady Jane's lips curved up.

"An excellent suggestion!" Elliot cried.

"I wasn't aware that I made any."

94

"Well, it's late," Elliot turned to Lady Jane. "Why don't you follow me? This young chap will take you home tonight."

Our retired, old groom materialized.

"Joseph is not young," I commented in Arabic.

Joseph grinned and crooned, "Master William, good to have you here."

"Good to see you, Joseph. I am glad that my brother has you in his employ, because I do have some questions about the health of Nick Bottom, our old donkey in the stables. Do you remember him?"

"I do," replied Joseph darkly. "Still alive, is he?"

"And full of energy. I'll be back to talk to you later then."

"You have a donkey? Named Nick Bottom? Shakespeare's infamous ass?" Lady Jane asked.

"I do."

"Why? I mean, why do you have a donkey and why name a donkey Bottom?"

"Because he's an ass!" boomed Elliot, pleased with his quip.

"Lady Jane, I have a donkey because Elliot and I found it tangled in wires and Joseph here, and a little stableboy called Ali, helped heal his lesions. It was mistreated and misused by tourists. So, he's a misused ass," I replied then paused. "Hang on. Do you understand Arabic?"

"One must. There's all that infatuation with the orient or should I say the East, or Middle East, nowadays."

"I see."

Elliot who seemed to be rather in a hurry blurted out a rather gruff farewell, "Lady Jane, stop by again," and led the beauty to the door, handing her over to the thin old man and his immaculately clean car.

Elliot returned and, leaning close, he asked, "William? How did it go? Are you all right?"

"Fine, I'm fine."

"Come."

Too tired to object, I followed with a sense of wonderment. "Elliot? Where do you find the time for all this?"

"Just get in the car, William."

Once behind the wheel, Elliot drove fast. "I don't like to leave the club unsupervised more than I have to."

"Where were you?"

"GHQ. Father needed my assistance."

"Assistance?"

"You know, sort through waste baskets, that sort of nonsense. He gets such hideous notions into his head sometimes."

"And so do you, when you fib."

Elliot maneuvered the narrow streets with ineffable ease until he stopped the motor. He parked in a slanted alley, the car haphazardly blocking either entrance or exit.

Few risked approaching this forgotten section of the ant-heap-like city.

Elliot marched up to a worm-eaten wooden door. A short knock summoned an apelike man who led us through endless corridors.

Plagued with lack of sleep and excess of drink on a hot September night in Egypt, I was hit with a sense of unreality. The car ride, the walk with Elliot, and the dark long galleries seemed unreal.

Finally, sandalwood scented wisps hung on the humid air over a grand pool in a fantastic hall. The misty recess sent up tendrils of steam. A man sat, dangling his legs into the rectangular pool. A woman with dark skin was anointing another man with oil. The man and girl were not clothed, and she was displaying her leg suggestively as his hands stroked her body.

"A bathhouse!"

Such places often celebrated a reputation of impiety, and my mind reeled at the prospect of a visit to a bathhouse and all that it implied. But what did it imply? I had no idea. My resentment was mixed with, and soon overpowered by, curiosity.

Our escort had disappeared.

Elliot clapped his arm round my shoulder and indicated that we should remove our shoes.

When our escort returned, he carried a tray supporting two glasses. My throat constricted with the liquid's rosy, unnatural flavor. But Elliot only smiled in amusement and raised his glass. He tossed the vile contents off neat and placed the glass on the tray with the eerie clank of glass hitting copper.

In somewhat of a panic, I drank the rosewater as fast as I could.

"Happy birthday, William."

"But it's not my birthday!"

"Don't argue."

"Elliot, where the hell are we?"

96

"Paying a social call on an old friend," he replied, then winked and walked into the mist.

A sense of loss gripped me.

The blurry outlines of figures now appeared to be in motion. I was surrounded by people, and yet, I was alone. Deciding to look for Elliot, my steps were heavy and misplaced. My head ached.

Then, Elliot and a large woman appeared. Guiding me into the water, Elliot laughed.

My jaw clenched as hot water penetrated my trousers, my leg hairs standing on end.

Elliot ruffled my hair, then led his lady away. His voice resonated across the hall and hung on the mist, breaking through my blurred senses. I listened to the layers in his voice and remained conscious.

Staring vacantly at the ceiling, then the wall, I imagined the crimson folds of the curtains take shape and move toward me.

The red masses were gliding, cautiously, but steadily. There was rhythmic rapidity to the motion. The folds of the curtains darkened then lightened as the fabric writhed enticingly, extending tubular arms bound with lace and rope. Something shiny glittered, and I stretched an arm to reach the twinkling light.

I strained to hear Elliot's voice. The familiarity of it comforted me as my body reacted to the opium derivative in the rosewater.

A slender foot came into the water by my side and drew circles on its surface with the toes. I stared at the ripples. The shapes in the water widened then disappeared, and my gaze shifted to the feet beside me, on the floor. There were tattoos drawn around the toes, ringlets of intricate design. And that was all the woman had on her bare skin. Feet suddenly apart, she crouched then entered the pool.

A sonorous chant accompanied the sound of water rising and falling and swishing. Elliot's voice was muffled, fading into the noise of cascading water. Soon, I thought of Salomé, her arms. I reached to wrap my fingers round her wrists. My sense of loneliness now gone, I pulled her close, pressing her to me.

The curtains were a shapeless waterfall of warmth and ease. The claret downpour sent tributaries that sloshed then pooled. And now the pool was purple and gold. I removed myself from the bench and pulled Salomé along, into that dark, deep purplish gold. I closed my eyes and enjoyed her slow caresses, warm and ethereal. She removed everything that I had on, even my socks. The curtains, a flowing river of endless, invariable tenderness, altered from longer to shorter folds and from plum to crimson. The girl's leg wrapped round me. I ran my hands over her body. I wanted her. I kissed her hungrily. Her hair was long and coarse. The flowing curtains became more fluid and steadier and pounding as I was touching, my fingers exploring short coppery hair. My arm went round her waist. My mouth covered her, moving from her lips to her neck, shoulders and breasts. Her legs tightened around me as I entered. The darkness of pooling tributaries engulfing us became darker and yet deeper until that darkness became unyielding, undeniable, and smooth, and void of texture, and serene.

Chapter 9: And No One Would Know

BY mid-September, Cook plunged into roaring lunacy. Soon it metamorphosed into authoritarianism. He ruled the crockery and dominated the servants, instigating squabbles, reveling in the misery. The pots rang, the silverware jangled, his clogs clapped as he caterwauled a composition of sour notes. And yet there was not much to show for all his noise.

As children, my brothers and I had disliked him. As adults, we avoided him because we knew that Cook's temper was an act, now a daily routine.

A short man, Cook wore clogs to add an inch to his height. His chest protruded at a cantankerous angle. The scars that marred his face and the mustache that straddled his lips capped the sinister look with a sure seal. Such were the man's looks and characteristics. Such were the events that Elliot's wedding set into motion.

One night in September 1942, I returned home from hospital exhausted and in low spirits. Passing the kitchen, I decided on some biscuits and a hot cup of tea, when I heard Cook bawl.

A little past midnight, Cook was shouting out orders at maids who should have been asleep. Was the scoundrel working his, our, staff well into the night? Why?

With a firm step, I turned to confront him, the women needed rest. But I was too late. A scuttle of feet brought Salomé hastily out of the kitchen with a clanking aluminum bucket, and it immediately became apparent that Ali had fallen victim to Cook's reign of terror.

"Ali! Sweep up broken glass. Don't leave it on the kitchen floor."

"But the glass broke next to the dust bins, outside. It's too dark to sweep now. *Malish.* In the morning."

"Nonsense! And, don't *malish* me!"

"It is dark outside. I cannot see a thing," Ali quailed.

"Shards of broken glass, protruding in every direction... You could die if you step on it." Cook advanced on Ali, threatening the boy in thunderous accents, twitching his mustache and eyelids. "And no one would know!"

The clink of glass hitting glass broke the silence following Cook's wrath.

Cook flew into a series of aggressive stirring and whisking motions, then a string of orders shot out.

I backed out to the dark, long gallery, all thoughts of biscuits and tea gone.

There was a terrible crash, as I toppled over someone.

Salomé, her chest rising and falling rapidly, held tightly to the empty, aluminum bucket that clanked when I fell on top of the girl. Pressed under me as I was stretched out, legs sprawled and arms extended sideway, she stared into my eyes.

"You all right?"

Salomé's veil fell off and her face was close to mine.

I felt a rush of excitement, at her pose, at her closeness, at her pinned under me, unafraid.

"Let's go!" Before I misbehave. But to Salomé, I said, "Before the kitchen knave comes after us."

With Salomé's hand in mine, I propelled us out of the dark house. We ran, both of us conscious and alert, to the courtyard.

An iron bench shone with jasmine blossoms in the semi-enclosed courtyard outside the guesthouse, hidden from view of the main house. We fell on the uncomfortable bench, breathing hard.

The girl looked about then her eyes settled on me.

"Damn the fellow." A nagging concern surfaced. "Just how often do you have to endure Cook's wrath? Do you even understand him? Do you understand me?"

Salomé just kept her hazel eyes fixed on mine.

"Shards of broken glass...Poor Ali..." I leaned back. "Why is he so caustic?"

A shiver ran down her body.

"Cold? Not in this heat!" But I gathered her in my arms, holding her close, rubbing her arms, then back.

How amazingly soothing was the motion of running my fingers through Salomé's soft, fine hair, tracing circles around the nape of her neck.

Then she leaned into me.

I took her chin and brought her face up. My gaze fell to Salomé's lips.

Her hand reached to clasp my hand. Her hand was cool and slender but no longer boney.

I was drawn to her. I wanted her. My fingers wrapped round her neck but as I guided her closer, I paused.

"Your cheeks are wet. Were you crying?"

She held my hand in place.

"Is...anything...wrong?"

She slid closer and the warmth of her body sent flames leaping up inside me.

"It won't do," I whispered. "You're kept here under my father's protection. And so young, too."

It was a calm night. In the distance, a jackal cackled urging other jackals into an eerie discussion.

Salomé brought her lips to mine in a gauche, inexperienced pucker. She really had no idea what she was doing.

But as I ran my hands from her neck to her shoulders, I brought my mouth down on hers, kissing her gently then deepening the connection, exploring her. Her body became pliant under my touch, and I lost track of time and place, and of what was proper. A serpentine-like wave of desire took over. I let go for a brief moment and looked at the girl, hungry for more. I picked Salomé up and brought her to my lap.

She closed her eyes and bent her head to kiss me again. Her motions were heady, drugged with need. Her hands ran over my chest, plunging me deeper into a whirlwind of desire. I opened her robe and kissed her neck. Brushing my lips gently closer to her breasts while she pressed herself against me in such inexperienced yet honest way that she threw me off momentarily as I recalled her innocence. She wrapped her arms round my neck and brought her lips to mine, her thighs pressing close to me.

"We can't," I breathed but her hands moved from my neck to my chest and to my back and I gave in, caressing her body, taking over her face then down her throat and even lower to her firm breasts. She gasped with unexpected surge of pleasure, when a sharp metallic clang cut through the dim haze fogging my senses.

"Elliot," I choked and hastily rearranged Salomé's robe. "Elliot is back from his club."

I felt stupid.

Salomé appeared confused too and nearly fell off of me as I made to rise from the bench. I slumped back down, Salomé by my side, and we stared at the bright beam of light swerving toward us as Elliot drove past the gate.

Elliot drove in slowly, parked the car, then running toward the kitchen, he whistled.

I looked at Salomé, then drew her back on my lap and in for another kiss, my hands then lips traveling lower along her curves, but we both nearly jumped off the bench when we heard, "William!"

Elliot, standing in a shaft of light by the kitchen back door, spoke again, "William."

"Coming," I grumbled, wondering if my brother's call was loud enough to wake up everyone in the house.

Salomé looked disoriented. She straightened up slowly.

I turned to her and grabbed her hand, "I'll see you later."

"William!" Another booming summon from Elliot penetrated our jasmine corner and I muttered an oath.

Elliot held the door open to the back of the kitchen as I walked past him.

"Excellent, Cook has been baking." He reached and tore a wedge of cake.

With a dull ache in my gut, I looked at the sad sight on the workbench. The freshly baked cake that had been nestled on a gold-trimmed plate and protected by a glass lid, now stood bare and exposed and ravaged on the rough surface of the wooden board.

"Elliot, how could you?"

Elliot, still chewing, studied me in silence then growled, "And you, William? How could you?"

"What do you mean?"

"I don't want my kid brother to be the ogre that pounces on the maidens of the village, that's all."

"Awfully judgmental from the brother who took me to a bathhouse, drugged me, and, set me up with a prostitute!"

"Not the same thing at all, William!"

\#

On the following morning, I had a vague notion to see Salomé and tell her that we could not repeat those passionate kisses and embraces of

102

last night. But when I saw her pacing outside the kitchen back door, an aluminum bucket in her hand, I only smiled.

"Have you breakfasted yet?"

She looked away from the kitchen.

"Are you afraid of Cook?"

Salomé lowered her gaze.

"He can't harm you, you know."

Salomé pointed to the irrigation canal.

"Time to water the gardens?"

The courtyard, still in shadows, rang with distant, lonely howls. A rooster answered the howls, and a duet followed. Cook clanked his pots and bellowed angrily at the sight of the ruined cake, while a workman outside our estate walls ululated a popular torch song.

"Let's go!" I made to grab her hand but held back, remembering that cake last night, an awful sight, crumbly and distorted by the uncaring hands of Elliot.

Salomé looked away; her head slightly bent.

"You're in the right to water the gardens in the morning. Evaporation would be slower, and the soil would have a better chance to retain the moisture. I'll turn the headgate."

Twisting the wheel, I opened the headgate, letting water into our web of narrow ditches. There were no obstructions and the mechanism was well maintained.

Downstream of the headgate, Salomé jumped into the mother ditch.

"I opened the gate. Salomé?!" I shouted then scrambled up the side slope, climbed over the diversion, and ran along the ditch.

Crouching in the ditch, the quickening current pounding on her back, Salomé held onto a thick root. She turned her radiant smile to me and the world was put to right.

Salomé watched the mayhem behind her. Her fascination with motion and noise amazed me since she did not seem to want to speak or get outside our estate walls. Was she really content in her silent isolation?

I jumped in and rolled onto my back, now drifting with the current.

Above, the sky was pinkish-red and bright.

How would Mother react to my adventures with Salomé? I could see her golden curls prick with consternation at my attentions to the girl. But dark clouds crowded over when I recalled Elliot's harsh words, "And you, William? How could you?" What did he mean by that? Did he disapprove of my attraction to Salomé or my handling of her? For Elliot, an encounter in a bathhouse was one thing but embracing someone like Salomé was something different altogether. Elliot categorized Salomé as an innocent, not a hostess at a bathhouse. But what precisely did he mean? Damn him, what did Elliot know about the girl?

Getting out of the ditch and dripping wet, I approached Salomé. "I best be going now." My voice, colorless and tense, scratched my conscience.

Salomé scrambled out of the water, her robe clinging to her body.

Helping her out, and aroused, I could hardly look away.

She stepped close and, like a child exploring something new, her fingers traced my lips.

With an effort, I held back. "I have to return to the house," I whispered, fighting the need to grab her and take her. So I walked away, my legs heavy underneath me.

#

"Something has to be done about that maniac!" I snapped.

"Effendi, he won't give her food because she did not dump wash water fast enough," the boy wailed when he met me at the hallway.

"And you, Ali, are you hungry too?"

"Yes, Effendi."

"Here. There's four English shillings, it's twenty Egyptian piastres, Ali. Get some food at the suk for you and for Salomé. Get enough for today and tomorrow."

"*Shukran*, Effendi."

With enough money for food and several cups of coffee jangling in his pocket, I was certain that Salomé would be hungry until dusk when Ali would stumble back from his rounds at the coffee shops.

I was wrong about Ali's promptness. Not much later, the boy delivered a greasy bundle to the stables.

"What is Ali up to?"

"I have no idea, Mother."

"Is something troubling you?" Mother asked as she put her hand on mine, halting me from switching the engine on. "You look terribly upset."

104

"No, Mother, I'm all right." I forced a smile, though, for some reason, anger at Ali bubbled inside me. "Where did you want me to drive you?"

"The tennis club."

"Right."

"William, your father needs you to escort Elliot for his fitting. Elliot always misbehaves at the tailor's."

"Because your tailor's a nightmare!"

"But he is the best."

"Have you ever entered his sweltering workshop? Walked through the wall of warm garlic breath? Withstood his pinpricks or his acidic remarks? The man's impossible. And Elliot swears that he touches him."

"He has to touch him," Mother innocently dismissed the complaint. "William, make sure that Elliot is not drawn into an argument with the impossible man."

"I'll do my best."

"A wall of garlic breath? Is that why your suits always reek of the East? Does that man eat a lot of garlic?"

"I should think he eats, sleeps, and bathes in it too! But who doesn't?"

"I don't!"

"No. And because we do not indulge in vast quantities of garlic and cumin and such we are devils."

Standing grim-faced at the shop window, Elliot stared ahead.

"So, have you stained the fabrics draped over you with sweat and blood already?" I asked my brother as I entered the shop.

"He pricks me in retaliation for the sweat! Can you believe that? It's Cairo. Everybody sweats!"

"Damn, it is only a wedding," I drawled.

"I can't wait to tell you that. Ah!" Elliot's retort ended with a cry of pain as a pin was driven into his thigh.

Stifling a laugh from the far corner of the shop, Father was enjoying a quiet moment away from GHQ, the Cairo Communiqué shielding his expression.

"Anything funny in today's paper?" Elliot asked.

"Stand still," growled the tailor.

Elliot and I exchanged looks. It was like the last time when he and I got pinpricked by the smelly old tailor.

"Why is Mother insisting on such a production?" Elliot complained. "Father, have you talked to her? Have you said anything?"

"You know how women are!"

"This nonsense of wedding preparations is jarring. Cook's been bellowing at night..."

"You never sleep at night," I chimed.

"He serves us slimy fish, glue-like mash, and..."

"There are people in this world who have no food at all much less a cook," the tailor interrupted with a bark.

"Your breath reassures me that at least you have a cook. And such a cook! Does he have to use garlic and onion in every dish?"

"Stand still," the old, sweaty tailor hissed.

Elliot's cry of pain echoed the tailor's demands. "That's enough!"

The cranky old man pricked my brother somewhere sensitive so Elliot ripped the confining fabric off and dashed out. "You have my measurements, now use a dummy! And you can't fondle me to get my crutch measurements!"

"Elliot!"

"Damn this place!" Elliot spat and slammed the door shut.

#

"William! Where have you been?"

"Where have you been? Father and I expected you to return. But you never came back!" I got out of the car, slammed the door, and turned to face a suspiciously curious Elliot. "What is it?"

"Not going to hospital today?"

"Later, much later."

"Good!" He grinned from ear to ear. "To the guesthouse."

"Elliot, what is it?"

"Hurry!" Then he cast a dark glance at me. "Why do you look so wan all the time?"

"I don't! Let go of me. Where're you taking me anyway? Another bathhouse?"

"What an ungrateful dog you are! Is this how you thank me for the treat?"

"A treat? Just what was in that drink? I was delirious for hours!"

106

"This is a bit much. What a queer question to ask! And from you! Haven't you been in hospital long enough to know, surrounded by narcotics as you are?" Elliot opened my bedroom door and pushed me in.

Turning to scold him, I brushed aside my hair, when I noticed that Salomé and Ali were seated on the floor.

A kingly feast from the suk, complete with *chai bil na'ana* was laid out. A soft trumpet twittered, and a woman's silky voice rose and fell.

Salomé was bobbing her head, enjoying the music.

"What's the meaning of this?"

Ali and Salomé looked up. Salomé appeared apprehensive, resting a renegade hand on a dish while Ali, never removing his eyes off of Elliot, slowly pushed her hand away from the Om Ali, his favorite dessert.

"We are celebrating."

"Why, I can see that!"

Elliot pressed his finger to my lips. "Hush."

I was happy to see them, especially the girl, only I was surprised, and a bit embarrassed. How did Elliot feel about what he saw last night? And how did Salomé feel about me? As for my part, I could barely keep my eyes off of her.

"We've been waiting for half an hour now." Elliot removed his finger from my lips.

Shifting my gaze from Salomé to Elliot to Ali then back to Salomé who sat cross-legged on my rug, I asked, "What's going on?"

"William, I've been thinking about what you'd said about Cook, tyrannizing the staff and us, and a brilliant idea hit me. Ali and Salomé helped, of course. Ali was at the suk today, and he found a black cat. A black parcel of bones! Ali brought it here to...Shh...shh, I hear the devil whistling. He's returning to the kitchen."

"Elliot?"

"Yes, well," he continued in a whisper, but attending to sounds coming from the kitchen all along. "Salomé locked up the kitchen...except for the back door. I need to lock the back door once I know Cook is inside. I can hear the cockroach clanking his clogs on the concrete."

"Oh, for God's sake, Elliot...was that onomatopoeia?"

"What? No! Of course not. Wrong word."

"Elliot, what about the cat?"

"The cat's in the cupboard!"

"It's a good thing Ali did not find a poisonous snake." I shot the boy a glance.

Ali flicked his wrist in a dismissive Oriental fashion.

"Now that you mention it, William... A cobra would've been some excellent sport!"

"You're not serious, Elliot, not a cobra! A visit from a black cat is clever enough. Cook is superstitious and to him a black cat means bad luck, misfortune!" I finally grinned. "Locking a scrawny black cat in the kitchen with Cook is certainly going to jostle the old horror's complacency. I only wish that the cat would not suffer."

"No, no, cat's safe! Oh, listen...He's in, and I'm off," Elliot choked, his voice cracking as he sprang out.

Ali bolted to the window, throwing suspicious glances at the delightful spread every so often but watching Elliot's progression eagerly.

Standing by the door, my stomach lurched when my head turned to the girl.

Salomé's smile, wide and serene, did wonderful things to my heart. She was lovely now that her bruises and scars had faded.

Managing to smile back, I took a step in her direction when Elliot crashed in, slamming into me as he shut the door behind him.

"Ouch!" I cried.

"He's inside the kitchen, and both doors are l-o-ck-e-d! You all right?" he asked.

"Never better!" Sarcasm laced my words.

"Well, pull out your whiskey, William. This calls for stronger stuff." Elliot nodded at my desk.

"Elliot, how do you know that I have whiskey?"

Elliot pulled a can of beer from his coat and opened it slowly, reverently. "Don't you?"

"When do we eat?"

"As soon as we get our cue," Elliot replied. "And, here it..." His last word was drowned by a cry blasting out of the kitchen.

Elliot chuckled.

Salomé grinned, and I reached to clink my glass against her glass, my eyes caressing her face. Elliot grunted and leaned over, his hand deftly replacing Salomé's veil back over her face while Ali fell upon the food, ravenous.

"Wailing like a banshee! This revenge's ten years overdue. Maybe longer, if you tally up James' grievances."

"William, this is just the beginning," my brother promised.

"If I didn't hate him so much, I'd feel sorry for him."

Shrieks and sounds of shattered crockery and toppled silverware crashed through the window. Loud angry yowls followed with the banshee still wailing.

Our glasses raised, Ali gurgled a blessing in Arabic.

"Cook found the cat!"

"And Cat's on Cook's head," I added, deciphering Cook's colorful expletives after the cat pounced, scratched, and vanished.

Rarely was I moved to rejoice in other men's misfortune, but I was elated that evening. Cook's wrathful imprecations were a song to the sweetness of the Om Ali that we savored after a hearty lentil and lamb stew and grilled chicken. The heavy cream drenching the nuts and batter was as decadent as the moment.

But while we were enjoying nuts and dried fruit, the banshee still wailing and banging at the kitchen door, Father's car roared into the estate.

"Well, that's unexpected," muttered Elliot.

I peeped out the window.

Elliot eyed Salomé's glass and pulled it to his nose. "Better stick with tea, Love." Shooting her a disarming smile, he took away her whiskey. "William, whiskey is too strong for the girl."

"Oh, Elliot! Father's going in! He just rushed into the house, probably to unhinge the iron bar."

"Damn, he'll rescue him," Elliot rasped in disappointment.

"Human or feline?"

A smile stretched across his face. "Feline. Father would rescue the cat."

The next day, the black cat curled complacently in my father's study, now answering to the name of Bruce.

Chapter 10: Of Circles and Cycles

WEDDING bells rang and for a brief moment Cairene street-noises were drowned out. Then Elliot led his bride to his car. Motorcar horns blew and donkeys brayed, the bootblacks shouted and merchants haggled as a long procession of motorcars followed to our estate, obediently plodding through the hot, dusty streets.

At the reception, one of the maids dropped a tray-full of glasses. Before the horrid cook could learn of the incident, she vanished into a taxi several streets beyond.

Following her, I called out her name. But when she looked back, the terrified expression on her face paralyzed me.

Elliot must have heard the crash and saw the young woman dash out of the estate gate, out to the wide avenue beyond. He sprang after her. When he passed by me, I grabbed hold of his sleeve. "She's a general maid. Cook would send her packing anyway."

"Oh, how I envy her."

"Why? Cook's wrath is not at all the thing to envy!"

"Not Cook! I envy her. I can't tolerate those tittering idiots."

"What idiots?"

"The bridesmaids."

"They sound more like yapping curs, malicious yapping curs. Do they have to criticize everyone and everything?"

Elliot looked away.

"Forget them, Elliot. Reception's in the courtyard, and there's plenty of space to keep out of their way. Besides, the orchestra is quite loud. You can't hear a thing. Elliot, the wedding guests are arrived and you have to dance with your bride."

He grimaced. "Yes, well, I was afraid of that, too."

"There's more to wedding and marriage than just dancing, you know."

"Oh, I know. And there's always the switch."

"Switch? What switch?"

"Light switch," Elliot elucidated and added the hand motion.

"You wouldn't bother with the light switch at all if you had married someone like Lady Jane."

As I spoke, Elliot grew pale and quite ill.

"I say, are you all right?"

"Dance with Mother, William. Then come get me."

#

It was only after my dance with Mother that I scanned the throng of wedding guests, looking for Elliot. With polite words and gestures tossed at various acquaintances, I escaped into the house and found Elliot traversing the hallways in low spirits, tugging at his neckcloth and eyeing the impressive Guardsmen standing about. Father had insisted on some measure of security.

"So, you're here." I pulled on his high collar. "And, what is this? A scarf round your neck? Or shall I call it a noose?"

"It's a fashionable necktie that carries with it the eau de cologne of Cairo, the ever-present garlic and cumin and curry." He sniffed, tilting his lips downward. His posture shifted somehow. His chest swelled and his bottom protruded out and this pose of his was accompanied by an ostentatious eyebrow lift that got my lips stretching into a grin.

"Curse that tailor. He exudes garlic and I cannot see why he bothers with ironing and pressing the damned suits and neckties and shirts if I can't even take a single breath without the repulsive fumes rising up into my nostrils!" His litany over, Elliot now sent me into peals of laughter, as his posture once again shifted. He displayed a particularly engaging smile. But his front top tooth was covered with a bit of a leafy green.

"I have a surprise for you, William. Come outside."

Music and chatter filled the air. The piano plinked, flirting with the trumpet. But Elliot and I left the house and its gardens and patios and courtyards and headed to the main irrigation canal, plowing our way through the reeds and mud.

Elliot pulled out a flask of whiskey and as the afternoon wore on, we sampled Elliot's whiskey, rum, and some noxious Arak cocktail. Singing crude songs, we rocked back and forth in bawdy camaraderie. Then, Elliot fished out beer from the reeds.

"Did you put the beer in there too?" I asked, surprised.

"I did."

"It's unfortunate that you did not have a table and chairs set up for us while you were at it," I commented, casting a long glance at Elliot's suit.

111

"It's ruined, you know. All this dark muck on your suit and the rips along the back and shoulder lines scratch you out of your own wedding party."

"Unsuitable," he laughed and handed me a dirty glass and poured the foaming liquid slowly. "Never-mind chairs. Drink. I am not in the habit of wasting good beer. Now if only we had some music here!"

"Elliot, you have to return to your guests," I reminded him as a sudden shaft of lucidity broke through the alcohol haze.

"All in good time. I just hope that I can change before anyone spots me."

"Why did you marry Elizabeth?"

"She has beautiful legs."

"You're incorrigible."

"Legs are an excellent excuse."

"Father's excuse was more convincing. He choked something like a suitable match."

"That too!" Elliot brightened. "Well, I better go dance with my suitable match and her fine legs." He stood up, not at all steady. But he made a great effort to return to the house.

The reception, from the sound of it, was getting jolly and overcrowded.

As I was unfit for the rigors of the dance floor, my legs led me to the stables.

A neigh drifted to me. "Oh, hello my Marlena." I walked to scratch Marlena then peeked in on Nick Bottom. "Still an ass, Bottom?"

Shuffling to Salomé's room, I called, "Salomé, are you in there?"

I grabbed hold of the sheet hanging at the entrance. But the sheet detached itself and, tangled, I fell to the floor. The solid earth under my body was consoling and I drifted into sleep.

Suddenly, I was wet.

"What...? Oh... You... So, you learned to dump water from Ali!" Looking at my ruined suit and at the pool of mud under me, I hissed, "Damn!"

Salomé gripped her empty bucket and backed against the wall.

"Was it necessary?"

Sobering up at the insult, I stood up, relieved to see that the worst was over. The earth was steady under my feet, and the spinning sensation subsided into a whir. Nervously, I ran my fingers through my wet hair. What was I to do now? The early evening was warm and pleasant. The wedding crowd, still in the courtyard, danced and chattered.

"Do you have something I can dry myself with?"

Salomé handed me a cotton rag. She watched as I passed the rag roughly over my face, hair, and neck.

Peeking at her from between the folds of the rag, I wished that Salomé would put down her bucket and get out. Damn it, she was a handsome creature when her face was unveiled.

"My trousers are ruined." I brushed mud off of my pants with brisk motions.

The girl inched away, interpreting my comments as temper.

I paused. "Come here," I whispered, holding my hand out to Salomé.

She stood still.

A popular waltz played.

I tossed the rag aside and walked to Salomé, reaching for her white knuckles.

She was still holding onto the bucket.

"Let go," I released her grasp and took her in my arms. "Do you dance?"

Following my steps, the girl was irresistible. She moved with me. Her head, held high, exposed a slender neck. And her warm body pressed against my chest while her scent filled me with longing.

I leaned forward to kiss her neck but, losing my footing, I tripped over a straw-bale. Tumbling to the floor, bringing the girl down, Salomé landed on top of me.

As she tried to brace herself with elbows at my side, I whispered her name.

Salomé's hazel eyes locked with mine. Slowly, she slid her fingers through my hair, bits of hay scattering near. My senses quickened as her fingers traveled down my cheek, my jaw, then further below. She traced an old childhood scar along the side of my throat, then back up, tenderly exploring my face.

With a groan, fighting to hold back, I rolled her under me. Finding our closeness difficult to resist, I gave her a hard kiss and quickly pulled her back up, ready to dance, as if nothing had happened.

As I drew her close, Salomé flashed me a smile, and I felt fine indeed. The dancing, the stables, the walls, and Salomé were real, tangible. Nothing was fluid except for our steps. The walls stood rigidly in place. The hay and the boxes were solid. Even the smell was that of earth.

The warmth of her body and her happy expression encouraged me. I led her in a waltz, making wide then short turns. Alcohol and waltzing meddling with my senses, my gaze caressed her skin peeking from under her sleeves and my arm resting at her lower back pressed the girl close, making no secret of my desire. As Salomé's sleeves fell back, exposing her arms, I brought my lips to her wrist. Brushing my lips against her arm then up to her throat and jaw and inevitably I cupped her face and covered her mouth with mine.

It was when I briefly glanced at the floor, that I regretted ever returning that raggedy yellow star to Salomé. Because there it was, shooting a yellow arm out from under the bale I had just bumped, reminding me that not all was well with the world. I faltered, stepping on Salomé's toes. Eyes averted, the yellow star still flashed before me.

Salomé pulled her foot from under mine, her long sleeves now covering her hands. Then she stood still, her eyes fixed on the yellow triangle sticking out.

What horrors must this yellow thing bring to her mind?

The music went on and incongruous, chattering voices filled the air.

I stepped back. When I opened my mouth, no words came out. And feeling gauche, I left.

#

The dirty suit scratched my skin, shaking me out of sleep the following day at dawn. My hair stuck up like a dried-up palm tree in a sandstorm. I dipped my brush into the water basin and remembered Salomé's impish move when she handed me the soggy brush she had used on the donkey. "At least I'm not as old as Nick Bottom and my teeth are intact."

And on that cheerful thought, and despite my headache and dry mouth, I made for the diversion.

Crossing the courtyard, I caught a glimpse of the stables. Did I really just turn round and left the girl? The memory of dancing washed over me, stripping me of my pride. Ashamed of my abrupt, clumsy departure, I regretted leaving Salomé without a word.

114

The main canal, irrigation water flowing in it, reflected the shadowy gray of the clouds above. Because clouds were a rare treat in the Cairene heavens, the dreary sky was a good omen.

I jumped in, letting the current carry me with it. But not far downstream, yelps and howls alerted me to a wild dog. Dripping wet, I approached a dry crevice where the horrible sounds were issuing forth.

Tufts of hair missing from the side of its neck, the little wild dog howled and barked, licking its hind leg. And when it noticed me, it gave a long heart-wrenching howl.

"How did you get stuck in there?"

Another howl and a yelp from within the depression was my only answer. The wild dog tried to get up, but instead of running away from me, it growled.

"What's the matter, little one? What have you done to yourself?"

It edged away and gave a long, sad cry.

"Let's see." I grabbed hold of the animal by the scruff of its neck. The dog's hind leg was broken, dangling at an awkward angle. "God, you must be in pain. And you are so young. Hang in there, I'll set you straight. You're lucky. I learned how to take care of curs like you growing up here, in Cairo."

The dog snapped its jaws, so I bundled the animal in my jacket and shirt and carried it to the stables while the little creature continued to snarl and snap inside the jacket, pathetic and scared.

Entering the stables, I called, "Salomé?"

Salomé did not answer.

"Salomé?" Now louder.

Still, no answer.

I laid the dog, swaddled in my jacket, in a vacant stall with a sturdy gate. "Stay where you are, little one!"

The mongrel answered with a snap of the jaws and a whiny howl.

My head aching and my mouth still dry, I ran to my room to get ether. And as I pulled my bed sheet off, I grimaced. "More gossip fodder for the maids."

The noise the dog was making had the horses unsettled. Nick Bottom was unhappy too. "I think that some ether is in order and, then, yes, some examining of what's happened to your leg."

Dog asleep, I stepped out and called again for Salomé. Where was she? I had not seen her by the diversion or in the courtyard and it was too early for breakfast. Cook and the rest of the staff were not awake yet. I called again then walked to her makeshift room.

Little droplets darkened the earthen floor and stains appeared on the sheet that dangled off of her bed.

"But what's going on?"

Salomé's face peeped from behind bale construction. She waved me away.

Dumb with shock, I spoke, my voice shaking with worry, "What happened?"

When she glanced at me once more, tears washed over her pale cheeks. Her hair clung to her face, a limp auburn curtain.

I felt a sharp pang in my chest. "What's happened?"

Her only response was to throw straw, as if to defend herself. So, I backed away, and Salomé drew back behind the straw-bales.

"But what's wrong? What's happened? Is it blood...Not your...?"

Her behavior unnerved me. She never pushed me away when she was injured.

"I...I found a dog. I'll need your help in setting its leg."

Silence.

"All right. You won't come out," I snapped. "I'm going now." I left, but quickly returned to add, "At least, let me see you."

A pathetic handful of straws fell at my feet.

\#

After the dog's thin leg was set in a splint, I entered the kitchen. Had Cook's temper improved now that the wedding was over? I doubted it. He had been a miserable wretch since I could remember. Anyway, I had much more pressing problems in the stables.

I caught sight of Rahma. "Rahma!"

"Effendi?"

"I need meat scraps and a cup of tea."

"Effendi?"

"Is Cook there?"

"No, Effendi."

"Hurry then before he wakes up. Scraps of meat and a cup of tea."

Her bewildered look at my requests got her only a nod.

I worried about Salomé. I could not shake the notion that her uncharacteristic behavior towards me was a result of what had happened during Elliot's wedding.

116

Leaving the sunny and warm day outside the door, I entered the stall where the wild dog was twitching.

"Here you are." I put the scraps close to the dog's face.

My new patient was little more than a puppy and extremely thin. "Poor lass," I muttered softly and examined her surroundings. The stall opening would need to be barricaded, but not today. The ether should prevent the dog from leaping out.

Outside, the sun was getting brighter, and there was none of that sweet morning dew in the air. From the kitchen, some disharmonious cacophony sounded Cook's return and temper.

"Thursday, first of October," I mumbled to myself and went to shower and shave and get to hospital.

Whatever occurred, Salomé would stay at the stables in her condition. But what happened? Was she bleeding from an injury? Would she suffer blood loss? Her looks had improved since the first time I met her. She had grown taller. She was thin, but not ghostly thin. Her body took shape, and she looked more like a...Oh, good God! A woman! She was a woman! How could I have missed it?

But, no, I did not miss her transformation.

I grew hot when I remembered how much I had enjoyed our embraces on the bench and the euphoria that gripped me while dancing with Salomé in the stables, her thighs against my body, her breasts pressed to my chest.

Relieved that I had an inkling of Salomé's malady, or rather lack thereof, I ran to the kitchen. By a stroke of luck, Cook had gone elsewhere. I pilfered the larder for crackers and bread, found some sweetmeats, nuts, and dried fruit, cheese and smoked meats.

I ran to my bedroom and grabbed towels, pillowcases, and shirts and as an afterthought a general human development textbook. I stuffed my loot into a pillowcase and ran back to the stables, elated that my commotion went unnoticed.

"It's me, William." I hurried in. "I know what's wrong with you. I mean, nothing's wrong with you."

Salomé remained hidden.

"This will help you." I placed my book close to her hiding place. "Take a look at this page."

Salomé stuck her head out.

"Salomé, it's all right," I whispered and reached for her. "Your body is changing, maturing, rather. It is a good thing."

She stole back behind the straw.

"Why are you hiding?" My words had an unusual echo though. The dog was dreaming, rhythmic whimpers filling the air. "I must go now. I have to get to hospital. I left food, water, and linen. Your tub has water and soap. You should wash up. I'll be back before nightfall." I left the stables, peering over my shoulder, hoping to see her reach for me. I wanted to help, but I was a man and, traditionally, not the person to help Salomé with this matter.

#

A vicar's daughter and newly married, Abigail Wright was one of the more generous and compassionate women of my acquaintance. She was a nurse who found time to work in hospital as well as volunteer at an orphanage and she never shied away from cleaning bedpans or gangrene. She learned to recognize eye maladies, eczema, dysentery, and typhus as easily as a common cold. And she was on duty when I arrived at hospital later that morning.

"Mrs. Wright, may I have a word with you. In private."

Although surprised, she agreed politely to join me for tea in the cafeteria.

"Mrs. Wright, I need your opinion. And your help."

She stiffened.

"A young woman I know..." I immediately regretted my choice of words. "It's not like that! She is fourteen or fifteen..."

"Really, Westbrook, I thought better of you."

"It's my choice of words...Hear me out. My acquaintance is an abandoned girl who just had her first or second cycle, and she doesn't understand what's going on with her body. She's scared. She has no mother, or female relation. I ask for your help," my words tumbled from my mouth quickly, some slurred with speed, but Mrs. Wright understood.

Mrs. Wright's forehead crinkled a bit and she appeared pensive, but not unkind or unwilling.

"Maybe it was a bad choice. I'll go to Madame Sukey. She'll know what to do." I knew that Mrs. Wright did not approve of Madame Sukey despite Madame's generous contributions and gifts to the staff and patients.

"No," she started, rather loud. "Where is she?"

"Madame Sukey?"

"No, silly, the girl not the dragon!"

"Madame Sukey is not a dragon. I do wish you'd stop..."

"All right, you don't have to be so beastly about it. Where is the girl? Is she here?" and so saying, Mrs. Wright looked about.

"She is not here...I'm here, and I need your help."

How much information should I reveal? Surely, some exaggerated gossip would reach my mother before her next social engagement. Face flaming, I asked, "Look, why don't you write some explanation of her condition? What it is, and what to do..."

Mrs. Wright blushed too, but her olive skin tone hid her darkening color.

"Perhaps include a list of materials...procedures."

"Mr. Westbrook, I'll see to it. I don't need any more instructions from you."

"I need to know what to get for the girl."

"Meet me when your shift is over. I'll have it ready by then...sealed." She gave me a stern look.

Did she think that I needed the letter and products for myself? Her behavior seemed absurd. Nevertheless, I was grateful.

#

"What is that unholy wail coming from the stables?" Mother asked.

"She's coming out of it, I suppose. I heard that some do that."

"Who?"

"The bitch."

"William, you cannot mean to tell me that you drugged that poor little girl?"

"Girl? No, no, a dog. I found a bitch with a broken leg this morning. I set her leg after I anesthetized her. It was all rather simple, you know, I have done that sort of thing in the past, when we were younger and forever picking up strays. Joseph taught us."

"Joseph, our old groom?"

"Yes, he was a genius in the stables and with anything in it!"

"Including my sons. Oh, William, do go and...and, oh just make it stop. I cannot bear it any longer."

"All right, Mother." I left the dinner table for the eerie stables. I stopped for a moment at the stall and threw some meat to the dog who

119

was still howling, giving a shuddering cry, her little body twitching in her sleep. The noise filled the stables, and as I passed by the horses, both shook their heads in disapproval.

Salomé's room was thrown into shadows. Salomé was sitting on her bed, leafing through my book. She was wearing one of my shirts. And she was clean now, too.

My stomach lurched; the girl was so beautiful. I stood by the door, afraid to intrude and uneasy about the snarling desire rising inside.

Her movements were slow and a tear ran down her cheek. With a sniff, Salomé wiped her face with her sleeve.

"Salomé?"

The book fell off her lap when she tried to rise, lethargic and gauche. "I'll get it."

She brushed her sleeve roughly across her face.

Gazing down at her, I had to push aside the urge to hold her in my arms and comfort her. "I have a letter for you from Mrs. Wright. She's a nurse."

Salomé's head hung low.

"The letter explains what you're going through, that is, if I am correct, and ah...what to do about it."

Salomé's fingers wrapped round the envelope.

"And this package is also from Mrs. Wright... for you."

When I turned to leave, Salomé sobbed again. She had opened the letter but now held it up.

"You cannot read English? At least, not Mrs. Wright's handwriting... I don't blame you."

Salomé could comprehend much of what was spoken through tone and expression and an increasing vocabulary. She could probably gather a surprising amount of information from pictures in a book. She even appeared to understand text, but a hand written letter in English was probably a challenge. Had I not realized that already? What made me forget? Perhaps it was the relative ease of communicating with Salomé that made me oblivious to her handicap.

"I'll read this letter to you, then."

Grappling with the spiny text and referring to pictures in the book and even some of my own, I explained the female reproductive cycle. When I reached the procedural details, I plunged into the parcel, heroically pulling out each of the mentioned bits of paraphernalia.

Blood rushed to my head as soon as I read the opening line of the letter. Mrs. Wright's writing had all the hallmarks of the feminine gender. Her elucidation was written with care and compassion and patience but there were dots and circles instead of punctuation marks. And, the paper was scented. But it was my attraction to Salomé that made me uncomfortable more than anything else.

Salomé was now a woman.

When I saw her next, Salomé was by the diversion, attacking weeds and pests in the shrubbery.

"Salomé!"

Her little veiled head popped up.

I ran my fingers through my hair, not as an absentminded gesture, but to comb the messy tangle. What was happening? Was I trying to impress the girl?

Salomé ran toward me. The sun shone brightly over her head. And as she ran, her veil had come undone, wrapped itself round her neck and fluttered playfully.

The now familiar warm pain in my chest took hold.

"All right?"

She nodded.

"Let's check on the dog, then."

She pointed to a patch of straw under a tree. The dog was nestled within the straw, busily licking her bandages.

"Well done! How did you get the mongrel over here? I thought that she'd be long gone!"

Silence.

"Here." I pulled a brown package out of the inner pocket of my jacket. "It's soap and rose oil."

Salomé sniffed the package. She then turned to the main irrigation canal and washed her hands, arms, and face. Then, she opened the bottle and poured a little onto her palms and rubbed the oil on her arms and face.

Mesmerized, I watched until, collecting my scattered wits, I turned away, back to the house.

\#

Sitting cross-legged on the verandah, Elliot clutched a dark cup of coffee and stared into the horizon.

The morning was drawing to an end, and the sky was clear. The intensity of the sun gave Elliot an exhausted look. Sweat beaded on his forehead and zigzagged down his temples. His lips barely parted to let the steaming beverage in and never once did he bother to wipe the runnels of sweat off his face.

"Hello." I reached to grab his cup of coffee, but he held grimly on.

"William," he croaked.

I put my hand on his shoulder, giving him a little shake. "You all right?"

Silence.

"Elliot?"

"She paints her legs."

"Sorry?"

Elliot lit a cigarette.

"Paints her legs?"

"That's right. She paints her legs."

"Elliot, are you by chance talking about Elizabeth?"

"Yes."

"She paints her legs?"

A nod.

"What on earth for?"

Elliot's mouth twisted into a grimace. "Stockings are rationed. So, she gets her legs painted. The seam gets painted on, too."

I did not know how to respond to his complaint. And the grim set of his countenance and his slow, controlled motions seemed a bit much for some leg painting grievance.

"It's my sheets, William, my sheets."

"What about them?"

"They're a mess."

I did not believe a word of it. Something upset Elliot, something very bad. And he was keeping quiet about it.

Elliot got up. "I just wanted to warn you of these things. The paint, I mean. I best push off, I'm on the next train."

"But you have not shaved!"

"No," he admitted in dry tones then left.

"Elliot? Where're you going?"

Elliot was already down the stairs, heading for the gate.

122

What was he up to? And what sort of mischief was forthcoming? Because as I watched Elliot disappear, I realized that Elizabeth would not paint her legs. Why would she? Her father was one of the richest men in Cairo! Rationing simply did not apply to her nor did it apply to many of us here in Egypt. And why was Elliot away from his bride? And why was he so morose, almost lifeless and yet complaining of non-existing leg paint and stains and filth?

Chapter 11: Luna

"DON'T fall out."

Turning from the window, I faced my brother.

His stalwart form filled the arched doorway, and although he strove to appear as cheerful as ever, there was bleakness to his countenance now and his movements appeared stiff. "Why dangle yourself out the window when you can simply walk over there?"

"Shut up."

"Were you searching for something?" He leaned close, adding, sotto voce, "Or someone?"

"What is it, Elliot? What do you want?"

"That's no way to greet your brother now, is it?" Elliot lit a cigarette, casting a dark glance at my desk.

Early October of 1942, scarcely a day or two after Elliot's and Elizabeth's wedding, brought shocking news.

Elizabeth Baker and her father, along with their posse of servants, were bundled out of Egypt under charges of treason, with irrefutable evidence.

Although often absent, Elliot managed to pop in at our estate for quick visits at odd hours. When he was home, Elliot's somber mood permeated the house. His ever present, strong smell of brandy lingered, following his footsteps, shadow-like.

Elliot was restless and edgy and there was none of that mocking glint in his blue eyes, and his smile, wolfish or otherwise, was rare indeed. On his visits, Elliot paced, squinting and scratching, as if in inexplicable pain. On some occasions, and those were the worst, he appeared numb, expressionless.

My bedroom window faced the stables and as my brother spoke, I darted glances to the window. I had been in the habit of looking out for Salomé. Elliot's innuendo pinpointed my motive for standing by the window.

"What is it, Elliot?"

"Perhaps you'll offer me something to drink?"

I shook my head.

"All right. Refreshments forbidden." He deposited himself on a leather armchair. "William, what do you know about Tom Sullivan? Is he still in hospital?"

"No. Why should he be? He was discharged months ago."

Elliot bit his lip, as if realizing he'd just made a solecism. "Where is he then?"

My thoughts were still focused on the stables and the girl inside.

"William, where's Sullivan?"

"Why do you ask me?"

"Who else would I ask? Salomé? She wouldn't have an answer anyway."

"Leave her out of this! Are you tight? Again? How much did you drink?"

Elliot tilted his head. "Haven't had a drop of alcohol, if you must know."

He took out another cigarette. Finding it difficult to light it, Elliot tossed the unlit cigarette. "William, I need Sullivan. Where is he?"

Both Sullivan and Tate were dispatched to Kabrit, a training camp by the Bitter Lake. I knew that. But I kept silent.

"Well don't just stand there like a prudish maiden aunt!" Elliot snapped. Then, he fished another cigarette and, shakily, lit it. "She is delightful."

"What?"

"Was it not her you were watching just as I walked in?" he asked, a thick trail of white smoke escaping his mouth and nostrils.

"Get out."

"William? What's the matter?"

A torrent of questions rushed out. "Elliot...Why did you marry Elizabeth? And how is it that she was charged with treason days after your wedding? And don't think that you can fob me off with some excuse about excellent legs, because her legs were fat and exhibited all the hallmarks of psoriasis! And why are you looking for Sullivan? What is it about Aziza's granddaughter that intrigues you so? What keeps you so often away from home? And why do you have such odd patches of sunburnt skin? Why can you never give me an answer? Just once for God's sake!"

The exhaustion that plagued my brother surfaced, but only for a moment. It was the kind that accumulated over the course of several months, if not a year, or longer. His ashen face and his narrowed deep blue eyes and the sallow hue of his sunken cheeks spoke of days without restful nights. His albatross hung over his neck, forbidding Elliot to share his burden. And only now, in my company, in my room, Elliot dropped the facade. He rubbed his eyes, cigarette hanging loose between two fingers, ash dropping on the floor.

My questions hung in the air, unanswered.

"Elliot, he went back. Sullivan's in Kabrit, by the Bitter Lake. Tate's with him, too. Training for some sort of...well, you know what they do."

"No, they're not in Kabrit. But it doesn't signify." Elliot grunted a thanks. "Don't just watch her. Tell her how you feel. But do it properly. Don't make a mess of things! She's a courageous, compassionate woman. So do it properly." His last words were swallowed by a fit of coughing.

"Elliot, we best get you outside. A long walk by the diversion would do you good."

"Yes."

Pushing reeds away and stepping over blocks of concrete rubble, Elliot exclaimed, "Your mongrel's been civilized!"

"What?"

"Look at that beautiful white dog over there! Isn't it your mongrel?" Elliot's gaze trained on a dog, loping along by Salomé's side.

"Not mine, no. More like the girl's pet."

"I know that she's an Egyptian cur, but just look at those well-shaped ears!"

"How can you see her ears under that black veil?"

"The dog's ears!" Elliot growled. He then let out a loud whistle.

Hearing such summons, the dog bounded up to Elliot, tail wagging and head lowered with ears resting back then upright again, trying to gauge her reception, yipping and whimpering all the while.

"Come." Elliot stretched his hand out to the Egyptian cur. Soon the dog was happily leaning against Elliot and enjoying his attentions. "Will you answer to Argos?"

"Argos won't do. Salomé is not Odysseus."

The dog settled to lick and bite an itch on her rear, twitching and yipping in idiotic bliss.

"Besides, this is a bitch," I objected.

126

"A beautiful lass, but I see what you mean!" Elliot again bent to pet the dog, running his hand over her back and scratching behind her ears.

"Check your fingernails. Probably full of livestock by now!"

"Does she have fleas?"

"Certainly."

"Are you sure?"

"She lived in the wild."

"Can't you do something about it?"

"No." And then I delivered my *coup de grâce*, "Aren't you itchy?"

Elliot cried out then ran to the canal and jumped in. When he stuck his head out of the water, he asked, "Fire ants? Again, William? Flicking fire ants at me again? How old are you, seven?"

And within seconds, I was an immobile lump over Elliot's shoulder until he threw me into the canal.

"What was that for?"

"Your cheek!" He jumped in to wrestle me.

But the dog reached me first. Teeth gripping my shirt and paddling paws scratching my skin, she tried to pull me ashore, pull me to safety.

"Stop! The dog, Elliot, the dog! Stay back!"

Once ashore, I caught sight of Ali.

Ali stood only steps away, hand raised with a revolver trained in our direction.

"Ali! What are you about?"

"Were you going to shoot me?" Elliot asked, wrathful, canal water dripping down his face.

"The sick dog attacked the Effendi."

"Drop it," Elliot snarled.

"Ali," I approached the boy and gently, but firmly, removed the Webley revolver from his hand and let Elliot have it.

Just then, the dog got out of the canal. And after she finished rolling in the tall reeds and yipping with delight, she approached us, shaking, spraying Nile water. Very quickly, she noticed Ali. Raising her hackles, she issued a low growl.

Elliot held onto the scruff of the dog's neck.

"It's all right. The poor creature wasn't attacking me, and she isn't going to attack Ali now. Elliot, you can let go of her. She's a good-natured animal. She tried to pull me out of the water."

"Wild dogs cannot be trusted," Ali hissed.

"Nonsense," Elliot snapped.

But I recalled that Faraj had once commented that, in Egypt, dogs rarely enjoyed favor in the eyes of the Prophet's followers. Faraj had to force his cook to give scraps to the curs in the suk.

"Where did you get this? It's ancient! And a Webley!" Elliot asked, examining the specimen with his free hand. "It's an old model. Very old, indeed."

The dog continued to growl.

"From friends." Ali reached to retrieve the revolver with a jerking of his shoulder.

Still holding onto the dog and all along directing soft, comforting noises at her, Elliot gave the revolver back to Ali but not before a final growl, "Don't you ever point this thing at me again. Or any other type of firearm."

As Ali stalked off, I followed him. "Why did you point the gun at my brother?"

"How long will Elliot Effendi be staying in Egypt?"

"Is something up with Elliot?"

"No."

"So why ask? Why the gun, Ali?"

Ali's shoulders were slouched. "What had happened to Elliot's wife? And her father?"

"Elizabeth? And her father? Well, since you ask, they were both charged with treason."

Ali grunted.

"Look, Ali..."

But Ali cut me off. "What about your thin one, Effendi? She is not from here. Is that not true? She is not an Egyptian. She does not belong here!"

I halted and looked at Ali.

Ali extracted a used cigarette from his deep pockets. Nothing in his posture betrayed his motives, or emotions.

"Are you threatening Salomé?"

He shook his head, "No, of course not." Then, turning away, the boy threw over his shoulder, "But, Effendi, no one is safe anymore."

#

"Hmmm...Salomé," he spoke, examining the sound of the name on his lips. Then Father pushed his morning paper aside and leveled his clear blue eyes on mine.

"Father, she is a foreigner. I know that. And what's more, Ali'd made mention of Salomé not being from here. Ali also mentioned Elliot. He even asked about Elizabeth and her father."

"Did he indeed?" He put his napkin down by his plate. "Well, I see that I have to have a talk with our little stable boy. I wonder about him. Is he in earnest or is he playing some deeper game?" Getting to his feet, Father patted me on the shoulder. "William, I best be off. I've a long day ahead of me at Headquarters."

Staring at the coffee carafe and the row of untouched toasts, I was now alone at the breakfast table. The hour was early and I felt edgy, and certainly upset that Father chose to share so little with me about his work or, more importantly, about Salomé.

So, I went to the stables to saddle up Marlena and go for a morning ride.

Made of mud-bricks, the stables were erected by the original owners of our estate, my grandparents. The bricks provided good insulation while the windowless openings circulated fresh air. Tranquility came from the rustling of the scraggly fig trees nearby and the warm breath and soft sounds of the animals. The building had once served a dozen horses and three mules. When I walked to the stables that morning, it housed two Arabian horses, an ancient donkey, a white mongrel, and a thin girl. Not to mention a fair amount of vermin.

The dog wagged her tail and undulated with happiness on Salomé's bed when she saw me enter. She had made herself right at home and nestled into a tight ball by Salomé's side. Now that I approached, the dog rolled over to expose her belly, sneezing and wagging her tail.

"Come."

The dog leapt off the bed and wagged, yipping and licking my hands.

At the same time, Salomé rose and sat cross-legged on her bed with her sheet wrapped round her.

"Here's a biscuit and some tea. You were not at breakfast with the rest of the staff. Are you excused from duties today?"

Her eyes widened in gratitude. Gulping her tea thirstily she then split the biscuit and offered a piece to me.

"No, thank you." As the words left my mouth, the dog leapt up and snapped the biscuit out of Salomé's hand.

Salomé was unveiled, and she had slept in my old shirt, the collar cut off. She looked healthy, and her heart-shaped face was attractive.

My reaction took me by surprise. "I better be off," I mumbled and made for the door, afraid to get carried away like I had done on the bench that eventful night.

But Salomé shot out of bed and stood before the exit.

"What is it?"

She was taller now. She took a step closer and slowly rested her head against my chest, her fingers grabbing hold of my jacket.

"What...?" My arms wrapped round her and I was paralyzed with excitement.

The dog poked her long nose at my thighs. The animal was a wonderful companion to Salomé. Her parents' whereabouts unknown, Salomé was a refugee of Nazi Europe. She was a servant in exile, brutally attacked at the suk, and the list could go on. But she was alive and healthy, I reminded myself. She was sheltered and fed and, although rarely, she had my company, or Ali's. But Salomé was lonely.

"Ride with me. Marlena can handle the extra weight." Detaching myself, I handed her the oversized, rough cotton, black robe. "I'll turn round. You'll have privacy."

The warm, white shirt she placed on the straw-bales beside me shot an electric need up my body that was wonderful and awful all at once. Her scent drifted to me, and I forced down the raging hunger for the girl.

My old complacency returned just in time as Salomé, in her characteristic calm, slipped her arm into mine and pressed her cheek against my shoulder.

"What an affectionate creature you are!" And trusting, jeered a voice in my head.

The October air turned cooler by the cultivated fields. The dew and mist glistened on the crops that swayed softly against the arid vastness beyond.

Salomé sat in front of me on Marlena, gripping my arm and pressing hard against my body. I had an arm round her waist and the other directed the mare, and all along I tried to subdue the cravings that pulsated through me.

130

When we stopped by the main irrigation canal, I dismounted and helped Salomé down.

"Sore?"

With a broad smile and a dazed look, Salomé took several stiff steps towards the canal.

"Allow me." I knelt by her side, wound my arm round her thighs, and picked her up.

For a moment, when I looked up at Salomé, desire roared. Her bright eyes and grand smile weakened my arms. I was lightheaded. "Well, I can't have you looking at me so," I said and heaved Salomé over my shoulder, marching to a deep pool. "Ready?"

If she could scream, she would have done so just then. The water was cold, and the pool was deep. Salomé's arms flailed. The dog jumped in, but I was quicker. Fully dressed, I swam to Salomé, to shield her from the mongrel's paddling paws.

I grabbed her wrist and pulled her close. Our bodies came in contact. "Float by my side but hold on. I'll get us over there. It's shallower by the bank."

The current was swift as it guided us into an eddy. And as the dog paddled by my side, I called, "It's as good a time as any for a proper swimming lesson. Here, hold onto the root. Now, watch my legs, Salomé. I'm kicking the water." Then, I took her hands in mine, my eyes drifting to her lips. "I've seen you do this before. Use me as a float and kick. And breathe!"

"And breathe," I told myself because getting out of the water, was a challenge. While instructing Salomé, the girl's thighs and arms clung to me on several panicky occasions. Her lips were often unbearably close to mine.

Dripping wet, I squatted by the sand bank.

As water pooled over a thin clay layer, I pushed and stirred the water, sand, and clay with a stick. "Watch the cracks in the soil vanish. The water is trapped in the complex clay layers and so the soil swells. It's slippery now and I can actually form clay balls. Like so. If Elliot were here, I'd pound him with mud balls. But you, Salomé, you wouldn't like it." And perhaps worse, I shuddered at the memory of Salomé's reaction to my salute. "We'll build a pyramid instead."

Salomé watched.

131

As the pyramid took shape, Salomé wrung the hem of her robe over it. She smoothed its sides running her palms up and down. Her knees and hands, now covered in a layer of mud, were a fierce shade of reddish brown. She enjoyed herself and she did not mind that her robe was also the same shocking shade.

"Need to make it sandier, ah, ouch!" I clutched my trousers. "Fire ants!" The growing pain, prickly and burning, was familiar enough. I had to remove my trousers and shake out the ants. "No, stay back."

Salomé tried to come near.

"No. Turn...Ahhh..." The ants crawled all over my body. I howled as more bites sent warm waves of pain that made my jaws clench. Thrusting my clothes away, I bolted into the canal.

Salomé leapt to the bank. She noticed a bloated carcass of an ox appearing round the bend. She clapped then extended her hand.

I hesitated.

She made to remove her robe.

"Don't! Keep it on you!" Last thing that I needed was her naked body by my side right now.

She took off her robe anyway.

Unable to resist, I watched.

But underneath, she wore a short black slip of thin cotton. It clung to her body. She clapped again, darting anxious glances at the carcass.

I dove under and, pushing hard, I swam to the bank. I clawed up the slippery clay and heaved my body out of the water.

Muddy robe stretched out, she wrapped it round my waist. Her shoulder then her breast made contact, electrifying me. Her hair brushed against my lips. The invigorating swim and her closeness caught me off guard. I wanted her. An odd, opium-heavy memory of a girl aroused me. What was I to do?

The dead ox was gone, floating far downstream.

Leaning forward a bit, I snatched my trousers and walked back to the river. I plunged the dirty trousers in and out of the water, ants and mud trickling out, as I struggled to stifle my desire.

Salomé, clumsily matching my movements, plunged my shirt into the river.

She was beautiful. Her pale arms outstretched, she was unafraid of the water that had recently hosted a bloated carcass.

I smiled, and she indicated that she wanted to do the same to her robe.

"Not just yet. Let's wait for my clothes to dry. I'll hang my trousers on the reeds. Besides, I rather enjoy the freedom in this tunic."

She made to retrieve the robe. I evaded her attempts. She chased me, amused.

"Not just yet!"

#

Wet and filthy, I entered the kitchen through the back entrance. I grabbed a handful of dates and walked to my room, praying that I might remain unnoticed. My chances were good. I heard Mother improvising at the piano.

But in the corridor, Elliot stood in wait.

"Where have you been?" His truculent mannerism showed signs of lack of sleep.

"Come inside."

"Where have you been?" Elliot walked to the window, his tall figure blocking the light. "Shut the door."

"Is something the matter?"

"Mother has been looking for you."

"I took breakfast with Father. Mrs. Judd knew of it."

"Father has been gone for some time now. Where have you been?"

"Such concern for my whereabouts! Tst, tst, it isn't like you, Elliot."

Elliot sighed. "Get changed. Wet and muddy, you are in no position to stick to your claim to have breakfasted with Father. Obviously, you went riding, swimming, and, God knows what else." Elliot turned to look out the window again.

"You hit all the important points. Why ask then?"

Elliot fell back on my bed staring at the ceiling. "Mother has been looking for you. She received a call from hospital. Did you forget that you had signed up for an early shift today?"

I swore, feeling chastened. "And I know that the staff has been gearing up for recommencement of hostilities in the desert. Gearing up for another bloodbath!"

"Well, GHQ wants an offensive along el Alamein before October's end."

"I better go to hospital right away."

133

"William, you know that I have long ceased to interfere with your *affaires de coeur.*"

"Really?"

"It's Mother. She went looking for you. And Mrs. Judd told Mother you went riding." Then he added, "With a girl, on horseback."

"Well, you can't expect me to ride Bottom."

"Mother's in a state."

"And you are here to warn me. How touching!"

"See here, William. Be reasonable. And put your trousers on already. She cares for your reputation. She is also surprised by your failure to report for duty. Don't look at me like that, I am quoting. William, let's not quarrel. We better come up with some good explanation."

"Any suggestions?"

"Perhaps you found a girl, a fellah, and offered to take her to her village?"

"I'm not such a saint."

"Be serious for once. You are in for it." Elliot lowered his voice. "I am terribly sorry. Envy, it seems, makes me care more than I ought. I was out last night, but unnoticed and no one looked for me."

"So, where were you? Indulging in another Paphian debauch?"

"Of course not. I was at work," he replied with a most innocent expression.

"I won't fib. Mother will have to accept what happened this morning."

#

It was rarely a conversation with my mother. She had a sermon for pretty much anything that could go wrong in life. Her latest was reserved for me and it heavily featured family pride, my reputation, women, and my association with them. "You owe it to your family, William," closed the list of my duties as the son to Sir Niles and my many attributes and accorded privileges, which, no doubt, was designed to soften what followed.

Homily still ringing in my ears, I could not help but wonder at the injustice. I was not to approach the stables, or rather, the person inside.

#

"It scarcely matters since you hardly ride Marlena these days," Elliot breathed the words out as he lit a cigarette later that evening when I returned from hospital. "Let's go to Faraj's. It's been donkey's years since we visited the man." His cigarette hung at the corner of his mouth.

"It's not just that the stables are denied to me, as well as the 'person' inside the stables. Elliot, you cannot imagine the mess I'm in!"

Holding his cigarette away now, he pulled me close. "Trouble at your hospital, William?"

"They need me there."

"Because of el Alamein?"

"No, not just that. There's been a steady influx of jaundice cases."

"Jaundice?"

"One of the symptoms for infective hepatitis! And the paperwork is suffocating. Tedious."

"Tell you what. I'll join you tomorrow. Two competent men can achieve marvelous things. But it would do you much harm to lollop round the house just now. You fret too much. So, we go to Faraj's. We might even meet your darling Madame Sukey!"

"Does Faraj know Madame Sukey? I've been out of touch! When and how did it happen? Your doing, Elliot?"

"My doing? Not so sure but they hit it off splendidly."

"Faraj and Madame Sukey?"

"What a pair! And they certainly keep each other well entertained."

#

The suk teemed with life, loud and smelly. Early evening crowds of American tourists risking wartime travels swarmed the marketplace. Clusters of soldiers huddled outside shops, waving their fly whisks, staring at the noisy merchants, and marveling at the Egyptian heat wave.

Although inured to crowds and noise, the stench of the suk lent speed to Elliot's step. He detested the reek of dried dung and rubbish and grease, the sour smell of unclean human bodies, and stale breath. Never faltering, staring steadfast ahead, Elliot lengthened his stride until he reached his destination.

Wartime atmosphere had penetrated even Faraj's quaint coffee shop. From the exposed leaky plumbing and the cracked concrete walls to the squinty-eyed customers who watched us enter.

"A bit hostile, aren't they?"

"Just walk on, Elliot, no need for heroics."

"*Mes amis.*" Faraj waved and thundered a "*Marchaba.*" He ambled to our table, his big brown eyes watching Elliot, loaded with warmth and concern.

Faraj clapped his palms and Jamal materialized with a polished copper tray laden with three small cups and a pot of Turkish coffee, potent and hot.

"*Aywah, tfaddle,*" Faraj said as his faithful Jamal served. "I have a story to tell."

Faraj enjoyed a willing audience when he had time to spare.

"We are in luck, then, William."

I smiled.

Faraj made himself comfortable on his cushions. "Nargilleh?" he offered.

"It would please me very much and William is certainly not going to object."

Faraj's eyes returned to rest on Elliot, kindness twinkling out of his dark orbs. "When you walked into my shop today, I remembered something that happened many years ago. I was your age, William, *mon ami,* when I first laid eyes on Luna." He pronounced Luna's name with deliberation.

I glanced at Elliot and his tilt of the head and almost imperceptible incline towards Faraj assured me that he too was as of yet unaware of 'Luna.'

Gurgling with delight, Faraj waggled a finger. "I have many stories and no you have not heard them all."

"Faraj!"

"Yes. Well, Luna. Luna was a star. Her skin, white as milk; her hair, long and dark. A beautiful woman. She would brush her hair standing on her balcony." Faraj closed his eyes, reminiscing. "Her father owned a restaurant. A well-respected old man."

"Go on," urged Elliot.

"I had a wonderful dream about Luna one night. And, I had the same dream again the following night. My heart burst with joy because I felt that my wonderful dream was a good omen. *Vous me comprenez, mes amis?* So, I hurried to Luna's father. 'Monsieur, I must have a word with you,' I told him. The old man invited me in. So, I came in and told him about my visions, not in detail, of course."

"Of course."

"I was fortunate and Luna's father agreed that I should spend time with his daughter. As I left his establishment, he promised, 'I shall give you my blessing to wed my daughter. But before I do so, I must warn you. Enjoy your evening, then, we will talk about your future. Luna requires a lot of effort.' Effort? Effort," Faraj sighed and his nostrils vibrated. "So, I took Luna on a boat ride. Luna had to maneuver her position in the small boat. You see," he explained, seeing our perplexed expressions. "Luna's side of the boat was low in the water, and my efforts to row did little to move us along. The oars could but reach the water. She required effort, as her old man had indicated. She had to move to the middle of the boat. So, it was not as romantic as I had hoped. But soon we returned to Cairo for our meal. Luna was a dignified woman. She hardly opened her lips while we were on the boat. Then, when we sat down to eat, her mouth opened, and I saw half of a grilled, tender chicken vanish before my eyes. The bowl of slow cooked rabbit and lentil stew also disappeared. Breads, date cakes, another half a chicken, again breads, rice, lentil, onions and fish came and went. And, so fast! I was sweating, 'Yah Allah, how was she eating such a large meal?' Then I understood. Luna loved food. Loved food! My heart ached. I was in terrible pain. I took short gasps of breath, like this..." And Faraj demonstrated his anxious breathing with strokes of his fist to his chest. "I loved Luna. So white, like milk, with sizable arms, soft skin, scented with patchouli." He made a surprisingly crude gesture with his puckered lips in reminiscence of Luna's marvels. "But she loved food far too much. She could not possibly love me and so it was not meant to be," he concluded on a sigh then gave a wail, "Luna, yah Luna," and hoisting his great bulk up, took his leave of us.

When Faraj returned to the clink and clank and 'Oy!' and 'Yassu!' of the backgammon game, Elliot commented sotto voce, "That was an unexpected story."

"I'd say."

"Who was the girl, William?"

"What?" I sputtered between coughs, smoke and coffee constricting my throat.

"Who was your 'Luna?' Who did you go riding with this morning?" Elliot made a bawdy gesture.

"Elliot," I began then felt faint.

The walls at Faraj's shop were lavishly bedecked with tin ware and kilim. A strong cloud of smoke slapped my face, and I leaned back on the soft cushion, feeling unwell.

"William? We better get some fresh air."

"Fresh air? At the suk?"

"It's the caffeine that has your head spinning. Or the tobacco. That was a particularly strong blend."

Outside, Elliot stepped into a stagnant puddle. Muttering complaints about heat, hunger, and several other matters of discomfort, he marched on, a trail of smelly footprints following his steps.

"Elliot, I'm sick. Oh, damn..." I gasped and in two short bursts I splattered the gritty wall with vomit.

As Elliot waved onlookers away, he growled, "Damn it, William, can't you get away from the fish monger?"

The peddler, hovering over a tin pot that sizzled with frying sardines, looked up. Then, he saw my affliction and hissed.

Elliot barked at him. "Your sardines aren't any better."

My stomach hurt. My head ached. I shivered uncontrollably and, then, the silent stupor came.

When I was conscious again, soft linen bedding tickled my cheek.

"It must have been the heat." Elliot's voice came to me from the leather chair. "Two boys helped me get you into a taxi and I brought you home. You better get some sleep. We're going to be busy tomorrow in hospital." Then he added, "You are not having a great day, are you?"

"No. But I had a marvelous morning."

#

"I did not tell you this but the Second Battle of el Alamein began today." Elliot's face popped up from under a metal cot.

Elliot was helping orderlies and nurses with setting up cots. Grateful for any help, the hospital staff welcomed my brother. And seeing his enthusiasm and infectious good cheer, we took heart and indeed achieved marvelous things. "British naval forces are engaged and the Australians are advancing along the desert roads with RAF coverage."

"How do you know all this? You have been stuck here all morning with me. Disinfecting bed pans." I often marveled at Elliot's breadth of current knowledge. It was uncanny.

"Oh, I popped into GHQ earlier." His voice hardly above a whisper, he warned, "William, it's going to be hellish here in the next few days."

"Not as hellish as it is in the desert and along the coastline."

On the following day, terrible news cascaded on Cairo.

The Germans hit Allied tanks. Fresh horrors made it to the newspapers, and into hospital.

But by the end of October 1942, Allied armor finally and at great cost broke out of Rommel's minefields known as Rommel's Devil Gardens, and advanced into Libya.

Chapter 12: We Never Had a Victory

04 November 1942 and the British were victorious at el Alamein.

Within two weeks, the Soviet Union launched its counter offensive against the Nazis. The Pacific War, however, remained undecided. News of unprecedented genocide at extermination camps throughout Nazi Europe became mainstream knowledge. In mid-November, many believed that the apocalypse was imminent and that, despite the victory at el Alamein, Britain had countless demons yet to fight.

Clutching a letter from James, my oldest brother, I summoned Father and Elliot to the study.

"From James," I said. "But, it's postmarked months ago."

"Well? What is it?" Elliot eyed the letter warily.

"Terse and cryptic."

"Read it to me William," Father asked.

"Father, I am well. The North was impossible. I am closer to you now. Regards, James." I read it once more then tossed it onto the carved mahogany table.

Elliot looked as if thunderstruck. He opened his mouth, closed it, opened it once more, then squeaked, "But what could he possibly mean by it? Doesn't he know the difference between writing a proper letter and dictating a telegram?"

Father and Elliot stared at the letter.

"I'm off. Hospital." And walking out of the study, I heard Elliot growl as the heavy doors shut behind me, "Cryptic. Terse and Cryptic."

"And what will your mother say about such a letter?"

#

Staring down the hospital ward, down the neat rows of metal frame beds, I turned cold. Men were killing men. And somewhere in their midst, was my brother: Patching up soldiers.

James, an army surgeon, patched up damaged bodies.

I did the same thing. My duties expanded daily, demand dictating need for experienced medics. Working with the medics in London during the Blitz had given me experience most young men my age would only acquire after years of school and training.

140

Shells, mortars, mines, grenades, booby traps, bullets: All agents of misery with the results of severe, multiple injuries and burns if one actually survived.

"I hate minefields," escaped my lips, visions of mine wounds twisted and turned in my head.

Mine wounds were grave, destructive to the face and feet. Shelling wounds were ghastly too, and the smell was indescribable.

"I find myself wishing that warfare had never progressed beyond the bow and arrow," Mrs. Wright confessed next to my shoulder. "But it's not just the shelling or the minefields that I dread."

"No?"

"Infection," she whispered.

"Poor bastards."

Ignoring my foul language, she pressed on. "Here in Cairo, we have the luxury of warm water and soap. We irrigate the wound. We apply a solution of iodine, with mackintosh guards for protection. What do field surgeons do?"

Field surgeons?

Mrs. Wright continued, a numb lecturer, and I her only disciple. "They use mackintosh guards, yes, if they can find them, and whatever antiseptic solution is at hand. And if luck comes their way, then they use sulphonamides as bacteriostatics." Her head dipped.

And as Mrs. Wright and I stood crammed, pressed together at the entryway, each hearing the echoes of Mrs. Wright's words reverberate in our heads, I recalled a conversation I once had with a patient, who was a field surgeon himself. He had confessed that treating wounds in rugged desert conditions took practice and ingenuity. And that he did not always get it right. He gave the example that, early on, surgeons removed too much of the skin. Later, experience demonstrated that only the thinnest slice of skin should be removed with, of course, the exception of late or septic wounds, as to aid healing.

But war damaged more than just the human body. Beyond physical injury, war reached down deep, into a hellish state of body and mind and, almost always, alone, in private. The patients put a brave face and did not want to be a burden on the staff. But at night or under drugged sleep, I could sometimes get a glimpse into their nightmares, their damaged souls.

Chapter 13: Gathering Storms

"IT'S a bloody squall out there!" Elliot swung into my room through the courtyard window.

"Where're your clothes?"

"I gambled them away. Damn evil luck. Well, don't just sit and stare. Shut the window, William."

"All right, but you best remove what's left of your undergarments. And get a towel, dry yourself. You don't want to catch the ague." I slowly closed my Penguin, shut the window, and watched my brother.

Naked, Elliot looked gaunt and sinewy, his movements quick and somehow brusque.

"What is it?"

"Well, William, I'll need something to cover up with, now that I've dealt with your ague concerns!"

"Here, use this."

"A bedsheet?"

"Did you want my eiderdown?"

"Clothes, William, I need clothes. I have no use for a bed sheet unless you intend it as a toga. And I should doubt it very much whether Mother would appreciate her son turning out in a diaphanous gown like some Bedlamite."

"Would she like you better naked?"

"Don't be an ass. Have you any trousers that'll fit? You are a trifle narrow at the waist."

"And you a Viking?"

"Shhh!"

"Was that a rap at the window?"

Elliot nodded then withdrew from view and secured the sheet round his body while I peeked out the window. I let out a cry.

Face upturned, Salomé hung onto a rain gutter. Her fingers, white with strain, clutched the pipe and she struggled upward.

"Elliot, help me. It's the girl!"

"Pull her in, William." Then he swore as he thrusted his hand out and hauled Salomé inside.

Lightning pierced the sky and lit up the courtyard. It was soon followed by a startling crack of thunder.

"What is she doing here now?" Elliot asked, staring at Salomé.

"No idea. And why tonight of all nights people are entering my room through the window? It's not an easy climb!"

"What is it Salomé?"

Salomé's arms flailed, and she dragged me back to the window. She made a gesture to follow her.

"Elliot, what do you make of this?"

"Whatever it is, I need to get dressed." He rummaged through my wardrobe. "Salomé?" Unsure how to get his point across, he barked, "Turn round."

The trousers he now wore flirted with Elliot's ankles. The shirt buttoned tightly across his chest. And so Elliot directed Salomé back out the window rather stiffly.

"Smart girl you have here," he said as we were slipping down the gutter pipe. "Has she been visiting you? Is this her nightly routine?"

"Of course not. This is the first time she has been here. She probably followed you in!" And then, as an afterthought, I added, "I wonder what's happened."

Elliot's pants ripped loudly and seconds later thunder boomed above us. Elliot growled.

"My trousers! You ruined my trousers."

"Among other things..."

Salomé tapped Elliot's hand and silenced him with a dark stare. And as soon as I dropped onto the wet mess of tangled vines and mud, Salomé sprang to the estate gate, pushed it open, and bolted down the avenue.

The storm pummeled rain and hail on our heads while Elliot's rear anatomy, exposed and bare, shone with uncanny indecency in the wavering street light.

But there was no humor in the situation.

The limp form on the sidewalk before us was Ali's.

I rolled him over onto his back, and Ali's ripped shirt opened to reveal crossed lines etched into his skin across his chest and abdomen.

"Good Lord!" Elliot breathed, thunderstruck. "It's a swastika cut into his chest."

143

"You cannot possibly be certain that it is. It must be the rain, Elliot. It's playing tricks on you." Kneeling by Ali, I grabbed his wrist. "He's alive."

Salomé was bouncing from side to side, as if searching, or looking out, for someone.

"What is it?" I asked.

Salomé pushed Elliot toward Ali.

"William, can we move him?" Elliot's voice sounded choked and distant.

"Yes, nothing's broken."

"Where do we take him?"

"To the stables?"

Salomé shook her head at my suggestion.

"To my room, then." I glanced at Salomé. "I never saw the girl so agitated before, Elliot."

"Blood," Elliot croaked as a stream of vomit flew out of his mouth. Then, swallowing hard, face averted, Elliot picked Ali up, and carried him.

Salomé, nervously looking this way and that, led the way through the shadows of the tall rose bushes, back to my window.

Elliot groaned. He laid Ali down, then his eyes met mine. "The smell of blood turns my stomach! How do you do it, William, day after day?"

Salomé pressed close to me.

"You get used to it. Elliot, we can't take Ali through the window. We'll carry him through the main house."

But Salomé stayed under the window, motionless.

"Looks like we must. She must have..." Elliot's nocturnal senses were sharp, so I was not going to protest when suddenly, and without warning, he swung his arm and flattened us against the wall.

Three figures prowling the courtyard came into view.

"I don't have my revolver. I gambled it away!"

The dark shapes stopped and looked in our direction.

Rain drops rolling off her nose, Salomé stood still while Ali was on the ground in a dead faint.

Could the three intruders have known? Were they the people who abducted Salomé? Did they recognize her yellow star? Was that why Ali had a swastika on his chest now? Was the attack some form of revenge on Ali for working for us? Or was it less personal, perhaps a warning signal for Father, a representative of the British government?

The intruders turned away, toward the stables. Salomé raised her head and gave me a concerned look.

"The dog."

Elliot scanned the courtyard, biting his lips. "Where's the dog?"

"The stables, I'm afraid."

"The dog might chase them away, damn it all, and I need to catch the bastards who did this," he pointed at Ali. "Ali needs attention, immediate attention. Get him up, you two. I will distract them. Get him up, fast."

The pressing weight that pinned me to the wall lifted.

Salomé made to hold him back, but Elliot slipped past. "Keep her with you."

"Come here," I whispered as I wrapped my fingers round Salomé's wrist.

The noise of fabric ripping sounded, followed by the obligatory wrathful imprecation. Elliot was on his own, with or without trousers, and sprinting to the stables.

Despite Salomé's uneasiness, I carried Ali to my room through the house. By the time we got there, the sound that I had been dreading resounded through the storm: gunshot.

Dog barks and snarls confirmed that at least the dog was still alive and now angry.

Another gunshot.

The girl and I stood still for an instant, wondering what was going on? Who fired the shot? Was Elliot safe? Were the intruders hit?

Immediately after the second shot, light from Father's room flooded the courtyard.

Salomé had been peeling away Ali's clothes, slowly, carefully.

"Stay with Ali, Salomé. I want to catch Father before he runs outside."

In his study, Father was already unlocking the door to a musty glass case.

"Father, it's Elliot."

"Shooting or getting shot at?" With smooth motions he withdrew a rifle.

"The latter. They are at the stables, Father. Best hurry."

"Stay here with your mother."

"But I'd..."

"Stay in the house, William." And he took off, an antique hunting rifle of doubtful functionality in his hand.

The dog had been barking ferociously since the first gunshot. Still, there was no evidence that Elliot was safe or otherwise. I stood undecided in the long gallery when a light touch startled me.

"Mother?"

"What is all this racket?"

"Burglars."

"Cairo's changed. It's infested with burglars like a pack of rats in one's cellar back home."

"Mother, you never had rats back home."

"Certainly not, dear. Mr. Hall kept terriers!"

"Mr. Hall? Who's Mr. Hall?"

"Groom of the stables. Didn't I tell you about him?"

"No. Mother, Elliot and Father are outside sorting it all out. Will you be all right by yourself?"

"I will. But, William, don't you think you ought to summon Cook to help them?"

"Cook? What could he do? Threaten the miscreants with a pot? No, best leave it to Father. He has his rifle. That should put the fear of God into them, don't you think?"

Silent, Mother stared into the gloomy long gallery.

"Mother, will you be all right on your own?"

"Of course. But, William, do go help them."

"I will help." My legs, however, took me to my room, where I knew I was needed.

Opening the door, my eyes fell on Salomé leaning over Ali. Her hands were pressing together a deep gash on Ali's chest.

Outside, the dog was still barking but at least the rumbling thunder wavered.

"Here, use this. Sulphonamides."

Salomé disinfected the cuts then watched me dress the wounds.

Ali twitched and groaned and opened his eyes. His was a penetrating stare, not malicious, not resentful, but unnerving.

"Ali?"

"Effendi."

146

Salomé kept busy, her lower lip between her teeth.

A rifle was fired in the distance and then the dog ceased her barking. Straight away, Salomé jumped to the window.

"Stop. Where are you..."

She opened the window wide.

Elliot, dog in hand, scaled his way up. His thighs and bare feet clutched the drainpipe and thick vines as he pulled upward with one arm.

Elliot shoved the dog in and then, oh, then he flung his leg into the room. The rest of him followed with the sad remains of my trousers when a renegade lightning flash lit up his predicament. The pants were torn along the seams, leaving two pieces of fabric cut in the shape of men's trousers but no longer sewn together.

"This is not the time, William," Elliot snapped when my smirk turned into a nervous giggle.

"Oh, but you must see it!"

"I don't."

I looked for a distraction and found the dog trying to lick Ali's cuts. "When did the dog and Ali become friends?" I asked.

"No idea."

I grabbed the animal and led her away. "Stay," I ordered and returned to sit by Ali on the floor. "Elliot, get some trousers! And for God's sake, get some underpants."

Elliot's head turned sharply in my direction. The wet hair landed on his cheeks with a spray of water. His lips pressed shut, and he was solemn.

"I'm not putting on your pants. Certainly not those appalling y-fronts! Just give me a...No, I don't need a woman's robe." He pushed Salomé's robe away, shocked at her offer. "There, I need that one, hand it to me, will you girl?" he requested of Salomé. "What the devil is going on here? Why is she offering me robes? And why is that boy on the floor?"

"We have to staunch the bleeding and clean him up a bit before I allow Ali on my bed!"

Elliot stripped then snatched the underpants Salomé brought him. I was surprised at how at ease she was while a naked man was marching to and fro, whispering gruff orders and spitting oaths.

"No, Effendi," Ali moaned.

"Hang in there, Ali, it's the last of the dressings. It's holding your skin together."

Elliot rushed to Ali, the dog slinking ever so closer to Elliot, trying to lick his hands, "Not now, Love," he patted her on the head but held her back firmly. With his knees on the hard floor, Elliot leaned over the boy. "Ali, who were these thugs?" He placed his palm over Ali's forehead, and brushed aside Ali's wet black hair.

"Mahmud...he's back," Ali croaked.

Salomé took a step back, her eyes dilated with fear.

"Mahmud? Who? Damn it. The same man who took the girl?" Elliot's voice reflected his surprise.

Ali blinked.

"Elliot! You know about that?"

"About what?"

"Salomé's abduction."

"I'm not blind."

"Why did you keep quiet?"

"You did well enough. There was no need to get involved."

"But, damn it all, Elliot, who is Mahmud? Why did he carry the girl away and abused her so?"

"He's some bastard. I'm going to go and collect his sorry arse."

Ali's eyes opened wide. "No!"

"No?"

"I will deal with him," Ali rasped.

"All right, but you are in my brother's bedroom, bleeding all over the shop, and my father is firing his hundred-year-old rifle at shadows. Do you have a better plan?"

"Sir Niles?"

"Yes."

"Effendi! Get Sir Niles! They are after him." Ali made to rise, but Salomé put her hand on his shoulder.

Elliot walked to the door then turned to my closet. Grabbing a pair of trousers at random, he got dressed and walked out.

Salomé wanted to follow him, but I turned round and stopped her. "Stay with Ali. I'll go."

Her brows furrowed.

"Ali needs you. He's bleeding. Who knows what the dog will do to him without you nearby."

148

Salomé eyed the now sleepy dog, who gave a lazy wag with her tail. "I'll go. It's my father out there."

#

The storm had drifted to assault another part of the city and left behind a wet courtyard with broken branches scattered about.

Despite my haste, Elliot was already by the stables when I reached him. He was sitting on a bench, his arm wrapped round a man's shoulders.

"Father? Elliot, what's happened?"

Elliot glanced up then nodded toward a body strewn across a rose bush that was, until the storm rolled into town, in full, passionate bloom. Now, rose petals littered the paths.

My father did not shoot at shadows. It was probably the first man that he had ever killed; and I searched for words of consolation.

"Would you feel better if you knew that this man had attacked Ali?"

My father stared.

"And, according to Ali, this dead man and the other two Neanderthals are, ah, were set on capturing the famous Sir Niles simply because you, Father, are a British diplomat. And no doubt, they planned to extend the same hospitality they'd extended to Salomé."

"William, you do have a way with words! How do your patients feel about your bedside manner?" Elliot rejoined.

#

His retching left Elliot shaky. "I couldn't identify the dead man. But it's not Mahmud. Damn."

"And you think that you could recognize Mahmud?"

"Father did not shoot his face."

"That's not what I meant. Never-mind! Here," I lit a cigarette and jammed it between his lips. "Elliot, how much of it does Father know?"

"Not sure."

"So, now what? What did you tell the police?"

"Not much. Not more than they need to know. How is Ali?"

"He'll live."

"Yes, and he'll complain about it for the rest of his life. What a tiresome boy he's become!"

"Leave Ali. What about Father? And where are the other two?"

Leaning on a palm tree, I watched the policemen prepare to remove the body.

"Father is fine now. And the other two, ah, Neanderthals escaped when this one got it." Elliot drew on his cigarette, exhausted and ill. "Where's Mother?"

"Mother's in the house, in her bedroom, and under the impression that burglars infest Cairo like a pack of rats."

"What?"

"Like a pack of rats in one's attic back home. No, in one's cellar."

"Is she serious?"

"What would you've told her?"

Elliot then flicked the cigarette butt into the rose bushes. "William, how can you stomach the smell? Everyday! How do you do it?"

"Blood or vomit? Or excrement? Pus? Gangrene?"

"Stop!" Elliot gave a shudder of revulsion.

"You get used to it. But we have water, soap, and electricity. Can you imagine James' daily routine?"

"No." Abruptly, Elliot turned and headed to the guesthouse. His back was bare and wet, and his pants reached just above the ankles.

A sense of unreality seized me, and I felt that I was an outsider, circling round the periphery of another world in which I had no part.

#

Standing by the window, swigging brandy and giving it not a thought, I glanced at two guards stationed at our massive gate.

Their interest was fixed on Cook.

Cook and Mrs. Judd were having a row.

I became aware of the monotony of Cook's arguments. No, he would remain behind, but Mrs. Judd had to get him spices. Spices? Yes. Anything else? No, but...perhaps some produce, meats, fish and...Mrs. Judd refused, well acquainted with Cook's shopping demands, his stringent budget, and ungrateful ways.

A colorful session ensued.

The guards remained entranced, watching the scene unfold.

Cook was going to bully Mrs. Judd, then shout and berate her upon her return for, of course, anything she would bring back would be unacceptable.

"So, you say that you'd kept watch, Ali?"

In his bed in the servants' quarters, Ali enjoyed his hot mint tea.

"She was in danger," he repeated. "It's the way she walks, Effendi. Her head is like this." He indicated Salomé's upright posture and tea dribbled on his chest. "Effendi, Mahmud and I belonged to the same order, the same party."

"What?"

"Our party rallies the cause of a sovereign Egypt."

"Nice words," I commented. Did the boy know their meaning?

"I was allowed to join the party because I worked for your father. I was ordered to find a weak point in the household."

"Must have been tough on you."

Ali nodded, unable to look me in the eye.

"So, torn between loyalties and party demands, you decided to ill-advise your party leaders?" At fourteen, the boy was naive.

Again, eyes averted, he nodded, whispering, "I did not believe that any harm would come of it. And before the incident in the suk... Effendi, I informed the leaders that Salomé was your lover."

The glass broke in my hand and the brandy trickled down my wrist. Did the boy know what a lover was? Angry and sad all at once, I released the shards outside the window, hoping that I had not scared Ali back into silence.

"I did not think that they would actually hurt anyone."

"But they did."

"Yes. Lady Westbrook and Salomé were with me at the suk. But why Mahmud grabbed Salomé, I do not know, Effendi."

"Had Mahmud's intended victim been Lady Westbrook?"

"Yes. But the girl stood closer to the devil. I kept Lady Westbrook shielded. But not the girl."

Months after the incident, Ali learned why Salomé was abandoned outside Mahmud's dwelling. Something had gone wrong for the activists because Mahmud was a wanted criminal.

"Effendi, a policeman recognized Mahmud in the suk and followed him and Salomé to Mahmud's house. Salomé would not answer Mahmud's questions. Well, how could she? Mahmud beat her, and made demands on her when the policeman gathered enough courage and arrested Mahmud."

"What demands?"

Ali ignored my question. "The party leaders do not like foiled plans, Effendi. The party looks weak. Mahmud was released a week ago. I suspected that he would try to get to Salomé again, or to you. Mahmud wanted to get the leaders' trust. There is good money in it."

I made an irritated gesture.

"The plan was to get to Sir Niles." Ali looked uneasy as he disclosed that similar ploys were planned for other British officials.

"You cannot be serious! Is this party so bold as to begin trouble with Cairo's prominent British families?"

Ali nodded. "There are influential businessmen supporting the party," Ali warned.

"But the businessmen's primary goal was to gain political recognition!"

Ali shook his head.

And then I recalled past incidents during and after the Great War. Politicians and their families were made targets by such nationalist groups. Some were released for ransom and some were hung in public places as a display of power over British rule.

"Effendi, Mahmud knew to look for your girl..."

"She is not my girl!"

"I shook Mahmud off once before, but the night of the storm was different. Mahmud and two others entered the Westbrook estate. They entered the Westbrook stables." He paused for dramatic effect. "Effendi, I do not know why they went into the stables. Could they have known she lives there? Salomé was not in the stables. She was in the kitchen, sneaking scraps for the dog, and the dog was tied outside the kitchen. Lucky dog! Had it been in the stables... But I was in the stables. The three of them attacked me! Do I look like a little girl?" Ali wailed, ending his sentence with his typical flair for melodrama.

"But they must have recognized you! Were they angry with you? Disappointed perhaps? Did anyone know that you brought me to Mahmud's house to collect Salomé?"

"I have no idea, Effendi," he replied, miserably.

"What happened next?"

"The girl heard noises. She got to the stables and threw rocks at the men through the open windows. They panicked. They thought that they were being attacked. They dragged me out and down the avenue. Elliot drove in just then and parked his motorcar by the gate. The men kicked me. Next, I woke up in your room, Effendi. And, I saw Elliot Effendi, his, oh ..."

How difficult it must have been for him to admit to his ties to the nationalists while working and living here on my father's estate!

Nationalism was a powerful force indeed. But I could not help wondering what would have become of Ali if he had not worked for us, housed and fed behind the protective walls of our estate? Surprisingly, throughout his confession I felt nothing but pity for the gullible boy.

#

The Eighth Army captured Benghazi in late November of 1942, and lit a worldwide spark of hope for the Allies.

On our estate, as the Yule season of 1942 approached, Ali, recovered. Back on his feet, Ali decided to climb a ladder.

Unaccountably, Mother stood still, observing the youth at his work.

"Mother?" I walked to her.

"Where are you going, dear?" Mother asked.

"To hospital. I won't be dining with you and Father."

"I wanted you to know...I am proud of your efforts."

"Thank you." Impressed by her praise, I stayed for a while longer by her side. "What is Ali doing?"

"Shutters. He's repairing shutters. Cook said to watch him. He's sure to miss a few, he'd said."

And here she was, the lady of the house, obeying Cook's command. Why?

Ali wore a dark robe under a tweed jacket. He stood on a rickety ladder and his cigarette precariously dangled from the corner of his lips, toying with gravity as did he. His work ethic, once work commenced, was impeccable. His smoking was hurried. He simply breathed through the cigarette and exhaled through his aquiline nose. Unexpectedly, the long, undisturbed length of ash dropped on Ali's foot, caught in the sandal straps, and seared his skin. He leapt with a choked cry of pain, landing on the ground. The ladder remained unmoved, leaning against the stables' wall.

"Well done!" I called.

Ali nodded, sneaking a quick glance at my mother.

"I'll leave you to it then."

Walking out the gate, I suddenly felt Elliot's heavy hand on my shoulder.

"William, come. Quickly."

"Look, can't it wait?"

But Elliot simply took off at a run so I followed Elliot back to the house where I could hear howls and shrieks.

153

"Do you smell it?"

"There's an odd scent to the air," I agreed.

"It's coming from your room."

The howls also seemed to emanate from there.

"What on earth is this?" I demanded as Elliot flung the door open. The white dog stood in the middle of the room, howling.

"For god sake's William enter and shut the door. She is in heat. What the devil did you rescue a bitch for?"

"I wondered why I have noticed more dogs skulking nearby. Hang on, do you intend to keep her here? In my room?"

"Of course I do. We don't want another ten thousand puppies running round here, do we?"

"Damn. I didn't think about that."

"Females breed." And on that bit of laconic wisdom, Elliot sauntered off, leaving me staring bleakly at the howler. How long would that particular state last? And is that the reason Mother is staying out of doors?

Chapter 14: Winds of Change

"WINTER'S over. Brace yourself, William, the khamsin is coming."

"Would 1943 prove to be a hot one?"

"It's possible. Sand and wind hit Cairo every springtime, but some years seem to pack more dust and heat." Elliot's back pressed against a palm tree in our courtyard.

"Are the stables secure enough against a dust storm?"

"She'll be fine in there. The stables could use curtains or more shutters, but the structure should hold." Elliot grinned. "Mother is at the club. Why don't you take the girl along with you and buy some cambric or canvas? I'll help you nail it to the window frames this evening."

"Right."

"There she is. I'll leave you to it then. You'll be back before sunset?"

I nodded.

"Good." Elliot slapped my back.

#

Outside the cinema house, a group of British soldiers chorused to the Egyptian national anthem a derisive and bawdy verse about Egypt's King Faruk, his testicles, and a large hook. The poem was vulgar, but it rhymed.

"Don't worry about the soldiers, Salomé," I said when I noticed her wary glances at the young men. Putting an arm round her waist, I directed her onward. "They're on leave and their clever little ditty amuses them immeasurably. Besides, it's the beggars that are getting to me at the moment."

Dusty, dirty streets under our feet, and beggars and bootblacks on all sides, I soon sought relief from the grabbing hands -young and old- and the unholy din of shrieking demands for money.

"Let's head in here, it looks deserted. Hurry and maybe we'll shake off the last of the bootblacks."

Treading in rubbish, we kept to the abandoned, filthy alley. The stench was astonishing. I lifted Salomé onto a low stone wall and removed her veil. "Egypt is largely an Islamic nation, and alms-giving is a religious virtue, so begging has become a profession. Are you thirsty, hungry?"

She nodded.

"Let's get your veil back on then."

But Salomé cocked her head, then narrowed her eyes and pointed to a naked toddler.

"Oh."

Salomé hopped off and went to the boy, stretching her arms to him. Although it took a few silent moments, the child was finally perched on her hip, leaning his head against her shoulder, while Salomé frowned at his leg.

"Bring him here."

Under the dust and grime, the child's leg was an angry shade of red with patches of scaly and cracked skin exposing tender pink flesh and dried blood.

"Skin ailments are the least of Egyptian youth's problems," I explained.

Chronic diarrhea and malnutrition buried close to half of the native toddlers. But poor sanitation, inadequate diet, and enteric diseases were just a part of the problem. Opium, cocaine, heroin, and even excessive hashish stripped numerous infants of their parents, leaving them homeless and alone. And homelessness left the children at the mercy of their surroundings. As Egyptian population statistics infiltrated my thoughts, I wondered how best to illustrate the plight of the native newborn to Salomé. "Oh, Salomé," I whispered.

Salomé lowered the child's leg.

"Let me see." I took the child in my arms.

"Where is your mother?" I asked him in Arabic.

He did not respond.

"He doesn't want to talk either, Salomé. You're well suited for each other then."

She glared at me.

"Salomé, this toddler looks hungry and it's getting late. We'll get food then fabric for your window. After that, we'll take the child someplace safe, before we go home."

I was not sure how much Salomé understood, but my holding onto the child and resolute tone cheered her up.

After we ate, we stopped at a booth that sold Turkish delight and tin cups full of doubtful red syrup drink.

"Not so clean, is it?" I commented. Leaning against the vendor's stand, I closed my eyes and drank. The salty street fare and heat acted as loyal agents to the popularity of such drinks. The tin cups were filthy and no wonder. When we returned them to the vendor, I realized that he never washed them after each use.

Being tall and fair in coloring with a woman and child by my side, I attracted the wrong sort of attention. Even the linen shop proprietor cast disapproving glances at the dirty child in Salomé's arms. Then the child pulled off Salomé's head veil. The proprietor gasped with shock at the girl's fair skin, freckles, and cropped hair. A torrent of questions ensued. She was Italian but her poor Arabic was not a hindrance to her investigation. Was I looking for fabric for the woman? Who was the child? What was my relationship with the young woman? What business had I in Cairo? And, then, after she tired of all my lies, she complained about the khamsin. While she spoke, Salomé had been admiring a particular roll of blue cambric, running her fingers along its intricate purple and gold embroidery across the middle.

"We'll take the blue cambric."

Later, at the apothecary, Salomé and the child kept me company in silence.

"There is not much that she can do but clean him up and put the cream on his legs. God knows every scratch a child gets in Egypt turns septic. Here, have her apply this," the chemist handed me the cream that I was after. "Mr. Westbrook?"

"Yes?"

"Here's a list of clinics available to her and the child. If you are in a position to do so, encourage her to go. The mother's condition does not appear to be better than the child's." The chemist indicated Salomé's ankles.

Salomé looked down at her feet. And feeling rather chastened, my gaze fell to her irritated ankles. I should have addressed her fleabites long ago.

Outside, motorcars plugged up the main streets, bullying donkeys and camels out of their way with noxious fumes and loud horns.

"We cannot take him with us to the estate, you do understand? You do, don't you? Orphaned children swarm Cairo. Many live on the streets or even on roof tops, Salomé."

I avoided mentioning that some orphans grew up in brothels, eventually providing services themselves, male and female alike.

"Here," I pointed to a rescue shelter for children. "We'll get someone to look after the child here."

Reluctantly, Salomé handed the child over as the boy wrapped his swarthy arms round my neck.

"I'll take him in. It's possible that they'll find him a home. While I'm gone, don't bring me anymore babies." I wanted to make her smile and ease her tension.

Instead, Salomé scowled, and I leaned to kiss her head. She had grown taller since the last time I had kissed her head. Now, I wanted to gather her into my arms and kiss more than just her forehead.

Salomé and I returned to the house after dark.

"It's too late to hang the curtains. And Elliot's probably at his club by now. We'll do this tomorrow, or, actually, I better check my schedule. I'm on duty tomorrow. You look tired. You better get back to your room."

But Salomé tapped my shoulder and pointed to her ankles.

"Ha, but I thought of it already." I pulled out a thin tube from my pocket and a bar of soap wrapped in colorful paper. "I got these. The ointment is for your ankles."

#

On the following week, I checked in at the stables. Smug and complacent, Ali had already informed me that he covered up the open windows in the stables. And so I stepped into darkness. I announced myself, but only the horses acknowledged me.

Leaning my head against Marlena, I rubbed the mare halfheartedly and listened to her heartbeat and exhaled breath. Shutting my eyes, I slid into oblivion, thinking of nothing at all.

A rustle of robes finally drew my attention.

"Salomé!"

Her scent never failed to electrify me. It was the subtle combination of fresh hay and rose oil soap.

Salomé, hand outstretched, drew me into her room. In the semidarkness of her makeshift room, she presented my anatomy book.

Wrapped in one of my old pillowcases, the book had dried rose buds marking several pages. One of the pages was the reproductive system and childbirth and I recalled the evening I had spent trying to explain the feminine cycle to Salomé.

Heat flushed through me like a shock wave.

"I must be off. But this copy is yours."

Salomé smiled and with her overflowing excitement skipped from side to side, clapped, then, taking a leap forward, she wrapped her arms round me. She lingered. Her warm body pressed against my chest.

My mind, clean empty of thoughts, drugged with the fragrance of her soap and straw, reeled. Fire seared through my body in a rush of hunger. Heartbeat thudding, I pressed her close and, drawing her head back, I brought our lips together, her taste flooding into me as she parted her lips, innocently inviting, seeking more.

Her fingers slid into my hair, then moved to my neck and shoulders, leaving a streak of hot ice wherever she touched. She kissed me, pressing closer, now exploring my chest, throat, with warm lips.

A choked moan escaped me when I tried to whisper her name. I was fighting to catch my breath. Part of me screamed to stop but I quickly clamped that bit of noise down because Salomé was often on my mind. I wanted her, ever since our passionate kisses on the bench so many months ago. I wanted her. Somewhere between delirium and reality, I took off her robes, and with throbbing, surging need I reached for her.

Chapter 15: The Hazard of Hazards

MR. Kelly Evans was an American war correspondent convalescing at the British military hospital, despite his nationality and occupation, through the winter of 1942 and spring of 1943. And while recovering from burns and bullet wounds, he made journalistic use of his time in bed, interviewing his neighbors.

Upon his arrival, Mr. Evans explained that the bullet that grazed his arm took him by surprise while he photographed the mêlée in the Western Desert. But doubts lingered regarding the events leading to, and surrounding, Mr. Evans' bullet wounds. And one particular wound's location on Mr. Evans' body was an enigma.

Tucked under hospital sheets up to his neck, a truculent Australian in Mr. Evans' ward, eager to express his opinion, delivered a less valorous account. "Evans was underfoot. He followed us when we were sent to put down the riot by Cairo University. I say, most likely he shot himself in, where'd he get it?"

A Tasmanian patient with thunder-like voice would then cough, "Arse."

Roars of laughter would follow. The audience, nurses and patients nearby, enjoyed the joke.

The parody repeated itself frequently.

Even Madame Sukey, who had visited the hospital with parcels of sweets and wine, cigarettes and cards, had enjoyed the show. Especially now that the war in the Western Desert was swinging into a decisive victory for the Allies.

A gregarious, easygoing man from Boston in his late thirties, Mr. Evans charmed the nurses in the style of Rudolph Valentino. Like a 1920's Casanova in a Hollywood production, he showered the nurses with unctuous chivalry.

But although charming enough, Mr. Evans often irritated me. And one afternoon, to my great annoyance, Mr. Evans asserted that he captured the 'spirit of war.'

"Spirit of war?"

His toothy, American grin flashed.

"Here," I held up an artificial leg. "Photograph this!"

"Westbrook!"

"And while you have your camera out, photograph this chap. That should give you the 'spirit of war' all right." I pointed to a twenty-year-old with a disfigured face. "This scarring is complements of the Afrika Korps' shrapnel. And Mr. Evans, could you photograph her? This nurse hasn't seen her daughter back home for an entire year now. And what about him right there? But, really, tell me, could your photographs describe the smell? Could your snapshots capture the hair-raising screams at night? Or the twitching? Infections? Crying? Loneliness? Fear? Exhaustion? Hunger? The vermin? Or the shits?"

Silence fell on the ward.

"A Jewish chap, lying downstairs since no one would have a Jew in their ward, lost an eye and his other is infected; burns cover your third neighbor, over there. I can photograph them, since you're in bed. With burns and bullet wounds in..." I clamped my mouth shut then whispered a heart-felt, "Damn."

The ward was still.

One fellow had an unlit cigarette stuck in his chapped lips. His fingers cradled a deck of cards. He never blinked as his clear blue eyes watched me with cool detachment, the unlit cigarette a testimonial to his stillness. The horrors spewing out belonged to a world that he and his comrades only recalled in nightmares.

I hated the slaughter, the sights and smells in hospital. And endless charts and inventory lists along with the infuriating squabbles over supplies, even at teatime, disgusted me.

"You're right, Westbrook. Of course." Mr. Evans then apologized, loud and clear, "I am sorry, boys." He lowered his eyes then reached for my arm. He shook it with his left hand.

#

The battle over North Africa continued.

In hospital, Mr. Evans' cheer prevailed. His charismatic ideas drew patients in and a new evening tradition blossomed: Stretcher Racing.

"Your first time to watch their Stretcher Racing, Westbrook?" Mrs. Wright asked.

Standing at the entryway, mouth open in astonishment, I replied, "But it must be stopped!"

"The boys are happy."

"It's inhumane!"

161

"It cheers them up," the nurse whispered, keeping a firm hold on my arm.

As in all races, Stretcher Racing had a finish line, judges, and, of course, competitors. Tied pajamas, the finish line, stretched cheekily across the corridor. Mr. Evans and a junior officer made the panel of judges.

"What an unsightly lot!" I remarked.

Queuing up for a race, six volunteers with their two stretchers fidgeted. Each stretcher had a 'stretcher bearer' tied to it at each end.

"Mrs. Wright, the straps are made of torn fabric. It can't be torn bed sheets!"

Biting her lip, the nurse quietly stared at the straps fastened to the stretcher and worn by the bearers in a double sling over the shoulders and torso.

"Bed linens are rationed and counted."

"Don't..."

"You're rather fond of the game!"

"Westbrook, it's a game."

In addition to the two patients on each end of the stretcher, there was a third racer: the 'dead weight,' the chap on the stretcher.

During the first heat that I witnessed, two heavyset Englishmen were the 'dead weights.' One of the bearers was an amputee. Another bearer was hobbling with broken ribs and recovering from severe burns.

Mr. Evans inspected the knots which had to be just right, to accommodate the physical condition or injuries of the participants.

"The stretcher bearers look ghastly!"

"That's a bit harsh." Mrs. Wright's reprimand was barely above a whisper.

"Are the dark stains on their gowns blood?"

"Let them be."

Mr. Evans' noisemaker commenced each heat.

A Tasmanian man, the same man who would cough and grumble "Arse" whenever the question of Mr. Evans' location of wound arose, called out the results. He looked wild and half crazed with a kerchief tied round his head. Lying belly down on a bunk at the end of the hall, half-naked, he dangled from the narrow end of the bed. Holding a walking stick and a bedpan, he clanked when one of the competing trios reached the finish line.

Shoving his cigarette in his mouth, Mr. Evans would then twist the noisemaker. Accompanied by the obnoxious wailing and rattling of the toy and the hooting of the passionate crowd, he would call out the results, collecting and redistributing the winnings: torn cigarettes, bits of chocolate, or cards with naughty pictures.

"Mrs. Wright, where are they getting the wine and chocolates?"

"From your generous benefactor, Madame Sukey!"

"Worse and worse!"

A spin-off of the horrific stretcher parties, Stretcher Racing was undoubtedly amongst the patients' favorite activities. The lamest patient would often volunteer to race, while a corpulent comrade would be the 'dead weight,' lying on the stretcher, face down, barking encouraging words, then, trading insults with their opponents.

Stretcher Racing became a sport and a gambling outlet. Sometimes the nurses agreed to play the 'dead weight.' The irony triggered more laughs, and the stakes became higher.

#

"Chin up, Mr. Evans. You'll be discharged soon."

"Westbrook, I've lost interest in Stretcher Racing."

"Look, I wasn't criticizing the races. I only wish you'd pick stronger participants. Mr. Evans, my shift's over. I best be off."

"Care to accompany me to Palestine, Westbrook?"

"What?"

"You're burned out and tired of this mess. You look ill. What you need, kid, is a vacation."

"A holiday? In Palestine? Is this another of your little jokes Mr. Evans?"

"Well, not exactly a vacation in the restful meaning of the word. More like a change of pace, a change of scenery. You're tired of this hospital. Admit it! Even an innocent, playful game offends you anymore."

"The game is dangerous. That boy collapsed in your queue!"

"He should have taken better care of his tie-ups," Mr. Evans dismissed the unfortunate incident. "The two of us can cover a lot of ground together. We'll be out there, the real theater, the battlefield."

"Palestine's hardly a battlefield."

"Palestine's Armageddon!"

"Mr. Evans, I must go."

163

His left hand clutched my shoulder and, using me as a crutch, dragged me out to the courtyard, lowering his voice with feigned conspiratorial nuances. "William, may I call you William?"

"Why not." Anything to get Mr. Evans to put an end to Stretcher Racing and to let me go home.

"William, there are forces at work in Palestine cooking up a witch's brew. The British government is scrabbling for its mandates in the oil-rich Middle East and the Palestine mandate has often been difficult to maintain peacefully."

"Is this criticism of the Mandate?"

"Of course not."

"Then?"

"The Arabs in Palestine riot, hurting the British and the Jews. Zionists want the national home that was promised to them in the Balfour Declaration years ago. But Jews will not fight England. Not now. English Prime Minister Churchill is the only man who stood against Hitler."

I bit my lip.

"European Jews are being exterminated, massacred. Other groups, also. Gypsies are brutally murdered throughout Europe. I've been getting nightmarish reports about homosexuals and mentally ill Europeans who are being molested and murdered, even experimented on, by the Nazis. Either death or vicious handling is applied to anyone with any abnormality as defined by the Nazi leadership. Political prisoners, or anyone or group opposing Nazi rule, fall under the same category of abnormality and are therefore persecuted. Even certain Christian sects if you can believe it! What's more, brutality aside, I want to know what happens to all the money and property the Nazis confiscate? Where is it all going?"

"Where are you getting all this information?"

"It's my job to get information. I wish that it were nothing but rumors, but it's real, it's unprecedented, and it's happening now. Humans are dying in the most inhumane ways in Europe. And all over the world. And in great numbers." He scowled up at the sky. "Have you given any thought to the Bedouin tribes?"

"They're nomads."

"The Bedouins roam the deserts. They herd to some extent and loot villages along their way. But they are at war, too."

"War?"

"They are at war with villagers throughout this region, partially because this is what they do, but also because the Bedouin elders sense that their way of life is going to change once this war is over. They know that they wouldn't be able to roam the deserts much longer. They are fearful of change and some are even interested in lands with oil."

"What difference would this particular war make on nomadic tribes in the deserts?"

"The aftermath."

"Do you mean more borders arbitrarily drawn across the map of the Middle East?"

Kelly nodded. "Much like the arbitrary borders drawn after the Great War. Lines in the sand, dictating how much oil, land, and water are held by the victorious countries. Maybe the Bolsheviks would be better artists."

"Will the Russians win this war?"

"Who knows? But it's clear that some foreign agency will set the borders regardless of religion, social or economic structure or even geological structure. What do you say, kid, care to see for yourself? I already have a handful of assignments lined up. You must write well. You have impressive schooling."

"So do many of my colleagues. Why me?"

"Because you confront a patient when he's out of line. You're compassionate. And, I took a fancy to you the day you had me censured. Look, William, I know who you are. You're Westbrook's kid. He's quite an influential man here in Cairo. But you care for none of it. You work hard; and you don't need to... Socializing is low on your agenda."

"Mr. Evans..."

"It's Kelly, not Mr. Evans. And, I'm not talking about Regimental Brothels or hashish stands. Damn it, William," he added, somewhat hurt, "You look dreadful! You're overworked. Your schedule is rough. I see its effects on you. Tell me, when you go home, do you get to sleep at all?"

"Don't worry on my account."

Mr. Evans, or Kelly, persevered. "What about informing the world of what is really going on?"

165

"I must go, Kelly. My shift is over. And I can't be late for dinner. Cook would never forgive me."

#

Waking up after surgery, a patient sobbed in his cot. The young man discovered that his leg had been amputated. He panicked, and as I leaned close, he grabbed me and swore, demanding his leg back.

"Stop it at once!" Mrs. Wright sallied forth in alarm after she'd summoned help. "Westbrook, you need to leave."

I did not leave. Instead, I watched the patient being sedated, his face finally relaxed.

"I had nothing to do with it. Not this one," I confided to the nurse.

"Think nothing of it, Mr. Westbrook. Get some rest."

"I am exhausted."

She handed me a glass of water. "Perhaps they'll grant you leave."

Did Kelly have the right of it?

I worried about Elliot and his bewildering activities. And where was James, my oldest brother? Why was he uncommunicative?

But there was also another matter. Salomé. I wanted her and yet I could offer her affection and nothing more. My family would never allow such an alliance.

#

"Well, isn't it your American, over there, lolloping by the swimming pool?" Derision lacing his words, my brother pointed at Kelly. "Your description fits: a pale-skinned man, severely sunburned. Doesn't he know it's deadly hot here at the end of April? Yes, and here's his jolly face with large American teeth."

"Don't point, Elliot."

Elliot grunted and approached the journalist.

Smiling into the sunlight, Kelly, as he introduced himself, explained that he was staying temporarily in Geziera. "It's a fine place, this is."

"This is a fine place indeed," Elliot agreed. "But Palestine is not nearly as welcoming. What have you there? Why take my brother with you?"

I shot Elliot an angry look. He was well aware that I made up my mind to leave our estate, to leave Egypt. But Elliot never believed that I would choose Palestine.

Sipping his sweet red cocktail while making little clicking noises, his tongue rubbing against the roof of his mouth, Kelly eventually allowed,

"Palestine is less than half a day away by train. Should William find the place unsatisfactory, I 'll buy him a train ticket home."

"The choice is not mine. I prefer Egypt...But, as William always says, *à chacun son goût.*"

Kelly raised his glass.

"Well, it's a comfort that the two of you have come to an understanding," I said.

Chapter 16: A Passage in Palestine

ALTHOUGH she had been living in Egypt for almost a decade now, neither Mother's light complexion nor upright stance had altered. Blonde strands of hair falling on her forehead and curling to tickle her cheekbones, she remained an embodiment of her nationality and social class, snapping, "Elliot, you are not his valet."

"No, of course not Mother," Elliot replied, cheerful in his work, handing my kit to the taxi driver.

Father, his arms folded across his chest, appeared unmoved. And his steadfast gaze kept his thoughts and feelings hidden.

Kit safely stowed in the boot, Elliot barked his final order to the driver. "Evans is at Garden City. Pick him up, then Central Station. Got it?"

Through a grimy window, I watched Elliot and Mother enter the house, arguing. My father remained by the rose bush, his arms still folded. But now, next to him, with arms folded in a similar manner, stood Salomé.

She was his miniature, a feminine reflection of Father. Her eyes fixed on the retreating taxi. A rope was clenched in her fist, with the other end tied round the neck of the white dog. Then she shifted, her arms by her sides, one hand caressing the dog. And the wild dog, seated and pensive, was watching the taxi, letting the thin hand rub her fur. To Salomé, the dog had become the friend that I would never be, and perhaps the only friend at the estate. Loyal and at hand, she would love Salomé unconditionally.

I had avoided Salomé before my departure. Ali must have told her that I was leaving today.

Was Salomé angry with me? What did she think about all that had happened between us? I tried to stay away, knowing full well how improperly I had behaved and that I would certainly take advantage of her innocence the next time we would be alone.

#

Trains outside Europe were anything but prompt. The Haifa Express ran from Cairo to Haifa, a port city in northern Palestine. The name of this train, the term 'express,' plagued me with the direst foreboding.

At the Cairo Central Station, Kelly ejected himself out of the cab. As he plunged into the crowd, several incoherent requests drifted to me. "Tickets...sleeper car...meet me...booking clerk!" And he vanished into the sea of heads, caps, bowler hats, head wraps, and fez. Chasing down the porters, who had nimbly removed our luggage and were now hurrying away in the wrong direction, Kelly's head appeared bobbing through the throng.

The swarming mob of bootblacks, militia, travelers, horse cabs, porters, and vendors blocked the way to the booking clerk. Jostling and cursing, I pushed through when a fly-whisk stung my cheek.

"What...?"

The vendor knelt and bowed. "Two piastres...ah...one piastre?"

Swearing, I dove into the mayhem, head held high, cheek burning.

The whisk vendor's unctuous smile hardened. He paused, hesitating. But this cost him dearly and so other hawkers nipped at my heels as I queued up.

Kelly was now haggling with the porters. Hands flailing, the gestures became rude. Kelly shouted and threatened while the porters matched his style, all to the delight of the onlookers.

Ahead of me in the queue, a gaunt old man tried to light his cigarette. Match by match, his veined hands struggled to produce a flame. He was getting angry and his displeasure fueled his oaths. When he finally managed to light up a match, I was certain the flame originated through the sharp imprecation he hissed through tense lips. Then he drew on the cigarette, satisfied. After he got his way, the old man was happy.

Was the old man so very different from the swarthy child with eczema whom Salomé had once rescued from life on the streets? He, too, was happy with simple pleasures, a bowl of *fuul*, some Turkish Delight, and someone holding him above the rubbish.

The booking clerk's shrill voice jerked me out of my messy thoughts. I jabbered gibberish, a Babel-like confusion of French, English, and Arabic. The clerk seemed to learn or forget languages mid-sentence, the booking clerk's method to reduce the passenger load and increase his baksheesh. Tickets were hard to come by, and the trains were severely overbooked.

169

By a miracle, Kelly and I boarded on time, at three thirty in the afternoon.

"I still doubt we would be in Haifa by nine, the morning of the next day."

"Maybe. But we're lucky to have our tickets, William. How did you get us room in the sleeper car?"

"From Cairo to Kantara, we can relax in the wagon-lit. From Kantara on, only one of us has that luxury." I pulled out a coin. "Heads or tails?"

"No need. We'll switch places midway."

Train travel harmonized with the tawny, rolling dunes, shifting into a blurry, scene of oriental torpor. The ceiling fan wobbled, synchronizing with the sound of droning flies. The swarm and blades coordinated some clockwise flow that intensified and subsided capriciously.

Kelly wished for a fly-whisk when several bluebottles landed onto his head and got tangled in his pomaded hair. He cursed and stammered. He was not a tall man, and, at the moment, seemed even shorter as he bent over to shake flies out of his hair, waving a magazine with Casablanca's lead actor on the cover.

The battle against the flies over, Kelly settled down. "People should always have a choice, William."

"Sorry?"

"Keep democracy alive."

"Dear me, am I going to get a political lecture?"

"Go to sleep," Kelly smiled away the insult, chucking his magazine at my lap.

After crossing the Suez Canal, we changed trains in Kantara. I let Kelly take the wagon-lit.

The train was overbooked. Seats in the train main carriage were occupied by at least one person. But as I fruitlessly wandered about, to my astonishment and delight, my former patients and friends, Bill Tate and Tom Sullivan, clapped their hands on my back and drew me in a tight embrace.

"What on earth are you doing here? Didn't you two go back home?"

Indeed, most of the Australian troops had already headed back to Australia. Japan's vicious campaign in the Pacific had Churchill sending the troops home.

"No, no, we stayed here."

"We're kind of used to it now. And we'd rather not rot in the jungles of Burma."

"What do you know of Krak de Chevaliers?" Tate asked.

"The Crusaders' castle? Not much."

"We are on our way to Krak de Chevaliers," beamed Sullivan.

"Why go there?"

"My mates visited the site. Fancied the topography, aqueducts..." Sullivan replied.

"And the restaurant. I read something about it in T.E. Lawrence's accounts. He wrote favorably of the experience, but, really, it's just something to do while we are on leave," the older Australian, Tate, explained.

Tate was Elliot's age. He towered over Sullivan, his younger friend, by a head. Although I was curious, I never asked Sullivan for his age. He looked boyish in his uniform, with a pale halo of unkempt hair, freckles and slanted blue eyes heavily fringed with pale eyelashes.

"Listen mate, there's a restaurant car here. We'll try to get in. No point standing," urged Tate.

"It's locked."

Apologetic but undeterred, Tate worked the lock. Within a few minutes, the three of us broke in.

"Westbrook, bolt the door. I don't want any visitors," Tate said as he settled among the dangling ladles and clanking pots.

"What a relief, eh?" Sullivan sighed. "And there's jam."

Tate snorted with laughter. "Don't..."

"I'll share," Sullivan promised Tate.

"Don't..."

Finally, exhausted, we fell asleep and woke up as we passed Gaza, when the car heated up unbearably from the morning sun.

Sullivan splashed noisily in a water-bucket, his flaxen hair darker now and his freckles more prominent on his thin face. "Blimey, we were supposed to be in Haifa by now."

"I was exhausted last night. William, why are you going to Palestine? Are you traveling alone?" Tate asked.

"Not alone, no. I'll introduce you to Kelly Evans. Actually, you may have met him already. He's a journalist..."

Tate hissed. "Those damned journalists think that they understand desert warfare. They hop from one unit to the next in one evening. Then they return to Cairo to report a pack of lies."

Tate and Sullivan somehow stood even closer to one another now, united by a strengthening friendship.

I was happy to see my friends once again and happier to see them close. Elliot was correct when he once commented that war was ugly but sometimes humanity triumphs.

"William," Tate lowered his voice. He threw a quick glance at Sullivan then plunged into his disclosure. "William, you should know something."

Sullivan's eyes kept steady on Tate's as his lips turned white under his biting front teeth.

"Your brother," Tate continued and I stiffened.

"James is with the LRDG," Sullivan interjected.

Tate caught Sullivan's eye.

"James? And you tell me this now?" The ground was falling from beneath me!

"His Commanding Officer died in his arms so to speak. He might need you," Tate garbled out and turned his guileless face away.

The ensuing silence was uncomfortable as I was sure Tate was about to disclose something different, possibly far worse than what Sullivan allowed him to say.

"Was my brother close to his Commanding Officer?"

"Yes."

"I see. When will he go on furlough?"

"Any day now," Sullivan offered.

Chapter 17: Jerusalem

"DID I tell you, William, that I managed to book two rooms at the King David Hotel? An advantageous home base."

I stared. I had not been able to forget my last, hurried conversation with Tate when he disclosed that my brother James was with the LRDG, the Long Range Desert Group.

"British General Headquarters is just down the hall."

"Yes, well, at least Elliot would be satisfied. The amenities rival top European accommodations."

"We are fortunate to have such generous employers."

"Kelly, I'm here for a short while. I must return to hospital by mid-summer. It was rather generous of them to grant me so much leave."

"You will not be idle, William!" Kelly's American accents echoed within high ceiling halls and arched entrances as he walked from the dining salon to the bar, ordered a red parsnip wine cocktail and marched outside to the English garden that hid behind the first-floor bar and lounge.

Staring at the fashionably dressed crowd, Kelly remarked, "Anglo-Palestinian society at our fingertips."

"What of locals and Bedu chieftains?"

"I must be thorough. A journalist cannot focus on one or two points of view."

"I seldom read an article that is not biased one way or the other."

"Well," he began then fell silent.

"You're in the right, Kelly. I won't be idle. I recognize a few of the ladies. I'll get you an introduction."

"That will be grand."

So, I agreed to help Kelly interview and write. And in return, I had an excuse to stay away from Cairo, away from Salomé.

\#

"Look at that YMCA building!"

"That stone-structure with the tower peeking over the roofs?"

"What a mammoth! Phallic!"

I stared at Kelly.

"And it blocks city views."

"Kelly, you would be glad to know that this building has a street-side terrace. And that by the look of it, a favorite with Jerusalem's high society. Lots of ladies to pounce on."

"I don't pounce!"

"You left a string of broken hearts in Cairo after you'd left hospital."

Kelly grunted, reminding me of Elliot. "The nurses probably missed the wine and chocolates I managed to procure."

"How did you do that, by the way?"

"Secrets of the trade." Grinning, he led me to our next assignment, an interview with a local politician who was beginning to gain notoriety in the city for his affair with a certain English lady.

While we waited, Kelly flipped through a National Geographic issue. "Page after page dedicated to Jerusalem. But look at the absurd photographs of oriental costumes! Jewish Yemenites in wedding garb, the Grand Mufti, robed Arabs, the Russian Archbishop in his traditional costume, and their likes," he lamented. "William, have you observed anyone dressed like this on the streets?"

"Not once."

"This article is a disservice to a dynamic city!"

Kelly's favorite word was disservice. He was in the right, of course. But the world was unprepared to accept the Holy City as a modern town, a home for common men and women, a host to slack washing lines and noisy rock quarries.

"They need more hospitals, more hotels!" he opined.

"But who would care to read about *Tsena* in the Holy City?"

"Food shortage? But, William, *tsena* is the least of Jerusalem's problems at the moment!"

"Yes, I know. And fewer people still would like to read about dysentery and prostitution in Jerusalem's slums. Kelly, the popularity of the orient, the exotic, and the holy sell, as you'd said so yourself."

"But this desire to glaze over problems is interfering with the world's accepting Jerusalem as a city like any other and treating it as such, at least politically. Jerusalem is misunderstood. And it needs some industry."

"An industry?"

"Jobs."

"The religious calls of the various creeds must employ half the city. It's a daily battle between the ringing bells and the nasal muezzins."

"And the Shofar once or twice a year."

"Shofar?"

"Jewish tradition. A horn they blow on certain holidays."

Everyone fought to be heard, but no one was listening. And the clamor for gods became unbearable around sunset. Yet the cries of those in need went unheeded. Few saw the desperate conditions in the city and the plight of the inhabitants.

I did Jerusalem a disservice too. I rarely noticed its beauty, its aroma, that crisp dry mountain air laced with scents of pine and baked bread. Instead, I often remarked the stench of latrines.

When I was not chasing after officials to interview or curbing Kelly's harsh words on paper, I thought of Salomé. And I wondered about James and Elliot. Thinking about the girl and my brothers, and about my mother's disapproval of my intimacy with Salomé, hurt. And being left in the dark as to my father's and Elliot's activities outside General Headquarters and my brother James' connection to Tate and Sullivan with the LRDG amplified my unease. I felt handicapped. And so whatever leisure hours were left to me, I spent those hours at the tap.

#

"William?"

"Here!"

"William, you can't do that. Not now! Put your drink down. We'll be dining with an acquaintance of mine."

"Another acquaintance?"

"Chava," he barked.

Was Kelly clearing his throat?

"Chava's a visiting professor at the university. She's a kibbutz member."

"Chava?" The name sounded like an ache in the windpipe.

Kelly sighed, removed my glass from my hand and set it aside. "William, your line of work is catching up with you. The horrors that you saw and lived through are surfacing now that you have stepped away from the front."

"The front? I was never there!"

"I watched you work. I was there when you had to hold that young man's legs down so the surgeon could saw his feet off."

175

"He would have died otherwise."

"And pulling maggots and draining puss and holding the basin while..."

"Those were my duties."

"Yes, well, there you have it." He adjusted my tie, then tugged me out of the bar and into the hotel's dining salon.

Chava was a historian. She and Kelly had met at a seminar.

"I didn't know you attended a seminar."

"You nap in the afternoons, and I work. Some partner," Kelly grumbled.

"Nap? I've been waiting for you here."

"At the bar!"

Chava intervened. "We attended a symposium, not a seminar."

My eyes rested on her tanned freckly face, noting that the simple sandy plait on her shoulder showed streaks of grey.

"Delegates of the Kibbutz and the Jewish League met to discuss the unrest within Palestine itself," Chava explained in accented English, running her rough hand across the starched tablecloth.

"And I begged Chava for a history lesson. We could both benefit from her extensive knowledge of the history of this antique city. Without knowledge of the past, it is hard to visualize a future, and impossible to understand the present."

"Is that a Chinese proverb?"

Kelly shot me a warning glance. "Chava can give us a brief overview, and tomorrow, William, you and I will visit her recommended sites."

"Will you join us?" I turned to Chava.

Her dimples slowly appeared. "It's harvest time. I have much work at the kibbutz."

Gently, Chava described the horrific timeline of Jerusalem. The city was built, then razed, then rebuilt, then razed, cyclically.

"Jerusalem has undergone a string of sieges and fires and resurrected itself as the legendary bird, the Phoenix, time and time again, rising up from the ashes of utter obliteration," Kelly remarked.

"Consecration of the First Jewish Temple is believed to have occurred around 950 BC by the Hebrew King Solomon," Chava said, without poetic embellishments and I wondered how would Kelly rephrase her prose in his next article. "The Temple was built to house

176

the 'spirit' of the Hebrew god. But there were previous mentions of Jerusalem earlier than that in the Old Testament. William, how familiar are you with its contents?"

"Not well versed, I'm afraid."

"Well, Abraham was said to receive bread and wine from the king of Salem, a region later known as Jerusalem."

"Who's Abraham?"

Chava and Kelly exchanges glances. The twinkle in their eyes died. They just realized what a daunting task laid ahead of them.

"Agnostic, are you?" Kelly asked but he knew the answer so, with a sigh, Kelly elaborated, "Abraham, William, is the founder of both the Hebrew people and the Arabs. And, Abraham, unlike others who approached the city, received a warm welcome."

Chava continued, "Over 350 years after the First Temple was erected, Jerusalem was invaded and destroyed by Babylonian troops. Many were banished, some to Babylon."

Kelly interjected, "Actually, this is when the concept of the Messiah arose out of a need for hope."

"Hope?"

"Hope to return home."

"Hope came but fifty years later. Pilgrim Jews returned to the Holy City and rebuilt the Temple for the second time."

Chava and Kelly took turns, so I got to hear historical account in soft feminine tones accented with guttural names and sounds, and interspersed with deep American timbre, surely mispronouncing other guttural expressions.

Historically, each warring nation imposed its beliefs and architecture on Jerusalem only to abandon everything years later when a stronger foe prevailed.

"Persian, Hellenistic, and Roman rule came and went destroying the city and inadvertently turning Jerusalem into the capital of Jewish memory."

"Bravo," I clapped. "But, Kelly, you focused primarily on Jewish history. What of Christianity and other religious sects? What of Islam?"

"We're following a loose timeline," Kelly explained and he and Chava continued to tell their tale of a city.

Approximately 300 years after the crucifixion of Jesus and under Byzantine rule, Jerusalem saw the height of Christian splendor. The

177

Holy Sepulcher was built. This was a grand gesture by the newly converted Roman Emperor, Constantine I.

And 300 years later, Arab conquests tore the city up again, annexed Jerusalem, and adopted it as a holy city to Islam, third to Mecca and Medina. The Arabs built the Dome of the Rock and destroyed the original Holy Sepulcher.

But the Crusaders re-established Christianity in the city once more, a thousand years after crucifixion.

A hundred years after that, Muslims took over again only to be later defeated by Mongols.

Turkish rule began in the early 1500's and so did the decline in the splendor of Jerusalem.

And before my two companions could go on, I interjected. "At the end of the Great War, control of Jerusalem was relinquished to the British in 1917. You two look exhausted."

"I am exhausted," admitted Chava. "History repeats itself. And I can't help but wonder, why?"

"Jerusalem's string of names also suggests the city's Phoenix-like attributes. The city has been recognized as Salem, commemorating the ancient Canaanite deity of the evening star and son of the god El. And El, if you ask me, William, is none other than an earlier version of the Jewish Jehovah. El was believed to be the god of heavenly and earthly order, and was often referred to as *El-El'yon*, which, in Hebrew means 'most high God.' High as in either height or status; the Hebrew language does not make the distinction."

"Shouldn't you stop for breath, Kelly?"

"William," he growled then pressed on as Chava grinned at my quip. "In the Middle Kingdom, 1900 BC, it was believed that the city took on the name of Urusalim. The name translated as the foundation of the god Salem, or peace. So, it's a mystery why the Hebrew King David renamed the city Zion." Kelly paused as if perplexed by the changes in names and gods. But his silence was momentary. "And, this brings me back to Zionism. Jerusalem became known as Zion. Now the word Zionism makes sense, stemming from the desire to return to the immortal city, the capital of Jewish memory, Zion." Kelly's voice cracked.

"No more Kelly, I can't take it all in!"

178

Chava rose, smiling. "Well, it's my cue to leave. Good to meet you, William. Shalom, Kelly." She leaned over and kissed Kelly's cheeks.

When Chava walked out, Kelly stood watching her go with boyish adoration.

"You amaze me, Kelly."

Kelly jerked round to look at me. "Why?"

"Are religions on par with fairy-tales and folklore for you?"

A smile brightened his features and he gave a quick nod.

"You remind me of my mother, then."

"Lady Westbrook?" Kelly's expression was awe mixed with horror and he probably did not appreciate being compared to a woman.

"Religion, for Mother, is a vehicle of socialization and a tool to move and stir the masses."

Kelly stared.

"Neither of you dislike religion. You accept religion. Mother was raised in India for some time. She came from a wealthy family of English land owners. Married Father. Gave birth to three sons."

"And she is one of the most beautiful women I ever beheld."

"You've met Mother?"

"Admired her from afar."

#

Next morning, Kelly hustled us to the Old City with entertaining anecdotes to fuel our footsteps.

"Here, Kelly, when did you acquire such extensive repertoire of Middle Eastern lore? And how is it that you know so many Hebrew phrases?"

"Books! Boston has loads of bookstores. William, look."

"Where?"

"The Dome of the Rock."

Squinting in the blazing sunlight, Kelly fell silent.

In several of the sites we had visited earlier, we had to either remove our hats or shoes. "Which bit of clothing we'd have to discard this time?"

Kelly took a last draw on his cigarette and ground it out with a methodical twisting motion under his foot. Then, he wiped the sweat off of his face and handed me the canteen. "Lemonade?"

"You all right, Kelly?"

"This is the crux of it all, William. Under this gold-plated dome...under the green and blue peacock-like hues of this building, there lies a rock. A rock, William. Just a rock. But it is no ordinary rock; for I can recall few others that have enjoyed as long a list of documented events, tales, and beliefs as has this rock, right here." He pointed to the structure before us. "Four thousand years during which this rock saw at least eleven transitions from one faith to another. The rock was an antique sanctuary, already an established legendary monument, when David, King of the Hebrews, purchased it from the Jebusites for fifty silver shekels." Kelly smiled sheepishly and admitted, "I...I looked it up several days ago, otherwise, I would not have been able to recite the amount paid." Kelly winked. "I have already explained to you that Jewish lore designates this rock to be the rock on which Abraham was about to offer his son, Isaac, to the god Jehovah. Of course, the Muslims disagree on the identity of the son, and maybe the location as well. To them it was Ishmael who was to be sacrificed. And Ishmael was Abraham's son born to Hagar, Sarah's maid. Alas, I am making this too complicated. Besides, Jews and Muslims will never agree on that point. So, let's see. Muslims believe that their prophet, Mohammed, arrived at Jerusalem riding his winged, white steed over a night's journey. Here..."

"He soared to Heaven! Kelly, I'm familiar with the Koran. And, you've already mentioned it."

"Indeed, what of Christian belief?"

"God only knows!"

"William," Kelly rasped.

"Jesus was said to have had his last supper in Jerusalem. Then, he was crucified by the Romans. But, the location of crucifixion and resurrection is still under debate. You know, Kelly, our own gallant British General Gordon had made several claims to a hillock nearby, only a number of years before he was beheaded and mutilated in the Sudan."

"Oh, you were paying attention last night!"

From the Dome of the Rock Kelly and I walked to the Wailing Wall. As we approached, an argument turned into an outright brawl between the robed Arabs and the rabbis in dark suits and hats.

"This is what I mean when I say disservice to the city. Four thousand years of known history about the city, four thousand years of rubble piling high in the nearby ravines, four thousand years of strife and blood, and people continue to quarrel."

"What's happened?" I asked.

A British constable stood watching the scene. He replied lazily, "Someone defecated near or on the Wailing Wall."

"Let's go," Kelly nudged me. "I don't much care to find out whose feces they smeared on the Wall. As shocking as it might seem to you, this is not all that uncommon."

"Kelly, you've been here before! Your familiarity with and knowledge of Jerusalem has to be the outcome of a former visit, or visits!"

"Several times. As a child, too! Did I not tell you? My father was an archeologist. And I had previous assignments here, before the war."

#

Next day, the Judean hills peeked through a misty morning, nonchalant, as the sun lingered lazily below the horizon. The early summer sunrise was silvery, awakening the domes and towers first into silhouettes, poised and waiting for the day to dawn.

The milkman already on his return trip, walked along the alleys, crooning nasally with his jingling donkey a step behind. His "*As salam alaikum!*" punctuated his loud song. And nearby the hotel, the milkman would call, "*Salam ideek*, Madame Chasam!"

Every morning Madame Chasam's hands were blessed. And every morning, she would recite her poetic gratitude, a Semitic oath to my ears, wrenching me out of my hellish sleep.

One morning, as soon as Madame Chasam's hands were blessed and Madame made her reply, I shot out of bed to shout, "Shut up!"

But unaware of my misery and shouts, the milkman pulled his clambering donkey away. The milkman's silvery hair streamed, glowing in a shaft of light.

"*Salam ideek*...Chasam...be damned!"

"What on earth are you shouting about?" Kelly stood akimbo at the door.

"I cannot find my writing tablet."

"Do you call your tablet Madame Chasam?"

"No, no. Never mind my rude behavior. What do you think about it?" I asked, pointing at the article Kelly was clasping.

"What could we do? What could we, here, in Jerusalem, possibly do?" he quoted, stepping inside my room. "Brilliant! It was a sad day

181

indeed. How do you report the reaction of the residents of Jerusalem to the information about German concentration and death camps throughout Europe?"

"Firsthand information. There were some sixty prisoners of Nazi camps here in Jerusalem. They were sent in exchange for captured Germans."

"Conveying the horrors of Nazi regime to Jerusalem!" Kelly remarked as I looked away.

"Yes, well, Jewish shop owners closed their shops that day."

"William, put it in perspective and consider the physical distance from the tragedy. Besides, the daily grind here in Palestine for many of its native residents is difficult and there isn't a Bastille at hand to storm, either. Many Jews joined the British army. Thousands of men and even women."

I lit a cigarette.

"Your article is well composed, and with your restrained though accusatory thread tying the piece together. It's remarkable."

"Accusatory thread?"

"Well, it's obvious. Is it not? You want the Jews of Jerusalem to take action. You want the world to take action. Am I wrong? Did I misinterpret your article?" Kelly placed a hand on my shoulder. "Brilliant!" Then he turned to leave. "I'll see you at the suk in ten minutes. Get dressed and meet me at the gate."

#

A veiled young woman sat cross-legged at an herb stand, listening to her toothless, cloudy-eyed harridan who shook a handful of dill over a portable smoking chamber that burped out hateful steam and smoke.

As I passed by, the young woman pinned me with unblinking eyes. Almond shaped and framed with a thick line of Kohl, her eyes held me in a liquid brown spell. I was hypnotized. And I wanted to see more, to remove the veil, to see a face, to see...

Stinging pain on my wrist brought me to my senses. It was a fly-whisk, skillfully employed as a whip by the dragon.

"Go! Leave my granddaughter, Inglizi!" Her buckshot voice rang and she spat at the word Inglizi.

How did that crone know I was English? Wasn't she blind?

She waved the whip again and croaked a complaint to Allah.

"What is your name?" I asked the young woman.

182

The young woman was surprised that I spoke Arabic and even more confounded by my disregarding her dragon.

"Sharifa," she answered, and immediately my ear and upper cheek smarted. The whip hit me hard on my face. And I realized that I was bleeding. "Really!" I called out in anger.

The matriarch shouted, "Go!"

A black mustached native constable appeared. "What's going on?" He placed his baton before me.

The matriarch's whip disappeared.

Once again clutching a bundle of wilting dill, the dragon mumbled, "Inglizi molesting my child, shaming her name." Now, her wrinkly hand reigned deftly over smoldering herbs as she jabbed at the smoking chamber and the smoke grew whiter and thicker.

"Nonsense."

"What did you say?" The constable brought his baton to my abdomen, in a threat, when a familiar voice called out.

"Wait a minute!" Kelly, several stalls away, spotted the disturbance.

Glancing at the young woman once more, I drew back. She was trying to catch my eye, looking amused. Her eyes, now cheap and dull, repelled me.

"Stay, William. Respect," Kelly whispered. Then, he added loudly, "I have some questions if you please."

The constable eyed me warily, slapping his baton into his palm, waiting to see how the Inglizi was going to squirm out of trouble.

"Did the young man touch anyone?" Kelly asked.

The women shook their heads in the negative.

"William, were you trying to get the kind women's attention so you could interview them?"

"Yes."

"Look here," Kelly concluded looking up at the constable and handing him a handful of coins then dropping more at the lap of the crone. "My colleague was only doing his job. He's a journalist, you see. No harm meant. He never touched the girl. You cannot arrest him. What charges have you, conversing with merchants?"

Despite the threat of an arrest and the noise and commotion, I was already elsewhere. In my mind, I was in Cairo, with Salomé. I missed the girl terribly. I ached to see her, to be with her. I wanted to look into

183

her eyes, to behold her compassionate gaze. And to have her in my arms.

A savage dog tore at a limp body shrouded in indigo rags. No one called for help. Silence. When the dog turned round, its saliva turned to foam, dripping down its jaws. Its face was monstrously large. And, as it turned to look at me with empty sockets for eyes, I screamed in terror.

"What happened? What's the screaming about?" Kelly burst into my room. "Were you attacked?" He scanned the room, the windows, then me. "Well?"

"Bad dream."

"Some kind of a night terror, I suppose. Come, let's get you medicine."

"Medicine? I'm all right. No need for...What medicine do you have in mind?"

"A stiff whiskey."

Still shaken, a sheen of sweat covering my naked body, I pulled my trousers on and followed Kelly downstairs, to call on the night desk clerk.

Night terrors, as Kelly would call my nightmares, became a frequent phenomenon. And Kelly and I became frequent visitors at the clerk's office. Once or twice a week, the three of us would indulge in cheap arak. Kelly often remained sober. I did not.

"Have you ever had night terrors before?"

"Never."

"It must be delayed shock."

"Shock? Kelly, Palestine is not so bad."

"Laugh if you must. But we need to do something about this."

My condition rapidly deteriorated. Soon, work and sleep were possible only while I was numbed with alcohol.

Chapter 18: James in Cairo

"KELLY, what's this?"

"Telegram. From Cairo!"

Dread washed over me. During war, telegrams rarely bore happy tidings.

"Read it, William, get it over with." Kelly leaned over my shoulder then summed it up, "James is back in Cairo and Elliot urges you to return. But, what's the hurry to return to Cairo?"

"My brother James had enlisted at the onset of war. I haven't seen him since."

"I see."

"His last letter to my father indicated that he was all right. And nothing more."

"Well, our Jerusalem piece is due tomorrow and we can make arrangements to leave."

Two days later, I received a letter from James. James wrote that his leg got hit with shrapnel and that Father sends a slim girl to help. James' questions, "Did you really name her Salomé? Why such a Biblical name? Was it her beauty and pliant body that aroused the image of the dancing Salomé in Herod's court?" hit me hard. His words of praise, "William, I had heard of your excellent work both at the Citadel and Helwan," went unnoticed as a wave of jealousy made me bilious.

Later that night, lying in bed, I heard an officer yell Otzer, British accent mutilating the word. Heavy boots. Gunshots. Loud bangs. Shrill cries. Then, a call for help. More running hither and thither. Curses in English and curses in Arabic and Hebrew. A man shouted in German, accusing the soldiers of wrong doing. I could not tell what.

Men were fighting in the streets outside while I grappled with thoughts of James in Salomé's company. Reaching to remove her veil. Looking into her eyes.

I sat up all night, fuming. And when the heavy cover of night lifted and Kelly barged into my room, I said, "Kelly, I'm not joining you today."

The wireless was playing incoherent news reports.

"I must go back to Egypt."

"You stayed up all night again? How much did you drink?" he asked as he briskly walked to the window and thrust the shutters open. "I need you here, not in Egypt. You speak Arabic and French with fluency, and your German is good, too. Besides, your articles are popular."

Light flooded the room and a cool breeze flushed the fetid air.

"William? What's going on?"

Kelly's voice echoed in my head. It was followed by a roaring hum.

For a moment, I lapsed into euphoric emptiness, free of noise, light, and pain.

"William? Are you all right?"

"Never better."

Moments later, I hit the floor but felt no pain.

#

Cosmopolitan social life in Jerusalem in the early forties flourished. English personnel of higher civil and military ranks assembled at the King David's lounge and bar and dance halls. Popularity of tea parties on Saturdays never faltered. Arabs and Jews who could afford the King David's prices joined the jolly gatherings, while travelers or journalists spiced up the hotel's parties.

Throughout the war, hotel guest waiting list grew. Hosting British administrative offices boosted the King David's cachet. Some travelers jested that they mistook it to be the rebuilt temple of Solomon. And, yes, the King David's was an impressive structure indeed. But then it was designed to be just so, from the construction of a wide avenue, bearing King George V's name, to the hotel's legendary kitchen and service.

Kelly attended the parties and dances with enthusiasm, meeting with leading figures of the British Mandate in Palestine and elsewhere.

On the afternoon following my sleepless night and fainting spell, Kelly and I went to a dinner party after a long day of research and interviews.

"Well, William, what was it that ailed you so this morning? It was no night terror or I would have heard you screaming. What upset you last night?"

Fatigued, I reached into my pocket and handed Kelly the crumpled parchment.

"This is the answer then?" Kelly scanned the letter.

Staring into space, I let exhaustion wash over me.

186

"William." Kelly's voice scratched my consciousness. "Besides this piece of writing being somewhat short, I see nothing upsetting, nothing extraordinary. You were in a sorry state this morning, kid. What's in this that bothers you that I fail to comprehend?"

"I..."

Kelly and my surrounding blurred every so often.

"Well?" Kelly was not to be put off easily.

"I...He can be laconic. I mean, James."

I wanted Kelly to know about Salomé, about Elliot and James, and about me. But would he understand? After all, Kelly was an American.

"I hope that you're not planning to convince me that you sat up all night, probably drinking, because his letter is short!"

"No."

Leaning forward, Kelly scanned the parchment again. "James is your brother."

"Yes."

"He is injured."

"Yes."

"Severely?"

"Hard to tell. Probably so, if he was sent to convalesce in Cairo."

"Tell me, who is Salome?"

"Salomé."

"William, who is Salomé? She is not an infant, nevertheless, you, William, named her? Recently? Who is she?"

"It's not an easy tale to tell."

"I've got time."

"But will you understand it all?"

"Try me." Leaning back, settling comfortably in his chair, Kelly watched me, his American mannerism almost comical.

And here was Kelly's time to shine. He passed no judgment as I spoke. He listened until I was through, until I said as much as I was going to say. His friendship, in his mind, dictated he would do nothing less.

"Is this the end then?" he asked as I concluded with James' return to Cairo.

"I don't know."

"So, here is a tale of mystery. A girl hiding on an English estate in Egypt finds love in the youngest of its sons. While the other two sons do their best for their King."

"Well, James, yes, but not Elliot. Elliot does his best for Monnayeur's."

"Are you sure about that? Seems unlikely that a man of Elliot's caliber would be content to run a club, to be left out of this war, left out of an intriguing game that could set things right. And what about his engagement and wedding to Miss Baker who mere days after the wedding disappeared? Her father's gone too."

"That's Elliot for you. When I pluck up enough courage to ask him, Elliot rarely answers my questions about himself."

"But my dear boy, what about yourself and your Salomé?"

"I doubt my family will accept a formal relationship between Salomé and I." I kept quiet on my ugly suspicions regarding James and Salomé. "Kelly, I better stay here. Maybe I'll forget about her."

"Do you want to forget her? William, wars change many things, not just political boundaries. Look here, we have one last assignment to follow through, then you best return to your family's estate. You have a couple of decisions to make and timing is going to be on your side. I had no idea you had a sweetheart at home."

"I need to work things out in my head first."

"And, get some sleep. Tomorrow, we leave Jerusalem. We'll visit Tel Aviv. From there, we'll split up for a short assignment."

Kelly had already outlined an article that was to become a documentary. He was enthusiastic, mainly because the Jerusalem pieces were a financial success.

"But this rubbish we concocted about Jerusalem as a city of exotics and holiness is a misrepresentation, and, Kelly, it's a disservice to the city."

Kelly grinned. "But that's what sells. And booze is expensive, kid!"

#

The following morning, our bus crept down the mountainside, gears shifting, grunting and shuddering at every switchback, chocking pines and boulders with spewed fumes.

"William, my diary is in a compartment at the bottom of my case."

"You keep a diary?"

188

"Don't you? William, should anything happen...You'd know what to do."

"What could happen? Afraid of a donkey braying in your ear? Besides, you're traveling with a medic."

"How convenient for me!"

The bus breathed a sigh of relief as it reached the coastal flats and the roadway lay before it, horizontal and straight.

Tel Aviv was largely a Jewish city of recent construction, and, usually, clean and well-planned. Instead of shadowy, narrow cobblestone passages, Tel Aviv boasted wide boulevards that answered to higher European engineering standards, with gardens and squares to serve the public.

Today, a slinking, shiny barbed wire concertinaed across Allenby Street.

And when British military policemen flagged the bus to halt, sweat beaded on the bus driver's bald pate. "*La'azazel!*"

Why was the bus getting pulled over and, possibly, searched? Did I miss anything on the news?

Kelly made to disembark.

Holding Kelly back, I whispered, "MP's."

Kelly fiddled with the straps of his kit. His face blanched as British military policemen tramped the narrow isle, asking for identification documents and poking into passengers' belongings.

One of the policemen stopped before us. "Papers?"

Extracting Kelly's papers out of his sweaty palms, I handed our identifications to the young MP. Though I smiled and nodded, Kelly seemed upset.

"Kelly Evans?"

"That's my colleague."

"Can your...colleague speak for himself?"

"I'm Kelly Evans."

I hoped that I was the only one who could detect Kelly's anxiety, his scratchy voice, and rather belligerent pose.

Why was Kelly so distressed by a commonplace search? We had been through a few searches while in Jerusalem. Besides, Kelly was an American with permission to remain in Palestine as a journalist.

"America?"

"Yes."

189

"Where?"

"What?"

"Where in America?"

"Why do you ask?" Kelly was gruff, defensive.

"Steady on," the young man stiffened and I found myself nudging Kelly.

"Kelly's from Boston," I replied into the deafening stillness of the bus.

A spotty comrade of our policeman edged close. "American? From Boston?" He leveled his gaze at Kelly, his lips disappearing into a thin line after he quickly peeked into Kelly's papers.

Finally, the young policeman handed our papers back. To my surprise, however, none of the bus riders were paying the slightest attention to us.

A tall officer stopped by an elderly woman.

She had thin legs that popped out of a linen dress. The dress was loose fitting, to allow room for the woman's belly. Her feet were strapped in sandals, supporting an overstuffed sack that rested between the woman's legs with produce peeking out.

The officer asked for the elderly woman's identification cards. She drew a tattered piece of paper from her bosom. Our spotty MP glanced at the document and, crouching, searched her bag. Then, the officer asked the woman to stand up.

As the old woman creaked up, she looked coldly up into the officer's eyes. She stared at him as he ran his hands from her silvery hair downward, and over her dress.

Chagrin, mingled with panic and fear, pulsated through the silence on the bus.

The young man rummaging through the woman's shopping bag emptied its contents. Tomatoes and onions rolled out, and bundles of dill and cilantro fell onto the dirty bus floor. But there were other items that did not roll out. Three revolvers were fished out of an inseam in the bag.

Bedlam erupted.

The officer dragged the woman bodily, barking orders at his men. She resisted. A man stood up and demanded the woman be handled with respect but his words drowned in the woman's screams. Her English was fluent, and she swore, delivering hideous ill wishes carefully, loudly. Then, she paused and in a maniacal voice demanded, "Where is my sister? Hitler cannot kill us all! Where is she? My sister!" Several of the passengers hissed at the soldiers and added to the elderly woman's expletives. "English gentleman? Pooh! You promised us a national home!"

Then, before her last step off the bus, the woman held her head high and called, "Am Israel Hai!" She shook her cuffed fists, silver strands of hair falling on her face. But she was quickly subdued by the young officer.

After the last MP disembarked, silence fell. The bus driver turned the ignition key. The machine's old engine groaned and the bus lurched forward.

When there was no sign of the red berets, Kelly mumbled softly, shaking his head. Uneasy, I recognized the woman's words, "Nation of Israel Lives!" on Kelly's lips.

Kelly, the passengers, and the driver were shocked. Few spoke, and many passengers had shiny eyes and wet cheeks. A mother held tightly to her son's head, caressing his golden locks while he talked on and on in Hebrew, his tone of voice questioning and concerned, and the mother's tears darkened his hair. Her husband, or companion, collected the scattered vegetables and herbs, mumbling prayers, his freckly hands shaky.

Hearing the old woman's declarations, and seeing her thin, silvery hair come undone made me view her as a human being, as an elderly woman, and nothing else. I wondered whether she belonged to a clandestine organization. Kelly had told me about the *Machteret* on our way to Palestine.

"The what?" I had asked him.

"*Machteret.*"

"Need a handkerchief?"

"William, *Machteret* is a collective name for underground or clandestine organizations, but Haganah, Lechi, or Etzel are the individual names...Underground networks of Zionist groups, preparing."

"Preparing?"

"Defense."

"From the Germans?"

"Come now William. If Germany wins the war, few Jews will survive. But, if the Allies win..."

"What? Fight the British? That's absurd!"

"No. Either diplomatically send the British out of Palestine after the war's ended or...which is more likely, defend themselves against opposing Arabs, or maybe both scenarios at once, or some such combination. Diplomacy can only go so far."

Someone rang for the driver to halt, and I was shaken back to reality, back to the bus plowing through Tel Aviv.

"Was that our stop?" I asked.

"Ah? We'll...oh, here we are, come along now." Kelly motioned the driver to wait.

Walking along Allenby Street, each with photography kit and a holdall pulling at our shoulders, sweat trickled down our temples and backs.

Tel Aviv was warm and humid.

"William, our last article will be a panoramic of the people of Palestine. Bedouins, city Arabs, Zionists, city dwellers, villagers and farmers, soldiers, young, old, men, women. I will use it to write a book."

"You? Write a book?"

"Why not?"

"It's a lot of work. Solitary work, Kelly, and I can't see you sitting and typing a book-length manuscript, skipping on social events."

"We will see. In the meantime, William, we will set about to investigate how people feel about their village or city, country, their neighbors. You are charming," he added, appraising me through narrowed slits. "The ladies fall at your feet. Why do you not talk to them? Get fanatics to talk to you. They're such fun. Approach people, William. Go, talk to her." Kelly gestured to a girl standing by a crosswalk, clutching nervously to the sides of her dress.

"She's ten."

Kelly nudged me.

"She is ten, Kelly, what would you have me do, give her a sweet?"

"Watch!"

Kelly approached the girl and exchanged some words with her.

She looked up at him and nodded.

He offered his hand and together they crossed the street.

When Kelly returned, I placed my cigarette between my lips and applauded.

"A Moroccan Jew...eleven years old. Scared to walk home alone from school because of the busy street crossing."

"And?"

"William, you missed my point."

"Did I?"

"Opportunities that your arrogance makes you miss out on. Arrogance! You are proud, restricted by social codes. You are a victim of a strict social class, of your family and nationality, of your pride."

Chapter 19: Beersheba

THAT evening, on the train platform in Tel Aviv, Kelly asserted, "Beersheba will be good for you."

"How so?"

"Mingle with Arabs of the desert, William. Hear their conversations, their political outlook, land ownership laws, and water distribution methods. If you're lucky, you'll meet the nomads, the Bedouins," Kelly explained, and thus oiled out of telling me why Beersheba was my assignment.

"A rare treat!" I eyed him, incredulous. "So, this is why you kept the last assignment secret. You're sending me to Beersheba, to nowhere."

Kelly had the decency to look away. "A desert rat such as yourself should relish such a chance."

"Beersheba, Kelly?"

"What's more, booze is hard to come by!"

"Kell..."

"I'm going north. I'll be expected to work. Hard. I'm going to Yagur."

"Chava's kibbutz?"

"Yes. She promised me hard labor for firsthand accounts of Zionist ideals and impressions. Clever, eh?"

"I don't see you working, Kelly. Not on a farm. Will you have to milk a cow?"

Kelly looked up, alarmed.

"It's harvest time too."

Smug smile gone, Kelly grunted.

"By the way, are all kibbutz members Zionists?"

"No, not all. Yagur is reputed to be ... involved with the cause."

But why Kelly would bother with Zionists was beyond me.

"The Zionists are idealists. Are you an idealist, Kelly?"

"Certainly not. I need photographs and spicy accounts of life in Palestine. That's all. I'm a historian. And trying to get paid for my work."

I wondered about Kelly's infatuation with wages. Although his earnings were high, Kelly rarely looked fashionable. He owned a single fine tailored suit that he kept impeccably clean and pressed. He wore it to his social outings. His expenses were paid for by his employers, an American magazine and a prospective publisher. And although he enjoyed the occasional liquor, Kelly rarely overindulged. What did Kelly do with his fortune?

"William, are you with me?"

"For another sermon?" I tried to focus, or at least pretend.

"Write down precisely what you're told."

"Of course." I lit a cigarette.

"Remain neutral, kid. Stay safe. Keep your interviews neatly filed and we'll work on our research when we meet again, someplace safe."

Why was Kelly worried about safety? And, safe from whom or what?

Wiping his forehead, he said, "William, listen. Don't be a hero." He squeezed my arm, his eyes fixed on mine.

"Kelly!"

"Regardless of what happens next, go on with your assignment or get out of the country. If you feel you're threatened, get up and run. Hear me? Get up and run. You're young, so run fast. You write well, and the information we collect is useful. Should anything happen to me, you'll publish my work. You know my contacts in Boston. Promise?"

Without giving it a thought, I nodded. "Of course."

Then Kelly boarded his train.

My cigarette smoldered at the side of my mouth as I stood watching the commotion on the platform, numb.

\#

Numb, I stood now, recalling Kelly and his ill-timed sermon.

The taxi driver dropped my holdall under a feathery tamarisk tree, abandoning me on the outskirts of Beersheba. A flash of his toothy smile demonstrated his satisfaction with my payment, and the dust his tires kicked up made me regret paying.

Above, eagles helmed the empty sky. Below, a tawny wasteland.

Beersheba was a heap of sunbaked undulating sand hills with dust devils, tumbleweeds and scorpions. Stretched nearby, the desert crossroads lead to the Negev desert or to the Dead Sea. But there were few travelers. Sure, there was the local magistrate, but there were none of the frequent tea parties as in Jerusalem. And alcohol was scarce and overpriced.

\#

I lodged in Beersheba's town center with an old friend of Kelly's. My room overlooked the Ottoman-constructed Governor's Mansion.

"I interview the Governor today, just before lunch. But where can I gather bits of gossip?" I asked Kelly's old friend.

Gold necklaces and earrings jangling, her wrinkly red lips lifted up. "The café," she replied, her voice gravely with tobacco and age. "Yes, the cafe and the carpenter's workshop next door. They always have a crowd. Go to them today. They love visiting young men to argue with!"

The following morning was Wednesday. As she did the day before, the café proprietor greeted me with throaty blessings then shot a command, "Inglizi likes news!"

The wireless sprang to life, sputtering incongruent news reports. And half an hour later, the music came through with perfect reception.

When she saw the dregs of my coffee, the proprietor sidled close, clasping my shoulder with a gnarled hand. "Tomorrow's Thursday. Do you know about Thursdays?"

I shook my head.

"Bedouin Market. Go there!"

"Bedouin Market?"

"For trade. Important for Beersheba. There's vegetables, meat, and spices. And there's good bargains! But don't let the old goats fleece you!" she howled then shuffled away, chatting with her other customers.

Moments later, the proprietor was cackling and gesticulating, apparently bullying one of her costumers to represent her interests in the suk.

In the afternoons, layabouts sat cross legged at the entrance to a carpenter's shop, playing backgammon or rolling strings of beads between their dusty fingers and arguing or crooning, outdoing the saw, the hammer, and the sanding paper. And with supreme self-assurance, the men waved their hands in dismissal or approval, clapping every now and then.

Sappy torch songs burst out of the Beersheba wireless with the unshakable theme of love, women and their admirers, dead or alive. The layabouts, in harmony with the head carpenter, ululated nasally, reaching a peak in the melody that ebbed into a soft whisper of licentious dreams.

"Damn you Kelly," I cursed as a smile of understanding stretched across my face. Kelly had selected Beersheba. Why? Because this assignment was a short stop, a chance to rest and recover from the hectic lifestyle of Jerusalem. And, practical as always, he must have considered Beersheba's close proximity to Cairo. Kelly was a true friend. Why had I not seen it before?

That evening, I visited the British military cemetery. A lugubrious old man shuffled toward me, hunching over graves now and then. When he came upon me, he grabbed my hand and with no hesitation plunged into speech.

Like Coleridge's wedding guest, I found myself in the clutches of a possessed man.

"I study religions," he wheezed.

"Which religion?"

"What religion? There's Islam and then there's...the others." He waved an impatient hand while the other tightly clutched my wrist. "Beersheba. Here Abraham dug a well. And so he did. Then came the Philistines and covered up the well. Others opened up the well later, just to cover it up again. And this is what our world revolves around: Water wells. Sand, land, here take all you want, we have that." He waved his hand as if generously offering sand and dunes. "But, wells, water wells, we fight for water wells." His last words had a solemn, sinister ring to them. And his gray eyes were hard and hollow.

"What of religions?" I asked.

"Water," he barked then disappeared among the tombstones.

Shaken up, I left the cemetery right away.

After a salty meal of fava beans and egg, my stomach twisted up in knots and my head buzzing with coffee, I gathered up my notes in my room, shutting out the heat, and the muezzin's "Allahu Akbar."

I was lonely. I was nearing emotional breakdown. I was in Beersheba for less than a week and already I was desperate to leave.

That night I dreamt of Salomé and yet I could only recall terror then inability to feel or move, fear wrenching me out of restless sleep.

My land lady, Kelly's friend, must have taken the proprietor of the coffee shop into her confidence and told her of my night terrors because when I walked into her cafe that morning, she shouted, "Inglizi likes news!" then served me her own version of hellbroth: Steaming goat milk, cardamom, and god knows what else. Once the milk cooled

197

enough to drink, she swooped down on it and inserted a fork to fish out the skin. "That's for my pregnant daughter," she squawked, plunking the skin on a brass tray.

"Lady Proprietor, where can I talk to Bedouins? I tried the suk but they were all so busy."

"Inglizi boy, you can go to the Azazma tribe, they have an old sheik. Not far! They camp just south of Beersheba. Hire a camel and a guide."

Armed with little sleep and stomach-churning coffee and boiled goat milk, I hired Ayyad, my Bedu guide.

Ayyad reminded me of the dragomen of Cairo, hiring themselves as guides and translators to European tourists. He provided a camel, bedecked with woven red rugs and tassels. There was also a square head cloth, tied with thick dark wool ropes, for my head.

"I look ridiculous."

Ayyad disagreed, "You are handsome in this kafiyya," and showed me his teeth. To my horror, he then magically produced a robe. "Galabiyyeh. Wear it. For protection."

Although flee ridden, my galabiyyeh was indeed excellent protection against fine particles of sand that assaulted us until we reached the encampment.

The Bedouin encampment of long black goat hair tents billowed in the wind. It was a noisy place. The donkeys brayed, the camels grunted, and children cried. It also had a strong odor of goat, dung and campfire smoke.

Seated before the Bedu chief, the sheik, I expected long speeches. But the old man blinked at my camera, then fell asleep, his head nodding lightly, innumerable whiskers twitching on a sonorous snore.

The rank smell of goat hung in the dark tent, and my nerves were wrought. "Ayyad, wake him up. He can't fall asleep now. He hasn't even opened his lips, except to snore, and I'm short on time."

"At least you got to photograph him with his eyes still open. You wanted to talk about life in Palestine?"

"Yes."

"You came to the right place then."

"How so?"

"We can talk."

I cast my eyes to the sleeping sheik.

"You do not need a sheik to tell you about life in the desert, life in Palestine, life of a tribe following water and grazing grounds."

"Among other things."

Ayyad flashed his mirthless smile again. "It's not as romantic as Rudolph Valentino had it on film."

"Rudolph Valentino?"

"Look around you, Effendi. Tell me, what do you see? Children who already have disease in their eyes. People my age with few to no teeth. I still have mine. I spent some time in the city. I went to school. Every now and then, I see a doctor. They," he pointed vaguely at the camp. "They do not see doctors unless the English doctors come to them."

"English doctors?"

"Yes. They bring a lorry and set up a clinic nearby. But, most of my tribe does not believe in English medicine. They are not used to taking care of themselves like so. Last time the Englishmen were here, I had to drag the children, one by one, to the doctor. The doctor examined their throats, ears, and eyes. Do you know what the children did?"

"No."

"Screamed. My people need to learn about medicine, about water, about land. They need to watch American movies. Things are changing and they need to adapt because my people will not be allowed to roam much longer."

"You say my people. Why?"

"I am next in line," he replied easily, his hand raised in the direction of the sheik.

#

Before sunset, I left the Azazma tribe with pages of notes, a sheep, and a stomachache. I mailed my notes on the Bedouins and my accounts of life in Beersheba to Kelly in Yagur on the following day. The sheep became mutton-chops for the pregnant daughter of the coffee shop proprietor. But the stomachache remained for several days longer. It was the Palestinian version of Gyppy Tummy: Sharp abdominal spasms, recurring chills, and frequent vomiting and running.

A few days later, when the pain subsided, I approached the carpenter.

"Take me to the train station in Gaza."

"Can't," wailed the carpenter, a proud owner of a rickety motor scooter.

199

Clutching my stomach, I assured him that I will pay handsomely for the ride.

"Oh, no," he replied slowly. "No, I cannot drive you to Gaza. I am terrified to go there. Gunshots and bombs! Nothing but trouble in Gaza even during Ottoman times! But I will find out who's going there and let you know."

Chapter 20: Kiwis in Ma'adi

"*GAMBARI, istakouza hayya!*" a barefoot man with rotten teeth advertised his shellfish.

My stomach gave a lurch at the sight of the slimy creatures laid on top of a block of ice. The goods were laced with flies.

"Would you look at that!" Elliot cried out, approaching quickly.

"I can't."

"Not the shellfish! No, I mean you! Wasn't there a looking glass in Palestine?"

"Elliot, what are you on about?"

Facing me on the platform of Cairo's Central Station, and with his usual blunt manner, Elliot announced, "You look dreadful." He made a gesture, looking for anything that should have been behind or next to me and found nothing. "Your suit is stained. Where's your holdall? Where are all your suits? What happened to your kit?"

"No room for it on the carpenter's motor scooter."

Elliot pulled at my lapel, "What a mess!"

"Never mind my holdall, Elliot. It's not much of a loss."

"Oh, but it is, William, it is! Just think, this necessitates a visit to the tailor's."

"Damn. I never thought of that!"

As if on cue, a bootblack pulled on Elliot's jacket. The boy's hands were stained, and he held a filthy rag and a tub full of doubtful shoe polish. For a piastre the boy offered to shine both our shoes.

"Make his boots shine, and I shall give you two piastres."

"Elliot, no. You don't know what's in his shoe polish."

But the boy had already tucked his blue striped robe between his legs, knelt by my feet, and, with amazing dexterity, applied the cream.

"My boots are red-black now."

"It's terrible, and the smell! Still, I must pay up. Look here William, we better hurry before we're besieged by what looks to be all of Cairo's hawkers."

"And if we are, we have you to thank for it! Oh, damn it. It's all over my trousers and hands now!"

"The blacking? Looks like blood."

A horde of hawkers came our way.

"Elliot, we better run for it."

Breathless and with a horrible stitch in my side, I ran alongside Elliot until he said, "William, slow down, they're gone."

Grateful for the respite, I breathed deep and asked, "Elliot, where's the invalid? Where's James?"

"What...Well, James, right. It's the war you know. Look, William, we'll catch the tram, I can't stomach the thought of haggling with another taxi driver and I can't keep on running in this heat."

A filthy, narrow street connected us to the tram station. Two story buildings loomed on both sides, the top floors on the verge of collapse. I recalled Tel Aviv and its modern construction and wide, paved roads. Suddenly and sadly, Cairo appeared cheap and shoddy.

"And how is everyone else?"

"Why all the questions, William? Missed us? You hardly wrote."

"I telephoned you."

"Yes, to let me know you will be arriving today! Father was in a right state." Then Elliot wrapped his arm round my neck, pulling me close, and kissed my head.

"So, what ails James, his leg?"

"Not the leg, not very much." Elliot paused then touched his head then his heart. His smile faded. Then, springing to catch a moving streetcar, he pulled at my jacket.

"It's the wrong streetcar. Where're we going?"

"Ma'adi!"

#

Ma'adi was a suburb on the outskirts of Cairo crowded with estates of the newly rich. Over the years, the New Zealanders had erected a military training camp nearby and, by 1943, the Kiwis had a general hospital, a chapel, a swimming pool, and, of course, an entertainment tent.

Now, Ma'adi and the Kiwi barracks shimmered in the desert heat.

With dunes and pyramids for backdrop, Elliot and I trekked two-mile to camp. Just ahead of us, a couple of slim figures flickered in and out of view.

Passing by big ugly dust bins, we arrived at camp, and suddenly Elliot growled, "Look over there. Isn't it Ali?"

202

"What?"

"It is Ali! And there's she!" Elliot's voice, unsteady, reflected surprise.

"Salomé?" I croaked but Elliot drew me behind the bins.

"Observe."

A girl shrouded in robes leaned on a steel drum, watching a soldier approach.

The soldier searched for piastres in his pockets. He cocked his head to steal a furtive glance at the girl, then shot a smile at his comrades.

"What the devil is going on? Why is Salomé here? And why so filthy?"

"I don't know. But Ali looks exhausted."

Arms folded across my chest and biting my lips, I stretched my neck and watched. "Are they selling flowers? I mean, is she selling flowers?"

"Let's see what happens next."

"But why?"

"Why what?"

"Why would soldiers from New Zealand buy flowers? Why come all the way out here to sell flowers?"

"Is that what those wilting green things really are?"

"Of course it's flowers! She is selling flowers to that man! Elliot, why is Ali crouching on the roof? Is he watching over Salomé? Why is she here? Where's she getting the flowers from? Do they not get paid for work at the estate? Why is Salomé selling flowers?"

"You can't possibly expect Ali to be the flower girl."

Elliot's jest left me groundless.

Salomé was charming. Her robes fluttering in the wind every so often clung to her body. And when the wind exposed her arm or a bit of ankle, she was enchanting.

Another soldier smiled at Salomé. Mischievously pulling out a flask of whiskey, he tilted his head back, though clearly drinking little. The flask was capped when he presented it to her.

Salomé shook her head.

"The whiskey is for your flowers. They could use a bit of a drink." A chorus of laughter swallowed his words.

Salomé played along. She coyly dabbed the flowers in the whiskey then, lifting her hand to eye level, examined the wilting blossoms. She shook her head. No, the drink did not help.

The Kiwis were enjoying the act, and more of their piastres trickled into the slender hand of the flower girl.

Elliot chuckled.

Now, a group of Kiwis in shorts, holding long bayonets, approached.

"This is not the first time they've seen her," I remarked gravely.

"No, look at them march right up and wave a hello. Well, time for us to say hello, too." Elliot stepped out to join the Kiwis, but in unpredictable Egyptian fashion, the wind picked up.

The wind blew puffs of fine grit, whirling debris and dried twigs and the blowing airstream snaked round Salomé. Silence fell amid the soldiers as they watched in anticipation. But the flower girl tucked her robes in a flowing motion, now leaning against the barrack's wall.

The sand settled, and the newly arrived Kiwis were already forming a fresh semicircle round Salomé. They were bartering. A leonine chap handed Salomé soda water. Salomé took the battered tin mug, gave it a sniff, shook her head, and returned it, nodding at a flask of whiskey.

The Kiwis roared with laughter.

"Whiskey, mate!" the short soldier with the whiskey barked, giving his flask a little shake.

And the onlookers snorted with laughter again.

"She'll have them all stand on their heads soon," Elliot grinned.

I glared at him.

"Lighten up. You cannot be angry at Salomé for entertaining the soldiers. She has charm. Besides, Ali's guarding her."

"Look here Elliot, we've got to put an end to this charade." But before I could do so, Elliot swore, sprinting into the assembly.

A strange man spotted my brother's approach. He pushed out to escape and knocked over two New Zealanders. The crowd round Salomé stirred when Ali leapt from the rooftop, grabbed Salomé, and, together, they fled.

"The devil take that man! It's Mahmud!" Elliot cried out then shouted a long string of Mahmud's unsavory filial relationships.

I followed Elliot.

The Kiwis followed me.

And, so it began.

Mahmud, now armed with a short knife, kept after Ali and Salomé; Elliot closed in on the villain; and the Kiwis and I, boots pounding on sand, were catching up.

Elliot bore down on Mahmud.

Ali dragged Salomé off in the other direction.

It did not take long.

First, Elliot grabbed Mahmud's shoulders and spun him round. A swift kick to his shin brought Mahmud to his knees. But the simian devil quickly got up, knife exposed and ready to attack.

"Elliot!"

"Don't worry, mate, we've got it." A sinewy New Zealander, hardly out of breath, proudly extended his weapon of choice. "We've got perfectly good bayonets here."

Advancing upon Mahmud, the soldiers encircled my brother and Mahmud so that Elliot was swallowed up by a ring of khaki within seconds.

The odds were in their favor. Still, the New Zealanders impressed me. They had perfectly good bayonets, but the weapon was inconsequential. Their discipline, synchronized motions, and silence spoke well of their training. None of the soldiers looked sideways. All eyes focused solely on the threat, a man with a knife.

Of course, Mahmud dropped the knife, terrified. He scanned the circle in search of a weak link. There was none. And, so, Mahmud raised his hands in the air.

#

"Who's he?" the sinewy New Zealander inquired.

"He's been threatening our friends for quite some time now." Elliot lit his cigarette, but not before he offered one to the officer. "He's a thief, a conspirator, and a scorpion. The police have been searching for him. Of course, we filed a complaint, too." He eyed Mahmud, as if disgusted by the petty criminal.

"He's been after our flower girl? Why? How do you know all this?"

"This man's been after the girl and the boy. They won't tell me why. They work for us, you see."

"Work for you? But we saw them in Cairo, collecting kids off the streets so that's why we help them. Do they really work elsewhere? We figured they needed money to buy food for the street orphans."

"Stableboy and maid," Elliot replied dismissively, then asked, "What do you mean by 'collecting kids' and when did you see them in Cairo?"

"We were astounded when we saw it! They walk into alleys then walk out with children! They feed them and take them away to the nearest church, mosque, synagogue, even hospitals. We followed them, you see, because it was a most peculiar sight. They simply popped out with kids, babies even, from dirty alleys. We were amazed the first time. But we noticed them on several other occasions and so that's why we support them, in our own way."

"I see. I had no idea. But what of this scoundrel? What should we do with him now?"

"Well, we are not the police. We'd rather not have him on our hands. But we can see to him until the police arrive." He commanded, "Pryde, make our guest comfortable."

Pryde nodded, saluted, and, bayonet extended grandly, approached Mahmud.

"Give him a hand. Bulford. Sampson," came the next command.

Elliot pulled the tall New Zealander aside and continued a hushed discussion.

The other two soldiers rushed to assist Pryde. They tied Mahmud's hands behind his back.

"What's next?" Bulford asked.

Pryde flicked a glance at his commander, now discoursing with Elliot. There were no further orders coming forth, so the trio was confused. But resourcefulness prevailed and Pryde located an upturned steel drum. "The drum?"

"What? Shove him in?" Sampson asked.

Bulford grinned. "Let the wog stew!"

Stewing in the drum, hands tied, Mahmud received three pats from each of the three Kiwis then watched the men return to their commander. Mahmud sighed with relief. It could have been a lot worse.

"I doubt that he'll have a good time once we hand him over to Cairo police," the officer remarked. "But where're my manners? I'm Sergeant Gleeson."

"William Westbrook and you have been conspiring with my brother, Elliot. By the way, what are you lot still doing here?"

"We're the last of our forces in Egypt. In charge of repairing flash flood damage. Can you believe our rotten luck? The rest of us are in Tunis, marching with General Freyberg and the British Major General Bernard Montgomery."

"Rotten luck."

"Care to swim?" Sergeant Gleeson's arm shot to the sparkling blue pool.

In no time at all, Elliot soaked the New Zealanders with a cannonball, only to be outdone by the Sergeant's belly flop. Elliot, good-natured and amiable, cheered and offered his hand to the New Zealander and fished him out of the pool for another round of diving.

"This is paradise," a young man flashed a smile at me and I agreed before diving in again.

As the water flushed my worries, I was happy to be back in Cairo. Recalling my discontent during the weeks preceding my travels, I realized that I felt remarkably better now. A holiday from hospital duties and Kelly's optimism to tugboat me through hurdles worked wonders.

My feelings for Salomé had not changed. And there was no doubt about it, I wanted Salomé. I accepted my attraction. So why did I watch her from a distance? Why did I not talk to her? Was I so concerned with propriety, with pride?

But what of Salomé? What would she think of me? Her circumstances were vague. She was in hiding, shrouded in rags and veils. I knew only a few things about her. She was somehow rescued from Nazi occupied territories. My father was involved and would not or could not talk about it. She was sheltered in our estate. She was attacked by Mahmud in the suk. And, she was nameless at our estate until I named her Salomé. But one thing was certain: I loved her.

Chapter 21: James at Arms

MOTHER'S hand flew on my shoulder. "He's coming." Then the door to the dining hall flew open and she rushed forward.

If my mother had a male rugger twin, then James would have been him. Like my mother, James was fair. He had golden glow to his cropped hair and wide-spaced clear-blue eyes that stared at the world, interested and intelligent. And his features were regular.

"James, my darling, William's back."

James beamed a smile at Mother then redirected it to me. But as he shuffled closer to the supper table, I noticed a slight stoop to his once broad and erect figure, and he had a limp. His face shone with sweat. His crystal blue eyes were a bit glassy.

Working at a military hospital did not prepare me to face my injured brother, and I was sorry for that. I took his hand in mine and grasped his shoulder. "Good to see you."

"And you." James' expression rested on me then brightened. I must have betrayed my anxiety because he then said, "Don't look so worried, William. Some days are better than others. You know how it is." Then he turned to Mother and winked. There had always been a close bond between James and Mother. They communicated with their own secret language.

"Yes, I do."

A loud bellow from the long gallery drowned my words and Elliot marched in. "Welcome back!" he boomed, pulling me into a tight oriental embrace.

My father entered, shaking his head. "Everyone's here. Let us begin then!" He positioned himself at the head of the table and raised his favorite palliative in a toast.

Dishes came and went and none of them palatable though we did our best. James eschewed the seared fish since the inside was still raw, and I, of course, balked at the heavy, greasy sauce drowning the shallots.

"Father, how long will the British mandate hold in Palestine?"

"Things are restless." He glanced at my mother.

"Why do you ask, William? Are you planning to go back for your holdall?"

I threw what was left of my watercress at Elliot, but missed.

"William!" Mother gasped.

"Ah, rotten luck. Try again?" Elliot's cheeky grin flashed.

"That's enough," rumbled my father as James coughed, "Incorrigible raff."

#

A ring of clouds converged on the moon. Before darkness settled on the courtyard, I caught a glimpse of the stables. I remembered the girl's unfortunate stumble, and the donkey's response and disobedience; I recalled her gazing quietly at the fields; and, then, her playfulness. And shivering, I yearned for her touch, her feel, and her lips.

Elliot remarked, "She's not there."

"Who? What do you mean she isn't there?"

"Salomé. She is not in the stables now."

"Where is she then?"

"Out."

"With Ali?"

"Probably."

"Does she trust him that much?"

"William, all over the world, little boys like Ali are manipulated to do abominable things. Terrible things. Ali is a good boy. He may have had his loyalties put to the test, but he is good enough."

"If you say so."

"What did you think of James?" Elliot abruptly changed the subject.

"It could be worse, I suppose. What's happened to him? Why is his face scared like that? Where's he been?"

"Oh, the scars are nothing. Desert sores. Or, that's what he says." Elliot looked away. "He's not the same person. He's changed. Maybe the long stay out in the desert did it but somehow he's changed." Elliot's gaze fixed on the gate. "The official records indicate that James' leg was injured. I am not at all medically inclined, but I don't see how he'll recover. Does he have to medicate himself so much?"

"Healing takes time. A lot of time. And it is rarely the same afterwards."

"Never back to the original, as one Australian boy once told me."

"Sullivan?"

209

"Yes."

Something bothered Elliot. But what?

"Elliot, whatever happened to Elizabeth and her father, Mr. Baker?"

"Mr. Baker and Elizabeth were charged with treason, you know that. But, don't worry. Our family is not implicated in the affair and Cairo GHQ silenced it all admirably. Even Mother hasn't complained."

"But, you Elliot, how are you?"

"Busy."

"Busy?"

"Monnayeur's!"

"Elliot! Your wife..."

"Don't, William. Yes, she was my wife. But you know how it is."

I did not know how it was or what he had meant. Apparently, Elliot wanted the matter to fall, so I held my peace though the relationship between Elliot and his former wife certainly baffled and unnerved me. And what of Lady Jane? What of that Aphrodite of his? Where was she?

Just then, chains jingled and a dark form slipped through the iron gate and into the courtyard.

Pulling at my dinner jacket, Elliot heaved us into the rose bushes. Elliot's breathing became inaudible and I bit my lips as barbs dug into my skin.

A shadow tripped by the roses and disappeared down the paths to the stables.

"What..."

"It's her." Admiration lent a slight warble to his thunder-like whisper.

Seconds later, a muffled yip followed, then the stables door shut.

My pulse raced. Every bit of my body demanded to go to her but my legs would not budge.

"Damn. Another dinner jacket ruined." Elliot extricated himself from the bramble then fastidiously pulled thorns out of his jacket.

"Two. I'm wearing one of yours!"

"That horrible tailor, damn him."

"Leave the tailor, curse the man. What about Salomé?"

"I found her one night outside Monnayeur's. She was persuading a girl to come along with her. A bit difficult when she cannot communicate well. I watched, but did not help her. I'm sorry about that

210

now. That little girl whom she was trying to help was found unconscious the next morning. Hunger, disease, or something worse altogether got her. Anyway, after that night, I followed Salomé whenever I had time, which isn't much," he admitted.

"What else has she been up to? And why did we hide in the rose bushes?" My hands were shaky and cold, so I pushed them into my trouser pockets. Breathless, I awaited Elliot's response but he marched past.

Then, he threw over his shoulder, "We'd better go see James."

"At this hour?"

"He's awake."

"Elliot, you cannot force a person back to health."

He snorted.

"Do you recall the epidemic influenza you'd contracted when you were sixteen?"

"How could I forget?"

"Why did you refuse medication? Why embark on a rigorous routine of exercise?"

"Just some sprints round the park."

"You're mad! You ran in rain and fog, and I, running alongside like a fool, dreaded that at any moment you'd simply collapse."

"Well, I survived, didn't I? And you, you ungrateful dog, got much needed muscle tone. You were fair into being a gangly youth otherwise! Pale and spotty! Quiet now, here we are."

James' room was dark and silent.

"He's asleep."

"Not he." Elliot flicked the light switch on.

James' eyes popped open, glowing orbs, quickly hidden behind his arm. "Oh, no, not you!"

"So, you're awake after all."

"It's an irksome habit!"

"What?"

"Popping in and out of here like a jack-in-the-box at all hours of the day!"

"But you are awake," Elliot insisted.

"Well, what of it? What is it to you?"

"Very well, I'll go." Elliot turned to the door.

211

"Incorrigible raff are we?" I asked, approaching James, reaching for his wrist to take his pulse. "What has Elliot been up to?"

James brushed my hand away, looking chagrinned, then pulled himself up into a sitting position. "Besides his fibs about Aziza?"

"Fibs?"

"Let's see, he's been stalking servants at night."

"And a stableboy, too!"

This utterance sent James cowering back into the sheets, muttering wrathfully.

Elliot stretched a roguish grin.

"Were you stalking Ali too?" I asked him.

"For sport." Elliot waved his arm to stress the simplicity of his answer. "James was bored."

"Bored? I scarcely dare leave my light on to read a book! I am pounced on at every hour and pulled into impish ventures I want no part in!"

"William wants to know all about the girl and her walks through neighborhoods." Elliot turned to me and gave a conspiratorial wink. "The best parts of the evenings, or nights actually, are the chases..."

"Chases?"

"Guards," James elucidated.

"Guards! Elliot, do you mean to tell me that you let a little girl roam Cairo at night?" I asked, outraged. "You're aware of the dangers. Why?"

"A little girl? Aren't you overdoing it? She's a young woman and free to roam, free to wander. It's not up to us to inhibit her adventures. Besides, I kept an eye on her." Elliot glanced at James then turned to me. "You recall the thug we rounded up this afternoon in Ma'adi? Mahmud?"

"Yes?"

James groaned.

"Well, you may have already suspected this, but he's been behind several incidents involving us." Elliot turned to James, "I've told you all this before."

"Congratulations. You finally caught the villain," James breathed out the words, listlessly.

"Don't overdo it, James, your leaps of joy and all that might do you an injury!"

212

"But that reminds me, Elliot. When you had mentioned this at dinner, you nearly gave Mother an apoplexy!" I said.

"I would've been wiser to mention the matter to Father in private, but you know my temper."

"Don't I!"

"William, the first of the incidents was the kidnapping of Salomé in the suk and the second was the attack on Ali during the storm. I paid a visit to that house in Al-Khalifa."

"You, Elliot? How did you know about the house in Al-Khalifa?"

"Managing Monnayeur's puts me in touch with the right people. Mahmud is Syrian born. Years ago, he came to Egypt to study at the University of Cairo. He fell on hard times and embarked on a criminal career. But then he joined a gang of radical nationalists. I call them a gang, but I am in the wrong. They are a party, a political party. They get support from the Germans and successful businessmen who want the British out of the Middle East for monetary gains. Contrary to Ali's impression, Mahmud is no ordinary thief. His main duty was to get hostages, British officials or their kin," he spoke briskly then added in a lowered yet serious voice, "William, do you know what they do with hostages?"

"I do. And they used Ali to get to us."

"Quite."

"Elliot, how did you learn all that?"

"I called on Mahmud. I paid him a visit at his house and had a little chat. But the bloody wog got away. He managed to slip out from under me."

"Literally," James intervened.

"What's that?"

"He slipped away!" Elliot growled.

"Some filthy teenager came in with a gun and distracted Elliot long enough for Mahmud to wriggle out of Elliot's grasp. Elliot got to the damned kid, but too late. Mahmud had already gone."

"And the kid?"

"The bastard spat into Elliot's eyes."

"Worse!" Elliot cried.

"Yes, and the boy's old Webley Revolver was not loaded."

"Were you there?" I asked James.

"Of course, and a mighty poor sport it was for me! I had to chase Mahmud."

"Mahmud fled?"

"Over difficult terrain of low walls and dustbins!"

"James! You ran? In your condition?"

"James' leg's been hurting since...and he blames me for it. He blames me because his stitching came undone or something like that!"

"My stitching is fine! But, you, Elliot, you were careless."

"Oh, I've had enough!"

"Why add so much flourish to your moves? By the time your leg and arm came to a stop, the villain took off!"

"What ungrateful dogs you two are!" Elliot shot a hurt glance at James, then at me.

"Leave me out of this! I wasn't even there."

"A simple blow to the head would have knocked the fellow out."

"But then how could I have interrogated him myself, James? Once in custody, it is unlikely that the police would let me near him," Elliot explained. "Oh, well. He's tucked away now." Elliot pulled out a flask of whiskey and passed it round.

I lit a cigarette and walked to the window.

James' back was against the wall. His night shirt hung loosely over his shoulders. His neck, extending out of the dark fabric, was pale. "Elliot, it is fifteen minutes past two in the morning. Get out of my room," James croaked.

"William fancied a chat with you, James. Won't you amuse the fellow?"

"William has better sense than that. Go away."

Chapter 22: In the Canal

AUGUST heat slowed my steps to the guesthouse at sunrise. When I entered, Elliot peeked out from under his thin blanket.

"Elliot?"

"I see you've cleaned yourself up. You shaved, too! Good, now, go away."

"Oh, no. You'll join me for a swim in the canal."

"We were there just a few hours ago."

"It's much more interesting at dawn."

Elliot swung his legs out, pulled his trousers on and slid his feet into his boots. "The diversion? She'll be there."

"Who?" I asked, playing for time.

"Salomé bathes early in the morning."

"I'll take my chances."

But near the brush by the diversion, Elliot pulled me back. "She's here all right." He stood, silently watching Salomé. "She is not an Egyptian. I asked Father. I confronted him, you know, after that night, the shooting, then I followed her..."

"What have you learned from him?"

"From whom?" Elliot asked. He was staring at Salomé bathing in the canal. "Look at her skin. And those lovely thighs and..."

"That's enough." I pulled him away.

Elliot pushed my arm away and went back. "Not jealous are you, William?"

"Of course not."

"You fancy this girl, and you know it, William. You..."

"Shut up."

"What would Mother say?"

"Trap it."

"Steady on, William, it is socially unacceptable. And Mother is so strict about such things. To Mother, the girl is a servant, a person, regardless of extenuating circumstances. How will you pull it off, I wonder?"

"Keep your voice down."

But it was of no use. The girl turned to look at us, and aware of our presence, she dressed.

Embarrassed, I instinctively turned to Elliot and gave him a shove. Elliot retaliated, and somehow my fist collided with his ribs. Elliot swung at me and I fell on my back.

"Get off my stomach, Elliot. I'm sick. Get your arse off me."

"Temper, temper," Elliot flicked his finger under my chin and lit a cigarette.

"You are perverted!"

A long trail of smoke escaped his mouth as he leaned closer. "I am..."

But I never learned what he was because at that moment a woman appeared behind Elliot's frame.

Flushed with strain under Elliot's muscular body, I stared at the young woman. Soft, hot wind blew about. I was uncomfortably aware of Salomé's curves, slightly hidden by her robe, fabric clinging to her body in certain locations with moisture.

Salomé smiled, raised her hand to greet me with a whispered hello.

Chapter 23: She Speaks!

CROUCHING on one knee, his arms stretched out, Elliot boomed, "She speaks!"

"And I breathe! Damn you, how is it that you're so heavy?" I got to my feet, dusting my clothes, trying to hide my shock.

"What a scandal!?" Elliot continued his buffoonery, his voice a piercing falsetto.

"Amusing, aren't you?"

"William, do not approach her. She's an afreet, a jinn, a ghost."

Salomé's smile wavered. She took several steps back, confused by Elliot's loud antics.

"Perhaps," I conceded in a whisper, my eyes fixed on the girl.

Elliot was too excited to hear my disclosure. "Step back, my boy," he called and swung his arm round. He had no idea that I had stepped forward and was now close to him. His muscular arm struck me, bringing me down once more.

My head hit a rock.

#

"William?" Elliot's cobalt gaze swam before me.

Standing behind my brother, Ali clutched a bucket.

"You devil," I rasped then closed my eyes.

"More water, Ali!"

Still weak and giddy, I barely opened my mouth when another bucketful of water cascaded on my head. Then, spluttering and swearing I asked, "Damn it, before you hit me again, answer this. Where is she?"

Getting up, shaking his boots and wiping water off of his face, Elliot sighed, "James. She's fetching James."

"James?" I leaned on my elbows.

"Why not? He's a doctor, isn't he?"

"But I'm fine."

"Then aren't you going to thank us for all our efforts to revive you?"

"If you're looking for thanks, think again. You, Elliot, knocked me unconscious. I suppose that I should be grateful to Ali. But I'm not. One bucket would have been quite enough. Two is just for amusement."

"Three buckets. Three!" Elliot wiggled three fingers.

Ali, still in attendance, shot an indignant look. His thick eyebrows furrowed as his dark beard twitched.

"I can't stand cold water. I am cold and wet. And it gets into my nose. And I am cold..."

"You're overwrought." Elliot was now brushing the sand off of his trousers. "I just wanted to surprise you. She speaks. And now if you will excuse me, I have a rather busy day at GHQ."

As I watched Elliot hurry away, I regretted my temper. I had a painful lump on my head, but my dizziness subsided. And the damage now seemed minimal.

Ali remained by my side, playing with his beard.

"So, what will you do now that Mahmud is not around to threaten you?" I asked, looking up at him.

"Lady Westbrook has taken a fancy to riding."

"Which of the horses? Not my Marlena?"

Ali nodded.

"Could you not have persuaded her to choose or even purchase another? You know how fond I am of my Marlena."

"Effendi, I don't have kitchen duty anymore. I have been assigned to the stables. That horrible cook can't touch me there!"

"Some friend you are. Marlena? She does not have the right touch. What if she breaks her leg?"

"But Effendi, I drive well now. I would take her to hospital, right away!"

"Hospital? You will need a veterinarian for Marlena, you cur!"

"I spoke of her Ladyship."

Behind my back, I had been preparing a ball of wet clay. As I slowly got up, I launched the wet lump and hit Ali's chest.

"Effendi!" he shrieked then ran to the canal, got water in his bucket, and chased me to the courtyard.

Later, walking through the courtyard, wet, but, as I had told Ali, refreshed, I heard the white dog bounding to me, tail going in full circles, she yipped and barked.

"Good girl. You came to welcome me back?"

The dog put her front paws on my chest and wagged her long, curling tail.

"You are gorgeous!" I patted her head. Her sleek fur was soft. "So, the white mongrel had transformed into a lovely pet. Not wild anymore, are you?" I let the dog follow me to the door. "I better go inside now. Señor Marcelo is visiting today. But you give my love to your mistress," I whispered and rubbed behind her beautiful upright ears.

#

"Well, breakfast was a nightmare."

"Indigestible," Elliot agreed.

"I wonder why Señor Marcelo is here," I remarked, recalling the last time I saw him. "What business has he with Father?"

"He'll regret it soon enough, so don't trouble yourself with that fellow." Leaning into his dining chair, his breakfast dish pushed aside, Elliot picked his teeth and eyed me askance. "Besides, what have you with an old man? What I would like to know is why haven't you gone to your maiden of the stables yet?"

"What are you on about?"

"Salomé. Why have you not gone to the stables yet? You know, she inquired about your head. She asked to see you, but...You were quite all right, I told her. Didn't think that she should see you at your worst. You really should control your temper, William." Then he reached his hand out and put it on my shoulder. "You showered and shaved. Great. You're cleaned up. That's good. But now, you mustn't keep her waiting."

How do I confess that I could not pluck up the courage? Now that she spoke, I could find myself in an awkward situation. What would she say to me? And in what language? I looked at Elliot's eager face. "I'll go. No need to push me."

"Well, don't delay. After all, she speaks now. This is your chance to talk to her."

"In what language?"

"Her English is good enough."

"How did she start speaking? When? How did it come about?"

"Does it matter?"

"Of course it does! I've spent hours reading to her, talking to her. Countless interminable monologues!"

"James, I guess. They spent hours together and then one afternoon I heard her call for the dog. Nadia is her name now."

"What?"

219

"Nadia is the dog's name."

"Nadia? Good, a proper name."

"A perfect name. That dog is something special. So, are you going to go, or not?"

"I'd wanted her to speak for so long," I blurted.

"Afraid that her words might not be what you want to hear?"

I nodded, miserably recalling that I had left for Palestine soon after we were intimate.

"Don't. Tell her how you feel. Better yet, show her how much you care and tell her of your resolution. Now, run along with you."

"What resolution?"

But Elliot already drifted away as he threw his last words at my unsteady feet.

The sun cast stubby shadows as I crossed the courtyard, wiping sweat off my forehead.

My hand pushed open the door to the stables, transporting me into another world altogether.

At that hour of day, the atmosphere in the stables was magical. Inside, the air was cool, suffused with earthen smells.

Salomé was feeding Nick Bottom, the old ass, while a child perched on an upturned bucket nearby.

As I entered, the dog rose and shook loudly, her ears pattering. She trotted to greet me. Bowing into a stretch and licking my hands, the endearing creature was determined to get my attention. I thanked her for providing a distraction, and, while I was petting and scratching her neck and sending her into idiotic bliss, I was at ease. "What a beauty you are! And you have a proper name now. Nadia suits you."

The two horses popped their heads out, then raised and lowered them, as to greet me. The child crooned softly, eating a bowl of *fuul*. I took a seat on a bucket next to the stranger. The dog curled up beside me, resting her chin on my boots, while the child's curious gaze followed my motions.

"The first time we met was here. You were brushing Nick Bottom and offered to groom me as well." Somehow, the memory cheered me and I smiled at Salomé and then at the child.

The child turned to stare at Salomé.

220

Salomé beamed a smile, left the donkey, and approached the little girl, stroking her straight, dark hair.

"William," Salomé pointed to me. Then, she pointed to the child. "Lulu."

"It's a pleasure, Lulu."

Lulu returned to her bowl.

Feeling on edge, I got up as the dog shook her head and body, ready to follow me.

Salomé quickly placed her hand on my arm. "William." She spoke in slow, accented English. "Will you stay?"

"Yes, all right."

"How is your head?"

"Not bad."

She smiled.

"Salomé..." I began uneasily. "Well, first, what should I call you? I mean what's your name? You had a name before you came here. What's your name, Salomé?"

She stood motionless. "No, call me Salomé."

I clasped her hand in mine, my eyes fixed on her face.

Her hair, flirting with her shoulders now, caught the light and shone with coppery radiance.

I looked at the soft curves of her lips, then her jaw, and back up again to a faint indentation on her cheek. I wondered why I never noticed that she had dimples, faint dimples.

Cupping her chin in my palm, my thumb gently traced her jaw.

Her lips parted.

I knew that I had to step back, away from this beautiful woman. But all at once I wanted to bring her closer, touch her hair and her face, kiss her lips.

"I thought of you often," I whispered, holding her in my arms, bending my head to her face.

"William," she whispered as my lips touched her cheek, then her lips, and lingered, my mouth covering hers. I drew back and my eyes held hers. "Salomé," I breathed. Then pulling away, I asked, "Not angry with me?"

She cocked her head, perplexed.

"I'd left."

"You are back," came her reply, barely above a whisper.

My hand slid to the back of her neck as I pressed my mouth to hers again. A sharp intake of breath as her familiar scent drugged me.

She drew closer and once more I was drowned in her, deeper now, my hands running over her body, seeking, wanting. Her body responded to my caresses and she arched like a curved bow against me, her arms round my neck, then running her fingers through my hair. Her lips responding to my touch, excited and searching and without a trace of hesitation. There was a quiver running through her when my hand reached under her robe. Searing pain of desire seized my stomach, as my lips moved down to her neck then back up to her lips.

It was Nadia who gave us the alert. She stood up noisily and pointed her nose and ears at the entrance, then gave a sharp bark when Mother walked into the stables in her riding kit, talking to Ali and Ali responding in hurried, "Yes, my Lady."

Releasing Salomé from my embrace, I stepped aside as Nadia's hackles rose up on her back, a low growl at the ready for Ali.

Salomé's flushed face turned to me and I took hold of her hand, reaching at the same time to sooth Nadia.

"William!" Mother gasped.

"Mother."

"A word with you. And in private. No Ali, stay inside." Her icy staccato sent shivers down my spine.

I let go of Salomé, who set to quiet Nadia.

Outside, the sun governed the empty sky, scorching the earth.

Perspiration and flies clung to my face, but I could scarcely register the discomfort.

Although Ali remained inside, Salomé came out of the stables. With quick, hurried steps she headed to the gate, the child crying miserably in her arms, and Nadia, still in attendance, trotting alongside, her curly, sassy tail upright.

I watched Salomé leave as Mother's words of disapproval turned into indistinguishable noise, distant from my consciousness, but slowly condemning me in more ways than verbally. To my mother, the girl was a maid, a servant. And a maid was not a suitable girl, not a suitable match for a Westbrook.

Salomé walked out of sight, barefoot. Followed by a dog, she carried a child in her thin arms as the heavy estate gate creaked shut behind her.

222

My mother, put her hand on mine.

"I hear you, Mother, but you are in the wrong about her."

I was slightly sick and numb. I was not angry, not with Mother. Mother had different and rather old-fashioned ideas about marriage. I wanted to talk, to explain, but the words stuck, and would not come out.

Chapter 24: Lost

AUGUST wind pushed and shoved the clouds out of the sun's way. Fine dust choked the garden. And, in listless indifference, roses hung their heads. The gardens needed shade and water. But there was no shade, only sun and blistering heat. And there was no water coming from the ditches.

Salomé did not return to water the gardens.

Days went by, but Salomé did not return. The dog was gone, too.

"Elliot," I called as my brother swung his legs out of his motorcar and sprang to his guesthouse.

He paused. "The girl? Any news?"

"None. I've been out looking for her all day."

"Where?"

"I crisscrossed the main avenues near here, then had a notion to check in poorhouses and orphanages. Elliot, you followed Salomé at night while I was in Palestine."

"Yes. But she's been gone for days now. And I just can't see her out on the streets. Not for such a long stretch as this."

"Ma'adi?"

"No, Sergeant Gleeson would've rang me up. He knows who we are and that the girl is our maid. But, William, why did she even leave? Why did Salomé walk outside the estate in the middle of the day? It's unlike her!"

"Mother walked in on us in the stables and you can imagine what a perfect scene it all was."

"I'm glad it wasn't me!"

"Yes, well, it was me. Elliot, I must find her."

"Why not look into government-run clinics for the sick and destitute?" Elliot continued the original thread of conversation.

"Would they remember seeing her?"

"Of course. The nurses or assistants at the clinics would certainly remember an uncommonly tall young woman even if her face is veiled. Besides, she speaks English. I haven't heard her utter a single word in Arabic, except perhaps *chai bil na'ana.*"

"Mint tea? Is that all she can say in Arabic?"

"Something's just occurred to me, William."

"What?"

"Cairo is a giant of a city!"

"And I still have hospital duties. I cannot disappear again."

Restless, Elliot lit a cigarette. "I'll go. And, I can check out some charities."

"Where?"

"Mosques, churches, temples or other such religious institutions with charitable inclinations. But first, some of those governmental clinics..."

Late at night, Elliot returned disappointed and taken aback. Crashing into my leather chair, he groaned. "No such woman happened into the clinics."

"What happened to you there?"

Elliot grabbed his whiskey and made horse-like snorts as if trying to shake off a terrible memory.

"Which of the clinics did you stop by?"

"Which? All that I could get to, of course!" His voice cracked.

"Out with it then! What happened?"

"One damned clinic...A wretched rubble on the outskirts of Birket Street..." Elliot poured himself another glass. "The British government, in its infinite wisdom, legalized brothels. And there are clinics nearby. And in the places, William, where the women would seek refuge, they find swine!" Elliot lit a cigarette. "The greasy swine at the front desk...She leaned forward, her meaty breasts oozing like poison on the counter...and then she reached out and pulled me close. My chest, William, my chest flattened against the counter. Her arm got to my arse, groping me! Sizing me!"

"Never mind! Did she say anything? Has she seen the girl?"

Elliot's lips curled. "Well...She asked me how many like her I wanted because by the size of me I could use more than one. She had girls available, at any price, any description, any kind. What the hell were you thinking sending me there? Damn you! Damn it all!"

"It was your idea. But I thought that it had great potential."

"What about you? What have you got?"

"The dog."

"The dog? Nadia?"

"Nadia and Sullivan."

225

With a shout of laughter Elliot cried, "I don't believe you! Where are they then?"

"In your..."

Whiskey sloshing in his glass, Elliot whooshed by me, dashing to his guesthouse.

"Elliot!" I held him back. "Elliot, Sullivan is rather upset."

"Still?" he called out in exasperated tones then bit his lip, regretting his outburst.

"What do you mean still?"

"Soad," he groaned.

"Which Soad? There are millions of Soads in Cairo."

"Joseph's dancer."

"Joseph? Our old groom? What has he to do with a dancer?"

"Joseph plays for me at Monnayeur's."

"Yes, that was good of you to hire him as a flute player at the club but what has he to do with a dancer and Sullivan and a Soad?"

"Joseph recommended Soad, a dancer, a fantastic belly dancer. Sullivan and Soad met and one thing led to another, and...She got pregnant. However, she has left to America."

"Well?"

"It's Sullivan's child."

"And he will not marry her?"

Elliot gave a sad smile. "Sullivan begged her to marry him and planned to take her home with him. She laughed and treated him like a naughty school boy, telling him that harsh farm life in Australia was not at all to her taste. What would he have her do? Belly dance for the kangaroos? There was a terrible quarrel. But she picked up her tambourine and cymbals and left."

Dumbfounded, I wondered at the fool of a woman refusing a man like Sullivan. "Well, good riddance to her!"

"Yes. But he loved her, you see, and she loved him only not enough to cross the ocean to Australia. And he is still upset about it, you say?"

"He is upset. I had no idea about the Soad Affair. But Sullivan was certainly not as cheerful as I remember him."

#

Four days had passed since I last saw Salomé. Nadia, the wild dog, had returned with a bullet wound a day earlier. Tom Sullivan too returned to Cairo and was staying with us while on short leave. Elliot was

226

now pacing his room while our friend leaned against the window and watched the sun set.

"She might return." I hardly believed my own utterance. "Nadia came back."

At the sound of her name, Nadia cocked her head, staring up at me, setting her tail to a gentle wag.

"The dog came back wounded, grazed by a bullet," Elliot remarked darkly and knelt to scratch her head. "Aren't you just gorgeous? Bullet wound and all. My lovely Nadia."

The dog's tail now wagged with earnest rhythm, thump, thump, on the floor. She watched Elliot with adoring eyes ready to follow his slightest command.

"Even female canines fall like ninepins before you, Elliot!"

"Still, it's no indication that the girl got shot. To most people in Cairo, shooting a dog is different from shooting a person," I argued.

"Madame Sukey!" Sullivan called out. "Does not Madame Sukey have a school for rescued girls?"

"Madame Sukey?" I repeated idiotically, recalling all the amazing things Madame had been responsible for in and around Cairo and her generosity to the patients in hospital and to the soldiers' families.

Elliot, after a moment of recollection, shook his head. "No, Madame Sukey's girls come from Siwa and one or two other oases. The girls aren't Cairene."

Sullivan turned from the window. "Can't Sir Niles help? He's well connected here in Cairo, and well respected. One word from him and the entire army is at your service."

"No, it'd take several sentences to get the army out of the Western Desert, especially now!" Elliot attempted a chuckle. "No, Father cannot help us."

"Perhaps we should try looking outside Cairo?" I suggested.

"If she's still alive, then she's in Cairo."

"How can you be so damn sure?"

"Because I am!"

"What sort of an answer is this?"

"All right you two," Sullivan spoke again. "Who is this girl anyway? I know that there must be more than what you're telling me. She cannot possibly be a hired maid. No one goes searching for servants. Not with so much concern and diligence and with great effort to keep it hushed up."

Dim rays of light stabbed the room. Suddenly, Elliot's face caught one of those feeble streams. It was remarkable. His chin tilted sideways and up and Elliot appeared regal.

Sullivan noticed the effect, too, and he leaned back against the windowsill, as if in reverence.

"Sullivan, the girl is dear to us. She's a child fished out of Europe." Elliot pronounced Europe with disgust. "You are our ally, our friend, helping us in our search, and you are entitled to know."

"Where would she spend her time? I mean, where would she go when she wasn't here?" Sullivan asked.

Elliot glanced at me, then recited a long list of places he had seen Salomé roam, either by night or, rarely, by day.

I added to the list our excursions to the irrigated mud flats and the suk.

At the mention of mud flats, Elliot raised his eyebrows. His lips moved to shape the word 'Luna.'

Sullivan did not see Elliot's lips move vulgarly because he turned to the window just then and, pointing, asked, "What about that young man?"

Elliot and I rushed to the window and stuck our heads out. "Ali?" we asked in unison.

"Would he know anything?"

"He might know everything or nothing at all. But how do we approach him? How do we figure out what he knows and how much he is willing to divulge?" Elliot mused.

"Ali?" I asked again in disbelief. Why did it never occur to me to ask him before? "He stayed behind, in the stables, when Salomé left. Would he have a clue? Would he know her whereabouts?"

"Let me think on it. I'll find the right moment and the right approach. Just don't say or ask anything yet. Ali can be a bit tricky to handle sometimes. He's at that awkward age, you know. Agreed?"

I nodded.

"All right," replied Sullivan. "But who is he?"

"Stableboy, more or less."

"But he has his nose in everything," I added. "So, don't delay too much, Elliot. The right moment and the right approach should come about sooner rather than later."

"Oh, don't you worry," replied Elliot, a mischievous grin lighting up his face.

#

'A child fished out of Europe' was hardly how I would describe Salomé. But I could hardly tell that to my family and friends, could I?

Between shifts at hospital, I searched for Salomé. I missed her terribly and felt responsible for her disappearance. Fear gripped me and I became frantic in my search and irritable with my surrounding. Again, my nights became restless. But this time, in familiar territory, my insomnia drove me outside, out of the estate, to the busy, noisy nights of Cairo, where I walked up and down filthy alleyways looking for Salomé, calling her name.

Chapter 25: Naji

"WILLIAM, James can't know Salomé's gone."

"Don't say gone!" I snapped.

"Mental anguish is the last thing James needs at the moment."

"Do you suppose that I'd gladly go blabbering to him about her?"

"Not at all, not gladly blabber but you do rather favor the comprehensive!"

"Elliot!"

"Look, we'll go on a pleasant drive with James and keep him talking."

But James and Elliot developed the hateful habit of quarreling. They bickered and bantered in a confusing whirlwind, seesawing between disagreement and drollness. On our manic drive to Faraj's, as Elliot wove between cars, lorries, a pile of machine guns that fell off and onto the motorway, cabs, camels, and bleating goats, James effortlessly tested Elliot's good humor.

Exhausted and in a temper, Elliot pulled into Faraj's alley, switched off the engine, and rushed into the coffee shop.

"I'll get the door, James," I said.

But as James straightened up, Elliot returned, shaking his head. "No, no, he's not here. Not now. We'll go to Shepheard's. It's not far."

"Are you sure? Is he not in the back room?" James asked.

"Quite sure."

"Let's go to Shepheard's then."

"Let's..."

Flaunting its seemingly disarrayed furniture, the terrace of Shepheard's Hotel buzzed with activity, its unpredictable and unlikely crowd shifting, buzzing about. Men in business suits or officers in full regalia drank beer, open newspapers fluttering in their hands. A balding businessman squashed his dark wicker chair, his hands never touching the square-top table before him. He puffed on a cigar and checked his watch frequently, casting expectant glances at passersby. A group of young men entered, exchanged a few words with the fat man then trooped away, their expensive shoes clattering on the ornate, almost confusing oriental theme of the terrace floor.

The only piece that appeared consistent was the uniformity of the servers. The tall, dark-skinned waiters were adorned with white robes, a wide band hugging their hips, and their Egyptian head cap lending them additional height.

"James, how did you get to Cairo so soon after your injury?" I asked. "Father hinted that you were in Europe."

"I wasn't in Europe."

"Where were you then?"

"I crisscrossed North Africa with the Eighth Army," James replied thoughtfully.

So, James was not going to talk about the LRDG.

A slight smile brightened his features. "Before that, I was in Iraq for a month. Lots of cases of heat exhaustion and of course the troops contracted some of the appalling diseases endemic to the area. Malaria, yellow fever, hepatitis, typhus, smallpox, dysentery, venereal diseases - a whole array of those!"

Elliot and I exchanged glances.

"In Iraq, I met an orphan. He used to loiter by the lorries outside hospital, looking for free meals and driving lessons. Naji was eleven years old. And a prankster."

Elliot leaned close.

"Naji had a grudge against one of the Arab drivers. His opportunity to get back at him came when one day the driver made a special delivery. The dead."

"What dead?" I asked.

James had a whiskey in his hand with a cigarette wedged between his fingers. "Iraqi leaders, and the Grand Mufti, collaborated on organizing riots. The violence was directed at us, at the British. Uprising against British presence in Iraq was craftily designed to offset balance of power in the Middle East and shift much needed troops to Iraq instead of the Western Desert. The Germans were hoping to weaken the Allied front in Egypt."

"Sounds familiar. Cairo and Tel Aviv and a score of other cities experienced similar attentions."

"The Iraqi riots produced a pile of dead people. So, the bodies were quickly loaded into a lorry to be transported. The cemeteries were out of town."

"Transported away to prevent more diseases?"

"Yes."

"Naji?"

"Oh, yes. The driver entrusted with the dead was the same driver who tormented Naji. So, the boy crept into the back of his lorry. Somehow, he managed the smell and horror all right. But when the driver reached a desolate stretch across the desert road, Naji pulled himself up. He knocked on the window that separated the cargo from the driver, howling and screaming, calling out the driver's name. The driver, a boorish fellow and already uneasy with a load of corpses in the back of his lorry, had a fit. He stopped the lorry and ran. We never saw that driver again."

"And Naji?"

Silence fell and James drained his whiskey. Then a whisper escaped out of his lips, "We best be going."

James' eyes were shaded under his heavy brows and the angle of the sun. His shoulders drooped and remorse washed over his features. What was it that he regretted? James was only twenty-eight years old, but where were any signs of youth? And then a dawning realization struck me. Could it be that my brother's interest in Salomé was merely longing for his young friend? Could it be that he saw the girl as a child, and nothing more?

"What about North Africa? What were you doing in the desert? Any interesting cases?" Elliot pressed on. Was he challenging James? Did Elliot know about James and the LRDG?

"The Nazis nearly got me in November of '41. The Germans overtook the British garrison at Tobruk. The explosion knocked me off my feet, and there I was believing that it was all over, wondering why I can still feel pain. A massive arm grabbed hold of me. It was my Canadian friend, Dr. Roger, dragging me out to sea. Once in the water, I revived and together we swam out to the last Royal destroyer leaving Tobruk, only moments before the garrison was captured by Rommel, that devil. How did he know where to attack and what our plans were?"

Elliot shifted uneasily in his chair as the waiter brought another round of drinks to our table and stole a furtive glance at James.

My brother's long, thin fingers shakily held a smoldering cigarette, hiding his wan face. While recalling his service in the desert, James talked about surgery conditions, scarcely mentioning the fighting. "William, you must have seen some of the men we'd sent to Cairo."

"What was left of them," Elliot growled.

"We did the best we could. Working in a field ambulance and a MSU while shells exploded nearby, surrounded by minefields, and explosives was a bit challenging. Sometimes, we had no antibiotics. Hygiene was non-existent. We carried out our operations in a lorry with a tarpaulin suspended over the back. We did not have gloves; ah...pentothal, we had pentothal, and, if we were lucky, ether. William, did you see the supply kits the American soldiers were each carrying?"

"They had Sulphas!"

"The American first aid kits saved lives by merely preventing infections. Those supply kits were splendid. But there was little we could do about the swarms of flies and the intense sun and heat."

Elliot leaned back into his chair, watching his brother talk about splints then move to internal injuries.

"The biggest battle was with men suffering stomach wounds. It took us some time to realize that patients after surgery must rest for several days, no motion at all, to have a better chance of survival. Of course, we gave them no food or drink, only intravenously. We kept them immobile otherwise."

"For how long?"

"Recovery on the front was a rare luxury. Stretcher bearers were picking up the wounded in the midst of the firing and piling them on Bren-gun carriers then into ambulances. You see, at first, we would transport patients to the base surgeons immediately. We assumed that hospital care superseded the need for rest. The ambulance plowing across the desert terrain nearly killed the boys with shock."

"Jolting?"

"It was a rough terrain."

Elliot decided to make one of his flippant remarks just then. "Do you mean to tell me that if the Germans did not kill the Tommies, then you had a go at them; and if that didn't work out, the ambulance ride was a sure thing. And, if the poor chaps survived after all and made it to Cairo, then it was William's turn?"

"Don't!" I snapped.

Elliot had no notion of what it felt like when young men looked up at you with anticipation, and several hours later they were dead. James and I did. Australians, New Zealanders, Canadians, Indians, Scotts, South Africans, British, Free French, Fighting Czechs, Jews from Palestine, Greeks, and others. They were a spirited lot. They were young. They wanted to live, wanted to be victorious.

"The Germans were using a dreadful weapon: Shells that exploded several yards above and sent down fragments of hot, burning metal. One such monstrosity got my leg," James continued. "Every night the sky was up in flames, and the air thick with smoke and noise. We had a dug-out in the middle of a minefield the Germans had laid before retreating. Sometime in the middle of it all, I realized that the men were fighting, resolute to fight until death overcame them. There were men and there were supplies. I don't know if there was enough of either to overcome the Germans and the Italians." He raised himself up and leaned over the table. "One scrawny chap showed up with a piece of shrapnel embedded in his eye. He stood before me, covered in mud and blood, 'Palestine' hardly visible on his epaulettes. He was young and undersized. He asked me how long would I need to remove the metal. I said twenty to thirty minutes. He waved his arms to reject treatment. Instead he asked that I numb the pain. He said: 'Twenty minute's too long. They can still use me out there; my post is unmanned. Just give me something that'd numb the pain. Will you do that for me?' That's what he said, and that's what I did. That's what I damn did! I put drops in his eye. He ran back to his post. Such a scrawny man. When he ran across the minefields, he was as a boy running between rain drops. Except the drops weren't rain. And he got hit. They shelled him. He was only a driver. But the post was unmanned, so he took over. He was a driver, and the bastards shelled him. There wasn't much that was left of him. There wasn't much that was left of any of them."

When we left the hotel, traffic was heavy.

Barely able to tolerate our slow progress, Elliot observed a tragic camel cross the road, tufts of hair, long lost, exposed patches of scaly, dry skin. "Amazing," Elliot murmured, eyeing the camel with awe.

"What's amazing?" James asked.

"The size of it!"

"It's nothing unusual. It's a small camel when measured against its kind," James commented.

"No, no, not the camel! Look at its willie! It's grand!"

"You're mad, you are," James snorted with laughter.

"Completely dotty," I agreed.

#

"Elliot," I breathed, staggering into Elliot's room.

"What is it?"

"James..."

"You didn't tell him anything, did you?"

"No, of course not. Elliot, I don't see how this can remain quiet. Don't you think we should tell him? He keeps asking after her."

"How did you avoid an answer?" Sullivan asked. When in Ma'adi, Sullivan made it a habit to visit us, and to reassure us that he continued to search for Salomé.

"Well, what do you mean?" I asked Sullivan. "Are you looking for her? I'll just step out and see."

"Clever."

"Yes, clever, but not good enough! It only bought me another hour or so, I suppose."

"I'll tell him."

"I don't see how keeping this secret protects James."

"William, you recall how he acted when I asked what happened to the Iraqi boy..." Elliot stopped, frozen into his chair. He stared, horror struck, at the doorway.

I turned to look.

Leaning against the door, James' tall, thin body took shape. "Naji," he croaked, "was taken away by a rioting mob, and I never saw him again." He lit a cigarette and stepped into the room, then thick smoke came out of his nostrils. "Where is she?"

#

Now there were four of us searching for Salomé. Elliot, James, Sullivan, and I looked into Cairo's charities, orphanages, social service houses, clinics, public gatherings, and even mosques, churches, and synagogues. Two weeks passed, but our search was fruitless. Sullivan's leave came to an end, and he bid us farewell.

August ended and September brought hot dry winds. Feeling the strain of the search, Elliot suggested that Salomé was gone from our lives forever. So, I confronted my father.

"How much do you know?" Father asked.

"Quite enough. What I need to know now is why was she here? And who brought her here from over there? And where is she now?"

"Señor Marcelo rescued her. His was the role of a transporting agent." Father tapped his pipe, and then continued to pack tobacco into it, carefully and meticulously. "I agreed to keep a child here, until the war was over. I did not know that the child was a girl. I only knew that it was a child. And that was all that mattered. Your mother, however, objected to having a girl here while you and Elliot," he sighed, "while Elliot's in residence. She worried about Elliot though I believe that now she is worried about your attentions to the girl. At any rate, Señor Marcelo could not shelter her. He is a war correspondent. His duties take him to places a child cannot follow. Thus far, he has been to every port city from Beirut to Tripoli. Earlier in the war, he was in central and eastern Europe."

"Father you..."

He was digressing, but I clamped my lips shut.

"Señor Marcelo's already aware of this."

"Well, what's he doing about it?"

"I haven't the slightest idea, William. And I cannot offer to help your search, either. You must not bring attention to yourself, and our association with the girl. Take care because information in the wrong hands, William, could be fatal to Señor Marcelo or our family."

Checking my temper, I asked, "Father, is someone after her? After you?"

"The war is not over yet. Señor Marcelo and I," and in an afterthought he added, "and our organization, are still involved in several missions. They are arrows against...but..."

"Our organization? Father what organization?"

"No, William. The less you know, the safer you are." He fixed me with a stern gaze. "And, I want you to be careful. The child is out of our hands now. But this should help you along." A folded piece of paper came into view. "Now, if you don't mind, William, I'm rather busy."

Shutting the heavy door behind me, I left Father alone in his study. In my hands, I clutched a copy of his journal entry for December 9, 1941, a peculiar account of Salomé's arrival at our estate written in the third person! But the note could not 'help me along!' It gave no additional information, nothing useful, except as a tool to eject me out of my father's private study so he could quietly go to Mena House Hotel to

236

meet with our Prime Minister and the President of the United States, business as usual.

Chapter 26: Suk Ballads

CHRISTMAS of 1943 was fast approaching. Tom Sullivan and Bill Tate were training in Palestine with the SAS. My brothers and I once again walked out of the same horrific tailor shop, after getting fitted for suits for the upcoming parties of the new year.

"The devil take the filthy man and his garlic oil," James swore darkly. "Why do we go to him? There're plenty of other tailors in Cairo."

"Mother."

"Do we have to please her so?" My question surprised my brothers.

Elliot worked on a response when James coughed out, "I better explain this to you both," he began. However before he could shape his next words, Faraj emerged from his shop.

"*Marchaba!* Hello. *Bonjour, mes amis!*" His welcoming ceremony in three different languages herded us into the depths of his shop.

I caught Faraj observing Elliot, a minute scrutiny full of compassion, maybe remorse, too. Then it was over and Faraj and James settled for a brisk game of backgammon. They tossed the dice and blew on them for good luck, shuffling disks rapidly, hands and minds flying to and fro.

"So, my young Elliot, have you found your Lady yet?" Faraj asked.

What Lady? Salomé? A fleeting, frantic thought gripped me. Surely not!

Elliot shook his head in the negative.

"He's still searching." James looked up from the board momentarily to examine Faraj's expression.

"Did you follow up on the rumors I mentioned? Did you go to the village up north, Elliot?"

"I did."

James intervened. "She'd been there. She deals in eye ointments. She sells noxious salves to the poor fellahin as a cure for trachoma. But it's a scam. Trachoma is a bacterial infection of the eye. The ointment is nothing more than a bit of petroleum jelly and scented oils."

"You don't know that it's a scam. The ointment works!"

Faraj sighed. "She is just like her grandmother. Aziza the Beast had a fountain of such ideas."

And as Faraj's voice rose in praise of the Beast, James' last piece landed into the long row of pieces already out of the board.

"It's only the first round!"

"Yes, only it would have to be next time my dear Faraj. We promised William a ride to his hospital," James made our apologies.

Faraj waved his arm and a waiter materialized with a wooden crate of wine bottles. "William, you take this to your boys in hospital. And have a happy holiday! *Inshalla*, you will visit me again soon. With God's will, you will come again."

"Thank you," I shook his hand.

James held out his hand. Faraj drew him close and held his hand for a moment in a strong clasp and managed to whisper in his ear while James smiled.

Elliot reached to shake Faraj's hand, but the latter pulled him into an embrace, and kissed both Elliot's cheeks while holding his head in his large pudgy palms and it seemed like much more affection and mutual understanding was passing between them than a simple embrace.

Walking to the car, I asked, "Does Faraj seem to you quieter somehow?"

"Quieter?"

"Where are the chuckles and gurgles and claps? Where's the happy satisfaction? He doesn't do all that anymore."

"No, he wouldn't," Elliot agreed sotto voce.

And suddenly I suspected that it had something to do with Lady Jane, the beautiful woman whom I had not seen since our last meeting at Faraj's inner sanctum.

A Cairene diva ululated seductively on a popular wireless show. Her anguished wailing rode the flutes and violins reaching an orgasmic crescendo. The sounds echoed from shop to shop, and off of the stone walls.

"Look at that barber." James' chin jutted out.

The mustached barber serenaded with the radio diva, snapping his fingers. His head swayed with pleasure while his scissors and combs protruded from a pocket sewn to the front of his apron and jingled in disharmony.

A client sat patiently waiting for the barber to finish the job.

But the barber waved a hello, a cigarette between his fingers. Undisturbed, his suk ballad and dance continued, his client clean forgotten.

Elliot turned to James and picked him up, singing with the barber and the diva. He looked into James' eyes, as the latter fought Elliot's arms round his bottom.

James was writhing with shame. "Quit manhandling me. You're mad!"

I put down the heavy wine crate as a memory flashed across my mind: The Beersheba carpenter and his menagerie of clients and their daily performance. What a collection of crooners! And here in Cairo, more crooners ululating in such a raucous clatter, desert and pyramids looming in the distance. "I shall only love you once more tonight," cried the singer, the barber, and Elliot. And I could hear the Beersheba carpenter and his entourage echo their words with, "All night, with no day, my dove, she who holds my soul captive." Oddly, even James' cries of, "Let go of me," were quite fitting. His anguish, a parallel reflection of my own need to escape Beersheba, Palestine, Egypt, or even myself. But here I was with my brothers in Cairo and just now, my brothers and I were together: Not entirely happy, certainly shattered, but together, bawdy and ridiculous.

#

"Westbrook, you better deliver these to your boys."

"On my own?"

"Your brother phoned yesterday and sent his compliments and apologies. He cannot help us today."

"Elliot?"

"Yes, Elliot."

"But he planned to help me deliver the Christmas gifts and food parcels. I haven't seen him for a few days but that's not that unusual. Damn him. He offered to bring in entertainment from his club."

"Not today. Mr. Elliot Westbrook could not come. Madame Sukey will be taking his place, I suppose, but she has not made an appearance yet."

"Then, come with me, Mrs. Wright," I urged the nurse. "I don't want to march in there on my own."

"Of course. We'll grab Lady Lampson's British Red Cross Committee parcels too."

240

"What about the mail?"

"It was such a job sorting it all!" she replied.

"I've been on leave only for the summer but I have not quite settled into a routine yet."

Mrs. Wright looked up. "Westbrook, I've been here all along and there are days when I feel a bit out of place, out of sorts. Cheer up, it's Christmas." Her arm flew to my shoulders in a rare show of warmth.

The patients and staff were enjoying food and fruit, even fresh flowers, paper streamers, canned bear, and stuffed olives. And by midday, more crates of oranges and boxes of nuts and dates arrived from local organizations while Madame Sukey's and Faraj's wine stole the show.

Chapter 27: News from Palestine

LIKE a tyrant, the sun lingered in the sky to set everything ablaze.

"William, over here," James opened the gate. "Long day?"

"Not too bad. What's this?"

"A letter for you."

"Kelly Evans' still in Palestine! His letters are droll. You'd think that a successful journalist would master the art of letter writing! Here, I'll read it aloud." I directed James to a bench.

"My dear William,

I'm awfully busy in Yagur. I must have mentioned that the shores of the Mediterranean Sea are not far, a trek through fields and orchards. The foothills of Mount Carmel are beautiful with early blooms. Kibbutz members are a swell bunch. Their idealism strengthens their souls and hands. There is so much to do, to build, to plant, to grow, to reap. There is much work, but not enough people and not enough food. I drink weak coffee or tea for breakfast and hit the dairy farm. And, by noon, when my hands begin to shake with exhaustion and hunger, a comrade arrives on a buggy to take me to the communal dining hall. Lunch is generally home-grown vegetable salad, a slice of toast with margarine frugally waved in the air somewhere above, and another cup of weak tea. Certain days, we're allowed to have an egg. As you must remember, Palestine has two meatless days. In the Kibbutz, we are lucky to have two meat days. The youngsters jest, then penitent, they work harder after they rant. Watching Yagur's youth, I regret that you are away. You ended up in Beersheba. How did you ever escape the clutches of the graveyard lunatic? What did you call him, Coleridge's Mariner? And you, the Wedding Guest?

Will it surprise you that I am learning Hebrew? The tutor is a severe specimen. She pulls her hair back into a silvery ball at the top of her head. Her posture is like that of a bantam cock, complete with impatient expletives. And her eye-rolling when students stutter their answers bring to mind your infamous 'Cook.' She's Elsa.

Elsa habitually enters the classroom after dinner with a slice of toast impeccably wrapped in her handkerchief. She rests it on her desk, quakes 'open and read page seven,' then walks out to gossip with the gardener. She returns thirty minutes later to rush through the last fifteen minutes, explaining pronunciation in heavy Slavic accents. When her forty-five minutes of class time are up, she quickly unwraps her hardened toast, and begins to chew. Anyone seeking help with the lesson risks toast shrapnel ricocheting head on.

Well, I've had it! So, last night, while Elsa gossiped outside, I unwrapped Elsa's toast, brought it to my lips, and took a sizable bite, classmates cheering. I wished that I had a fat worm to place atop the leftover bread!

Once back inside, Elsa finished her 'fifteen' and reached for her toast. After one look at the mess that I left, she marched out, yelling in Russian 'hooligans.'

William, come to Yagur. Bring Elliot, too. This is the Palestine you should have experienced. Impatiently awaiting your reply,

KE."

"I cannot see Elliot in a Kibbutz, can you?" James commented.

"They'll send him packing once they realize just how much he eats!"

"And drinks. Your Evans never mentioned alcohol."

#

Little did I know as I was reading Kelly's lively letter that I would be receiving a telegram from Palestine only two days later as 1943 was ending. Again, James met me at the gate.

"William, a telegram. It's for you."

The message was from Kibbutz Yagur but signed by a stranger.

Kelly was dead. He was killed on duty. His grave was in Yagur. Kelly's kit and articles and books were left to me. Kelly had wished it so.

His hand on my shoulder, James was silent. He must have known all along because he gently drew me to him, his clean scent of freshly laundered linen filled my nostrils as he rested his smooth cheek on my head, his strong arms enveloping me.

#

"You'll write when you find her," I whispered to Elliot.

"I'll phone you." Elliot bid me farewell and reminded me not to worry about my leave from hospital. "Father took care of it. So, you can be easy. Fulfill your promise to a friend and come right back home, William."

Elliot had driven us to Cairo's Central Station and helped with my kit. James purchased my ticket. But when the Haifa Express departed, I realized that all three of us barely accomplished what Kelly had managed alone. We lost my hat. James queued up twice to barter with booking clerks in Arabic, French, and English about the validity of my travel papers. And Elliot ran into trouble because of his parking spot.

Chapter 28: Yagur

1944 burst on Tel Aviv's shore with rough seas and unsettled skies.

Warring thoughts about Kelly Evans, his unpublished work, and the time I was taking away from Cairo, from hospital, and away from my search for Salomé slashed at my conscience.

Where was Salomé now? She must be alive! But how can I be certain? And Father was vague about Salomé. He had offered no help. Why not?

"Where the hell are you?" I growled into the wind and hearing my own voice jarred me back to the stormy Tel Aviv shore.

With a secured ride to Yagur on the following morning, I hired a room for the night. Now, marching doggedly along the Mediterranean Sea in the rain, I hoped to avoid pestering prostitutes and to be left alone with my thoughts.

But there were three figures huddled close to the thrashing sea. Whores? In this weather? Tel Aviv's sandy beach had become an extension of Jaffa's vices.

Two soldiers haggled with a woman. The soldiers had military rain gear. The raindrops rolled smoothly off of their shoulders, and there was no visible shiver to their stance. They had boots, too. And, they were going to go someplace dry, although overcrowded and loveless.

I glanced at the arguing trio.

One of the soldiers shook his head, probably in an attempt to be rid of the ice that stuck to his hair. But his gesture reminded me of Kelly Evans when he had shaken flies out of his hair on the Haifa Express. And I knew then that I would publish Kelly's work, come what may.

#

Jostled on a lorry to Yagur, Kelly's words reverberated in my head: "There are forces at work in Palestine cooking up a witch's brew."

A witch's brew it was indeed! A powder keg would also fit the bill.

January 1944 was an awkward time in Palestine. The threat of a Nazi attack subsided after the Allies' decisive victory at the battle of el Alamein and the successful march to Tunis. Now, anxiety ran rampant over British blockade on immigration into Palestine.

Zionists opinions were divided. Some erected colonies on lands they had purchased from local Arabs. Some Zionists actively joined the British cause and supported the British military offensives. Jewish men and women, fluent in European languages, joined British special forces behind enemy lines. At one point, there were thirty thousand Jewish men and women from Palestine as volunteers in the British militia.

But heavy tidings from Europe, fueling the need for a homeland for Jews, also fueled two factions of Jewish organizations to launch attacks on British police in Palestine, aiming to gain recognition and British support for a homeland. Though while the British were fighting the Nazis, they would not attack British militia.

Clambering out of Tel Aviv northward along the coast, the lorry lurched and swayed. Next to crates and sacks, a lugubrious passenger shared my narrow bench. He was thin and in ragged clothes. One of his cheeks was bruised and as the road got worse, he clutched his lower back.

From Tel Aviv to Haifa, the roads were in good condition; the British military forces saw to that. But north of Haifa, the lorry rattled over potholes. The whipping wind too became sharp and cold.

The thin man groaned as the driver pulled to a sudden stop.

"Which one of you is British?" the driver asked in gruff Arabic, popping his head out.

"I am."

"*Shu esmach?*".

"William Westbrook.

"William? Good! I need you to talk to the British MP. My English is poor, and there is often a check point on this road. They always give me a hard time. By the way, I am Jacob. You can sit in the cabin now."

His request seemed odd. He spoke English well enough when I had first met him at the Tel Aviv bus terminal. Nonetheless, I obliged.

A young woman climbed out as I approached the cabin. She was Jacob's daughter.

"Plenty of room here... for all three of us," I offered.

The daughter looked at her father questioningly.

"It's more comfortable here. Stay," he agreed.

Squeezed between daughter and father, I silently watched the road. The woman sat pressed against the window, clenching her teeth. Much like the chap in the back of the lorry, she slumped, exhausted.

"Jacob, do you live in Yagur?" I asked.

"Yes. You?"

"Cairo. I'm here to collect my friend's belonging. Kelly Evans."

"I met Kelly Evans. Elsa quit teaching because of that wild American. He caused a bit of a stir in the kibbutz."

"Do you like living in a kibbutz?"

"I love it. But, life's hard, especially in the Galilee region. It's harsh. I lost two sons. One died at an early age of malaria and the second son died a month before his eighteenth birthday, in the same struggle that claimed Kelly's life."

"What struggle?" Suddenly, the brief telegram phrase, 'killed on duty,' made sense.

"Syrian men attacked Yagur. Kelly was on night guard."

"Why were you attacked?"

"They came at night, you see. They struck hard, killing indiscriminately, then dispersed. So, you ask me why? I don't know!"

Just then there was a loud bang, and the lorry shuddered. The driver gripped the steering wheel and eased the machine to the side of the road.

"What's the matter?"

"*Pantcher!*" Jacob growled.

"Puncture," I corrected his pronunciation when I saw the flattened tire. "Do you have a spare?"

"Yes." Jacob handed me his wrench. "Here. I'll get the spare. You can unscrew the bolts." Then he turned to his daughter. "We will stop here for a while. There are bushes if you need to..." Jacob pointed to a patch of low-lying bushes off to the side of the road.

A slow smile was the daughter's only reply as she headed to the vegetative cover. Then she paused, her gaze falling on me.

"Go ahead. I'll help Jacob grab the spare."

The tired-looking chap had somehow disappeared.

"Where's the other passenger? The other man..."

"Who cares?" Jacob grunted again, and pulled and tugged at his crates, looking for his spare. "He'll turn up soon enough."

By the time we replaced the tire, the sun set. Squinting ahead while clutching the steering, Jacob commented, "We'll arrive before seven. There should be some scraps left to eat."

I was anxious.

Jacob's daughter was fidgety.

Suddenly, a beam of light flooded the road.

"Damn it!" Jacob cursed.

"They're still here?" his daughter gasped.

The brakes smoked malodorously as they let out an eldritch screech, stopping before concertinaed wire that slunk across the road.

Three men in khaki uniforms and red berets appeared. Two of the British MP's approached with their Tommy guns and a torch.

"Good evening."

"Good evening," I replied.

It now became clear why I was sitting next to the driver.

"Your papers."

I handed over three identification papers, one greatly different from the other two.

"Have you any other passengers?"

"No," I replied. The lugubrious man was gone. Had he fallen out?

"What are your names?" The MP kept asking questions, while his comrades reviewed our papers and checked our names with their lists.

"What is your destination?"

"Yagur."

Jacob and his daughter remained silent and motionless.

"Yagur? What have you there?"

"Look," I said, but Jacob cleared his throat as if to remind me to be polite. "A friend. My colleague asked me to pay him a visit."

"Your colleague?"

"A journalist."

The officer wanted to continue, but his comrades nudged him. "Mr. Westbrook." The officer returned our papers. "You may go."

Jacob did not need the command repeated and sped off.

Soon, twinkling lights shone as we approached Yagur. And an interesting surprise awaited me. The thin man reappeared when I went to get my kit. I opened my mouth, then shut it, and let the fellow be.

"You are not going to the graveyard right now. You have to get something to eat and then you stay in my house." Jacob put a rough hand on mine, extracting my holdall.

His daughter and the other passenger hurried off to a cluster of shabby tents.

"In the morning, I shall take you to Kelly's..." Jacob promised.

248

#

At the communal dining hall, Jacob ladled soup, fished out a fried egg, and scooped some salad. He even produced two slices of toast. "It's not much, but it tastes good." Then he nodded and pointed at a leathery, middle-aged woman seated at a table near the kitchen window. "Chava says she's met you before."

Noticing the familiar long silvery plait, I exclaimed, "Chava? The historian?"

Jacob nodded.

"I must say hello!"

"William," Jacob held me back. "She's had a bit of a shock."

Putting one foot gently before the other, I approached Chava. "Hello again," I said, softly.

But when Chava turned to face me, I gaped in astonishment. "Chava, what's happened to you?"

Chava smiled a crooked smile. "I'm fine, William. Just a minor incident."

"Minor? Looks like you were hit with hot oil!"

"I was. I'm better now. Are you staying? Do you have a place for tonight?" she asked, putting her hand on my arm.

"I'm staying with Jacob. He drove me here."

"Tomorrow, William, bring your kit over and stay at my house."

#

The following morning, on our way to the cemetery, I inquired about Chava.

"Chava lost her husband the night Kelly was killed," Jacob rasped. "And her son was recently imprisoned by British authorities for smuggling weapons."

At Kelly's grave, flowers had recently been planted alongside his tombstone.

"Pretty flowers."

Putting his hand on my shoulder, Jacob whispered, "Rakefet."

"I beg your pardon?"

Instead of answering, Jacob leapt from rock to rock, then called, "Shlomo, how do you say...Rakefet in English?"

"Cyclamen!" A deep voice resonated from the gorge below. It must have been Shlomo's.

"How?"

"Cyc-la-men."

"Cyla...cyca..." Jacob waved his hand in dismissal and returned. "Did you hear him? Well, good. Cycla...err...is our..." he groaned and, exhausted, bowed his head. "Well, we like the Cycla, and we liked Kelly. So, he gets the rakefet." He had his palm over his eyes, shaking his head. He was sorry for Kelly. He was miserable because Kelly's stone was inches from his son's. Then he handed me a smooth river rock. "William, put this on your friend's stone."

"What's this?" I asked, but then noticed several similar little rocks already on top of Kelly's grave.

Jacob was now at his son's tombstone, placing his own pebble and wiping off dirt from the grave.

Chapter 29: A Lorry to Acre

"KELLY'S friend?" A weathered man spoke in deep, low voice. It was difficult to determine his age because although his skin was leathery, his movements were agile. "You are a doctor, too?" he rumbled, an apple firmly clasped in his hand.

"No, I mean, yes. I was Kelly's friend, but, no I am not a doctor; I have not finished my studies."

"I'm Shlomo." He wiped apple remnants from his hand, then clasped mine.

"The voice of the cyclamen in the graveyard."

"Right."

"I'm William West...William. Did you know Kelly?"

Shlomo's reply rolled out after a long pause. Apple bits in hand, his mouth full of somewhat processed fruit, Shlomo conversed in an odd mixture of Arabic and English. "I knew Kelly. I knew him well." He lowered his eyes and continued to chew, albeit without the initial gusto and joy. "I grieve his loss. Kelly loved life. He was an excellent man. His jokes, no one understood, but everyone loved his gestures and his tales about Egypt and his Australians and the doctor. You? William?"

I made no reply.

"You are Westbrook, so you should know that he told us great things about you! He held you in high regard."

"Nevertheless, I am not a doctor. I studied medicine, true, then war broke out and I joined the rescue units in London. In Egypt, at the military hospital, I picked up skills and duties as they came along."

"Tell me, William, was there really a second bullet hole?"

"So, Kelly told you about that?"

"He...Kelly had asked me to contact you 'just in case.' And who knew? Who knows even now?" Shlomo deposited the apple core, little more than a handful of seeds attached to a stem, in the bin. "I sent for you. I have Kelly's belongings...his writings...I gave him my word to keep everything until you came. And here you are."

"Kelly left it all with you?"

"All of it. 'Westbrook would know what to do,' he'd said. He trusted you. So, you stay with me. Kelly did. He had his chores and training, and even those Hebrew lessons. But at night, he typed. 'The noisiest manuscript!' I'd called it but he called it 'Mandate Palestine.' It sounded good. Is that what you are going to do? Finish Kelly's work?"

Slowly, I tipped my cup of tea and sipped. How was I to answer his question?

Shlomo scanned the hall. "William, I have to ask... I have to ask because it is my son. Orie. It's Hebrew for 'my light.' He came into my world and brought light into it. I had lost hope in this vision of settling our ancestral land. Then I got Orie." Shlomo paused, marshaling his thoughts. "Orie is now in Acre. There's a crusader's citadel in town, serving as a British prison. Yes, Orie is incarcerated, and he's guilty as charged."

"Oh?"

"My son smuggled weapons, British weapons, into this country, and that's against Mandate law. Orie resisted arrest. Worse yet, he's cheeky."

"Cheeky?"

"Perhaps his behavior eases his shame. Our native youngsters are brash. At any rate, the guards won't let me see him. I go to Acre. Almost every week, I get denied a visit. I stand by the fence, and I look in. I get to hear that Orie is alive, but only just. I get to hear that the conditions are atrocious. But I never get to see my only son. I have no one else but him."

His rough fingers ran through his hair. "Maybe, if the guards see an English doctor, maybe...they'll allow you to take a look at our boys. Tell us what they need. It would help the boys...to know that someone cares. I know that Orie would appreciate to hear of you, Kelly's friend, from the others because he was close to Kelly. We are applying pressure for better medical services, but the process is slow." Shlomo then admitted, "William, our kibbutz doctor is too old for the drive. We could use a handsome young doctor here."

"When is the next expedition to Acre?"

Shlomo misunderstood my question. He leapt up, spilling tea. "Kelly's friends are grand! Chava! When are we going to Acre?"

Emerging from the depths of the kitchen with a ladle dripping potato batter, Chava replied, "In two days."

#

The north of Palestine was rural and hilly with cold nights that left a halo over the rolling hills. It was not a quiet place. Songbirds and roosters raised hell. Shrieks of laughter and some shouting resounded from the children's dormitory. And, as I approached the dining hall to take breakfast, clanking pots and loud voices drowned all other sounds.

By midday, sweat trickled into my eyes in a steady stream. The blisters on my hands oozed. I had little experience in farm labor, yet I volunteered to clean out the cowshed. Why?

A bovine eye stared at me. The gargantuan creature was chewing its hay, apathetic.

"William!"

"Over here!"

"Lunch!" Shlomo delivered me back to the communal area. "Why were you working in the cowshed?"

"I best earn my keep."

"You came for Kelly's manuscript and you are my guest. Leave farm labor for someone else! I'll have a word with..."

"It's all right, Shlomo."

A labyrinthine web of paths lead from one bungalow to the next, looping to the communal showers, dining hall, library, and meeting hall. Hills surrounded the kibbutz. Rocks and boulders strewn across the foothills testified to the harsh terrain the earlier settlers overcame.

When the Muslim cry for the midday prayer reverberated, my thoughts wrenched to Egypt, to my family, and Salomé.

As Shlomo and I entered the dining hall, he asked, "The delegation to Acre sets out tomorrow. Are you still up for it?"

"The kibbutz doctor has proper credentials."

"He also has severe arthritis. Besides, you are British. You can ask them to improve conditions in the jail, as a British citizen."

"I wouldn't count on it."

Then Shlomo hurried energetically to the kitchen, shouting, "Kitchen duty for me!" as if he had not labored since sunrise.

How bad could Acre be? I had never been to a jail before. Elliot had. And he had not enjoyed his stay.

After dinner, a Russian love song in guttural Hebrew penetrated my thoughts. Glancing up, I saw Chava and her comrades dancing, weaving through the dining hall. As they passed by me, a strong, callused hand clasped my arm, forcing me up. I was running and skipping, frantic to keep up. I stumbled several times, and people nearby toppled over one another, negotiating the strain, the imbalance, and the dining hall furniture. But to my surprise, the dancers kept on dancing, laughing. And even the elderly had joined the string of people, throwing caution and arthritic pain to the wind. And then it was over and most went back to their noisy chatter or bid goodnight to their comrades.

#

"It was good of you to join the dance." Chava's wide smile soon vanished by another jolt to her spine as the lorry hit a pothole.

"I had very little choice in the matter."

"It's just as well. Don't worry. Dancing in the dining hall is rare these days." She reached for my hair as the lorry's laborious trek down the mountain road thrusted her closer. She tucked the loose strands behind my ears, then combed my hair with her fingers, a soothing, comforting gesture.

Chava's son, Ami, was caught in the same raid that snagged Shlomo's son, Orie.

#

A hanging was scheduled so all visits were cancelled. The kibbutz lorry turned back with its disappointed cargo.

I looked at Chava, then at Shlomo, and I recalled commiserating with the parents of soldiers. I remembered the military hospital, and the stretcher parties, and the post that arrived from England, Australia, New Zealand, South Africa, India, from all over the world, for Christmas, for the sons, brothers, husbands, daughters, and wives lying or working in a dusty hospital, a world away. Every Christmas, I looked at a pile of mail sent to soldiers. Some packages remained unclaimed; their recipients dead or captured or missing. I had wondered what on earth I was to do with the mail. And now I saw Chava's grief, etched into her scarred, yet handsome face, and I convinced myself that I should do one thing to ease this mother's anguish.

I placed my arm round Chava's slumped shoulders. "I'll offer to join as an assistant to the medical officer...just for a bit. I'll see what I can do." I could not believe my words.

254

Chapter 30: Acre

OFFICER Morrison eyed me askance. "Your papers?"

Sir Niles Westbrook meant nothing to him until his superiors entered into the discussion, and I was, however reluctantly, signed on as assistant to the medical officer in Acre.

Kelly's manuscript on hold, I began work, protracting my stay in Palestine. I telephoned Elliot who, although appalled at my choice, assured me that he and James continued to search for Salomé.

And as the cobblestones wobbled under my feet on my way home one evening, my thoughts drifted to the infirmary in the citadel's northwest wing. Although on the second floor, it was damp. Plaster peeled and grit, hair, cobwebs and the previous flaking paint showed through the recent whitewash.

On my first day, I saw a boy from Haifa. Beaten and arrested at a local riot, his wounds grew septic. But my ministrations came too late. Today, when I called for the removal of his body, I learned that he was thirteen.

Late afternoon shadows over the jutting eaves cast a somber aura on my path.

A procession of gray donkeys clambered up the alley. Climbing in single file, tails swishing and heads bobbing, the donkeys persevered. Hessian sacks full of grains and spices hung on the donkeys' strong backs.

Is Nick Bottom all right? And following that thought, Salomé came to mind...

"Hey, you there. Stop!" A soldier thrust his hand to my shoulder. "It is you!" His accent betrayed his nationality.

"Sullivan!" I choked with surprise.

"William!"

"And where's Tate?"

The long pause and the pain in his eyes told it all.

"Gone?"

Sullivan nodded, his lips compressed.

"I'm sorry. But, look here, you never wrote me about it."

"Wouldn't have been a cheerful note, now, would it?"

"No. Does Elliot know about it?"

"Yes. But how have you been?"

"Back in Palestine, as you see. And now I'm working at the prison, as a medical assistant."

"William, you can't be serious! What about the girl?"

"Elliot and James." I headed to the seawall.

"You certainly have peculiar jobs, Westbrook. Does your mother know about this one?"

"No, and I won't mention it to my father either. Though he's probably already aware of it. I had to mention his name a few times to get my way."

"Last time you were in Palestine, you worked with a journalist."

"He's gone, too. Killed while on guard duty in a kibbutz."

Sullivan's slanted blue gaze drifted as the sky became streaked with shades of red and pink.

"I'll need a holiday soon enough." I leaned against the gritty seawall.

"And I'll accompany you."

"I hoped you'd say that!"

"I'm a driver now. Temporarily, but good connections with other drivers will get us places."

"Sullivan, they'll call out Otzer soon. Here's my address. Visit me as soon as you can." I threw my arm round him. His tall friend was gone. I wondered what had happened. I grieved his loss as I watched Sullivan shuffling away. His weaponry and other contraptions jingled. His heavy boots dragged a little, scratching the old stones.

#

Next day, a prisoner contracted typhus. Fearing the worst, a typhus outbreak, we immediately removed the infected man to a quarantine station in Haifa. An American missionary group promptly arrived, immunization and prayers for the Muslim and Jewish inmates at the ready.

Orie, Shlomo's son, was in solitary confinement when the prisoners were inoculated. I noted his absence in Orie's file and informed the medical officer.

"Let that fellow rot," he replied. "He's a nuisance."

Orie tormented his guards. He chanted ceaselessly some hellish ululation, nasal yet metallic. And as he caterwauled, Orie's eyes shone, a gargoyle-like grin etched across his thin face.

There were also the night calls. Orie felt obliged to disturb the guards, even at night, and for no reason at all. And so, his pranks earned him frequent solitary confinement.

#

Acre, a fishing town north of Haifa, was among the oldest inhabited cities of the world, dating as far back as pharaonic times. It overlooked the harbor, fatigued. Vendors, pedestrians, domesticated donkeys, and feral cats swarmed the streets. And the port hugged dilapidated vessels, shriveled fishermen toiling onboard.

Acre was also a Mandate stronghold. The prison was set up in the citadel, in the Old Town. The British Constable took over several other Ottoman structures. And military barracks and training bases spread out nearby.

On a blustery evening, my landlady, exuding garlic and fried sardines, met me at the bottom of the stairs. Unabashed, she produced a letter, edges frayed.

"And it appears that you'd already opened and read my correspondence. Yes?"

She was young and agile, and she clung to every opportunity to collide with me on the narrow landing, press me against the wall with her breasts, turn her face up to me, and simper.

Was she going to ravage me?

Quickly, I thanked her and sprang away.

The missive was from Elliot.

"Dearest William,

Greetings.

Our dear old James rescued Faraj today! A mob blasted into Faraj's shop, shouting insults, kicking and breaking things, and all on account of Faraj's religious beliefs. James muttered, "Cowards," and, before I knew it, he fired a few shots at their feet.

Did you know that James has been carrying a neat little revolver?

Mob scuttled off in a frenzy. One of them, however, lingered to draw a short dagger. James took two unsteady steps and with his walking stick brought the vandal down in an instant. The ubiquitous Jamal dashed

257

forward, knocked the fellow out with a well-placed kick, and removed the last rebellious miscreant from the shop.

I hope Faraj is not going to get in trouble with the Egyptian police. Lately, there have been vandal attacks on non-Muslim property with little interference from the law.

But, the devil of it all, William, is that Faraj's good spirits burn eternal. Faraj ordered tea and sweets to be left outside for the vandal. James asked our friend why the good gesture. Faraj replied, 'I am only human.' A pleasant twist to this popular sentiment, if only more of us were 'only human,' don't you agree?

No news regarding the girl. We put in a word with local clergymen. James reckons she sought refuge in a religious institute.

Ali continues to deny any knowledge of her whereabouts. Do I trust him? Only time will tell.

Monnayeur's is doing well. Gleeson's men frequent the place. They are not all officers but they behave themselves.

Be gracious and write,

Elliot

#

On my tenth day at Acre, I witnessed a hanging.

The room was whitewashed with narrow slits for windows. The size of the apertures was a precaution, but against what, or whom? A marking in chalk on a wooden trap door indicated the precise spot for the condemned to stand. A heavy beam hung above, a massive, immovable bit of lumber.

The condemned man shuffled slowly before a guard. With little time to contemplate, he was quickly led to the platform. A police officer confirmed the man's identity. Then, the warden read his sentence, fast and efficient.

My mouth was dry. Cold sweat dripped along the sides of my face, down my temples.

The trap door opened.

But the hanging was not over.

Although convulsing, the condemned man was not dead. Not yet.

I turned round and wretched hatefully, shudders of revulsion wracking my body.

Afterward, I decided that I must get Shlomo's son out of jail and quit Acre myself. Vomit still souring my mouth and gut, it was easy to convince myself that getting Orie out of jail was the only ethical thing to do. And why was I, a Westbrook, son of Sir Niles, here?

The warden correctly surmised that Orie was a ringleader. Now that the discord between British personnel stationed in Palestine and local Jews was mounting, law enforcement became stricter. Would not Orie's sentence change for the worse as soon as the warden tired of his antics? And would I be able to watch him falling forward and down, rebounding and jerking, slowly dying bit by bit while the warden, the guard, the Northern District Commissioner, the medical officer, and I stood watching?

Shlomo's son deserved a better death.

#

On the following day, Orie slumped into a chair in the hospital wing.

"What do you do when you are in confinement?" I asked him in Arabic.

The guard shifted uneasily. "English. You need to speak..."

"This man does not know any English. How else will I communicate with him?" I lied. Shlomo had already informed me that his son spoke several languages. English, Orie spoke particularly well.

"Nonsense. They all speak English. They..."

"I won't have you calling me a liar."

The guard jutted out his chin.

Head bent down, Orie asked, "Why am I here?"

"A journalist in Egypt used to play Stretcher Racing in hospital." Had Orie recognized Kelly's story?

Although howling in pain, Orie remained seated as I attended to an abscess on his neck.

Disappointed at Kelly for keeping quiet about 'Stretcher Racing,' I started draining the puss. "Calm down. It's for your own good, you know."

Orie squirmed with pain. "That's what you would say! Why not leave it alone?" he asked, his Arabic guttural and harsh.

I turned to the guard. "You there, hold this fellow down. I can't have him wriggling."

The guard's beefy arms held Orie in place.

Speaking Arabic once again, I said, "I'll tell you about my friend to ease your pain."

"I doubt that," was Orie's surly retort.

"My friend played tricks on his teacher, Elsa. He took a bite of her bread..."

Orie was aware of this tale. Kelly's biting into his Hebrew teacher's slice of bread must have left an impression. He paused long enough for the guard to become suspicious.

"What's this?"

"I told him that you'll shoot him if he howls again."

"Just the antiseptic to the infected area now. Here's the bandage. I'm through. You may let him go now."

"*Shukran...*" Orie rasped, his cries of pain silenced. Then, as the guard turned his back, Orie's lips moved, "Kelly? William Westbrook?" And for the first time since I met him, Orie smiled; not the travesty of a grin he kept while tormenting the guards, but an almost boyish smile.

He was now aware of an ally.

"*Aywah!*"

That evening, shocked, almost breathless, Sullivan banged on my door.

"Is something the matter?" I asked, pulling Sullivan inside. "Tea? I'm brewing up tea to fend off the cold. Is something the matter?"

"No, it's just that in your Egyptian mansion, you would have three or four maids serving you tea, with cakes and sandwiches! And you'd be wearing a proper suit, polished shoes, and perfectly combed and pomaded hair."

"It's not a mansion, is it?"

"It is."

"I never thought of it that way."

"You wouldn't. You grew up there."

January ended with swathes of rain drenching the North. Wisps of breath laced the icy air as we spoke in the frigid room. Without any source of heat, but the smelly kerosene stove, the walls remained damp, and we each wore two military blankets draped over our shoulders.

"Well, I don't have cakes or sandwiches, or three or four maids to serve you here but tea is ready. I left my suits safely in Cairo but here, put this on." I handed him another blanket. "Are you all right?"

"Yes, of course." Two raindrops ran down Sullivan's nose and onto the floor. "Look here, William, right as I walked in the building, your landlady caught up with me. She pinned me to the wall!"

"Damn her."

"She demanded to know where I was going so fast and ogled me all the while, I half expected her to reach into my trousers and grab me with her sticky cherry jam-smeared hands! What sort of a place is this? Is this a brothel? Are you living in a brothel?"

"Would I live in a brothel?"

"I don't know! These days, it's like falling through the Looking Glass. Everything is so queer now. Sons of Lords run round the desert with hand grenades and Lewis bombs and here you are, Sir Nile's pampered offspring putting up in a damp hovel and toiling for a jail quack!"

"Sounds rather awful now you put it this way." I grinned, then gave an inward groan that sounded out. "But who's the Lord with the hand grenade?"

"Lord Jellico, of course."

"Oh, him. He was with the SAS, was he not?"

"Special Air Services, yes, but now he runs the Special Boat Services, SBS. But enough about him. You look cold, mate."

"This room is close to the seawall. During a storm, I can feel the waves pound the rocks. I'm surprised the wall is still in place."

"Well, cheer up, mate. Never-mind the seawall and that jam-sticky landlady of yours. You wanted a bit of holiday, and I got approved for leave! Where are we going then?"

Handing Sullivan a mug of tea, I breathed, "Excellent!"

"I'll stop by camp in the morning to see if anyone is driving up or down the coast. Do you have a preference? North or south? Have you made any plans?"

I shook my head.

Sullivan held his cup with both hands. "Tate always wanted to go north, to the mountains. A skier."

"Skiing in the north's perfect. But, Sullivan...Sullivan...I need your word...that whatever I am about to tell you will remain secret."

261

Chapter 31: Broken Skis Broken Men

SULLIVAN'S eyebrows furrowed. "What are you on about?"

"Do I have your word?"

"Come now. You have my word, of course, but what is it, mate? Is it something to do with Salomé? She's some lost barbaric princess, or something?"

"No, not Salomé. I have no news of her. But there's a chap in prison...I'd like him to accompany us."

Sullivan's squinty blue eyes trained on me.

"I've been wracking my brain, trying to come up with a plan to get him out. And tonight, you show up..."

"You are not thinking of the medical officer, are you?"

"Good Lord, no."

"I'm not too keen on the guards, either, mate. They're a burly lot. Just now two of them chased me through the alleyways, for sport!"

"Most certainly not the guards."

"So, who's accompanying us?"

"Orie."

"Don't tell me. I can see it clearly. A prisoner!"

"Yes."

Sullivan whistled. "Oye mate, are you sure about that?"

"Yes. He's a prisoner all right."

"Be serious."

"I am."

Sullivan shrank back.

"I need your help. I need a lorry and a driver. But it is your choice, of course. Just say the word and you need not be involved. But before you decide, I'll explain. The plan is simple. Toiling for a jail quack, as you put it, has its privileges. And before I go on and tell you about my involvement, and whether you choose to help or not, I must ask you to swear to secrecy."

"Westbrook..."

"Give me your word."

"You have more than my word, damn you," he sighed, his boyish face suddenly alight with mischief, his eyes glinting under thick eyelashes. "When?"

"Tomorrow."

#

Driving rain pummeled Acre that night and through the following day. Crashing waves sent bits of sea foam inland across the seawall. Shivering in the gusty wind, I stood outside the Citadel's sloping rear entrance, and waited.

"What a wicked night," the tall guard complained, his thunderous voice echoing the storm. He looked like a Viking warrior, of great height and massive shoulders. And his voice was as loud as a foghorn.

"Newly arrived? You've been here no more than a couple of days, yes?"

The Viking nodded.

"Welcome to Palestine. Winter storms can be brutal. Especially in the northern reaches. And none of the structures are equipped to handle low temperatures and stormy weather."

"What about him?" the Viking asked, pointing at Orie.

Now supine on a stretcher, rain pounding on his shut eyes, Orie gave a moan, then fell silent.

"Should we get him out of the weather?"

"I doubt that anything we'd do for him now is going to help. Typhus, you know. This poor chap should have been inoculated with the rest of them."

Taking a step back, the guard asked, "Was he not inoculated?"

"No. The Americans claimed that everyone was inoculated, but this man was in solitary confinement."

"So, it is typhus."

"With text book symptoms. Look here." I pointed vaguely at Orie's wet blankets. "Here is the rash. He complained of headaches. Add his high fever and the list goes on. Look at his shining forehead. He's burning up. And the relentless moaning." As I spoke Orie put on a convincing act of pain, twitching and moaning.

"Is the medical officer joining us?"

"Not he. He's busy. Probably reluctant to come close to this one."

"Is it," the Viking paused then added, almost with a shudder, "catching?"

"Yes. I rang the Warden earlier and he agreed that I should remove the inmate to the quarantine station in Haifa. I've got the necessary paperwork filled out."

The Viking rubbed his nose. "Christ! Look at that seagull!" A large bird hovered in the air over the sea, struggling to get to safety. "It won't make it, I tell you. Damn it, where's the ambulance?"

Just then, an ambulance wound its way south, toward us.

"Ease him into the back. Then I want you to hurry back inside and disinfect yourself. Soap and hot water. Take care," I ordered the burly guard. "This is not trivial. Typhus is not to be toyed with."

"I am to accompany you, sir. These are my orders."

"Well, if you must. Just do me a favor. Don't get too close to him and, for God's sake, don't forget to disinfect yourself."

We deposited the stretcher in the ambulance, a dilapidated armored lorry.

"You best sit up front with us," I instructed the Viking.

"Thank you," he was pleased to avoid sitting next to the typhus case.

Finally, the ambulance departed in an unsteady forward lurch, a white cloud of burnt petrol fumes trailing behind it.

"You'll have to make the drive back on your own, you know," I told the guard.

"Sir?"

"My holiday started today. I'm doing all this as a favor to the medical officer. The driver knows to drop me off at my hotel in Haifa."

"That's lucky!"

"Yes."

"Will you be staying the entire time in Haifa?"

The giant Viking was only making small talk but I wanted to talk as little as possible about my adventure. "I'll be in Haifa and possibly go into the countryside." And pulling out the official papers from inside my jacket, I perused Orie's file.

At the quarantine station, I roused the night attendant. "The patient was an inmate. I need signatures and assurances that proper precautions are going to be made."

"Certainly. But why did you not ring me in advance? I could have been better prepared."

"It's an emergency."

The attendant, still sleepy, replied, "Yes, of course. Bring him inside."

On a rolling metal bed, Orie was now mumbling, as if delirious. The rain had kept his face wet, giving the impression that he was feverish and sweaty. His beard, too, helped his disguise. Behind bushy whiskers, his face looked thin and sunken in.

"When will they clean that wretched place up? This is not the first typhus case we've had this year from Acre," the attendant complained while I filled out the last of the questionnaires, and signed at the bottom.

"That's the lot, then. Good night." I nodded to the Viking and the two of us walked back to the ambulance.

#

Crates of bully beef and tea, our army staples, rattled in the back of the lorry. Sullivan, Orie, and I were on a night convoy heading north to Beirut.

"I say, William, I can't quite believe it," Sullivan whispered. "We pulled it off."

"The Viking, I mean, the guard, gave me a quick nod of farewell outside the hotel. I expected him to be inquisitive and ask a lot of questions."

"The rain must have finally broken his vigilance."

"I'm sure you're right because he just did as I instructed. Sullivan, how on earth did you find the clinic in the rain? I could hardly see a thing."

"They didn't make me a driver for my good looks, you know."

"What good looks?"

"Shut up. I have good night vision, and I can find my way out of a maze in the dark. Besides, I've visited the fishermen's quarters in Haifa before. I know the area like the back of my hand. Took the kid a while to show up, though," Sullivan said, grinning at Orie.

Orie's eyes widened. "I left my bed as soon as the curtain was shut. And I found the exit in no time. Well, there was a little delay..."

"What?"

"The sleeping guard was in my path, snoring. He blocked the back exit door. I had to blow slowly and lightly into his ear to get him to change his position without waking him up," Orie complained, scratching his now shaved face and tugging at his neck tie, readjusting his coat jacket. "Westbrook forgot to mention a guard in the rear of the facility."

"There wasn't a guard when I last visited the station. And I took care to observe the place as I had already begun planning to remove you from Acre. When I was at the clinic, I saw the rear exit, the garden, the back alley, but never was there a guard. It must have been a measure of precaution on your behalf."

"Did they know to expect me?"

"No."

Sullivan stared in alarm. "No one saw you?"

"No one saw me leave."

"Are you sure?" Sullivan asked, worried.

"I'm well trained. You and I were not seen together, and we will not be seen together in future. By the way, there's a road block on this stretch of road, did you know that?"

"Will they stop us?"

"It's possible."

Sullivan looked out the back flap of the lorry, sticking his head sideways, trying to glimpse the road ahead. "No sign of it yet," he reported, and returned to his seat. "Where did you learn English?"

"School," came the muffled reply as Orie wedged himself behind the crates and the back of the lorry, turning invisible.

#

Before noon on the following day, Sullivan, Orie, and I rode to the topmost peaks of the Lebanon in a maintenance vehicle with a plow on the front. The recent winter storm was over, but the mountain road was impassable for a taxi.

Winding up from sea level through orchards of olive trees, the notoriously hair-raising mountain road extended upward, horribly upward, evergreens and frozen cascades defying the steep slopes.

"Don't look down."

"Why?" I asked.

"*Presque perpendiculaire,*" Orie quoted an old record of a traveler's description of the road.

The account was true.

"I'd stayed here before the war," Orie said. "At a hotel called Mon Repos. It is nicely set in the mountain. Sullivan, you do know that we usually play this Bedu game with a knife!"

"Yes, only it's my fingers spread apart, so content yourself with a knobbly stick. I won't have a sharp knife flashing between my fingers while traversing the Great Lebanon on a *presque perpendiculaire* road!"

At the top, Orie jumped off and dashed inside the hotel. When Sullivan and I followed a few moments later, we paused.

"Mon Repos has changed," Orie remarked, crestfallen.

"Rundown and overcrowded." A thought flashed, and I blurted it out.

"You may stay here," the desk clerk drawled, chest protruding one way and buttocks another. "But you pay in advance."

And that was how Sullivan, Orie, and I went marauding for beds, linen, and a room.

At breakfast next day, I glanced at Orie's wan face. "How do you feel about joining us?"

"Oh, I will ski!"

"Are you fit?"

"I'm fit enough, my good doctor. A miraculous recovery from typhus!" He flexed his muscles. "I'll ski for a bit then melt away. It's a rare chance for me. And I do have to stay out of the country for now. The kibbutz would be searched. So, we may as well enjoy ourselves before we part ways and you and Sullivan return south."

And true to his word, Orie marched us up the mountain. Within two hours, when we were amid the Biblical cedars of the Lebanon, he trilled, "Ski time," checked the leather straps of his long narrow wooden skis, and plunged headlong in the snow, knees slightly bent, legs spread apart, and jaws clenched, closely followed by Sullivan in a similar posture.

When I saw him next, Sullivan stood poised above a snow gulch. Poles held tightly, he pushed off, letting loose, airborne and vulnerable. Soon, Sullivan was a rolling bundle of fabric, snow shooting out from under him and a wooden ski landing upright, meters away.

"Sullivan!"

On his back, legs up and head resting on down-sloping snow, Sullivan groaned.

"Anything broken?" Orie's voice came from between the trees as he popped out with a shower of snowdrift.

But Sullivan stared uphill, opened his eyes wide as he cried, "Watch out!"

Skiing at unchecked speed, a bright red mass croaked in French "attention!"

I sprang to pull Sullivan out of the way, but not fast enough. And as my poles tangled with my skis, the Frenchman collided with me.

Silence followed the impact, with a brief flash of hope that I would soon see those I loved. When I came to, my head throbbed. Muscles shaking, my body began to register pain.

"William," came a distant cry.

Orie swore while rubbing my body, checking for any broken bones. "Where does it hurt?"

"All over."

"At least that damned Frenchman went into some fantastic parabolic flight and is now motionless. Serves him right, the bastard!" Sullivan grumbled.

"No, he's coming to," Orie reported. "And with such language!"

The Frenchman was muttering a litany of obscenities that hung over his laboriously retreating form.

Orie asked softly, "William, shall I take you to the hotel?"

"It's cold and dirty inside. No, let me have a rest and I'll get up soon enough."

"Look," Sullivan complained, displaying the ripped leather straps of his skis. "I cannot ski."

"Nonsense. We'll get you another pair at the base."

#

Watching Orie's face pucker as he slurped the remains of his dinner put a smile on my face. "Bravo. And you may have my bowl of soup, too."

"Dinner at Mon Repos is bad but certainly an improvement over the food and ambiance in Acre. So, thank you both."

Sullivan slid his bowl toward Orie with reverence.

Orie's efforts reminded me of Salomé's efforts to eat Ali's hellbroth. "Good Lord, how can you tolerate it?"

"*Kolboyneek.*"

"What's that?"

"A *Kolboyneek* is a container in the kibbutz dining hall for leftovers."

"So, you're a well-trained disposal container," I choked as Sullivan snorted with laughter.

"I'll take you to Yagur, Sullivan. But tonight, I'm going north."

"So soon?"

"It's best if I keep out of Palestine for a little while..."

And so Orie quietly slipped away while Sullivan and I lingered at the bar.

"Is it the fruit machine you've been staring at?"

Sullivan nodded.

Unfortunately, there was a contingency of British soldiers by the machine arguing with the owner. They'd won, and he should hand over the winnings. They showed the owner the three plums in a neat row. No, he would not pay them a shilling! The soldiers cheated. No, they did not. Yes, they did. He had proof. Proof? What proof? They were not cheats, simple as that.

"Better wait this one out, Sullivan," I advised, recalling Cook's interminable sparring with the maids. "They'll be at it for some time."

By the following evening, Sullivan and I had settled into another military convoy going south, back to Haifa.

"Tom, you and Bill Tate saw me on a train to Palestine last year. Did I ever tell you why I joined a journalist in Palestine?"

"No. We did wonder though."

"The girl we looked for in Cairo..."

"I knew it!"

"What?"

"You love her."

"What?"

"At least one of you loves her. Why else go through all that trouble? But you are English, so you will never admit it."

"Sullivan."

"It's you, isn't it? You are in love with her! I should've guessed, because it could not have been Elliot, no not he. And James gives the impression of a monk!"

"Damn."

"Well?"

"After the Blitz, I left London and returned to Cairo. Then, I met a girl. She was terribly thin, so she looked like a little girl. But she was fourteen, or so. She may have been older. But because she was so very thin, she resembled a girl child." I lit a cigarette then drew on it. "I certainly saw her as a child, at first. But then something changed. I did not want to get involved, certainly not with her, not with some maid working on our estate."

How was I to explain the predicament to an Australian?

"But she was special. She wore Egyptian robes, but she wore them like a European, stumbling on the hem. She found solace in an old donkey and befriended a white mongrel. She always returned a favor, and she never begrudged my absence even when I was needed. She picked up homeless children in the suk and tried to help. And, yet, I saw her as someone I must never love."

"Pretty?"

I nodded.

"Did you...?"

"I couldn't resist...She was lovely. Elliot called me an ogre; can you believe him? Afterwards, my attraction for her only intensified, so I left for Palestine. You and Tate met me on the train."

Sullivan whistled softly.

"I missed her terribly. In Jerusalem, I could barely sleep at night. Then I returned to Cairo only to see her a woman...Stunning in every way. Well, the next day, she disappeared..."

"Remember James' reaction?"

"How could I forget!"

"He was livid with Elliot."

"I cannot blame him, can you?"

"No."

"My brother tried to protect James."

"Typical."

"Typical? How do you mean it?"

"Well, isn't Elliot the protective type? Won't he try to protect people he loved?" Sullivan stopped abruptly and bit his lip. "But, here, William, why are you here now? Why Palestine?" His tone was firm and abrupt.

"I couldn't bear to stay in Cairo. Then Kelly died. I had to return to collect and publish his work."

"Why?"

I smiled at his intense expression. "Why what?"

"Why did you have to return to Palestine and collect and publish Kelly's work?"

"I promised that it should be so."

"Must it be you? You, who is so very important in Cairo, in hospital?"

"I can't think of anyone else who understood Kelly's viewpoint better. Can you?"

"Are you going back?"

I had not yet decided what to do next. Why did I come to Palestine? To gather Kelly's kit? To publish his work? "Back to Egypt?"

Sullivan nodded.

"I haven't decided."

"Orie is remarkable," Sullivan commented, lighting a cigarette.

"I'd say so."

Sullivan sounded his careless laugh, his freckles disappearing into his laugh lines. Then, awkwardly, he flicked away his cigarette.

Watching Sullivan's guileless smile, I understood that he approved of all that had come to pass.

"It's like in a fairy tale," he blurted, watching his smoldering cigarette roll on the dirt road.

"What is?"

"I'm leaving a trail behind." His intense slanted eyes watched each discarded cigarette drop to the road. When he reached the last cigarette, he stood up, hanging onto the metal frame of the lorry. He lit his last cigarette. But Sullivan soon slumped against the metal, his eyes welling up with tears.

"What is it, Tom? Is it Bill?" I asked him.

Sullivan gulped. "I want him back."

"I know, Tom."

Chapter 32: Nevertheless

THE little bungalow was in shambles.

"Shlomo, what happened?"

Shlomo stood amid the wreckage of his bungalow, hands stretched in resignation.

"Why is the furniture upside down and broken?"

"Just a few days ago, William, they burst in here," he explained, using 'they' to indicate British policemen. "They searched my house. They looked for Orie all over the kibbutz grounds. Where is my son?"

"He escaped?"

"Yes." Shlomo shook his head, casting glances at the bits of broken armchair and its side table. "William, are you all right? Jacob told me that you came from the north road, from Lebanon, in a military lorry."

"I'm returning from the Lebanon. I came to collect Kelly's belongings. Acre, well, it's not my line of work, you know."

Dolorous, Shlomo agreed.

"It's going to be all right. Orie will turn up. Your son is resourceful and well trained." I held his gaze then reached for Shlomo's shoulder and patted it.

"What would you do with Kelly's..."

"Kelly mentioned a trusted editor in America. I want his work published. That's why I came here. I am bound by my promise to Kelly."

Shlomo's lips were a grim slash across his rugged face.

"Of course, I'll first review the material and ascertain that it is free of sensitive information. I would not want this to happen again," I remarked pointing to the broken furniture strewn about.

Shlomo shuffled to the bedroom. "William, in here." He crouched and wrenched at a floor joist. Soon notebooks and papers and photographs came into view, stacked in a neat pile at my feet.

"That's quite a lot."

"Yes. I had to keep it secure. One never knows when the British will drop by for a visit."

"I dropped by for a visit."

"William," Shlomo's words were choked with emotion.

"I won't betray you, Shlomo."

"I know, I know." He patted my back. "At the onset of war, I signed up to join the British army, but they sent me away. They told me that I was too old. Called me Uncle! Uncle?!"

"Shlomo?" Chava's voice drifted inside.

Shlomo ran his sleeve across his eyes. "Don't tell her I cried. She fusses. Women, you know." He then raised his voice, steadying with every word. "Here. Inside. William Westbrook is here."

Chava greeted me warmly then asked, "Would you stay for dinner, William?"

"Thank you but I must return to Acre. I want to learn what happened. And a lorry going to Acre is leaving soon."

"William is leaving Acre."

"I thought so. It's no place for someone like you," Chava reached to clasp my hand, gazing with understanding at me. She then inclined her head toward Kelly's belongings. "You'll take care of his work?"

"I will."

"Take care of yourself," Shlomo managed.

"And thank you. It was kind of you to look after our boys," Chava added.

"Chava, your son is fine and should be released before the end of March. And there are several organizations now that will look into conditions at the citadel. I saw to that, at least. The American missionaries in particular promised more inoculations and visits."

"William." Breathing my name, Chava pulled me into an embrace. "Take good care of yourself and come back." Chava released me and was now busy adjusting my jacket.

Shlomo squeezed my hand.

"Shalom."

Oddly, as Chava spoke, I felt that I wanted to stay, like a child clinging to his parents.

#

"Westbrook!" the warden's grainy voice summoned me to his office where the interrogation commenced.

Expecting something of the sort, I was ready for his questions.

The patient had fallen ill the night I was scheduled to go on leave. Coincidence, I insisted. "He belongs in quarantine, not out on the streets, roaming, infecting others."

The investigating officer eyed me with mistrust. "No doubt."

"The prisoner fell ill..."

"But they were all inoculated," the officer cut me off.

"Not he."

"No?" asked the warden.

"Confinement. It's in his records. Of course, I checked because of the prisoner's condition..."

"Where did you take him?"

"The patient was delivered to the quarantine station in Haifa."

"Who can vouch for you?" asked the officer.

The warden's eyes left me and fell upon the officer, "Westbrook left the prisoner with an attendant in Haifa, at a clinic. One of my guards accompanied Westbrook. You've already questioned him."

Unsatisfied, the officer peppered me with more questions.

I stuck to my story. I went to Lebanon. I went skiing with a friend.

The warden and the police officer quickly wrote down Sullivan's name, and with regret I realized that Sullivan, too, would be questioned.

Throughout the interview, I made a nuisance of myself. I insisted that conditions in the jail must improve. When the warden dismissed me, shaking his head, he sighed and murmured, "Westbrook."

In a hurry to sort out Kelly's papers, I rushed home, running up the steps two at a time but on the landing my landlady had me pinned to the wall. Her breasts pressed against me, one hand held out a letter and the other was holding on to my lapel. Her hands smelled of garlic and jam, and for the first time I noticed that her palms were sticky. So, Sullivan was right after all about the jam. But how did he specify cherry jam? Then, a flitting thought of revenge crossed my mind as my hands almost went to her bottom but I shuddered with disgust.

What would Elliot think of her? How would he describe her and in what awful tones?

Reeking of kerosene and garlic, bosom heaving and lust glinting in her eyes, my landlady finally relinquished the letter never missing the opportunity to run her hand against my body, bump her pelvis and breasts against me. She had opened and read the letter, I was sure, because there was no envelope.

274

The missive was from Elliot.

"W. Head to Jerusalem immediately. Urgent family matter. Meet me at the King David Hotel on the last day of February," Elliot wrote.

Could it be that he had found Salomé? A flicker of hope warmed me but I quickly extinguished my dream. Elliot would have mentioned such news.

It was mid-February. Good. I wanted to quit my work in jail. Now, I could explain to the warden that my brother would be in Palestine within days, and my departure would not appear so abrupt; especially after Orie's escape. I would show him the missive. And for once, I was grateful for Elliot's enigmatic ways.

Chapter 33: Jerusalem Revisited

IT was in a narrow, winding alley that I saw him again. Ducking into a doorway, I pressed hard against the wooden door and held my breath, listening to his footsteps.

My pursuer paused then edged slowly, closer to the crumbling brickwork of the house, probably cursing the dripping wash-line overhead. He stopped as he approached the bend in the alleyway, considering his options.

Taking pity on him, I popped out. "You can't follow a chap discretely in such flamboyant garb!"

Startled, Orie raised his hands.

"*Salam aleikum.*"

"I have been looking for you."

"Should I be flattered? Here, walk with me."

"You aren't in Acre."

"No, I'm here. The Holy City called me back. You know, it is incomparable to any other city that I had ever visited. Tell me, have you called your father? He was in a right state."

"I sent word. He knows that I'm alive and well. When did you see him?"

"On my return from the Lebanon, I stopped by to collect Kelly's work. Are you sure that Shlomo is at ease about ...?"

"Yes, yes, quite sure. William, what plans have you for Kelly's notes?"

"Publish his work, of course."

"Of course." Then Orie requested that I hand over the manuscript. "I'll publish it for you," he promised.

"Has liberty shifted your interests to prose?"

"You have already read it. Haven't you?"

"I have. No wonder you would like to, eh, publish his work."

Kelly's accounts of kibbutz life included references to clandestine activities and forbidden drills of the Haganah in Yagur.

Ignoring my cynical remark, Orie looked about him. The alley was filthy and it reeked of urine. "Why are we in this smelly alley?"

"I use it as a shortcut to my hotel."

Orie's adjective of the alley was short of the mark. This disgusting path defied almost everything that was charming about Jerusalem. Throughout the city, a cool, high-altitude breeze carried a Jerusalemite mélange of smells of brewing coffee and fresh-baked breads with oregano, fried fish, animal waste, rotting vegetable matter, and, alas, burnt petrol and other noxious fumes. This alley boasted rot and sewage hovering low in the dark, narrow passage without the cool breeze.

"Not very safe."

"No doubt. But see here, Orie, what are your motives?"

"Motives? Westbrook, I serve the Jews of Palestine and of the world."

I was silent. I was curious about Orie's motives for taking over Kelly's work. But here Orie was prepared to indulge me with a comprehensive lecture.

"Jews need a homeland."

"Well?"

"Kelly and I joined the Haganah. A defense force. Recognized by the Jewish Agency as such. William, like it or not, you too are already in."

"I have explained my position to your father..."

Orie waved his hand. "You've read quite a bit about us. I've no idea why my father let you do so, considering that he knew nothing of your daring activities. But he firmly believes that the British are our allies. I do too."

"You spent months in a British jail! You cannot expect me to believe that."

Averting his eyes from an unsightly pile of rubbish, Orie picked up his pace, giving me a light touch on the arm, hastening us both away. "You are ignorant of local history, so I forgive you calling me a liar! The Haganah evolved from the Jewish Legion, one of the Great War legions within the British Army. The Jewish Legion fought alongside the Allies against the Turks in Palestine. Jews living in Palestine trusted that the English would make better lords than the Turks. The general opinion held the British as civilized, trustworthy. In 1914, Hashomer, or the Watchman, was formed as a defense force of volunteers to protect Jewish settlements from retaliation by the Ottomans."

"Were the Ottomans so very bad?"

"Ottomans took vengeance on Jews assisting the British. But Hashomer also defended against Arabs taking advantage of the weakening defenses of Jewish settlements here. In 1917, the British government declared Palestine as a future national home for Jews. The Declaration was accepted by the United States, France, and the Arab peoples through a special Treaty of Friendship drawn up by T.E. Lawrence and signed by Prince Feisal on behalf of the Arabs. Two years later, however, Hadj Amin el Husseini was appointed 'Mufti of Jerusalem.' The British High Commissioner, a British Jew, Sir Herbert Samuel, appointed him. But instead of improving relations between the Arab and the Jew in the Middle East, matters turned from bad to worse. Jewish settlements in Palestine needed to re-establish a defense unit."

"The Mufti's a religious fanatic."

"Or just another politician."

"But he wanted to restore a Muslim caliphate over the Middle East."

"And so he does still. So Hashomer became Haganah after the Arab Riots of the 1920's."

"Kelly called the Arab Riots a massacre."

"It was. Well, clearly, we needed protection. Haganah means defense in Hebrew. But Palestine is under British rule now. And British regulations prohibit such organizations. So, the Haganah is an underground organization."

"Underground defense?"

"Yes. You know about that bit." He smiled but continued doggedly. "Then Nazi Germany invaded Poland in 1939..."

Here, I held my arm out to Orie. "I'm aware of recent events."

"I apologize. I wanted to be thorough, for a change. We never talked much, not about this."

"Go on then, but walk a little slower, I need to catch my breath."

Orie paused, casting a jaundiced eye over our alleyway. "Well, Westbrook, it was when Europe cowered under the Nazi war machine," he resumed with spicier metaphors, making me smile despite the gravity of our conversation, "that Britain fought Germany when all odds seemed to point to a Nazi victory. England alone, now led by her determined Prime Minister Winston Churchill, remained opposed to German aggression. And this is precisely why the British are my allies."

"There are others opposing Nazi dominance."

"Partisans, yes, but not as a formal, unified government. Anyway, regarding Palestine's position, the Mufti of Jerusalem joined forces with Hitler. Are you aware of that?"

"Mufti's in Berlin now."

"Westbrook, before 1940, the Palestinian Jews put together a Jewish Legion to aid the Allies. Over 30,000 Jewish volunteers from Palestine joined the British militia and are now serving side by side with the Allied Forces. The Haganah provided the majority of the volunteers."

"What do you know about the German work camps?"

"Work camps?" Each syllable came out with extreme effort.

"Orie?" I reached out to put a hand on his shoulder because his face turned deathly pale.

"How could this be?" he hissed. "Mass extermination of Jews, and other minorities I must add, throughout Europe! Modern, enlightened Europe! Up until Montgomery's victory at el Alamein, residents of Palestine were concerned with an attack on Palestine. Now we are sending our best boys and girls into Europe."

"And into British buildings in Palestine?" I challenged.

"I detest the sabotage attacks on British interests in Palestine! But since the later part of 1943, at least two other underground organizations want to move things faster."

"Why?"

"To urge the British government to establish a Jewish home in Palestine, or at least to allow refugees to disembark at Palestinian ports."

"Like the SS Patria?"

Orie looked away.

"What of Malcolm MacDonald's White Paper of 1939?"

Orie let out a growl. "The White Paper." He spat. "Such a stab in the back! The White Paper limits Jewish immigration into Palestine. It makes land acquisition nearly impossible. We understand that the British are trying to gain Arab support. The Arab oil is valuable. I understand. Nonetheless..."

"Arab oil is much in demand."

"Oil, land, crops, and more! But, why does it have to be at our expense? Well, we supported England, and we will continue to do so. As our leader says, 'We will fight the war as if there were no White Paper; and the White Paper as if there were no war!' As long as Britain fights Hitler, we support Britain and fight alongside the Allies."

"And when the war ends?" I asked. "Who would control this land? If the Allies win, what will happen if the British were to relinquish the land as delineated in MacDonald's White Paper? And what if the Germans were to take over? Oh, here we are! The hotel."

"Westbrook, what're your plans for Kelly's articles?"

"What have you got in mind?"

Orie glanced at the hotel's reception hall. "I am..." he began, but fell silent as a group of young women, well-dressed, scented, and chatty, appeared. Orie was dressed in the Arabic style.

"Improperly attired? No doubt. But I am hungry. Have you dined yet? Will you join me?"

"Perhaps another day."

"Don't be an ass. You are well trained, are you not?"

Although both courageous and intelligent, Orie was still a young man, barely twenty.

"Are you really scared of a group of pretty, tittering young things?"

Orie pulled out a white packet and selected a cigarette, unhurried, and deliberate. "Forgive me." Thin wisps of smoke laced his words. "I am a bit on edge. The articles..."

"Let's go inside and order first."

When the waiter disappeared into the kitchen, I leaned back in my chair and watched my companion's narrow, boyish face. "I can see that you're torn between what you want to do with Kelly's manuscript and your inability to force me to destroy my friend's work."

"Westbrook, you are aware that the matter is complicated."

"Complicated is an understatement," I commented. "If Kelly's descriptions reached British authorities, there would be quite a number of arrests and a large-scale raid on a number of kibbutzim. That's why I take great care at hiding Kelly's work wherever I go."

"Good. I am glad to hear that it's safe. And I'm in no position to censure your work. I can, however, make a request. Westbrook, will you go over it all, removing names and places, activities and schedules? In short, weed out all specifics that could lead to an arrest or worse. Here, I cannot make it any clearer, and I dare not ask anything more," he spread his hands in an oriental gesture of good will and resignation. "Maybe delay publication? Will you oblige?"

Chapter 34: A Nightmare

TIGHTENING my jacket against the mountain breeze, I glanced at my companion a day after we discussed Kelly's manuscript.

"You've eased my mind," Orie's deep voice rang.

Behind Orie, a tangle of barbed wire slinked across the street, casting odd shadows as clouds drifted about, letting the sun peek out then screen it from view.

"In his request, Kelly never demanded immediate publication nor did he forbid any editorials. After thinking the matter over, I can do both."

"Thank you. Your brother will be phoning you in a couple of days?" I nodded.

"Will you be leaving us then?"

"Will I be departing Palestine?"

It was Orie's turn to nod.

"I have something that I must bring to closure in Egypt."

"Chava sends her regards." Orie's mouth twitched into a reluctant smile. "Westbrook, I am indebted to you. In the few days that you have stayed here in Jerusalem, you managed to help me again, and it is tremendous help that will have an impact on many people."

"Orie, I only picked up some medical narcotics and sulphonamides from a hatchet faced Bedu woman. Then I delivered the lot to some doctor with strong Germanic accent. Do you trust the ugly griffin?"

"Shareefa, or the griffin as you call her, is well paid. I doubt that she will abandon such lucrative trade. She isn't handling weapons, just medicine."

I paled at the memory of an old woman on the Tel Aviv bus, her silvery hair disheveled, as an English officer arrested her.

"And the doctor?"

"He has good reasons to stay here in Palestine and help us. Personal reasons. He is a German doctor. He had served as a surgeon in the British Army and is now a Haganah member."

"You ask me to make one more delivery and I agree. But I will be leaving soon."

"How may I thank you?"

"Think nothing of it."

After twitching quite a bit, Orie finally managed to stammer, "Well, I'm much obliged."

I nodded.

"So, the Bedu woman is a hatchet-faced griffin. What about the German doctor?"

"A crashing bore. But you know that."

Orie gave a shout of laughter.

"Your doctor operated on patients from el Alamein in '42. Did you know that?"

"Yes, we're lucky to have him on our side."

"He was in Cairo. He worked at the same military hospital as I." I tried to hide the fact that my first meeting with the doctor was a source of annoyance. I remembered how the doctor mentioned, with a sardonic smile, that Rommel's Afrika Korps rattled our boys for some time. The Doctor's words, although meant to be genial, had a deep German ring to them that jarred on my nerves. "He mentioned a New Zealander surgeon who had worked with him in Cairo. The New Zealander went with the Eighth Army to the desert, and the doctor was wondering where his friend was. Orie, in the end, the doctor commented that 'once this terrible war is over, millions of people will be searching for one another.' Is your lot going to do anything about it?"

"Oh, certainly." Orie confirmed my suspicions that the Haganah was an intricate defense as well as political and social force.

A woman leaned out of a second story window. With an infant in her arms, she summoned her son. The boy protested: He did not want dinner, he wanted to play with his friend. The mother insisted: Young Avi had to bid Muhammad farewell for the night, get upstairs, eat, bathe, and get to bed. And, by inexplicable machination, I bid farewell to Orie, returned to my room, bathed and put myself to bed.

I fell into nightmarish sleep.

Cairo: Fellahin working in the fields and pyramids shimmering in the horizon, the bustling suks and dirty streets, our estate's gardens and water channels, Salomé swimming in the wide irrigation canal, Elliot arguing with James in the suk, Faraj's gurgling laughter, and my parents mingling with Egyptian effendis and suave politicians.

I was unable to interact. I reached for Salomé's robes as they filled up with air, cool, wet, and intangible. Then, the girl got out of the water and walked to the dunes. I called my father, asking for his help to get her back. But he turned to look at my brothers in the suk. Elliot and James argued. My father watched them. "Let them work it out."

I wrestled whatever force was holding me back. My father was the only person aware of my existence. But he, too, faded. "Father?"

"No. It's Sullivan," an Australian voice spoke. "Wake up, mate. It was just a dream."

Chapter 35: Awake!

STANDING by the window and silhouetted by the morning light, Sullivan turned, his hands behind his back.

"Sullivan?"

He grinned.

Though a cold mist hung over Jerusalem, I was hot and sweaty.

"What are you doing in my hotel room? How did you get in? I mean, I am glad to see you, but how did you get in?"

"I walked right in. Don't you lock your door at night?"

"I, I must have forgotten." Confused and disoriented, I groaned, "I have to wash up."

Under warm water and gritty olive oil soap, I relaxed. Then, I slipped into a suit. Stepping back into the room, I smiled at Sullivan. "Better?"

"Oh, for a moment there I thought you were Elliot. Dressed in a suit like this, you do resemble Elliot."

I turned to the looking glass.

"I heard from our convict."

"Really? That's odd. The kid found me in the suk just the other day. He didn't mention seeing you."

"Well, I got only a correspondence...He thinks that he's under surveillance; maybe he's not in the clear yet."

"Yes, I thought so. Last time we met I had a feeling of being watched. But I did not say a thing to Orie."

"Maybe you should have mentioned it. By now, the British MP knows that he is not dead," Sullivan continued. "Though, we're okay, somehow..."

"The magic of a title, perhaps?"

"Your father's?"

"Probably. There are times I doubt that they ever believed my story. I'm sorry to have pulled you in."

"It's all right. The cause is a good one, you know. But that's not why I'm here. I have a gift for the doctor." Sullivan handed me a bottle wrapped in brown paper. "It's for pain."

"Yes, I know." I reached under my bed and slipped the narcotic into my leather holdall.

"You know what to do with this gift?"

"Well," I replied with a deep Cockney accent, "'appy fuckin' birthday to me!"

Pain flickered across Sullivan's face.

"What's the matter?"

"For a moment there, you sounded just like... Oh, never-mind. Is it your birthday?"

"Just past."

"Look, there's a lot to tell you, but how about a spot of breakfast? I've got to be off soon. They're expecting me in Latrun."

"In Latrun?"

"It's not far from here."

"Yes, I know, but, Sullivan, Latrun?"

Sullivan put his arm round my shoulders. "Come. I need food."

Outside, a ray of sunlight caught Sullivan unaware, and he shaded his face. I looked at him, admiring the fellow. He was honest and frank, and his gesture to shade his face was representative of Sullivan, a man acting on impulse.

I took heart in having a friend by my side and quickened my pace to match his.

In the old city, we ordered Turkish-style coffee and pitas.

Sullivan sipped and made a grimace. "By heaven, I can't learn to appreciate this coffee. It jars on my nerves like nothing else."

"So, what brought you into my room so early this morning?"

"Aside from your calls for help?" Sullivan appeared rather pleased with his little joke. He stuffed his mouth with pita bread and then sipped his coffee. The absorbent dough sucked the liquid and soon Sullivan chewed nimbly on the sticky paste that formed in his mouth. "One of the blokes in my unit approached me. He gave me such a turn! But I must admit that he was efficient; he went straight to business. He asked me who I was and asked for proof. Then he said that he knew Orie and that I knew him well, too. I asked him, 'Who the devil is 'Oye'?' I was at a loss. Technically speaking, I wasn't supposed to know anyone named Orie. 'I don't know what you're talking about, mate,' I said then took off."

I watched Sullivan endeavor to drink the remaining liquid in his cup without the bread. He sipped and grimaced.

I pushed my plate at him.

"Wretched stuff that is. How..."

"Sullivan, you are in somewhat of a hurry, are you not?"

"On tenterhooks, aren't you? Drink your coffee. It's all right, you know. I won't let you down, Westbrook. That bloke made me realize that he is one of Orie's contacts. He had a message for me, or rather, for you."

"What message?"

"Today you are supposed to meet someone, is it not so?"

"Yes."

"Well, you'll have a luncheon with the doctor. At the YMCA... On the terrace, at noon. You lucky dog! I heard that the food is incredible."

"Lemonade's all right. I don't know much about the food, though. I've lost all appreciation to food."

"Why?"

"Cook. Damn him."

"That ugly horror in your kitchen in Cairo?"

"And everywhere else my parents have lived."

"Something has to be done about that creature! How can you tolerate the maniac?"

A skinny cat sauntered across the pale stone courtyard, nimbly jumping onto a balcony. It groomed itself and then gave a lazy yawn. I begrudged it. I wanted to saunter, too. I wanted to slink from trellis to balcony to roof and worry about nothing more than my next meal and female companions.

"Still, I wish I could join you," Sullivan whispered. "Luncheon at the YMCA."

"Are you getting involved with Orie's band of rogues? I want to strangle his skinny neck now. Is it not enough that I am in it, he had to draw you in too?"

"Westbrook, I came here because I wanted to see you. And if I choose to continue my acquaintance with our old mate or his 'band of rogues,' then it's my affair, just like it was in Acre."

"I am sorry, Sullivan."

"Sorry for what?"

286

"I got you into this in Acre. And now you're still tied up in their raffish world."

"Well, I do make my own choices, you know. I choose this. I'd rather this raff than some other... Don't apologize," Sullivan spoke his last words softly, all traces of temper gone. "I am happy. At least for now." Standing up, he clasped my hand. "I'll be going soon. Back into Europe."

"Back? Sullivan were you in Europe?"

"Termoli," he whispered.

Stunned, I let my mouth open and shut. Rumors of what the Allies went through in Termoli, Italy in June of '43 trickled into hospital, terror and horror for the combined forces on the front line. Was Sullivan one of the few men who survived that horrific landing and the consequent bloodbath? One surgeon hinted that most of the SAS men were blown up or murdered.

"Must be off, Westbrook. I'll write. Cairo?"

"Cairo, yes." I watched my friend walk away. I remembered the last time I had watched him walk away in Acre. Then, the posture was that of a bereaved man returning to his lonely barracks. His best friend had recently died just then, and he agonized over the loss. Now, he had a chance to help a friend, maybe even an entire nation. He slipped from view, erect and determined. Whether good or bad, whether in alliance with his country's political views or not, Sullivan believed that he was doing the right thing.

Was he? Was I?

#

"I am in somewhat of a hurry," I remonstrated.

"Yes, of course, Mr. Westbrook. But you had a visitor today. Your brother."

"That's right. Is that all?"

"Well, yes," the reception clerk nodded, crestfallen that his news came as no surprise.

I had little time to wonder about the clerk's comments. He had seen me walking out with Sullivan and I could only assume he mistook Sullivan for my brother because of our similar coloring. Once upstairs in my room, I grabbed my leather holdall.

Crossing King George Street, to the YMCA, I scanned the crowd. The German doctor gobbled biscuits in the center of the terrace, surrounded by patrons and tables and chairs.

Suddenly, Military Policemen gathered at the entrance to the YMCA. "Damn," I hissed.

Would the MP's conduct a search? Would the doctor have enough time to escape with the holdall?

Then the MP's walked into the building.

Safe for now. I stepped onto the terrace, somewhat hastily. But from the corner of my eye, I noticed a woman wave her hand. I turned, fearing it was a cue for the soldiers to return. But on my next step, I toppled over one of those unsteady round-top tables.

Drinks spilled and glasses shattered. A lady cried out. Her dress was stained. The waiter fussed. An old man in a dark suit yelled.

But I was in a trance.

The young woman put her hand down. She wore a blue wool coat. Her hat had a thin strip of veil round its brim, concealing one eye. Her shiny leather boots peeked from under the white linen table cover.

Astonished, I stared. Green leaves stuck to the sides of the clear glass mug before her. She was drinking mint tea.

She was fantastic.

And I had last seen her leaving our estate, barefoot, and with the hem of her robe splattered with mud. I could still hear the dog, gamboling and yipping at her heels. "Impossible."

I ran my fingers through my hair, fixed my tie, and pushed the leather strap of the holdall up on my shoulder. Then, springing up, ignoring the commotion, pushing chairs out of my way, I scrambled to the beautiful woman.

Her gaze never wavered.

"I seem to make a spectacle of myself every time we meet."

Face upturned, her eyes shone. "William," she uttered my name softly, almost breathless.

A waiter bustled demonstratively, picking up glass shards, clanking with consternation.

Grinning from ear to ear, I drew a chair, recollecting Cook in Cairo, his admonition to Ali about broken glass, and, of course, the wonderful night with Salomé that followed.

"Shards of broken glass, protruding in every direction, you could die out there," I mimicked Cook's outrageous linguistic blend of accented Arabic and English.

She smiled.

"Shards of broken glass..." My heart raced.

Ripples of mirth running through her coat, her eyes fixed on mine.

"You have a lovely smile." This surely was bliss. Had I the right to be so happy? I leaned close and brought her chin up. "I looked for you. Where were you? I missed you." My finger traced her cheek, my lips only inches from her lips.

"William," Salomé whispered. Her English was heavily accented but her voice was clear and composed. "They are watching."

"Who's watching?" I asked stupidly.

"The Red Berets. They are watching us, William." She gave me a peck on my cheek. "Don't look now."

My smile died as my gaze shifted from Salomé to my heavy holdall, the patrons, then the sidewalk, and back at Salomé.

Something was wrong.

Where was the doctor? Why were the patrons so silent?

My mouth went dry and my heart hammered in my chest uncontrollably.

I'd been so foolish. If the MP's conducted a search now, not only would I be arrested, but Salomé would be implicated as well.

I let go of the holdall and looked at the maître d'. His expression went blank and the tall lad stood still.

A company of half a dozen policemen marched towards the café, towards us.

With equanimity, the maître d' raised a hand to halt the advancing men. The café was not meant for their sort, clearly, they were aware of that.

The commanding officer had an immediate reply. "We're conducting a search. Step aside."

Then the maître d''s turn to appear surprised came: A search? Here, at his café? He was beside himself. There went his daily earnings.

The officer, of course, prevailed. "Attention everyone!" he called.

The patrons watched the stout officer.

"Place your bags on top of the tables."

Although putting on a terrific show of hauteur, everyone did as he commanded; everyone, except for me. I remained motionless. Should I run? Throw the lumpy holdall away, across the patio, into the bushes?

An array of purses and briefcases exposed itself to view.

A pale young man in khaki uniform approached our table. Salomé gestured with her hand at the bulging leather holdall. Hardly able to take his eyes off of her, he nodded and murmured an apology. He was a bit confused because of Salomé.

Salomé, calm and peaceful, was remarkably attractive. She could not have any idea that I was carrying medical supplies with no record or permission.

Bilious, I once again recalled my first visit to Palestine. An old woman on the bus to Tel Aviv had been arrested. The MP's found weapons in her bag of vegetables. She'd shouted, Am Israel Hai, impressing Kelly, who then repeated her words, his body rocking back and forth nervously chanting a crude translation of the woman's cry, Nation of Israel Lives, and I remembered the limp dill and parsley bunches on the dirty bus floor and the stunned silence punctuated by the little boy's sobbing.

I closed my eyes.

A zipper opened. The sound of it grew louder in my head. The ripping noise escalated in volume until it exploded.

My eyes flew open.

I resolved to repeat loudly the old woman's cries, because I admired her courage and because I really had nothing else better to say. I did not have weapons in my bag, but I had such quantities of syringes and vaccinations, pentothal and sulfas and narcotics - enough to send me to Acre.

But instead of uttering a loud cry, I choked. Looking at the holdall, the soldier, and the girl, I bit back cries of mirth.

As the unlucky soldier opened the bag, feminine products of the most private nature spilled onto the table and rolled about. Cotton wool and ladies' hygiene paraphernalia appeared first. Rose oil scent and patchouli filled the air as risqué undergarments in shocking shades of red and gold and pink emerged.

The young soldier's pale cheeks reddened, and so did his ears and throat.

Then, Salomé gave the soldier a forgiving smile, as the lad's shaking hands fumbled with more lacy undergarments, rouge and other mysterious cosmetics. He tried to get himself, and the bag, back in order. Again, he mumbled an apology as, hurriedly, he jammed in a packet of pain relief pills and cotton wool into the cup of a glittery bra and his fingers were caught in a tangle of lace that materialized as knickers all twisted round female contraceptives, condoms of every type and color, and some odd little balls that rolled out of a filmy pink negligée that had been somehow clasped to the knickers. Tiny pink feathers now floated above the bag, tickling the man's nose.

When the soldiers were off, all I could do was wonder at the miracle, for it was nothing short of an extraordinary trick...No, surely not divine. Sullivan? Had he the time to meddle with my kit?

I kept silent. I sat by Salomé and drank the familiar sweet mint tea.

When our tall maître d' reappeared, Salomé asked for scones and more tea. Flustered, he nodded and returned moments later with biscuits and coffee.

"The lady had asked for scones," I reminded him. "And some tea."

"Right you are." He withdrew to the kitchen and returned with another plateful of biscuits. A spoonful of jam was heaped next to the rolls.

The search must have rattled him, so, I thanked the fellow, buttering his palms with two pounds and five shillings. He looked at the money, still confused but now with a touch of elation at my generosity.

"You must think me a fool," I spoke quietly.

"Not you."

"Is there no end to my embarrassment?" I realized that before I could find out who had replaced the contents of my bag, I had to explain my peculiar cargo to Salomé. "I must explain, but not here, not now. We have quite a bit to say to each other."

"Yes."

"Let's go then, shall we?" I attended to Salomé's chair.

"Where?"

"Across the street," I replied then paused. "I love hearing your voice." I drew her close and put my lips on hers. With an effort, I pulled away, and she reluctantly let go. I reached for the embarrassing holdall. Then, as if in an afterthought, I tipped the plateful of rolls into the bag. I tossed the holdall over my shoulder and took Salomé's hand

291

in mine, pleased with the electric excitement her touch roused in me, and admiring the firm pressure of her clasp.

Together, we left the terrace. The breeze picked up as we crossed the street and my hair blew about. I felt like a fine chap indeed. I had a sack full of women's paraphernalia and plenty of rolls and biscuits. And, I had my elegant, beautiful woman holding my hand.

#

"Hang on, there is something that I must do." In the dim, long gallery outside the hotel room, I drew Salomé into my arms.

She met my gaze, anticipating.

My hands moved up to the back of her neck and I leaned to kiss her. Her lips parted and her hands reached for my face. I murmured her name. Only a force of nature could tear me away from her again. Her body pressed against mine, she ran her hands up my back, her mouth opening, yielding to me.

Without warning, a door flung open.

"Pardon!" he rasped.

The door slammed shut and then opened again. In the entryway, stood a tall, thin man. His sleeves were rolled up casually, and a soft gazelle-skin belt was tied round his waist, keeping his well-tailored trousers proper. He raked us with curious cobalt eyes, his mouth slightly open, curving up.

Chapter 36: You Go to My Head

"GOOD Lord, it's you!"

"And let's make sure that it's me and you and no one else." Elliot glanced down the hall, then pulled us inside and shut the door. He leaned against the mantle and exhaled his greeting. "William, at last." Elliot moved away from the door and took me in his arms. He then bowed to Salomé, "And a hello to you."

Salomé acknowledged him, a bit flustered.

"It's good to see you. But Elliot, what are you doing here?"

"You expected me."

"I expected you to phone, and not today, Brother, but tomorrow. How long have you been here?"

"Do you mean in your room, or in Palestine?" He withdrew a cigarette and offered it to Salomé.

She refused.

I watched their interaction. "This is too much!"

"Well, isn't it time for a toast? United again, eh, William? Salomé? Shall we head downstairs for a drink?"

Standing still, I realized that Elliot acknowledged Salomé without even a trace of surprise.

"Oh, come now, don't tell me that you two are not elated to have clapped eyes on each other from across the terrace," Elliot exclaimed, putting his hand on my shoulder, and giving me a little squeeze.

Salomé tilted her head, bemused. Her lips turned into a little circle. "Did you plan this together?"

"Certainly not! And I suspect that my brother has had a hand in our affairs and for quite some time now." I turned to Elliot. "Explain yourself."

Suddenly, the reception clerk's comment that my brother popped in for a visit made sense. The clerk had been referring to Elliot, not Sullivan. "Elliot, you altered the contents of my bag. But why?"

"Oh, I do get tired of lurking in the shadows," he admitted. "Shall we have a drink?"

"So, you planned this?"

"The MP's were unexpected. But no harm done."

"MP's?" I eyed him. "Elliot, are you behind my meeting Salomé?"

Elliot grinned.

"Elliot, you're trying my nerves. A simple note: I've found her, would've sufficed."

"But what's the fun in that?"

"Why, Elliot? What do you get out of it?"

"Oh, I don't know," he replied, soulfully gazing at the ceiling, dream-like. "The challenge, I suppose...Getting the pieces together at the right time. And to see my brother topple over that tiny table on the terrace...Oh, dear...casting smoldering glances at a girl, and the twitchy tall fellow cleaning up the broken crockery."

"Were you watching? Do you mean to tell me..."

Salomé's face lit up with a smile.

"It's not funny Salomé. Can't you see? You were one of his pawns too."

"But it is funny, William. That table! Your face!"

Swallowing back a sharp retort that sprang to my lips, I watched Elliot seat himself on my bed and light another cigarette in eccentric sang-froid.

"Elliot?"

"Yes?"

"Salomé and I were not the only pawns in your sordid plot. Who else? Sullivan?"

"Sordid? Hardly!"

"Who else?"

"Sullivan watched over you. And what a remarkable job he did with Orie, don't you agree? But you and he arranged that particular business on your own. Nothing to do with me."

"Who else did you use to set up our meeting? Orie? The German doctor?"

"No."

"Who else?"

"No one else!" he howled then became still and croaked, "Well..."

"What?"

"Two other commando blokes kept an eye on Sullivan. Ever since Tate's death, you know, Tom's been a bit odd. One of the lads is...was

Tate's cousin, on the English, maternal side. So, he and his friend took interest in Sullivan and made him their business."

"I had a feeling every now and then that either I or someone with me was being followed. I assumed that it was Orie. Orie, under some surveillance."

"I would not have left my kid brother in his company if that were the case!"

Salomé quietly watched us talk, her eyes resting on me.

Elliot tilted his head and it was then that I recognized the humor in the situation. Snorting with laughter, I chocked, "Why Elliot!"

Salomé and Elliot joined in.

"You must tell me, how did you pull it off?"

"I am thirsty. Let's go downstairs and I'll talk."

#

"Meat is scarce," I explained dryly as I wolfed down my food.

Salomé quietly transferred a good bit of her portion onto my plate, then offering Elliot the rest.

"Oh, I have long ceased to crave decent food in these parts. What with Cook's parsimony and 'art' and the food restrictions here in Palestine..." Elliot tapped his cigarette.

As Salomé gave a shudder, I erupted, "Cook's an obscenity at the dinner table. Don't mention the horror again. However, while I eat, you can talk."

"I have quite a bit to tell you, William. I reckon this is as good a place as any. But we best keep our voices low."

I nodded.

"I'll start at the beginning. You, William, received an urgent telegram from Yagur. You left Egypt. So now you and Sullivan were in Palestine. James and I looked in vain for Salomé in Cairo. We never gave up, but, by heavens, our hopes faded as time passed. I wrote you about our search. A while later, Father received a telephone call from Acre. The prison warden called to make inquiries about you. He was rather casual, but Father began to suspect that something had gone wrong, that you had gotten yourself into a delicate situation. The warden was singularly evasive about the purpose of his call. William, he called the day you took off to Lebanon, to the mountains. Father phoned the estate. He sounded rather uneasy. James and I rushed to his office. Father wanted to go to Palestine. He wanted to get you out of 'that damned powder

295

keg.' James was against it. So was I. Still arguing, we left the embassy and headed home. But we had another surprise awaiting us at the estate. Ali. The bugger! And he wore such a smug grin...I knew that he was up to something."

"Ali was made guard, William, did you know that?" Salomé asked me.

"Guard? Why? Have you been enjoying special attentions?"

"Not really," Elliot dismissed my question.

"So why did Ali keep watch? Hang on, how do you know?" I turned to Salomé.

"The attentions we had been receiving from Mahmud put Father on edge. Guards assigned by the British embassy were, apparently, not enough. British rule is unpopular in Egypt...Father was on edge, that's all."

"So, Ali?"

"It cost me a pack of cigarettes to squeeze the information out of the rascal. He'd met Salomé, he told me. While we were with Father, Salomé had approached the estate. She now resided in Palestine."

Salomé interjected. "Ali told me that no one was at home. I did not know if I should give Ali my address. He never asked. He just gossiped. I was sorry to hear about your friend, your Mr. Evans."

I still got a shock of pain when I thought of Kelly, his stone in Yagur among all the others and the cyclamen, bowing their delicate pink heads down like ballerinas in a wake.

Elliot continued. "I took the afternoon train to Palestine. I was scarcely a day behind you when you left for Lebanon. I learned all that I could while in Acre and was nearly raped by your landlady!"

"As bad as that?"

"Her garlic and kerosene knocked me out! Lord, I was helpless against her roving hands until they reached my..."

"Elliot," I growled darkly.

"So, I went north. By then, you'd been outside of Palestine for two days, and I worried about catching up with you." He continued as if he never digressed to describe my landlady's indecent scent and tendencies.

Salomé sipped her drink. The lamentable concoction was parsnip wine mixed with tart, indistinguishable, red syrup. She was rather enjoying it and all the while kept her rapt attention on Elliot. Noticing her interest must have prompted Elliot's detailed account, since he was rarely in the habit of admitting to his shenanigans.

"Luck followed me to Beirut," Elliot admitted. "I ran into none other than the person the warden was after. It did not surprise me to learn that he had been in your ski party."

I objected, "He wouldn't..."

"No, of course he wouldn't. He didn't rat on you, if that's what you're suggesting. No. My success was not at all thanks to your good chum."

"What did you find out then?"

"A question put to Beirut's taxi community told me all that I needed to know to put the pieces together."

"Of course. How obtuse of me! It would have been a simple matter to trace three men going up the mountain road after a storm, and easier still to distinguish the trio because two of the men had the unusual coloring of foreigners. But you must admit, Elliot, that three men in a taxi or a snow plow does not in itself prove guilt."

"True, but I know your tendencies. I am your brother, don't forget. I took the search more seriously than the authorities did, and I paid attention to details that only I knew to look for, being familiar with your altruism and being fully aware that you had Sullivan with you. You see, I looked for a trio. I must congratulate you. It was a daring move. I want to hear the rest of the details when I am through with my narrative, William."

"All right, but why did I not see you at Mon Repos?"

"Because Orie was keen to accept my help," he replied. "His men ran into a spot of trouble. But I digress. What's important now is that my business with Orie took me back to Palestine, and I gave up on direct contact with you. I could see that you had matters well in hand. Besides, you needed a holiday, and I had a reunion to arrange." Elliot gave a subtle wink to Salomé.

The waiter approached to clear the table. He offered another round of drinks. With the waiter's attentions turned to Salomé, Elliot glanced at me.

"You do appreciate my little joke?"

"Which one?"

"The lacy petticoat and the Russian condoms."

The waiter retreated.

297

Salomé returned her attention to Elliot.

"You devil!"

"Just funning."

"It was devilishly brilliant! But you gave me such a fright. How could you plan a meeting that would put Salomé in such danger?"

"Ah, but I took that particular element of danger out by replacing the contents of your holdall."

Looking at Salomé, I whispered, "I shudder to think what you must have thought of me. A bag-full of scented ladies unmentionables!"

"And pots of rouge and red nail polish!" Salomé shook her head.

"Among other things," Elliot added, sotto voce.

"So, Elliot, you somehow helped Orie; God help him. You set two scary English commando chaps to watch over Sullivan. Then you summoned me to Jerusalem. By heavens, Elliot, what did you do next?"

"William, it was not all my doing. I summoned you to Jerusalem because I learned that Salomé was here, or rather, living just outside the Old City."

"How did you find that out?"

Elliot reached for his drink. "Damn! Where's my drink?"

"The waiter just cleared the table."

"Well, didn't I order a whiskey?"

"No, you did not."

"Oh." Elliot looked searchingly across the dining salon.

"Elliot?"

"I'll be right back."

As Elliot walked to the bar, I turned to Salomé. "How did he know that you were here? How did you get here? I searched all over Cairo, looking for you. How did you get here?"

"I had no idea that you were looking for me, William. Sir Niles..."

"Patience." Elliot tapped my shoulder. He then turned to the waiter and thanked him. My brother took his time sitting down and distributing another round of drinks: Parsnip wine for Salomé, whiskey and soda for me, and a neat whiskey for himself. "Where was I?"

"You summoned me to Jerusalem," I replied in resignation.

"Right. Well, you came. And you busied yourself with Orie. Next, I had to get in touch with you to let you know the plan. So, the Australian was an easy messenger. You have good friends, William. Sullivan was eager to see you. He gave you the time and location of your meeting. He even agreed to deliver something from Orie to the doctor, that bottle you received this morning and whatever else was in your holdall. God, these items change hands countless times, bouncing about the Middle East. I would not be surprised to see the High Commissioner himself holding such items en route."

"So, Sullivan delivered, and?"

"Now, you knew to go to the YMCA around noon. Chasing down Salomé proved to be a bit more challenging. So, let me put it in order. Salomé approached Ali. No," he paused. "Wait a bit, I am skipping several events that took place prior. Salomé left our estate to go to an orphanage, to leave the child there. Perhaps you would like to tell this part of the story, Salomé?"

She shook her head.

"All right. When Salomé returned from the orphanage, Father intercepted her."

"Father?"

"Hush. Father took Salomé to Señor Marcelo's office. Señor Marcelo delivered her to a family in Palestine, the Millers; they are textile merchants. Father and Señor Marcelo figured that taking the girl out of Egypt was advisable. I found out about their scheme a bit too late, you may say. Ali approached me with the information Salomé left with him. I confronted Father...He admitted to his involvement..." Elliot sipped the last drop of his whiskey and hailed for another drink. "I assure you, William, that I was quite vexed with Father's actions. He let us search for the girl throughout Cairo, knowing all along that she had been removed to Palestine."

"By his own doing," I added darkly.

"I confronted him, and I admit that his reasoning was sound. The fewer involved, the better. What's more, Father preferred to spread the word that Salomé had left on her own accord, somewhere unknown to us."

"So that's it? He just decided that she should go?"

"Mother found her with you...in a compromising position."

"Compromising position? Elliot, Salomé was in my arms, yes, but we were fully clothed."

"William, Mother was concerned that you and Salomé were lovers. Well, but that's irrelevant."

"I don't think so. Mother's involvement in this shouldn't be disregarded. I'll wager that Mother was as much responsible for sending Salomé away as Father."

"Well, let us put it all on one side. It's inconsequential right now. William, I obtained the name of the family that Señor Marcelo arranged for Salomé."

"How?"

"James charmed the information out of Father. You know how he is and his patient ways."

"Don't I! James could charm a snake-charmer."

"Yes, but only when it suits him," Elliot grumbled then cheerful again added, "I got myself to Palestine. I knew how to begin my search and luck had it that Señor Marcelo was in town and he put me in touch with Salomé. With some effort, the pieces came together. I did not want to put Salomé at risk. So, the last step was to alter the contents of your delivery. Little did I know that my prudent character proved to be invaluable. The German doctor was a complication that I did not expect. Had I known that the German was under surveillance, I would have staged your meeting differently!"

"Under surveillance?"

"It is the only conclusion one may draw. Why else would there be a raid while you were at the YMCA? I never meant to jeopardize you and the girl. The doctor knew nothing of my plan. It was all a game." Elliot placed his hands behind his head and leaned back with satisfaction. "So, there you have it. I did my part. And the rest is up to you and you, of course." He directed a smile at Salomé.

"An impressive achievement, even by your standards, Elliot. We'll drink to you."

But Salomé was upset, and her cheeks wet.

"What's the matter?" I asked.

"Sir Niles would not let me go inside, to say my farewell to you. I wondered about that. He said that there was little time to waste."

"I'm sorry," Elliot apologized.

"It's not for you to apologize, Elliot," she soothed my brother. "I waited for a chance to join the Millers on one of their trips to Cairo. They travel to Egypt often. I came, looking for you. Ali stood guard. When he saw me approach, he looked at me as if he'd seen a ghost. He explained that no one knew where I was and that you feared the worst because Nadia came back days later, wounded. I believed that Ali was exaggerating. You know how he fancies the dramatics. But it did not occur to me that you were left in the dark...I...So, all along, you really had no idea where I was? For months, while I was here in Jerusalem, you looked for me in Cairo? Why would he put you through this?"

Elliot leaned close to Salomé. "Forget what's past. Your future is important now. Do you like Palestine?"

"My father used to look towards one wall in our house. It was never whitewashed, and the bricks were left exposed. He would look at the wall and say 'next year, in Jerusalem' and pray." Salomé's eyes shone. She could not go on and looked down, folding and unfolding her linen napkin. A teardrop fell and broke onto the starched surface.

"Marcelo brought her to Palestine." Elliot roughly rubbed his forehead. "It was donkey's years before he agreed to help me track down the girl's connections here. But the Millers are kind, are they not?"

"Oh, yes. Very kind."

"But how did you get here?" I asked Salomé.

She paused, struggling with her answer. Her ensuing recollection made Elliot lean closer. I remained still, my lips parting in disbelief.

She had misunderstood my question. "It was my brother," she began. "My older brother. It was he who threw me into a big pile of bodies. I lied inside the mound. After dark, I crept out. But I met the night guard. He was a Kappo, an inmate serving the Nazi authorities of the camp." Her words barely above a whisper, Salomé was not recalling her escapades in Cairo, but her time spent in a Nazi camp. But what kind of camp?

"The Kappo did not turn me in. He hid me in a hole. He had been digging; he had been planning to escape himself. A long time went by. I had nothing to wear. They stripped the corpses, and my brother had removed my rags before he hid me in the pile. I was cold, and I hurt. But it was better than lying among the dead. So, I stayed in the Kappo's hole. And sometime later, the Kappo showed up with a man's shirt with a yellow star sewn to it. The shirt was for me to wear. He told me to come out. It was night. He led me back to the corpses. He told me to take the shirt off. I wanted to run away. I did not want to lie with the dead again. Not again, not after I already ran away from their stares, and the smell. The Kappo got mad. He told me not to be foolish, and if I

301

did not obey, he would kill me. He made me take the shirt off, roll it up and keep it hidden, and go hide between the bodies."

Elliot stared at his hands.

"Soon, the tractor would come to take the bodies away. Someone will be waiting for me there. Señor Marcelo was the next living man I saw. Señor Marcelo took me to Egypt, promising to look for my brother and my parents but along the way, close to Egypt, I lost...I could not...my...voice. Señor Marcelo sent me to Sir Niles." She spoke in monotone.

Glass shattered. Elliot's palm bled as he released the fragments of glass.

"Elliot!"

The tablecloth reddened beneath his palm.

Salomé slowly took my brother's hand, pulling bits of glass out and then pressed her napkin against his palm. Elliot raised her hand to his lips and kissed it and I watched, as the blood trickled down Elliot's forearm. Neither Salomé nor Elliot cared. Neither was really there just then.

The waiter approached our table.

I sent the waiter back.

The waiter nodded and turned away, indicating that he will see to Elliot's bloody predicament and that our drinks were on the way.

I reached for Salomé's hand and removed it from Elliot's frozen grasp.

"Damn it all," Elliot rasped, surly.

The waiter oiled closer with our drinks and fresh napkins.

"Send the charges to my room," I instructed him.

The band abandoned the stage, leaving a pianist and a vocalist to produce a solemn version of 'You Go to My Head.'

"Dance with me." Elliot took Salomé's hand in his again and drew her to the dance floor as our tired waiter returned with our list of charges.

I was drowning in thoughts, unhappy. My father in Egypt was pulling strings as in a puppet show, steering our lives in secrecy. Elliot half-heartedly urged me to abide by the rules of the show, and return with him, to Egypt, and then to our homeland, England. My brother was rather clear about the message. His frequent glances at Salomé while he spoke were meant as a subtle hint. Subtle be damned.

Salomé would not join me. She was Jewish. Her simple reference to the unfinished wall in their house removed any doubts. The unfinished wall commemorated the fallen Second Temple. Kelly had written about a conversation with Chava, a conversation about rituals of the Diaspora.

Chava, Shlomo, Orie, Kelly, Sullivan, Tate. I repeated the familiar names. "What about Ali?"

Salomé and Elliot, bodies swaying gently, flutter of skirts, leaned against each other. Somehow, I was not bothered by Elliot's chivalry, if that what it was. I had a feeling that he was grieving, quietly, and in secret and had been doing so for quite some time now but had been keeping himself busy to keep the ghosts at bay.

I got up and walked to them.

"Elliot, have you heard from Elizabeth?"

"Elizabeth?" Elliot asked. He stopped dancing as if by merely mentioning her name I broke the binding spell between him and Salomé. "Elizabeth and her father are gone. Both collaborated with the enemy. And both were found out," Elliot replied in a matter-of-fact tone. "They're dead."

Salomé and I stared at him.

"What, what? Such silence? And from both of you?" he scoffed and clicked his tongue. "And what did Mother say? Unsuitable match?" Elliot looked down and gave a rueful smile. "Oh, but there is more shocking news to come."

"Shocking news?"

"Faraj is selling out. He's leaving Cairo and going to America, to Chicago. Wealth and connections open some doors. And, he is taking his Madame Sukey with him along with her ever growing entourage of rescued girls."

"Who is Faraj?" asked Salomé.

"Good Heavens, we never did introduce the girl to Faraj!"

"Don't be absurd, Elliot. Faraj owns a coffee shop frequented by men. Salomé would not necessarily be welcome there."

"Faraj then is a friend of yours? Why is he leaving for America?"

"He's Jewish. His business and his estate have been targeted by Muslim fanatics too many times for his taste. He's selling out and moving to Chicago. Apparently, he has a cousin in Chicago willing to 'sponsor' him and Madame Sukey," Elliot explained and I marveled at how generous Elliot could be with minor, nonessential details. "William,

303

take care of her." Elliot handed Salomé over before the girl would ask who was Madame Sukey.

"I can manage that." I drew Salomé close and rested my cheek against her temple.

The piano was still filling up the hall with the slow melodic rise and fall of "As Time Goes By," accompanied by the singer's husky voice.

Elliot sauntered back to our table.

"What do you think about it all?"

Salomé looked at me. Her hair was slightly disheveled.

"I missed you."

"William, so did I."

"What a shambles it all is!"

"Your brother made certain comments...about the future. I have not had much chance to think about what he..." Her sentence was cut short. Her expression became somber but puzzled, and she stopped dancing.

"What is it?"

"Elliot. He is leaving. But he cannot. Otzer."

Chapter 37: Elliot's Dilemma

I caught up with him just outside the front door. "Elliot, where are you going?"

"Back home." Elliot's simple reply winded me. Hands in his trouser pockets, he kept on walking. He was already outside the King David and heading through the walkway to King George Street.

"Don't be ridiculous." I gathered my wits and ran after him to pull him back.

Elliot brushed me aside.

"You don't know where you are going. Not in the dark anyway." I was out of breath keeping up with his long stride. "Look, you can't do this."

"Of course I can." He slewed to face me. "I did my bit, William. Now you do yours."

"Why don't you tell me what's going on? What is really going on? What are you doing here, in Palestine? Why did you go through all the trouble to bring us together? How come you're always popping up when I least expect you?"

My brother stared, silent.

I did not mind his secrets. I loved him. I loved Elliot. And, I was relieved to see him in Palestine. Why, then, did I not tell him that?

Then he snorted, "Pop up? My dear boy, I don't pop up!" His mirth vanished quickly though and Elliot placed his hand on my shoulder. "William, you have her."

"Elliot..."

But he raised his hand, silencing me. "I joined the SAS," he whispered.

"What are you on about?"

"I joined the Special Air Services."

"With Sullivan's bodyguards, those two scary British commandos?" Astonished, I choked. "You're unbelievable. What would Mother say?"

"I reckon that Mother and Father are well aware of it by now. I left a note before coming here."

"They can console themselves that you are not the only one of us who's done so. Lord Jellicoe is now commanding SBS, Special Boat Services. So, they can take comfort in that."

"Oh, he's not the only one of us attached to that unit. One of the founders is none other than David Stirling. Then Stirling disappeared. Rumors have it that he is a prisoner of war somewhere though it is hard to believe that he is still alive. Hitler, you know, has many new rules about commandos."

I clasped his hand in mine. "Elliot..."

"Worried, William? You shouldn't be. James' all right. And so will I be when this show is all over."

"James?"

"Yes. He was with the mobile squadron of the LRDG. The squadron that joined the SAS on their airfield raids. So you see, you need not worry about me."

Because there was something odd in his voice, I asked, "I thought that you and Lady Jane, your singer from the club, had some understanding. Did it not work out?"

"Lady Jane, a daughter of a war hero and an earl, is dead." Elliot's face was ashen and his gaze drifted away.

"A day after your wedding night," I whispered.

Elliot's head shifted almost imperceptibly.

"It's the way you looked. And it had nothing to do with paint on anyone's legs or sheets. Elliot, you need not morn and hurt and worry alone."

"But I do. In the line of work that I'd chosen, I do. Look, William, what will you do with your girl now? Take her to England?"

"I first have to find out if she will have me!"

"She will."

"How can you be so damned sure?"

"Didn't you once ask me this very question?"

"I often ask you this question. You say the most provoking things with such damned effrontery and assurance!"

Elliot grinned. "Something went wrong with us, William."

"Propriety," my reply was muffled as Elliot pulled me into an embrace. "But knowing you, you had everything to do with exposing the Bakers for the scum they are...were. I am proud of you, Elliot."

"I don't know what you are talking about."

"Do be careful. Life is too short but don't shorten it unnecessarily."

He grinned. "William, will you stay here, in Palestine then?"

"As good a place as any."

"But not here in Jerusalem, I hope. Go elsewhere. Go north. Go to Yagur, William. You're welcome at Orie's father's house, you know that."

"You know about Shlomo too?"

"We had a bit of a chat."

"I'll talk it over with her. Would she agree?"

"Salomé? She lives with a merchant family. A temporary arrangement. Father and Señor Marcelo are still searching for her family. If there's anything left of it. Genocide is too clean a word for what's really happening under the Nazi regime. But I don't see any difficulty in convincing Salomé to join you. You're charming enough."

"And James?"

"James? Why, he is not in love with Salomé!" Elliot exclaimed, and in a thoughtful, concerned voice added, "I hope that you know that."

"Of course, though for a while I had some doubts. But what of James?"

"He's going back to England, to that great old barn of a place, Grandfather's hunting box!"

"That big old rambling pile? Why?"

"Oh, James needs peace and quiet. He puts on a brave front but something shook him while in the desert. I am not sure what. But something shook him. Father and Mother too will join him. In a few more years, most of the British officials in the Middle East will be returning home."

"What about the estate? What about Ali? Damn, what about the dog, Elliot, the dog, Nadia?"

"Ali is staying in Egypt, of course. Father will probably leave him in charge of the house or some small part of it and sell the rest. He'll have to put up with Nick Bottom. In your absence, William, Ali took charge of your animals, excepting Nadia of course. She's been staying with me, and James will care for her until I return. Ali though has been dutifully caring for the rest of your beasts but at least he won't have to bother with Cook any more. William, Cook...damn it, man, I can't believe I'd forgotten to tell you this."

"Don't mention the horrible man!"

"But I must. Cook quit."

"Quit? Is it possible? You wouldn't have had anything to do with his departure?"

"Oh, I don't know."

"Well, it's about time."

"He'd seen one ghost too many and howled 'it is more than flesh and blood can bear' and marched out, arse twitching, clogs clopping, and Mother in hysterics."

"Oh, Elliot."

"We wished that you were there to see him go!"

"We?"

"James and I."

"And Mother? How is she now?"

"Did you know that Cook was part Indian, from Calcutta? His father served our grandfather in India and so Mother, in an odd sort of way, felt obliged to hire Cook! What nonsense!"

"You mean to tell me that we suffered that fucking arse for years and years out of a warped sense of obligation to some old retainer of Mother's father?"

"Language, William, language."

"Well?"

"Apparently so. How demoralizing, isn't it?"

I opened my mouth to relieve my anger with another filthy swear word but paused as Elliot nodded at someone behind me.

Salomé approached. "Otzer tonight." Her whisper was soft. "Otzer."

"Damn!" Elliot must have had a sense of the meaning of Otzer.

"We are not allowed outside. Not until tomorrow morning." Tugging at his arm, I urged, "Elliot, come back. You cannot go anywhere; not tonight."

Elliot stood his ground.

"Elliot?" Salomé spoke. "Where were you going to go?"

Elliot looked at her. He looked as though he wanted to answer her question, but something stopped him. His posture relaxed into a moderate slouch. "I was...going to have a smoke." His unconvincing smile faded rather quickly, and the cigarette he rushed to produce hung between his lips, limp. "Would...you care to...join me?"

"We better go in." I gave my brother one last tug, and he obliged, sulking half a pace behind me.

308

"Really, Elliot, I don't understand your behavior tonight." I leaned over the basin and stretched my skin, dragging the blade upward, along my cheek. "Where were you going? On your own, in the dark? Were you going back to Cairo tonight? Or to some unholy SAS outpost?"

"No doubt you imagined me flying down the desert road to Cairo on a motorcycle, riding goggles on, silvery scarves trailing behind and glimmering in the moonlight."

"Come now, why did you run out of the dining hall?"

"Westbrooks never run." His nude form emerged from a cloud of steam hovering over the tub. Then my brother took on the posture of the sand demon he had once pretended to be, scaring the Egyptian maids.

"Cover yourself up."

"Why should I?" Elliot then began his tuneless hum of Lilly Marlene.

"Come now, not your Lilly Marlene again."

Elliot's eyebrows shot up. "And why not?" Still humming, he added some uncouth hip motions. Did he get lessons from his belly dancers at Monnayeur's? He stepped out of the bath and left wet footprints behind him, his singing escalating in volume, and his body immersed in dance. He was producing his own version of the song and dance, ill-mannered and provocative.

And that's how he was going to evade answering my questions. Adjusting the towel round my waist, I pursued my infuriating brother, intent on getting some answers, true or false.

I was not to have such good luck, however.

Elliot gyrated himself out of the bath chamber and into the room. He could not have known that she never left. He assumed that Salomé had already retired to her room, adjacent to ours.

I was unaware of her presence, either.

Salomé stood open-mouthed when Elliot, nude and dripping water, his body still letting off wisps of steam, materialized before her, singing inappropriate lines of the song, thrusting his hips all about.

Well, there was not much for it but to run and hide. But Elliot would never run and hide. His style dictated otherwise. He slung his arms round me and performed a moving revue of his waltzing abilities. My towel hung on, but only just, as he twirled us about the room.

Salomé backed up against the wall, her palms on her cheeks. Eyes bright, her mouth stretched into her widest grin.

Elliot considered retreating to the bath chamber. But he did so slowly and deliberately. He was now humming the Blue Danube. Despite my language and demands, he would not let go of me until we were back in the bath after traversing the room and leaping over the bed a number of shameful times.

Salomé's laughter rang as we were catching our breath behind the door.

"Damn you, Elliot, I shall never forgive you for this performance."

"You mean to say, William, that you will never forget our performance."

I looked at my brother and choked, "Quite right."

Acknowledgements

A novel does not write itself and I certainly had a supportive community of family and friends. And so it follows that this book belongs to many talented people besides myself. Particularly, I would like to thank my grandparents who persevered and selflessly gave so much of themselves to their families and to the world; to my parents and brother who never failed me and championed me throughout. And since this trilogy has been in the works for over ten years, I would like to thank most heartily my husband and son for their unflagging support and trips to England and Israel to visit the British Museum, the Imperial War Museum, Acre and the Galilee.

When I doubted myself, Bethany Kapusta, a.k.a. the genius editor, and Flesché Hesch, MA, business strategist for moms, emerged like solid pillars of strength. And so did many of my friends.

But above all, this book belongs to those who fought the monsters of the Second World War in so many ways.

Made in the USA
Lexington, KY
17 October 2019